"All I want is for someone to trust me," Clay whispered. **"To believe me and know what I say is true."**

"Oh."

"I'm not sure if I've met her yet or not," he whispered.

"I can't choose you over my brother." Allie felt a moment's anger that he would ask that of her and then she remembered she had been the one to bring up the question about what he wanted.

"I'm sorry," she added.

"So am I," he answered.

He pulled away then and they stood there looking at each other.

She knew without asking that he would not compromise on this point. They were on opposite sides here.

Clay finally moved to open the door and they walked out of the barn.

Sometimes, Allie told herself, a woman had to stick with her family even if her heart wished she could believe something improbable. That was part of being a grown-up. Things did not always go the way one wanted.

A Cowboy's Easter Redemption

New York Times Bestselling Author

Janet Tronstad

&

Lois Richer

2 Uplifting Stories

Easter in Dry Creek and *The Cowboy's Easter Family Wish*

LOVE INSPIRED
INSPIRATIONAL ROMANCE

LOVE INSPIRED®

INSPIRATIONAL ROMANCE

Recycling programs for this product may not exist in your area.

ISBN-13: 978-1-335-62189-4

A Cowboy's Easter Redemption

Copyright © 2023 by Harlequin Enterprises ULC

Easter in Dry Creek
First published in 2017. This edition published in 2023.
Copyright © 2017 by Janet Tronstad

The Cowboy's Easter Family Wish
First published in 2017. This edition published in 2023.
Copyright © 2017 by Lois M. Richer

For questions and comments about the quality of this book, please contact us at CustomerService@Harlequin.com.

Love Inspired
22 Adelaide St. West, 41st Floor
Toronto, Ontario M5H 4E3, Canada
www.LoveInspired.com

Printed in U.S.A.

CONTENTS

Janet Tronstad grew up on her family's farm in central Montana and now lives in Turlock, California, where she is always at work on her next book. She has written over forty books, many of them set in the fictitious town of Dry Creek, Montana, where the men spend the winters gathered around the potbellied stove in the hardware store and the women make jelly in the fall.

Books by Janet Tronstad

Love Inspired

Dry Creek

Visit the Author Profile page at LoveInspired.com for more titles.

EASTER IN DRY CREEK

Janet Tronstad

And Jesus said, Father, forgive them;
for they know not what they do.
—*Luke* 23:34

This book is dedicated to my new friends
at the Covenant Village of Turlock.
Thanks for the welcome you've given me.

Chapter One

Snowflakes hit his windshield as Clay West peered into the black night, barely managing to see more than a few yards down the icy asphalt road that lay in front of his pickup's headlights. He'd exited the interstate and could see the twenty or so frame buildings that made up the small, isolated town of Dry Creek, Montana. This place—between here and the Nelson ranch—had been the closest thing to a home he'd ever known.

"Not that it worked out," Clay muttered to himself. He'd first come here as a foster kid, and he'd foolishly believed what the social workers said about him finally having a family. Of course, they had been wrong. Being a foster kid wasn't the same as being part of a family.

As he kept the pickup inching forward, Clay studied the road farther ahead until he gradually realized the town did not look the way he remembered. Four years had passed since he'd lived in this area. He'd been seventeen at the time. The heavily falling snow made it hard to see, especially in the dark, so that might have been part of his confusion now. And maybe it was because of the snowdrifts next to them that the clapboard houses seemed shrunken in the storm. But he didn't recognize the gas station, either.

Suddenly, he asked himself if he'd gone down the wrong road in the night. There were no traffic signs in this part of the state. There hadn't been many turns off the freeway, but he could have chosen the wrong one. Maybe he wasn't where he thought he was. Right then, a gust of wind came out of nowhere. The gray shapes shifted and the town's church materialized out of the swirling storm. "Whoa." He braked to a stop, his fingers gripping the wheel and his breath coming hard. He wasn't as indifferent to this place as he had thought.

The large white building had no steeple. Cement steps led up to an ordinary double door made out of wood. On the ground, a plastic tarp had been laid over flower beds that went along both sides of the church.

One thing was certain, though—he was looking at the Dry Creek church and none other. Every year the congregation here forced daffodils to bloom for their sunrise Easter service as a sign of their faith.

Clay let the pickup idle for a bit and took a few deep breaths. He wasn't going to be hurried through this town, especially not by his own bad memories. Just then a light was turned on in one of the houses down the road. He tensed for a bit and then shrugged. He told himself that whoever it was would go back to bed. He didn't need to worry. Clay might not be welcome within a hundred miles of here, but he had every legal right to be where he was. The paper in his pocket made that clear when it stated the terms of the early parole he would earn if he spent the next year working as a horse wrangler on the Nelson ranch.

The storm lessened as Clay kept going along the snow-packed road. Finally he came to the drive that led to the heart of the Nelson ranch. When he'd lived here, a locked metal gate always spanned the road just behind the cattle guard. The gate swung free now. Snow had filled in the ditches at the side of the road, but the height of the dead stalks told him that no one had cut back the weeds last fall.

Clay let the pickup sit as he took more time to look around. It was hard to maintain his upbeat attitude looking at the place. He saw a dim light coming from what would be the kitchen of the distant house, but the upstairs was dark. Old habits die hard, and he couldn't help but count across the line of second-floor windows until he found the one that marked Allie Nelson's former room. She was the rancher's daughter. Back before all of his troubles, Clay used to check that window every night from his place in the bunkhouse to see if she had gone to sleep. He never questioned why he did it, but it made him rest easier to know she was safe.

The first portrait sketch Clay had ever drawn was of Allie's young face looking out that window at night, her whole being showing a yearning that touched him in its simplicity. Looking back, he should have known drawing her had been a mistake. She was the one who had made him yearn for some of those promised family ties the social workers told him about.

As Clay pulled closer to the barn, he saw that it wasn't just the weeds that had been neglected. Several poles in the corral were down. He realized then that the windows in the bunkhouse looked deserted. They'd built that log structure the year before he'd been sent here. It was long, with two big main rooms and a porch along the length of it. If there were any ranch hands around, they would have been up stirring by now.

He looked out at the fields then. There used to be dozens of horses standing or galloping around the dirt track that lined the small field to the right. The Nelson ranch supplied stock to other ranches and even managed to sell a few to small racing stables. He and Allie both loved discovering which horses had the strength and speed to be racers. It's what bound them together. Now he saw no animals of any kind.

"Something's wrong," Clay said to himself as he kept looking around.

A light flickered and a woman stepped in front of one of the kitchen windows. Clay could see only her shape, but something about the tilt of her head made him think that it was Allie. His breath stopped at the thought. She'd been a girl of sixteen when he knew her. She had to be twenty years old now. Maybe even twenty-one since her birthday would have been last month. But it couldn't be her; he'd heard she was working at some fancy resort down in Jackson Hole, Wyoming.

He'd rather come up against a dozen raging blizzards than face Allie again. The fierce anger in her eyes at his trial had been harder to bear than hearing the judge pronounce him guilty of armed robbery. He might have endured the censure of the rest of the town if she had stood by him.

He'd been clueless that night about what Allie's older brother, Mark, was capable of doing when he was drunk, but no one believed Clay's version of what happened, especially not Allie. Everyone thought Clay had planned the robbery of the gas station, but it had been Mark's impulsive move.

Clay closed his eyes until the rush of memories stopped. He didn't like thinking about Mark. Allie's brother had been shot in the head that night in a scuffle with the store clerk. At first, everyone expected Mark to come out of his coma in time to testify, but it hadn't happened. The last Clay had heard was that the doctors were saying Mark was not expected to ever regain consciousness. He'd had some kind of fever that compounded the swelling in his brain.

Clay turned the engine off. The pickup jerked as the muffler rattled to a stop. He heard a cat's indignant hiss then and he looked down. He'd forgotten about his passenger. A starving cat had snuck into the pickup when Clay stopped for gas a few hours ago. She was too tame to be feral, but none too friendly, either.

He figured that big empty-looking barn over there might as well house the cat and the kittens that, if he was any judge, she'd be having soon. From the looks of the place, the ranch could use a good mouser. So Clay grabbed the tabby and, without giving her time to protest, tucked her under the coat he was wearing. Someone had left the sheepskin coat on the seat of the pickup that had been left for him in the prison parking lot.

Clay briefly wondered who his benefactor was as he opened the pickup door, stepped down and started walking. Then he told himself he was making too much of the kindness. He was a man who stood alone. That was unlikely to change here.

* * *

Inside the house, a thin trail of steam was still rising from the skillet that Allie Nelson had dropped into the sink water before she stepped over to push open the only window that wasn't painted shut in her father's cluttered kitchen. She'd spent the past couple of years working as a fry cook in a popular restaurant in Jackson Hole and, even with that, she had burned the eggs on her first morning back on the ranch.

She'd been in the hall tying her nephew's shoes, but that would be no excuse in her father's eyes. Despite her shouldering the loan payments for her brother's medical bills, which had taken everything she and her father had and which led to her father borrowing against the ranch to pay the rest, her father still treated her like she was barely older than young Jeremy.

The smoke from the skillet was disappearing. The winter air blew in through the open window, and Allie closed her eyes before leaning forward against the counter. She was tired to the bone, she thought as she stood there. But she couldn't give up. The next trip here to the ranch she was going to make sure all of the windows opened as they should. Then she'd get down some of those leftover building supplies from the hayloft in the barn and paint the kitchen walls a bright sunny yellow. She would not like Mark to see the house like this; it was depressing. She'd make their house look happy again before he came home.

Against all odds, her brother had started to slowly come out of his coma this past fall. For a long time the doctors said they expected him to recover. But, when he didn't, they decided things were worse in his brain than they had initially thought. However, Allie's father kept saying Mark had an IQ of 156 and that his son's genius brain would find a way to heal itself.

Allie had heard that IQ statistic so many times growing up that she figured it was seared on her memory. But she did not share her father's confidence in her brother's high IQ to heal him. She turned to someone more powerful. More than once she knelt at her mother's grave and pleaded with God to save her brother, promising she would take better care of him this time if she could only have one more chance.

Now Mark was coming out of his coma. The doctors couldn't explain it. They said it was impossible, but the swelling in his brain had gone down. First, a finger moved, and then some weeks later Mark cleared his throat and tried to speak. Finally, his eyes flickered and he started to eat through a straw. That had gone on for months. Everyone had kept Mark's progress quiet, though. In the beginning, his improvements were so slight that they weren't sure he'd stay on track with his recovery. Then they weren't sure he could take the excitement of other people knowing what had happened.

Allie had gotten back to the ranch only last night, but she was planning to drive to the hospital nursing home to see her brother on Monday.

"You making bacon with them eggs?" Her father's querulous voice floated down the hallway and interrupted her thoughts. "Jeremy and I like bacon with our eggs. Three slices for me."

She looked up but saw no one. Her nephew and her father were still in the back bedroom.

Allie turned to face the hallway. She heard the giggle of her three-year-old nephew and the creak of the springs on her father's bed, which meant that the little boy no doubt raced his plastic horse across the edge of his grandfather's mattress.

Jeremy was bringing joy to this old house, even if they saw him only once in a while. He and his mother lived in Idaho, and this was the first time that she had left Jeremy here alone. Allie had asked for time off from work so she could be here to help watch over him.

"The doctor said you can't have more than a small slice of bacon," Allie called to her father. She'd spoken on the phone with the doctor last week. "Your cholesterol is too high."

Actually, the specialist had said her father should have an aspirin every morning and start eating turkey bacon, but Allie was taking things slowly. Her father refused to consider eating what he called fake bacon. She was stretching the doctor's advice by giving him a small piece of the real stuff and two eggs.

It wasn't until she started back to the sink and passed the smaller window in the kitchen that she glanced out toward the barn and stopped midstride. She hadn't seen that pickup sitting there when she had arrived late yesterday. The pickup was usually parked behind the barn. She didn't know why her father kept the old thing after what happened with it that awful night when Mark had been shot. The pickup was practically falling apart, the red paint faded to mauve except on the dented bumper where the bare metal showed through in a long scratch.

She twisted her neck to get a full view of the yard. Sure enough, a man was walking toward the house.

"Company coming," Allie called as she stood back.

Her father must have lent the vehicle to a neighbor and the man was bringing it back. "Best get your robe on."

She picked up the long metal spatula that was lying on the counter. Whoever the man was he had most likely eaten breakfast already, but she didn't want to turn anyone away without some hospitality. Having company in this house was as rare as a party these days. She'd toast slices of the whole-grain bread she'd brought with her from Jackson Hole and pull down the crock of honey to go with it. The coffee was already brewing. She'd also get started on new eggs. Her father would want some even if the other man didn't.

She was pleased to know one of the neighbors had felt free to ask her father for the loan of his old pickup. Ever since Mark had been hurt, her father had stopped going to church services. He said it was because he had to rush to make it to the nursing home before visiting hours closed, but she knew, even though Clay West was clearly the one at fault, her father felt the whole family had been shamed that night. He'd been avoiding everyone since then. He had plenty of time to visit Mark after church.

Allie heard a sound and turned.

"Who is it?" her father asked. He was peeking out a door off the hallway. "I hope it's not Mrs. Hargrove. I'm not presentable. She said she might come by."

Allie would rather the visitor be the sweet older woman. She was the traditional Sunday school teacher for children of Jeremy's age, and Allie thought it was time her nephew joined the class, at least when he was staying with her and her father.

"It looks like a man, so your robe will be fine."

"Does he have on an old sheepskin coat?"

"How'd you know?" she asked as she twirled to stare. Those coats were no longer common. Everyone preferred puffy jackets in neon or pastel colors. For one thing, they were washable, and there wasn't a dry cleaner this side of Miles City.

"I'll put my overalls on." Her father turned without answering her. "I sent Jeremy to his room to get dressed."

Allie stepped over and opened the main door. No one had taken its screen off last fall, and the latch had gotten damp and rusted even more. There were enough things that needed doing in this old house that she could spend a month here instead of the two weeks she'd arranged to take off from her job.

Flakes of snow blew toward the house, sticking to the screen door, but she made no move to wipe them off. Allie shivered from the cold, and her breath was coming out in white puffs. It was difficult to identify the man walking toward the house because he had his head down. The leather coat flapped around his legs. The garment was half-open, and a gray plaid shirt covered his chest. He held one of his arms like he was holding something inside his coat. Worn denim jeans fit his long legs, and cowboy boots sank into the snow.

The morning was overcast, and a burst of wind blew the snow around. The man lifted his face, and suddenly a glimmer of sun came out.

Allie couldn't believe her eyes. It was like her thoughts had conjured up her worst nightmare.

"Clay?" she whispered even though no one could hear her.

His shoulders were broader than she remembered, but she'd recognize his stride anywhere. He was always prepared to take on the world, and it showed in the way he moved. Confident to the point of arrogance. He reminded her of her father in that way.

Clay's dark Stetson left his face in shadows. She couldn't see his black hair or his piercing blue eyes, but it was him all right.

He suddenly stopped midway to the house and stared at the open door. Surely the darkness in the house meant he wouldn't be able to see her clearly enough to know who she was. But he stared as though he could see through the screen and recognize her. He'd always been able to make her feel that he could look right down to her soul. It was those eyes of his.

Of course, that was nonsense, she told herself as she stepped back then, and instinctively slammed the door closed. He had ordinary eyes even if they were a startling icy blue.

"What're you doing that for?" her father asked, grumbling as he limped across the kitchen floor in his slippers. "We got company."

"It's Clay West," Allie said, leaning back against the door.

"Well, so what?" her father asked, his chin up like he was ready to argue. He held a rolled-up magazine in his hand.

"Clay West," she repeated. "You remember—he's the foster kid who lived here. He's the reason Mark is where he is today."

"You don't need to tell me who he is," her father said. "I was here."

"I was, too," Allie protested. She still remembered the night the sheriff had come to their door after midnight. Mark was already in an ambulance on the way to the hospital. Clay sat in the back of the sheriff's car, handcuffed and silent. He never looked up at her.

The sheriff told Allie her brother had been drunk on tequila, but she assured the officer that Mark had never taken a drink of hard liquor in his life. She would know if he had, she'd explained. She was a year younger than Mark, but she'd always been more responsible than he was. As her mother lay dying, she had asked Allie to watch over Mark and make sure he didn't start drinking alcohol. The family was unusually susceptible, she'd said. Mark might have gotten the beer that night, but the empty tequila bottle found in the pickup had to belong to Clay. Allie didn't know why Clay's alcohol blood level wasn't that high, but she knew that the tequila had to belong to him.

Allie's father reached for the door handle. "Clay's probably hungry. He'll want some bacon with his eggs. He's my new ranch hand. And they say he's an artist— sort of like Charlie Russell."

Her father waved the magazine at her.

Allie wondered if her father had started drinking again. He had promised he wouldn't. His fondness for whiskey had nearly ruined their family when she was young. There were no other indications her father had started drinking again, but the possibility had to be examined. She lived too far away to monitor him very well now, but she remembered the past. Alcohol always turned her father's mind fuzzy. He'd get foolish ideas and act on them. And what he said now was preposterous.

"We can't—" She started talking to her father, but he was paying attention only to the man standing outside their door.

Allie had thought she'd never lay eyes on Clay again. It wasn't fair that he walked around every day a whole man while Mark was lying in a convalescent bed staring at the ceiling and struggling to form a coherent sentence.

And now Clay was here—on their porch—and looking better than he had any right to be.

Her world had just turned upside down, and she didn't know what to do about it.

Chapter Two

Clay looked through the screen into the shadows of the kitchen, and his heart sank. For a moment he had thought it was Allie inside the room. Now he saw it was only Mr. Nelson reaching toward the door wearing denim overalls hooked over his white long johns. The unshaven man held a magazine in one hand and fumbled with the catch to open the screen with the other. A lock of his gray hair fell across his brow as he bent his head in concentration. There were lines in the man's face that Clay did not remember being there and dark circles under his eyes.

"Here, let me help you," Clay said as he jiggled the handle on the door from the outside. He had figured out how to make that latch work years ago. A person had to press it just right and it moved smooth as butter.

"You came," the older man said as Clay pushed the door open.

Clay nodded as he stepped into the warmth of the kitchen. It was just as well it was only the two of them. Maybe then the man would tell him why he'd sent for him. When Clay had been convicted of armed robbery, Mr. Nelson told him never to come back to Dry Creek. The old man had meant it that day. People didn't just change their minds for no reason. Maybe the church had put pressure on Mr. Nelson to bring Clay back.

"I can't take your job under false premises—" Clay started, suspecting the rancher would be happy to end this charade, too. He likely hadn't wanted to make the offer in the first place. "So if you plan—"

"Hush," the older man whispered. Then he turned and gave a worried glance at something behind the door. "We can talk later." The man's voice returned to normal. "You'll want breakfast first. Right?"

Before Clay could answer, he heard a feminine gasp.

"Allie?" Clay whispered as he turned to the side. The main part of the kitchen was filled with shadows, but he'd know the sound of her voice anywhere.

In the darkness, he saw her. She stood off to the side by the refrigerator with a beat-up metal spatula braced in her arms like it was a sword and she was a warrior queen ready to defend her kingdom. She used to love to pretend at games like that. Garden rakes became horses. Leaves made a tiara. She'd told him once that she had wanted to be an actress when she was little. Of course, that was before she fell in love with horses. Then all she wanted was to work on this ranch for the rest of her life.

Clay wished he had a pencil in hand so he could sketch her. A thin glow of morning light was coming through the window, and it outlined her in gold. Her posture showed her outrage and her resolve. She wasn't looking at him, though. Instead, her eyes were fastened on her father.

"I'm not cooking for *him*," she announced as she jabbed the long-handled spatula in Clay's general direction. It was a dismissive gesture. Then she crossed her arms, letting the metal implement stick out.

Well, Clay thought, trying to hide his smile, at least someone in Dry Creek believed in telling the truth as she saw it. He should be upset, but he couldn't take his gaze off Allie. She'd always fascinated him. Gradually, however, as he studied her, he realized the young teen he'd known was all grown up. The girlish lines of her face were gone, and she had the sleekness of a sophisticated young woman even in the faded apron she wore tied around her denim jeans. Her auburn hair was thick and as unruly as he remembered, although she'd tried to pull it into some order and knot it at the back of her neck. The pink in her cheeks was no doubt due to the cold that had come in from the opened door, but it made her look impassioned.

"I don't need to eat." Clay spoke mildly, and then he swallowed. This new Allie made him feel self-conscious. He wished he had taken time to get a haircut before he left the prison. "I do have something to say, however—"

"It'll do no good to say you are sorry," Allie interrupted as she stepped closer and stood in the light of the open door. She gave him a withering look. "Words won't make one bit of difference to Mark. And you should close the door."

"Sorry," Clay said as he reached behind him and did so. "But I wasn't going to apologize."

No one answered, and the tension in the room jumped higher. Clay figured a new haircut wouldn't have made him look much better.

"Now, Allie," Mr. Nelson finally said. "Clay's a guest in this house. And, of course, he's going to eat. Your mother wouldn't send anyone away hungry. You know that."

Allie turned to Clay, and he felt the air leave his lungs. She'd changed again. The sprinkling of freckles across her nose was the same, but her green eyes blazed. They showed the same fury that had consumed her at the trial. He had hoped the years would have softened her toward him.

"I'll make you some toast and you can be on your way," she finally said.

"I have no quarrel with you," he answered quietly. He missed the girl who had been his friend. "Never did."

"Nobody here is quarreling," Mr. Nelson said firmly as he frowned at Allie. "We know how to be civil."

Clay snuck another peak at Allie. The fire was gone from her eyes, but he did not like the bleakness that replaced it.

"I just want to explain," Clay said then. There was so much he wanted to say to Allie, and this might be his only chance to say anything. But he had to be wise.

"You okay these days?" he asked.

She didn't even blink.

He figured that all he could speak of was that night. "I should have convinced Mark to go back to the ranch earlier that night. But the robbery—it wasn't my doing. That bottle of tequila wasn't mine. I didn't know Mark had it with him. I was driving. It was dark inside the cab of the pickup. I thought he was still drinking his bottle of beer. We each had one. And I was pumping fuel into the pickup when he took the rifle off the rack behind us and went into the gas station. I didn't even see him at first. I had no idea what he planned."

"Are you saying Mark was the one at fault?" The fire in her eyes came back. Her voice was clipped as she faced Clay squarely. "That you didn't know anything about it?"

"I'm not saying he was at fault—" Clay stopped, unsure how to proceed. He didn't need an apology for the way anyone had treated him. He didn't want her to think that. He wanted her to believe him because she trusted him to tell the truth. Her opinion of him mattered, and he'd fight for it.

"It's cowardly to blame Mark when he can't even defend himself," she said, her voice low and intense. "I know Mark, and I know he wouldn't plan any robbery. It had to be you. I thought all those years in prison would have taught you to tell the truth if nothing else."

Clay studied Allie's face. She was barely holding on to her tears. He knew how that felt.

"I already knew how to tell the truth," he said softly. "I had barely stepped inside the place when the rifle went off. Mark and the station clerk were already struggling with each other when I saw them—I told everyone that at the trial. That's why all they could charge me with was being an accessory to the crime."

Clay saw the battle inside Allie. She never liked fighting with anyone, but he could see she was determined to blast him away from here. At least her anger seemed to have pushed back her tears. He could take the hit if it made her feel better.

"You were judged guilty," she said firmly. Her eyes flashed. "Everyone agreed. I don't understand how you can stand there and pretend to be innocent."

"I have no choice." Clay hoped his face didn't show his defeat. The two of them would never be friends again. Maybe they never had been. "I have to stand here and tell you what happened if I want you to know the truth. I'm sorry if you can't accept it."

Mr. Nelson cleared his throat as though he was going to speak. Clay held up his hand and looked at the older man. "I know my parole is tied to this job. If it doesn't work out, you can call someone and they will contact the local sheriff—I'm assuming Carl Wall is the one here. Anyway, since the pickup is yours, I have to leave it here. The sheriff will see that I get back to prison. Thanks, too, for having the vehicle sent over. You can decide."

Mr. Nelson was silent.

"You just got here," the rancher finally mumbled, looking uncomfortable.

Clay nodded. He still wasn't sure why he'd been asked to come, but he wasn't going to stay if it was a problem. He'd learned his lesson about making sure he was wanted before he stayed anyplace.

"Everybody knows—" Allie started to say. She stopped when Clay looked at her.

"Everybody doesn't know as much as they think they do," he finally said.

She didn't answer. It was so quiet in the kitchen that Clay thought he could hear the cat inside his coat purring. The heater in the pickup he'd driven over hadn't worked very well, and the tabby was likely content just to be out of the cold. Clay sometimes wished he could be satisfied with the small victories in life like that. A good dinner. A moment's comfort. They should be enough. Instead, he wanted people, especially Allie, to know who he was. And no one could claim to know Clay West if they thought he was a liar. He probably shouldn't care, but he did.

"Do they still ask people in the church to stand up and say what's wrong in their lives?" he asked. That was the only way he knew to address everyone in the area. He wouldn't need to stay for the sermon.

"You mean for prayers?" Allie sounded surprised. Then her eyes slid over him suspiciously. "You want to ask *us* to pray for you?"

"The church will be happy to pray for you," Mr. Nelson said as he waved the magazine in the air. "Everyone has read about you here. The hardware store got in a dozen copies. The ranchers are all talking about you as they sit around that stove in the middle of the store. You remember that stove? You're practically famous there."

Clay felt a sudden desire to sit down, but he couldn't. Not yet.

He never should have done that interview for the *Montana Artist Journal*. Allie was looking at him skeptically.

"That reporter exaggerated," Clay said. "I'm no Charlie Russell in the making—except for maybe that we both like to roam. I sketch faces and scenes. Simple pencil drawings. That's all." He'd had offers from a couple of magazines to print his prison sketches and had even gotten an art agent out of the deal, but Clay saw no reason to mention that. "And I'm not interested in anyone praying for me. I just want to set the record straight on what happened that night with Mark. I want the facts known."

One of the few things Clay remembered from his early life was his father urging him to always tell the truth. Both his parents had died soon after that in a car accident. Clay clung to that piece of advice because it was all he had left of his family. He wanted to feel that he belonged to them no matter where he went.

Allie looked at him. "I won't have you saying bad things about Mark."

Clay studied her. She no longer seemed to be as angry, but she was wary.

"I'll just tell what happened." Clay paused before continuing. "That's all I'm aiming for. And, after that, if you still don't want me here, I will go back. I can't make people believe me. I didn't have high hopes coming here anyway. I can even stay somewhere else tonight. Tomorrow's Sunday, right? Does Mrs. Hargrove still rent out that room above her garage?"

The older woman had been the only one to stand up for him at his trial, and he counted her as a friend. She had sent him cards every birthday and Christmas while he had been locked up. He'd done his best to send her cards in return. Usually he enclosed a few sketches; over time he'd sent her a dozen Dry Creek scenes. The café. The hardware store. Every main building, except for the church. He'd never managed a sketch of that. He wouldn't mind spending a couple of nights in her rental room before he headed back to prison. He had sold enough pencil portraits to other prisoners over the years to have a tidy sum in a savings account. He could pay for the room easily.

"Mrs. Hargrove?" Allie asked, frowning. "I'm sure the parole board doesn't want you speaking out and giving good people like her a hard time. She's having trouble with her feet these days."

"The parole board sent me here." Clay felt guilty that he hadn't known about the aches in the older woman's feet. "They had to figure I'd talk to someone. Besides, I can even help Mrs. Hargrove out some if I'm at her place. It could be a good thing. She probably needs logs for that woodstove of hers. The winter is going on long this year. I could get her all set with more firewood. Some kindling, too. She'd like that."

"The board probably doesn't realize the harm you could do here." Allie turned to face her father again, and Clay couldn't see her expression. "But we know."

Mr. Nelson cleared his throat, eyeing his daughter. "Don't look at me that way. We're not sending him away."

"Why not?" Clay asked softly. Father and daughter both turned to him in concern. He had to admit he was a little taken aback himself, but nothing was ever gained by dodging the truth. He spoke to Mr. Nelson. "When I saw you last, you were determined to make me suffer for what happened. I remember what you said. 'Let him rot in that black hole of a place. We don't want him back here.' So I'm asking straight out, what's changed?"

The rancher paled at Clay's words. "I suppose you want an apology from me, too, now?"

Clay shook his head impatiently. "I just want a plain-spoken answer. Why am I here?"

Mr. Nelson stood there thinking for a minute.

"For what it's worth, I am sorry," the older man finally said. "I said awful things to you and about you. No Christian should say such things."

"People say a lot of things they shouldn't," Clay said. "Christian or not."

Allie started to say something, but her father held up a hand to stop her. "He has a right to ask what's going on."

Everyone was silent. Clay watched as the older man debated something.

"I'm doing this for Mark," Mr. Nelson finally admitted, his voice thick with emotion. The rancher continued speaking, his eyes on Clay. "I didn't want to ask you, but I finally realized we need you. There's no one else."

Clay saw defeat in the other man's eyes. Clay had been in prison long enough to recognize the look on a man's face when he had no choice except the bitter one in front of him. The man was finally being honest.

"But you still blame me?" Clay asked. He wanted things to be clear.

The older man didn't answer.

"Will you help us anyway?" Mr. Nelson finally asked.

"I don't see how I—" Clay began to politely refuse the request. There were worse things than being locked up in a cell. Being around people who didn't trust him was one of them. He'd be free on his own terms in two years. He could wait.

Allie had been silent, but now she sputtered indignantly a moment until she found words. "Mark would be the last person to want *him* here to help."

Anger scorched the air.

Clay tried not to wince. "I should leave."

He decided he'd call Sheriff Wall himself if he had to. If it warmed up outside, he could hitchhike back to prison. He had more sketches to do there anyway.

Clay waited for Allie to turn around, but she kept facing her father with her back stiff enough to make her displeasure clear.

"Please don't look at me that way," Mr. Nelson said to her. "We have no choice. Mark wants to see Clay. Mark has always looked on him as a brother."

Allie jerked sideways. She could barely believe her ears. "What?"

Allie turned to look, and Clay seemed as stunned as she was. His eyes were wide and his jaw slack.

"They're not brothers," Allie swiveled and told her father crisply, ignoring Clay's question. She needed to put a stop to this nonsense. She hadn't been to see Mark for several months, but she hadn't heard him mention Clay before that. Of course, it was only recently that her brother was able to speak very complicated thoughts. And her father said Mark had improved since she'd seen him last.

Finally, she turned back to Clay. "Sorry, but that's the way it is. I don't know what went on between the two of you, but a brother doesn't do their brother harm."

Clay smiled grimly. "Believe me, I wish I'd tried to stop things. But I didn't know what he was planning to do that night. I certainly never meant for him to end up like he did. I worry about him just like you do."

Allie had watched Clay as he spoke. He wasn't lying. It didn't mean he was telling the complete truth, though. Maybe that was the way he thought it had happened, she told herself. He could have set everything in motion and then wished later that he had pulled back.

"I know you didn't mean for Mark to end up in a

coma." Allie could give him that much. And she knew Mark liked Clay; her brother had spent many of his evenings out in the bunkhouse since that was where Clay slept. They'd sit at one of the tables and play checkers. Their father hadn't liked it, but no one had stopped it.

Allie supposed it was money that had prompted Clay to plan that robbery. She had always thought that when he turned eighteen, he'd just stay on as a regular ranch hand. But maybe he was worried about his future. Then again maybe all he wanted was more beer to drink and he hadn't known how else to get it.

Clay hadn't responded to her, and she looked up at him. *Lord, what do I do?* she prayed.

Her father was right. She needed to be kinder to Clay. She wished she had known he needed more money; she could have turned over her allowance. After all, he hadn't had the advantage of having parents to raise him as she had. If the parole board was sending him back to where the crime had been committed, they must have their reasons.

Clay met her eyes, but his expression didn't soften. He certainly didn't act like someone who needed her charity.

"I still don't see what I can do for Mark, though," Clay finally said. She could hear the skepticism in his voice as he eyed her father. "I'm not a doctor. I don't know what to do about a coma. I don't believe in miracles, and I don't pray. God would never grant a request from me. I'm not a faith healer. There's not one thing I can do but say I am sorry that Mark is hurting."

Allie couldn't believe he was not going to at least pretend to help them. Not when it meant he'd be out of prison. She remembered now how stubborn he'd always been.

In the silence, her father spoke to her. "Mark told me a few weeks ago that he asked Clay to help him with the Easter sunrise processional."

She heard Clay gasp, but she focused on her father. He spoke slowly and deliberately, like he wanted a certain response from her. "You remember how Mark had been talking to everyone about that processional before the accident?"

"I do," Allie acknowledged as she reached over and put a hand on her father's arm. The poor man had aged two decades in the last four years. She was concerned about him. He carried a burden that never seemed to leave him. At least she was distracted from their family problems by working long shifts at her job.

"I doubt Mark means for you to worry," she said to her father.

"That's what he says," her father agreed. "And I know he doesn't know so much time has passed."

"I can't believe Mark is communicating," Clay said.

Allie suddenly realized that Clay still had that sheepskin coat wrapped around him. It had been cold outside, and she wasn't sure the heater in that old pickup worked very well. He must have been frozen when he stepped inside the kitchen.

When her father didn't answer, Clay turned toward her.

Allie nodded. Clay's eyes widened.

"So what, does he blink his eyes at you?" Clay asked her. "You know, the old 'once for yes and twice for no' kind of a thing?" He kept looking at her, but she gestured to her father, suggesting he was the one to answer. Clay turned to him. "I've heard of things like that—people pointing to letters in the alphabet. Is that the kind of thing Mark is doing?"

"Oh, no," her father said as he shook his head. "Nothing like that."

Allie could see the excitement leave Clay's face again. He was disappointed.

"Then what is it?" Clay asked.

No one answered. Allie wasn't sure what kind of a deal the prison officials had made with her father, but it would have to be canceled. They didn't need someone around asking probing questions about Mark. Besides, she couldn't afford to pay a ranch hand. And, there was no need for one anyway. The corrals and barn were empty. There were enough repairs to keep a man busy for months, but that work would have to wait.

"We don't talk much about Mark," her father finally said. "The doctors say to keep it quiet."

"You're going to have to tell me," Clay said then, his voice insistent. "You brought me all the way over here. And I'm not going anywhere until I understand what's going on with Mark."

Allie could have told her father that this would happen. But they couldn't protect Mark if they told everyone all there was to know about his condition.

Clay looked at her.

"My father knows more about it than I do," Allie said. She'd leave it up to him to walk through this mine-field.

"But you can tell him better than me," her father protested, looking over at her in alarm.

She shook her head. She wasn't the one who had invited Clay here; it was her father. She was tired of being the one who handled the problems in the family, especially when they were not of her making. She should go check on Jeremy anyway. She had heard the closet door open in the far bedroom some time ago. The boy was likely back there playing with those plastic horses of his. It wouldn't hurt if she stayed out here a bit, though, and saw how much her father was willing to share with Clay.

"One of you better tell me," Clay said.

He looked at her, pale blue eyes searching hers for answers. He wasn't afraid to push for what he wanted to know. A muscle along his jaw tightened, and she knew he'd not be discouraged.

"It's not my place to say," she finally managed to tell him.

She wondered if Clay had any idea how complicated life had become in the Nelson family since the day of that attempted robbery. There were many times since then when she wished Clay was still around so she could talk to him about the problems she had. He'd always seemed so steady in his advice. The truth was that she had relied on him more than Mark and certainly more than her father. Her brother had refused to acknowledge any issues in their family. Her father, when he was drinking, had been no help as he had often been the source of her concern.

After her mother died, Allie felt like she was the one in charge of keeping the family together. So far, she hadn't done very well.

Allie didn't like being on the spot again, because

one look at Clay's eyes and she knew he wouldn't be satisfied with some half-truth that she would tell him, hoping to satisfy his questions.

"Don't worry about it," Clay said to her softly then. "Your father will tell me."

Allie could only hope that would be true.

Chapter Three

The kitchen was gaining light, Clay noticed as he stood there in the silent room. The clock read seven o'clock. The room looked like it hadn't been touched since he left here four years ago. The same beige paint was on the walls, and the windowsills were a chipped white. He had noticed a nail by the refrigerator. It held last year's calendar, and it didn't appear like the months on it had even been changed.

"Tell me about Mark," Clay finally asked again as he turned his attention to the older man. "If he doesn't make some hand motions, how does it work?"

Clay figured the rancher must be imagining some kind of response from his son. The signs of depression were all over this kitchen. Even in prison, the officials became concerned when something as simple as a calendar wasn't kept updated. Clay guessed Mr. Nelson was telling himself he knew what Mark thought. It was like people who decided their cat was an opera fan because the animal sat there and purred when a song was being sung. He supposed it was very human to imagine that one could know the thoughts of a being who couldn't communicate.

Mr. Nelson didn't say anything. Allie, on the other hand, was standing there with a blank look on her face that was so uncharacteristic of her that Clay suspected she was unwilling to tip anyone off to her father's strange beliefs. Maybe she was embarrassed.

"I know it's been hard," Clay said, trying not to let his disappointment show. He might be having those flights of fancy, too, if he was father to someone in a coma. But desperate hope could mess with a man's mind; no one knew that better than men who had spent time behind bars.

"Oh, no, Mark is talking," Mr. Nelson said with strength in his voice. He seemed to have understood what Clay was thinking. "It's not easy. He has to come up with the words, and it's slow. But he's talking."

"He says actual words?"

Mr. Nelson nodded. "More now than when he started."

Clay looked at the man for a long moment. Then he turned to Allie. She nodded, as well. It was a wooden nod, like something was holding her back, but she did confirm the words.

"He used to just make sounds and we had to guess at the words," Allie offered.

Clay felt joy start to blossom inside him. "Well, what do you know?" Clay said as he lifted his fist in a gesture of triumph. Mark—his friend, his buddy—was free from the blackness of being in a coma. He'd heard enough stories from men who had spent the night in solitary confinement to have some sense of what that release must feel like to Mark. Not to mention the hope it would bring to his family.

Clay had a sudden impulse to wrap his arms around Allie and coax her into dancing an Irish jig with him. They'd done that once in the rain when they'd clocked a good time racing some of the horses. He, Mark and Allie, all dancing in a circle in the barn and laughing like fools. He needed to do something to celebrate. But he said nothing because he saw Allie was blinking back tears.

"What's wrong?" Clay asked anxiously. "Am I missing something?"

He supposed Mark could be talking and dying at the same time. That would explain the pinched look on Allie's face.

She shook her head. "Oh, no. These are happy tears."

Clay never had understood those kinds of tears. But he was glad Mark was apparently all right.

Suddenly Clay could feel the cat stirring. He put his hand over the place where the feline struggled against the coat, hoping to calm her until he could get her out from inside it.

Then he heard a sound and glanced down in time to see a movement out of the corner of one eye. A young boy was sneaking into the kitchen from the hallway. His flannel pajamas had pictures of galloping horses on them. His dark hair had a cowlick on the left side and was not combed.

The cat seemed to be calm now. Clay relaxed.

The boy slid forward and stood beside Allie. She put her hand on his head without even seeming to realize he was there. Then she stroked his hair in absentminded affection.

"I couldn't find my clothes." The boy looked up. "I want the blue shirt."

"So you've been playing instead of getting dressed like Grandpa asked," Allie said with strong affection in her voice as she leaned down to kiss the top of the boy's head. The boy nodded sheepishly. Then Allie straightened up.

Clay had never imagined that Allie would have a son. But just because time had stood still for him during the past several years, it didn't mean it had slowed for anyone else.

He knew Allie well enough to realize that if she had a son it also meant she likely had a husband. He supposed he'd never had a real chance with her, but it still left him empty. He'd pictured her so many times when he was in prison; there was something about her that reminded him of fireflies. Delicate yet bright, flitting from place to place. She always lifted his spirits. He would have given anything to be able to date her. Maybe give her a first kiss.

Clay must have shifted his shoulders as he stood there staring because the cat twisted inside his coat again. He saw that she'd pulled at one of the buttons until it was open. Before Clay could reach down and grab the animal, she flew through the air, landing on her feet atop the worn beige linoleum floor.

"What's that?" Mr. Nelson demanded to know. He looked around like more cats might be flying toward him from everywhere.

The tabby, its rust-colored fur bristling, stood there in the middle of the kitchen arching her back and looking pleased with her flight. Then she hissed. Clay had no doubt the cat was ready to defend herself from any scolding. But the young boy slid down until he was sitting in front of her.

"Don't touch her," Clay cautioned as he bent down and put his hands out to protect the child. "She's partly wild."

The cat had likely been tame at some point, but Clay figured she'd forgotten any softness she'd ever known. It had been a long time since she'd had an owner, and he knew how quickly home manners could be forgotten. The boy was already pulling the cat toward him, though. Once he had her in his arms, he rubbed his face against her matted fur.

The feline looked up suspiciously, but she didn't fight.

"I always wanted a kitty," the boy said and gave a satisfied sigh. "And this one has orange stripes. That's my favorite color. Does that mean she's for me?"

He patted the tabby gently, as though he'd already claimed her.

Clay was glad the boy had never seen a tiger.

"Orange is a good color," Clay agreed, noticing that the cat had relaxed in the boy's care. Maybe she remembered more than he thought. "It's the color for caution, though, so be careful."

Clay braced himself to make a grab if the cat started to claw her way out of the boy's embrace, but she stayed where she was. "I expect you'll want to ask your father if you can keep her."

Clay knew he shouldn't have asked it that way. But he wanted to know. He tried to keep his expression neutral. Allie looked like someone's wife, with her hair pulled back in a barrette and a faded apron covering her jeans. He hoped that whoever the man was he was decent toward her and the boy.

"We don't talk about his father," Allie told Clay and gave him a warning look. Her eyes darkened to steel as she stood her ground. She continued, speaking to the boy. "You'll have to ask your mother, though."

"Good," Clay whispered. He felt his face smile. So Allie wasn't the boy's mother.

Allie was studying him again now as though she was wondering at his thoughts.

"I—" Clay stammered. He didn't want her to know what he'd been thinking. She saw too much. He could tell by the questions shimmering in her eyes. He'd never been able to hide much from her. "The cat needs a good home."

That wasn't a lie, Clay assured himself. All those years ago, his father never had said anything about whether one had to always tell the entire truth.

"Everyone needs a home," Clay added to give more weight to his earlier words.

The pink on Allie's cheeks flashed red. "Are you saying we did wrong by you? We gave you a home as long as we could."

"I just meant the cat," Clay said gently. He was glad he hadn't made the mistake of thinking the color on her face came from warm memories of him.

"Oh," Allie said.

Clay turned so he didn't see her. He'd give her privacy if that's what she wanted. Everyone was silent.

"The kitty has too many bones," the boy finally said as he looked up at Clay.

Allie bent down, obviously relieved to have a change

in the conversation. "The poor thing's half-starved and is going to deliver a full litter any day now." Allie glared at Clay. "Don't you feed her?"

"She hitched a ride with me—that's all," he protested. "Someone abandoned her and no one would take her in. I did what I could for her. I bought some packets of coffee creamer at the gas station and fed her."

"Creamer?" Allie raised her eyebrow in question. "That's not enough."

"It was the middle of the night and I wasn't near any four-star restaurants. It was creamer, candy bars or coffee. Not much choice," Clay said. "And I scooped up a lot of packets."

The owner of the station had charged him plenty for the creamer, too. They'd found a glass ashtray and opened the packets of liquid and poured them into that. The cat had licked up three servings. Clay had to buy the ashtray, too, because the station owner said he couldn't sell it after it had been licked by a cat.

"I think she's still hungry, Auntie," the boy said.

"Speaking of hungry," Mr. Nelson said then, looking more like the man he had been when Clay knew him. "I'm sure we could all eat something." He glanced over at Clay. "How about we have some eggs and bacon to go with that toast?"

Clay nodded. "I'd like that if Allie's willing." He didn't want to press things with her. "Just this once. It was a long, cold drive over here."

"I'm glad you came," Mr. Nelson admitted.

It was quiet until Allie spoke to the boy. "Now, you go take the cat into the back bedroom and get dressed. There are some of your clothes in the closet hanging on the short bar. I think the blue shirt is there. Then get some of those old towels that Grandpa keeps in the bottom drawer of his dresser. The ones he uses to shine his Sunday shoes. They'll make a nice soft bed for the mama cat."

"But," Mr. Nelson protested, "my shoes—"

"I'll get you some other rags," Allie told her father. "We have plenty of old towels out in the bunkhouse. I just need to cut them up."

Mr. Nelson shrugged. "Well, okay then."

The little boy eagerly started walking toward the hallway.

Clay felt happy just watching him.

Allie waited until she heard Jeremy open the door to the back bedroom. Then she turned to Clay. She saw he had taken his hat off, but she refused to be distracted by the directness of his gaze.

"We try not to upset Jeremy," Allie told him. She hated to have to reveal all their family secrets, but she could see Clay was curious, and she didn't want him to start asking questions. "Jeremy's mother has just started letting him visit here by himself now. We don't want anything to stop that."

Allie watched Clay as he nodded slowly. The warm kitchen air had returned the color to his skin, but Allie noticed lines around his eyes that hadn't been there when she used to know him.

"The boy's mother?" Clay asked. "She's a friend of yours?"

Allie blinked. "I never really thought about it. She's more—that is, I only knew Hannah because of Mark.

They were both ahead of me in school—you know how it is. She and I didn't know each other really. But she grew up around here, too."

Clay had been her best friend back then. Not that he'd known it. Mark was gone so much, though, with Hannah, and the ranch had been lonely. Clay had actually been a good companion to her because he liked the horses, too. At least, she had always thought that was why they got along so well.

Her father grunted then. "Jeremy's mother is Mark's old girlfriend. The only one he's ever had."

Allie saw the truth dawning in Clay's eyes.

She nodded. "Hannah Stelling."

Clay was silent for a bit before speaking. "Jeremy is Mark's son?"

Allie nodded.

"Does he know?" Clay asked.

"We thought Hannah should be the one to tell him," Allie said. "And all she ever says is that Mark broke up with her and that's that. Case closed."

"But she's the one who broke up with him," Clay protested. "And Mark didn't say she was pregnant. I'm sure he would have mentioned that if he had known. He was just mad she had given him an ultimatum—marriage or nothing. That's why we went out that night. My birthday wasn't until the next day, but it was still a good excuse to have a beer and let off some steam."

"There was no good excuse for the two of you to have a beer," Allie said primly. "Neither one of you was of age." She had preached that to her brother until she ran out of breath. She saw now that she should have included Clay in her instructions.

"You got the beer?" her father asked then, more eager than Allie would have expected since he never wanted to talk about where the liquor came from on that night. She always thought he felt guilty for not cautioning them about how strong alcohol could affect them.

Clay shook his head. "Mark had it. He gave me one bottle and kept the other."

"It wasn't just the beer," Allie said, her eyes pointed to Clay. "It was that tequila, and we all know you had to be the one getting that."

"Why do you say that?" Clay asked incredulously.

Allie bristled. She didn't know why he couldn't just admit what he had done. "It's obvious. Mark had no way to get tequila. There wasn't a gas station around here that carried it. I checked. Besides, you have your ways. You probably learned all about how to get liquor when you were a kid in the big city."

It was the same place he'd learned all about girls, she thought. Mark had warned her that Clay thought nothing of kissing girls and so she should be careful around him. Unfortunately, her brother's warning had only made her more fascinated with Clay.

"Because I was a foster kid?" he asked, the edge to his voice making Allie feel a little nervous. "Is that what you mean? That I automatically break the law because I'm a foster kid?"

"It's not just that, but you have to admit—" she began.

"No, I don't," Clay interrupted. "I might have grown up rough, but I never was much on drinking. I never bought any alcohol. I wasn't of age, and I wasn't about to lie when someone asked if I was legal."

Allie paused and forced herself to swallow the ac-

cusations she was going to make. Clay had a point. She
knew he wouldn't stand there and lie to a clerk in a liquor store. She had always figured that the only reason
he had not told the truth about the robbery at his trial
was because he didn't want to go to prison. She did not
understand why he would not admit it now, though.

"It doesn't matter where the alcohol came from," her
father said with enough force to his voice to remind
Allie of what was important.

"The real problem was Hannah breaking up with
Mark," Clay added. "That's all he could talk about. She
asked him to go for a drive at noon and told him it was
over unless they got married."

"He should have known Hannah wasn't really breaking up with him," Allie said. "They'd been dating forever. She didn't tell him she was pregnant because she
wanted him to marry her for love and not feel like he'd
been trapped. But she wasn't leaving him. If you hadn't
been there to egg Mark on, he would have eventually
come around and seen how things were."

"But she didn't say any of that," Clay protested.
"What was he to think?"

"Most men don't think," she said, not expecting the
bitterness she heard in her voice. She was disappointed
by more than what had happened with Hannah and
Mark. Clay had thrown away their chances, too. "That's
the problem."

"Now, Allie," her father protested.

She lifted her chin. "Well, it's true. Men do what they
want and don't even always tell you what happened.
They just let the pieces fall anywhere."

Allie let her words hang in the air. She wasn't going

to take them back. She could see Clay measuring her words, like he wasn't sure what she meant. She saw the muscles tighten along his jaw, and she knew he had decided something.

"You're talking about me now, aren't you?" he said, no longer looking puzzled.

She didn't answer. As strong as her memories of him were, she had no right to question him. There had been no hint of romance in his manner toward her that time so long ago. He'd never even tried to kiss her, not even when she had bought tube after tube of lip gloss with enticing names like Sweet Pink and Red Passion. That should show her what Clay thought of her and kissing.

"I don't lie, and I wasn't letting anyone down," Clay finally said. "That night with Mark—no one was counting on me. There was no one to let down."

Yes, there was, Allie thought as she stepped back toward the kitchen sink. *There was me.*

She wasn't ready for all of this. She'd thought she'd never see Clay again. But he was wrong that no one had counted on him back then. Her father had still been drinking his whiskey, bottle after bottle of the same, and she used to tell herself Clay would know what to do if she needed help. Her mother had been the one to handle her father when he was drunk, and once she was gone, Allie never knew how to keep him steady. Mark refused to think there was a problem with their father, and so she knew it would be up to her to do something, if her father went out of control. That's why she'd been glad Clay was with them.

She'd worried all the time back then until one night when she'd seen Clay standing outside the bunkhouse looking up at her window. His gaze had seemed protective, and she told herself he was looking out for her a little bit. She knew he would come if she needed help. That's when she'd started her search for the perfect irresistible lip gloss. She had barely gotten used to the flutter of her feelings for him and then he was gone.

Deep silence filled the room.

Finally Allie turned around and spoke. She didn't look up, but she knew Clay would understand she was speaking to him. Those long-ago feelings were not important. She needed to help her family now, and she couldn't do that by mooning over Clay. "Hannah only took Jeremy to see Mark once a long time ago. Jeremy was scared of the coma, and so now she leaves him here with Dad when she goes. Jeremy doesn't know who his father is."

"You haven't told the boy?" Clay asked.

Allie shook her head. So many things had been left undone. "He hasn't really asked us. I think Hannah just told him his father was gone. Jeremy seems too young to care much."

"He's not too young," Clay said.

"I suppose not," Allie said. "I've wondered what he thinks about having a grandfather and an aunt, but no father."

"I wish there was something I could do," Clay said.

"Thanks," Allie said. "But in the end, it's not your problem. You're free now and Mark's stuck in that nursing home."

"Now, Allie," her father interrupted her. "Clay did his time in prison."

"Not all of it," Allie said. "He shouldn't be out yet.

I've kept track. If the parole board hadn't sent him here, he'd be serving two more years."

She had planned to send him a few hundred dollars just before he was set for release. She hadn't wanted to think he might be hungry. And if it was anonymous, no one had to know.

"I got him paroled early," her father replied.

Allie forgot the mellow kindness she'd been feeling and turned to look at her father in shock. "You did what?"

"It's called victim reparations. I called up the parole board and said we needed help on the ranch. They were reluctant, but I said there was no one here to work since Mark wasn't able and I asked them to send Clay. I didn't want to mention Mark's recovery. I figured it was best to keep it simple."

Allie continued to stare at her father. "Is that legal? You telling them to send him like that?"

She looked at Clay and saw him wince.

"I am okay with it," Clay said. "Especially now that I know about Mark."

"But he's the reason Mark is hurt." Allie stared at her father, willing him to meet her gaze. Everyone was forgetting what was important. "Clay should go back and finish his time. I can't believe you asked them to release him."

She'd been prepared to accept that Clay was sorry if he was getting paroled because the authorities thought he'd done enough time. But if her father had been the one to suggest it, that changed everything. No one else necessarily thought the time was sufficient.

Mr. Nelson kept looking at the floor. "What was I

supposed to do? Mark was asking for Clay. Besides, I need help with the ranch. It's falling apart."

She could see the condition of the ranch for herself. Each month she put what she could into a small savings account so she could save enough for some barn repairs.

"We'll fix things up around here later," Allie whispered fiercely. "We've got time."

"No, we don't," her father said, and he gave a proud grin. Her mother used to call that her father's Cheshire cat face. It meant he had done something no one would expect. And, usually, something her mother wouldn't have approved.

Allie had a bad feeling about this. "What do you mean?"

"I bought some more horses," her father announced. "Real cheap from a rancher over by Bozeman."

"You bought—" Allie gasped. She wasn't sure she had heard him right. "We can't afford anything. Nothing. You know that. Maybe some chickens."

Her father snorted. "We need more than chickens to turn this place around. Some prime horseflesh is what will put us back in business."

"You bought purebred stock?" Allie asked. She didn't even want to know how much that would cost. They had already squeezed the budget as tight as they could. The reason she wanted to start taking some accounting classes was to help with the ranch records. When Mark had received that scholarship and declared he wanted to be a doctor, she had felt free to stake her claim to the ranch. The horses themselves had lots of details that needed tracking. They'd need to buy more animals eventually, but not yet.

"The bank lent me enough to pay for them," her father said, a note of satisfaction coming into his voice. "I don't want Mark to come home and see the corrals empty like they are. We need some horses. They're being delivered any day now. I'm not quite sure on the time."

Allie stared at him. She couldn't breathe thinking about more debt. She could barely pay back what they had now.

"They're good horses," her father repeated himself, the dreamy look on his face telling her that he was lost in his own world. "The best bloodlines we can find. It's a deal. Four horses, three of them mares all set to have colts this spring. One of them is lame, but the sire, who is coming, too, is almost a purebred. At least that's what I heard. And one of the colts could be a racer. The others might go for range horses when they've had a chance to fill out. All of them for five hundred dollars."

She heard Clay grunt in astonishment, but he didn't speak.

"That can't be right," Allie finally managed to say. Her head was spinning. "That's way too low. Are the animals sick? Or was it five thousand dollars? Even that's not enough for that many good horses. Maybe you've got the numbers wrong. That happens, you know, when you've been—"

Allie stopped. She gave a quick glance over at Clay. This was private family business. She looked back at her father. "You know."

"I haven't been drinking," her father protested, sounding offended. "The man who sold them to me owed me a favor from way back. He's giving me a special deal."

"You're sure?" Allie's voice sounded distant to her own ears. It took a sharp woman to outwit a drunk. She'd searched the kitchen cupboards for alcohol and hadn't found anything. She always did that first thing when she got home.

"Of course I'm sure." Her father glared at her. "I'm going to go back and check on Jeremy."

Her father turned and went back into the hallway.

It struck Allie that, if it was true that her father hadn't been drinking, then he had likely been the victim of a scam.

"I need to sit down." She started to walk over to the kitchen table, planning to pull out one of the chairs. She wished she could remember how her mother had handled things like this.

Allie scarcely noticed the steady arm Clay put around her. Then he lowered her into the chair like she was made of fine bone china. Once she was settled, he bent his head until his mouth was close to her ear.

"It'll be okay," he murmured.

"Those horses are never coming," she said, letting her troubles spill out to Clay like she'd done so often. "My father gave someone money, and he'll never see anything from it."

"That's my guess, too," Clay said.

Then in the distance Allie heard the sound of a heavily weighted truck coming.

She glanced up at Clay. He nodded to show he'd heard it, too.

"If that is them and they're here, that five hundred is probably only a down payment," Allie said. "I'll... We'll be paying for those horses for the rest of our lives."

She was still looking at Clay. Suddenly the years fell away and his face seemed the same as it had before. His eyes were the same warm blue. His eyebrow furrowed a little in concern. He looked like nothing was more important at that moment than what she was telling him.

"That's ranching for you," he said.

"We're flat broke," she told him and then stopped to listen as the truck slowed down at what must have been the cattle guard where their driveway came off the county road. "I don't even want to look."

"I'll see about it," Clay said as he straightened up.

Allie wondered if there was any possibility that the truck would go by on the gravel road. It was the long way around to the Redfern ranch, but maybe whoever was driving was lost and was just slowing down to ask directions.

She watched Clay. He hadn't moved from where he stood.

"We haven't even had breakfast yet," Allie said.

Clay grunted. "If it is those animals, we'll need to get them settled first."

"You're a good man," Allie said as she sat there. "I have a little money saved. But not enough to pay standard wages to a ranch hand."

Clay smiled. "I don't think you're supposed to pay me. Free labor for a year. That's the deal."

Allie frowned. "We will make some arrangements. You can't work for free. I won't let you."

"It's fine," Clay murmured and then added hesitantly, "I think food is included, though. And I'll starve on toast."

She grinned. She saw the twinkle in his eyes. "Sorry

about this morning. And you will get a full breakfast just as soon as we deal with that truck."

He smiled back at her, and her day tilted until everything felt balanced in her world again. She wished with a fierce stab of longing that Clay and her brother had stayed in the bunkhouse playing checkers that night.

"My dad's not really an alcoholic," she whispered at last. She hoped this was still true. "I wouldn't want you to think that."

"It's not your fault if he is," Clay said and buttoned his coat.

She shook off her nostalgia. "That's kind of you to say."

The truck sounds grew louder.

Maybe it wasn't all her fault, but Allie knew she'd fallen down on her duty. She had liked the warmth of Clay's breath on her neck, but there was nothing about this that was going to turn out well. She couldn't recall a thing her mother had done when her father's craziness had already happened except for doing all she could to hide everything from the neighbors.

She wondered how they could cope with a bankruptcy. They had fought it off for so long, but she was tired. She really would need to paint the house. She'd always thought white with green trim made a house look prosperous. That might keep the pity from the neighbors down some. Or at least give them some doubt that the gossip was true.

Allie heard a vehicle door slamming outside. Whoever was out there was coming inside. And she wasn't ready.

She looked up and saw compassion in Clay's eyes.

She might not want him to know her father's weakness, but it felt good to have someone stand beside her in the troubles of this household.

Allie heard footsteps outside. She needed to remember that her goal these days was to see Mark recovered. Their family had been given a second chance. She wouldn't see alcohol or bankruptcy or problems from the past take it away from them.

Then her father cleared his throat. She looked over and saw him standing in the shadows of the hallway. His expression was so guilty that she wondered if there might be a bottle of liquor next to him in the coat closet.

"I should have asked you about the horses before I bought them," her father said.

Allie nodded. "We'll get by."

She forced herself to breathe calmly. She was only vaguely aware of the squeeze Clay gave to her shoulder before he moved toward the door. His brow was furrowed. His shoulders were hunched over in that sheepskin coat as though he was still cold even though it was warm in the kitchen.

A loud knock sounded at the kitchen door. Allie was relieved she didn't need to open the house and let anyone inside. Whoever was outside was going to give her trouble.

Chapter Four

Clay squinted as he opened the door. A sturdy middle-aged man, with a Stetson pushed down on his head and a red plaid shirt showing through the opening in his coat, waited on the steps with a clipboard in his gloved hands. Deep footprints showed where he had just walked through the snow. After studying the indentations, Clay guessed the snowfall was close to six inches deep. The man's black jacket had a logo and Farm Transportation embroidered on the front pocket, along with the name Stan Wilcox.

"This the Nelson place?" the man asked. His breath swirled up in a thin white puff. Even though the storm had stopped, temperatures had not risen yet.

"Yes," Clay admitted.

The man frowned and looked at his paper. "Mr. Floyd Nelson."

Clay realized with a start that he had never known Mr. Nelson's given name. He didn't remember anyone ever using it. "I'll get him for you. Stan, is it?"

The man nodded.

"I'm Clay West." He hesitated. "New ranch hand here."

"Good to meet you," Stan said.

Clay turned around then and saw that Allie and her father were walking toward the door. Clay opened the screen door for Stan. "Might as well come inside for a bit."

The other man entered and stood on the rug beside the open door. "We'll need to start unloading. I just wanted to check that we were at the right place and to find out where you want the shipment let down."

"Is it the horses?" Mr. Nelson asked as he walked closer.

"Yes, sir," Stan said. "This is them."

"I've been waiting." Mr. Nelson's face was as excited as a kid's on Christmas morning.

Clay smiled. The older man might be making a mistake, but he was at least enjoying it. Clay had to admit he wouldn't mind putting his hands on a horse again, either.

"I'll need you to sign." Stan held his clipboard out to Mr. Nelson.

Clay turned then and saw Allie walking over to the trucker and squaring her shoulders. He wondered for a moment about what she was doing.

"I'm afraid there is a change of plans," Allie said. Her voice was steady. "We need to send the horses back for a refund. I need to talk with my father some more, but we can't sign."

The man started to laugh.

"Someone will pay you for your delivery, of course," she added with a stiff smile. "Including the return trip. We honor our commitments as best we can."

Clay was proud of Allie. She'd obviously worked hard over the years to learn to speak her mind with confidence. He remembered how she'd hated to disappoint anyone and wouldn't confront them to say what she thought needed to be done.

Stan's laugh finally slowed to a rumble, and his eyes were kind. "That's not the problem, ma'am. These animals, though—there ain't no back to send them to. The man paid us in cash for the delivery, but then he got on a plane for Hawaii. Some messy divorce he's in. Didn't care how much money he lost. His ranch sold the day we left. He sent a few more animals over here with us. They were strays no one else wanted. If you don't want them, either, we'll have to shoot them."

"Goodness." Allie gasped. Clay saw the shock in her eyes. "We can't do that."

She turned to Clay, and he nodded in agreement. He knew how Allie was. She had taken injured birds and doctored them until they could fly again. She couldn't stand to see any animal hurt. She would never turn away an animal that needed saving. But Clay knew full well the problems that might be coming. He hoped none of the animals in the truck were ill.

"What do you need from us?" Clay asked Stan.

"For starters, just tell us where we should unload." Stan turned and opened the screen door. "We can sign the papers later. I'll tell my driver where he needs to park. Could take some doing, so you might as well stay inside for a few minutes. No point in all of us freezing."

Clay had never taken his coat off, so he was prepared. "I'll come give you a hand." He turned to Mr. Nelson. "Is the barn the best place to put them for now?"

The older man nodded. "The only place out of this cold. The weather report says the storm will continue off and on."

The kitchen door was opened again, and Clay stepped outside. He saw a long silver horse trailer and matching pickup sitting in the middle of the drive. A layer of snow had collected on top of the whole outfit. The sides were covered with dry mud, too, so Clay figured the vehicles had come some distance. In any event, he guessed it was too late to prevent any sickness from spreading if one of the animals had been infected with anything. They had all been together in that trailer.

"You're from Montana?" Clay asked as he walked down the steps with the other man. The sound of their leather boots was muffled by the snow. Clay liked the crisp air in his lungs. If the other man hadn't been in a hurry, Clay would have taken time to look around the ranch from where he stood midway between the house and the barn.

Stan nodded. "We came from over west by Helena."

Clay was glad that the trailer hadn't crossed any state lines. That might be complicated if there was illness in any of the animals.

A tall trail of exhaust rose from behind the pickup. Clay couldn't see much through the open slats along the sides of the metal trailer, but he saw dark shapes that were tall enough to be four horses.

"I'm assuming you have a ramp with you?" Clay asked Stan as they walked toward the vehicles. Clay wouldn't want to have to coax horses down a home-made ramp that was nothing more than several pieces of plywood laid one on top of the other. The ranch used to have something that worked pretty well, but he had no idea if it was still in the barn.

"We've got one built into the trailer," the other man said. "A couple of the horses are shy about using it, but we help them along."

Just then Clay heard a lot of flapping and squawking and the loud crowing of a rooster.

"Guess it's getting lighter inside the trailer," Stan said with a grin.

Clay noted that the sky was heavy gray still, but enough rays were getting through so that people—and apparently birds—could see.

"Big Red is waking up the crew," the other man added.

Clay heard the rooster again.

"You can't have chickens in there!" Clay muttered in protest. "I can't tell the guys I came here to babysit some old hens."

He'd forgotten about his few friends inside the prison, but suddenly he remembered his promise to send them postcards. They'd get a big laugh out of this. No one should get out on parole to tend poultry. He grinned some more at the thought of what they'd say when they heard.

What a day this was, Clay thought as he looked around. There were no telltale drips of snow melting off any roofs, but he supposed that would happen in a few hours if the temperature rose high enough. He heard the sounds of the front door opening, but when he looked, no one was stepping out to the porch yet.

"I suppose those birds are the animals you were going to shoot?" Clay asked. They were almost at the trailer.

Stan shrugged. "I was exaggerating a little about the shooting. I figure we can always give the chickens away. The woman at the café where we stopped to ask directions said she'd take them if nobody wanted them here. It's the goat that wouldn't find a home. He's an ornery old fellow. Name of Billy Boy. Thinks he's a dog. I can't believe how he tries to herd the horses. Him, we might have to shoot."

Clay groaned. "I think we can handle a goat."

Stan looked over at him. "Trust me, you don't want to cross him. He butts people when he feels it's necessary to protect his charges. I don't turn my back on him."

Clay heard steps on the porch and turned to see Allie coming toward them. She'd walked several yards when Mr. Nelson came out of the door, holding Jeremy by the hand.

It would be a family welcome.

"The boss lady won't let anything be shot," Clay said, keeping his voice low so she wouldn't hear. "Don't even talk about it around her. Or around the boy."

"She'll want to keep the miniature pig, too, then?" Stan asked thoughtfully. He arched his eyebrow as he looked over at Clay. "It's a little black Juliana pig of the teacup variety. About eighty pounds. The missus in the divorce at that ranch had the pig for a pet. I hear they're worth a fair bit of money, but the husband got him in the settlement. Cute little thing. They call her Julie."

"Please tell me you have regular horses in there," Clay said. His confidence in this exchange was shaken. "Nothing miniature or with a pet name. This is a ranch for working horses."

Stan grinned. "Wish we did have a Shetland pony or

something. My grandson would like that. But, no. The horses are full-size."

Clay nodded, but he knew better than to trust the man.

Stan called out to his partner behind the wheel in the pickup. "We're going to put them in the barn over there."

Then he pointed out the structure as though there was more than one barn in view. The red slats on the sides of the barn were rough with age, but Clay knew it would do well enough.

The partner dutifully started the engine and began backing up.

Clay figured he had done all he could to keep the proceedings sane. He was beginning to think that Mr. Nelson had been right, though. The older man couldn't manage this menagerie. And he sure couldn't afford to pay anyone to do it. As far as Clay could see, most of these animals wouldn't bring any profit to the ranch. No, Clay was the only one to tend them.

Allie stood in the drive for a minute, her arms crossed to keep warm inside her corduroy jacket, as she watched the pickup maneuver the horse trailer closer to the barn. The old structure was in fair shape, she thought, but the corrals would need to be fixed. Patches of snow covered most of the ground, but coarse gray dirt poked up here and there. They would need feed for the animals. Her father had sold the last of his horses three years ago, and the ranch hands had been let go at the same time. She mentally reviewed what might still be around and figured there were a few bags of old oats in the hayloft sitting on top of the plywood left after building the bunkhouse. The oats had probably gone moldy by now, but she'd check. She hadn't even gone out to the barn in over a year. With it empty, there seemed no reason.

They couldn't afford to feed a bunch of livestock for long. She'd already warned her father. They would have to sell the horses. As to the other animals that Stan had mentioned, she wouldn't send them to their deaths. But she couldn't afford charity. She'd work on finding other places for them.

Allie felt a twinge of guilt and then squared her shoulders. It was time she recognized that she didn't owe the whole world a living. She had enough to worry about with her father and Mark. And, Jeremy, of course, although he was nothing but a joy to her.

She looked over at where Clay was standing with Stan. A small frown crossed Clay's forehead. Dark stubble showed on his face. He probably hadn't shaved since he left prison. He looked tired. And it was only the beginning, she thought. Her father was right; they needed Clay for a while. What with the horses and Mark, they would be in a fix right now without him. Maybe after Easter, though, she could contact the parole board and find him another wrangler job near here. The Redfern ranch always seemed to need more workers. It would all work out.

Allie reached Clay about the same time that the pickup maneuvered the trailer into position.

"We'll need to close the side gate on the corral," she said, and Clay walked with her to do that. Then they opened the big barn door. The barn was like a large, dark cavern inside. A row of small windows was cut into each side of the barn, but the panes were dirty, and not much light filtered in, even on a sunny day.

"Smells musty," she said as she looked around. It was worse than she thought it might be. She should have at least aired it out when she came home to visit.

She heard the two men in the pickup setting up a ramp from the back of the horse trailer, and so she and Clay headed back to the front.

The rooster crowed again. This time Allie thought he sounded indignant.

"We haven't had a rooster around here for years," she said. They hadn't had hens, either. The ranch hands generally didn't like to tend to poultry, and they said the birds made the other animals nervous.

"He makes a good alarm clock," Clay said, glancing at her with humor in his eyes. "I thought you might not be too keen on him, though."

She smiled. "It'll give my dad a reason to get up and do the chores. I'll be in Jackson Hole, so I won't hear the rooster anyway."

Allie saw a flash of dark blue material in the corner of her eye and then heard her father grunt.

"I heard that," he said.

Then he came up beside them. "I don't need anyone to tell me when to do my chores. I've been working this farm for over sixty years."

Her father looked down at Jeremy, who stood beside him. "And this young fellow here is going to learn how to tend the animals, too."

Jeremy beamed as he leaned back and nodded.

"'ooster," the boy said with satisfaction as snow-flakes landed on his face. "I like 'oosters."

Allie noticed Clay smile down at her nephew.

"They call him Big Red," one of the men said as the other one opened the back door of the trailer. "Not sure what breed he is, but he's a pretty fellow. The boy will like him. All those copper feathers."

By then the two men were unloading a crate with what looked like a dozen white hens inside, although Allie had to admit it was hard to count with all the flying feathers and squawking. The men set that crate on the ground and pulled out a separate crate with the red rooster standing tall in it. One of the men turned and latched the trailer door behind them, and then the two of them started carrying the rooster's crate toward the barn.

"He goes first?" Allie asked.

"It is for the best," one of the men looked back and said with a chuckle.

Allie thought the golden red bird rode like an Oriental emperor, as though being carried along by two grown men was no more than what he was due.

"There's a chicken coop in the back of the barn," she called out. "You'll see the door on the right inside the barn. It goes to the coop. It's closed but not locked."

When the men disappeared into the barn, Allie turned to see that her father, Clay and Jeremy had all turned to stare at the open slats at the top of the trailer.

"Looks like Appaloosa horses in there," her father finally said.

"You didn't even know what kind of horses they were?" Allie asked in surprise.

"A man doesn't look a gift horse in the mouth," her father said. "I knew they were good breeding stock and that the stallion has next-to-pure bloodlines. Like I said, it's mostly a favor to get them at all for the kind of money I paid. That's why the bank gave me a loan on them. They figured I couldn't go wrong."

Allie kept her mouth shut. She'd let her father enjoy his bargain horses. If they had to sell them, and she didn't see how they wouldn't need to, she would tackle that problem after Easter. If her father wanted to continue the Nelson family tradition of supplying the horses to pull the wagon that carried the Easter cross on Sunday morning, then they would keep the horses long enough to do that. She would have a week after that to find a buyer for the horses before she needed to head back to work.

Clay walked over to stand beside her. It took her a minute to realize the storm had started up again and that Clay was standing where he was because it broke the force of the wind hitting her. A flurry of snowflakes had already been falling. She could see it on his coat.

"You don't even have a scarf yourself," she protested. "I should stand in front of you."

"Not tall enough," he replied easily.

He stood there looking like he was having the time of his life; but his ears were turning red. He had left his hat inside, too.

She shook her head. "We'll go in once the horses are unloaded and fed. I think there are a few bales of hay left in the loft. And some oats. I'm not sure how tasty any of it will be after all this time."

They heard a commotion inside the trailer again. It sounded like something was thumping against the inside wall.

The two men came out of the barn and ran back to the ramp area.

"Sorry about that," one of them said, breathless. "Billy Boy doesn't like to be left behind."

The men moved with an urgency that made Allie curious. She turned to Clay. "I hope they're not talking about any of those horses. We can't have a wild horse around. Not with Jeremy here."

"I don't think it's a horse," Clay said with a small smile on his face as he watched the ramp.

Allie turned her head and heard the bleating of an animal.

"That's a—" She leaned forward until she saw the thing's head coming out of the back of the trailer. "A goat?"

She looked up at Clay, and he grinned.

"Yup, it's a goat," he said. "Apparently he has appointed himself bodyguard for the horses."

"Horses don't need that kind of help," Allie said as she watched the dark brown goat with a white star on his forehead pick his way down the ramp. His hooves were each outlined with black. He let his displeasure known with every shake of his head as he made the trip. "Those horns look sharp."

"That they do," Clay said. "We've been advised to keep on his good side."

Allie noticed that the goat's coat was shining and the animal looked well fed. At least her father hadn't bought animals that had been abused. When the goat reached the bottom of the ramp, he turned and looked back into the trailer.

"Don't they need to keep him on some kind of a tether?" Allie's father asked.

"I don't think so," Clay said. "Looks to me like he's waiting."

The cold had settled in around Allie, but she was too absorbed in the animal show to feel it much. She decided Billy Boy looked like he'd been in the military and with a rank of some command. She saw why he felt so important when the first horse put its head out the back of the trailer.

A gorgeous Appaloosa stallion took one step down the ramp and then stopped, as if trying to get a sense of where he was. The horse's shiny black coat covered the first half of him, and his hind half was white with a spattering of black spots the size of a quarter. His head was lifted proudly in the wind, and his mane blew gently.

Just when Allie began to wonder why the horse didn't continue his descent, she saw the goat walk over and climb back up the ramp slightly until he touched the foreleg of the stallion. The horse lowered its nose to the other animal's back. As the goat made its way down the ramp, the horse followed.

"What in the world?" Allie said as she looked over at Clay.

He'd been watching the duo, too. "I think the horse is blind."

"And the goat is what—like a Seeing Eye dog?" Allie asked, astonished. "I've never heard of such a thing."

Allie noticed her father and Jeremy walking closer to see the horse.

Clay didn't answer her question, and she saw he was watching another Appaloosa horse walking down the ramp. This one, a very pregnant mare, took delicate steps. She seemed hesitant and swung her head often. Again, the horse's coat was sleek and looked well tended. She was spotted all over, a creamy white with brown splotches.

"She's lovely," Allie said with an appreciative sigh.

"Something is very wrong," Clay countered, frowning toward the ramp where a second Appaloosa mare was starting the descent.

"They look like someone took care of them," Allie said, turning to Clay. By now, the third mare was descending the ramp. "I know that only one of the mares looks pregnant, but the other two might be due later. Maybe it says something in that paperwork Stan has."

The third mare stood at the bottom of the ramp, though, her head lifted like she was hunting for some scent or sign. She nickered softly and waited as though expecting a response.

"She's looking for the rest of the herd," Clay finally said. "There had to be more than the four of them, and she was expecting the rest to be here."

As soon as Clay said it, Allie knew it was true. The mare looked distressed.

"She misses her family," Allie said softly.

He nodded. "Wanting to be with one's family is only natural—even if they're no longer there."

The driver of the pickup herded the mares into the

barn. Not that he had much to do since they seemed in-clined to follow the stallion and the goat.

"I never knew," Allie said softly. "If you missed your own family. When you came to our place."

She hadn't been very sensitive to Clay back then. He listened to all of her complaints and problems, but she didn't remember him ever talking about any of his troubles.

Clay shrugged. "It didn't help anything to miss my parents. They'd been gone a long time before I came here. I had no brothers or sisters. Not everyone needs a family."

Stan walked back to where Allie and Clay stood. Her father and Jeremy were still over by the corral, leaning against the poles.

"That's about it," Stan said. "Except the pig. I'll get her out now."

Allie was glad she'd have another moment with Clay. She wanted to say something even though she couldn't think of what it was yet.

"Those horses are blind," Clay said, making the man stay. "Why?"

Stan shrugged. "They have moon blindness. Not that uncommon in Appaloosas. Actually, the mares are only blind in one eye. It's the stallion that doesn't see at all. The ranch where they came from had a herd of over a hundred Appaloosas. These are the ones the buyer wouldn't take."

"So they were left behind," Allie said, her heart sink-ing. "They're used to a herd."

Stan shrugged. "They'll adjust."

Allie had no idea how to treat homesickness in a

horse. Not that it would be the biggest challenge they faced. "How sick are they in their eyes?"

"If you treat them with corticosteroid drops, they'll get some better," Stan said. "At least I expect they will. We have what's left of the medicine with us, and we'll leave it. The rancher had us bring over what feed he had, too. You'll do fine for a couple of weeks."

Allie nodded. They would never be able to sell these horses. No one would buy them. The horses themselves had no hope of becoming part of a bigger herd. "How much do those drops cost?"

She wondered if she could pick up another shift at work. Or maybe she could get work as a waitress at the coffee place in one of the big resorts and pick up some extra hours that way.

"I don't know how much," Stan said, and he turned to leave.

Clay was quiet for a bit after the other man left.

"I never did ask," Clay finally said. He'd turned to look down at her, his eyes serious. "Speaking of me coming here, why did your family ask for a foster kid back then?"

Allie smiled, remembering. "I was the one. My mother had died and I wanted—" She stopped then. She should have thought this through before she started her answer.

"You wanted what?" Clay asked. He didn't look like he could be put off, and she knew he wouldn't like it if she lied.

"I wanted a little sister. Someone to be silly with and do things like make cookies."

"I was to be your *playmate*?" Clay asked incredulously.

Allie shrugged. "They wouldn't give us a young girl because we didn't have my mother. They wouldn't give us an older girl, either. They thought any girl needed a mother in the house."

"So you ended up with me?" Clay asked.

He'd turned away so she couldn't see his face.

She put her hand on his arm. "I was never sorry that it was you who came."

By this time, Stan had put the horses in the barn and walked back up the ramp. He was bringing down what looked like a little dog now.

"I mean that," Allie said because Clay was still looking off into the distance.

"You don't need to worry about me," Clay said before taking a step toward Stan and that thing he was carrying. "I like my life."

"In *prison*?" Now it was her time to be baffled.

"I won't be in prison much longer," Clay said, staring at whatever Stan was carrying.

Allie realized it wasn't a dog when she heard the squeal.

"If you need money, you can always sell the pig," Stan added as he lifted the animal up so they could see it.

"This is Julie," Stan said like he was introducing them to royalty. "They call her a teacup pig because she's small. Only eighty pounds and she's full grown."

The black pig wiggled in the man's arms until she saw Allie. Then the animal lifted its head and inspected her.

"She's a princess all right," Stan said. "The woman of the house where we came from kept Julie inside the laundry room at night. Thought she was a guard dog. She's not, but her personality grows on you."

Allie just stared. "That's all of the animals, isn't it?"

Stan nodded and started to walk back to the barn.

Clay started to chuckle then, and she looked up at him. His laughter grew deeper, and his eyes danced with humor.

"You never know what you're going to get around here, do you?" he asked, his voice light and teasing. "One day a pig, another day a teenage boy."

"You were never a surprise like this," Allie interrupted, her voice firm. Then she saw his face and knew he was teasing.

"Oh," she said. "You."

"That goat looks dangerous and the pig way too intelligent for a barnyard animal," Clay continued.

Allie leaned over and whispered. "Shh—I don't think either of them see themselves as barnyard animals."

"Probably not," Clay agreed. "But they could mount a rebellion if they wanted. Mutiny in the cowshed. I can see it now."

Allie looked up and saw that her father was over by the corral signing the papers Stan had. When he finished, Stan sorted through them and peeled off a handful that he gave back to her father. Meanwhile, the other man had been pulling hay bales and sacks of grain out of the back of the trailer. He left everything just outside the barn door.

Stan started back toward Allie and Clay.

"We better get going," he said as his partner put the ramp up. "We want to get back on the interstate before the weather turns bad again."

Allie nodded. The wind had shifted again, and she didn't want to delay the men. "Thanks for the feed."

Stan reached out and shook hands with both Allie and Clay, then he ducked his head and turned around to jog back to the pickup.

By that time, her father and Jeremy had returned to where Allie stood.

"We better get everything inside the barn and dole some feed out to the animals," she said. Snowflakes were falling faster. "It's not going to get any warmer out here."

Allie heard the pickup and trailer drive out to the main gravel road as she led everyone into the barn. "It'll be quick work if we all do it. Then we can go inside for breakfast."

"With bacon?" her father asked eagerly.

"Just this once," Allie said as she opened the barn door.

"Nothing like a good crisp piece of fried bacon," her father said with a satisfied sigh. "The Nelsons have always liked their bacon."

"We shouldn't let Julie hear anyone say that," Clay leaned over and whispered in Allie's ear. "It'll make her nervous."

"What?" She looked up and then she giggled. "No one would dare turn her into breakfast meat. She doesn't need to worry."

Allie had forgotten how much she and Clay used to tease back and forth.

It was warmer inside the barn than outside, but they still worked fast. The wind had gotten stronger and rattled some of the windows as they led each of the horses to a stall.

"As I recall there are a few horse blankets here somewhere," Clay said as he was rummaging through the tack room off to the side.

"I think they're up in the loft," Allie said.

Clay walked out of the tack room and headed for the ladder leading to the loft. "I can find them, if the rest of you want to go back inside the house. It's getting colder every minute. It'll probably be zero degrees out there before long."

"Maybe you should take Jeremy inside." Allie turned to her father. He should be inside in warmer temperatures, but she knew he wouldn't go for his sake.

Her father hesitated and then nodded. "Don't be long."

He took Jeremy's hand and led the boy out of the barn.

By this time, Clay had reached the hayloft and had several old horse blankets in his arms.

"Look out below," he said and then dropped them to the main floor before scrambling down the ladder.

"Stan said the horses had their eye medicine already this morning," Clay said. "If we scatter one of those bales of hay and put these blankets on their backs, they should do fine until I can get back out here later today and get the barn more organized."

"Cleaner, you mean," Allie said with a grimace. "I had no idea we had let it go so badly."

Clay shrugged. "I don't mind some dirty work." Then he looked down at the sheepskin coat. "I don't want to get this messed up, though. I wonder where it came from."

"My dad will know," Allie said. "But, don't worry. We have lots of old jackets in the house."

"I need to get that pump running, too," Clay said suddenly.

"I forgot about that," Allie said as she started walking over to back of the barn where the valves were. "The water's turned off, so it will take some doing to get it back on." She stopped to examine the water trough and pump apparatus before she even got to the valves. Everything was frozen. At least the pipes had been empty, so they hadn't burst. "Maybe we're best to carry a few buckets of water out from the house until we can get the pump set up again."

"I'll come back," Clay said.

"We'll both come back," Allie answered.

Clay gazed at her sternly, and Allie felt like looking away, but she didn't.

"I'm the hired hand." Clay smiled as he studied her. "You don't need to outwork me to prove anything."

"I'm not going to leave you with everything to do," Allie insisted. For some reason, she felt shy around him. "Especially when you are not getting paid."

"I plan to eat a lot," he said.

"Still," she replied.

"You never could take help," Clay muttered.

"Me?" she protested, but he only laughed.

Within a few minutes, they were both leaving the barn.

"That wind's coming faster," Allie said as she ducked her head down.

The barn door had been hard to open, and it slammed closed behind them.

Clay reached over and put his arm around her, drawing her closer to his side. "I won't let you blow away."

Allie knew he wouldn't. She had never felt as safe with anyone in her life as she had with Clay. But she couldn't afford to lean on him. He'd broken her heart once when he left, and she didn't want him to break it again. That didn't mean she could let him do all the work, though.

Chapter Five

Clay felt invigorated as they fought the wind all the way to the house. He could move mountains with Allie tucked under his arm. He supposed it was nothing more than having a purpose in life again. One of the worst things about endless days in prison was the sensation of drifting, like it didn't matter whether he turned this way or that way in life. Now a few horses, a goat and a pig depended on him.

When Clay unlatched the screen door, he turned the knob on the main door as well so that Allie could hurry inside. She'd had her face pressed against his coat for the walk to the house, and when she stepped away he saw a long red mark on her cheek as a result. Her auburn hair had been whipped around her face and her lips were tight against each other.

"Cold," she muttered as she stepped into the warmth of the kitchen.

Clay joined her inside and closed the door behind them. They both stood on the rug by the door, stomping their feet and waiting for the tingling to stop in their fingers.

"It turned fierce out there all of a sudden," Mr. Nelson remarked as he came into the kitchen from the hallway on the other side of the room. He was in his stocking feet. Clay could see where the rancher had taken his boots off when he came inside and set them by the coat rack. A smaller set of boots was placed next to the older man's.

"Jeremy is in the back bedroom with that cat," Mr. Nelson continued, shaking his head. "He's worried she might be lonesome. I gave him a bowl of warm milk for the thing and fixed up a litter box."

Clay grunted. "I'm sure that old cat feels like she's landed in paradise."

"It's good for a boy to have a pet," Allie said from where she stood taking off her jacket. She'd patted her hair down already, and the red was fading from her face.

"That it is," Clay agreed, taking her all in—her tangled hair, bright cheeks and eyelashes that still shone with melting snow. She was beautiful.

Allie didn't respond and Clay figured he couldn't just keep looking at her, so he glanced around. When he'd been inside the house earlier it had been darker and he hadn't seen the place well. Now he saw it all. The walls were faded and needed paint. He had always imagined that this room was what a home looked like. The clock on the wall said it was eight o'clock. He used to wonder what it would be like to live in this house rather than out in the bunkhouse. Now he knew there had been trouble enough in here, too.

Clay was the first one to hear the distant sound of an

engine. Initially, he thought the wind was merely changing directions and had found a drain pipe or something to make a whistling sound.

"I hope it's not those two guys coming back," Clay said when the sound grew louder and Allie had stopped to listen, as well.

"The deal is done," Mr. Nelson said. "They can't come back and get those animals. They're ours now."

"I'm sure they don't want them," Allie said, looking at her father with a touch of impatience. "I don't know how we're going to feed them, either."

"You'll figure it out," Mr. Nelson said, and there was nothing but confidence in his voice.

The stress seemed to have left the older man's face. Clay wondered if leaving everything to Allie to worry about always took the burden from her father. She did seem to be the one who shouldered most of the troubles around here. Now that Clay thought about it, it had been that way when he lived here long ago, too. Mark used to say Allie was a worrywart, always fussing about something. Clay suspected now that the story had been different. No one else had worried enough. She'd been taking care of them all.

A knock sounded at the door and a man shouted, "Anybody home?"

Clay knew he'd have to open the door regardless of who it was, but he wished the door had a window in it so he could see who it was before that. He didn't want to make the man wait, though, no matter what his business was. The temperature was too cold for that. Since the visitor wouldn't be for him, Clay stepped back as he opened the door until he was in the same half shadows that had hidden Allie earlier.

"Is he here?" the man demanded before he even stepped inside. The screen was still closed, but the man was peering through the mesh. Clay thought the voice sounded familiar, but he couldn't place it. The man continued, "Someone was sneaking through town with their lights on low an hour ago or so, and I figured it had to be him."

With that, Clay knew there was little hope the man was talking about anyone else but him.

"I wasn't sneaking," Clay said at the same time as Mr. Nelson spoke.

"Of course Clay is here," the older man announced as he walked toward the open door. "We're just getting him settled."

"Besides, it's a public road," Clay offered up in his defense. "And my headlights were on high."

The man grunted, and Clay left the shadows in hopes that he could take a better look at the visitor. "Randy Collins? Is that you?"

The tall, thin man swiveled. He was still on the other side of the mesh, so his lean face wasn't as clear as Clay would have liked. Some things had not changed, though. A worn black hat sat pressed low on the man's head and the collar of his red wool jacket sat up tight around his skinny neck. The sleeves on his jacket were too short, and his hands were shoved into his pockets. Randy considered it a sign of weakness to wear gloves unless it was twenty degrees below zero outside.

"It's me all right," Randy said with satisfaction in his voice.

Clay smiled. This man had been one of the ranch hands who lived in the bunkhouse with him. Clay didn't know why he was pleased to see Randy again. The two of them had never been particular friends, even if they certainly had gotten along easier years ago than it appeared they were now. Clay wondered if maybe it was the simple fact that they had shared a fire on many winter nights that made him want to avoid any quarrel with the man. There was not enough space in a bunkhouse for bickering.

"You're letting in the cold," Clay noted, keeping his tone mild as Randy just stood there. Clay might not want to upset the other man, but he didn't want to add to the difficulties he could see Allie already tallying in her mind.

Mr. Nelson stepped closer and spoke to Randy. "I expect you came out to welcome Clay here."

Randy snorted and finally opened the screen door. His breath still blew white in the freezing air.

"I'd rather welcome a blizzard," Randy muttered. "Or maybe even one of those freak tornadoes where everything goes flying."

"You got a problem with me?" Clay asked as the ranch hand walked into the middle of the doorway and stopped.

"You said it," Randy exclaimed and turned to point at Clay.

The man's finger was so pale it looked half-frozen. The door stayed open as Randy just stood there glaring.

Mr. Nelson grimaced and then waved the man inside. "Mad or not, you might as well get in here."

"I've done nothing for you to be getting on my case

about," Clay said once the door was shut. Randy just stood there as the snowflakes on his hat and coat started to melt. At least he'd put his hands back in his pockets.

"You've caused me nothing but grief," Randy said, a hard note in his voice. "My life has fallen apart, and it's your fault."

"That's nonsense," Mr. Nelson reprimanded the other man sharply. "Clay hasn't even been here."

"I can speak for myself." Clay started turning toward Randy. He didn't get all the way there, though, when Allie walked past him, headed to the thermostat on the kitchen wall. Her face had more color than it had earlier. Just seeing her calmed him.

"I expect you have your challenges," Clay said as he finished the turn and faced Randy. Clay had learned some conflict resolution tools in prison and he thought he should use them now. He tried to visualize himself in Randy's place, which was not easy to do when his gaze wanted to settle on Allie instead.

"I sure do," the other man agreed, not seeming to realize Clay had other things to occupy his mind.

Clay forced himself to concentrate.

None of the ranch hands had been comfortable coming to the big house, Clay thought as Randy took his hands out of his pockets and rubbed them together. That much hadn't seemed to change. Clay thought it looked like Randy had the same pair of boots that he'd had when they were working together. They were certainly creased and scuffed enough to be the same ones. His jeans were frayed, too. Life hadn't been prosperous for him lately.

Still, even if money was scarce, Clay wondered what

could be that terrible about living as a free man in a place like Dry Creek. Randy might not be staying in the bunkhouse, but, if he was the one who had turned on that light Clay had saw in town earlier, he was set up in some house when Clay drove by tonight. The man had shelter and, likely, heat. Plus, there was lots of fresh air around. Good water. Enough quiet to think. Randy should try prison for a week, Clay thought to himself. That would teach him to be grateful for what he had.

Clay caught himself before he said anything. He supposed there were some problems in life for people who were not incarcerated, too. One of the key points in conflict resolution was to be open to the other person's experience.

"No need to get all upset," Allie said to the ranch hand as she walked toward the kitchen sink. She'd apparently warmed up. "Clay's going to be working with us for a while. That's why he drove out here."

"I can't see why you'd hire someone like him," Randy said, jutting his chin out in defiance.

Clay was going to say something, but Allie spoke to Randy. "You're welcome to stay for breakfast." Then she reached for the coffeepot and started the water running.

Randy looked surprised. "Thanks."

The men all listened to the water running for a moment.

"Anyway, I'm sorry if I disturbed you earlier," Clay finally managed to say. "We all need our sleep."

The other man shrugged. "I had to get up and check on things at the church anyway. There are some kids that have been messing with the daffodil tarps. So far they haven't done anything but look. I saw tire tracks behind the building. I think it's mainly that foster kid over at the Redfern ranch. He'll do worse than look if we give him time."

"That's not fair," Clay protested, trying to keep his voice mild. He didn't want people here to be afraid of him. The fact that he had defended himself against tougher men than Randy didn't mean he should let that be known. "Just because a kid doesn't have a family doesn't mean he's up to anything wrong."

Randy grinned. "What else can you say? You guys all stick together."

"Being a foster kid isn't like being in a gang," Clay said flatly. His fingers had formed a fist, and he slowly relaxed them. Even when he was here he could have handled most of the men working on the ranch.

Randy snorted. "Oh yeah? The kid moves here from Missoula and suddenly trouble starts to happen around here. I don't know what you call it, but he's a bad influence on others."

"Does he wrestle?" Clay asked. "This boy."

Randy looked puzzled. "I don't know. Why?"

Clay shrugged. "A boy would need some muscle to make much trouble around here." He remembered how people had their doubts when he moved here. "The teens here are big farm kids. No one tells them what to do—especially not some stranger. And they're not all perfect either. It could be any one of them doing stuff."

Randy eyed Clay. "I remember you said something like that to the judge at your trial. You led Mark down a path of crime, and when the whole thing went south, you blamed him. Always pointing to the other guy."

"I happened to be telling the truth," Clay said and took a deep breath.

He glanced over at Allie. She looked tired. Tendrils of her dark auburn hair fell from the twist she had in the back of her head. She had picked up the spatula again. He wondered if she was going to fry some eggs.

"You're just making excuses," Randy said, scoffing.

Clay felt his heart start to speed up. He knew how to keep his cool. But, it didn't mean that he didn't still get angry.

"Now, boys," Mr. Nelson said, sounding old and weary.

"Dad's not supposed to have any stress," Allie interjected from where she stood by the stove. "High blood pressure."

"Are you okay?" Clay asked the rancher.

Mr. Nelson nodded.

"He'll be just fine when you get yourself out of here," Randy said. "When are you planning to leave?"

"Not for some time." Clay didn't like how pale Allie's face was. "I have some things to do first."

"Like what?" Randy asked belligerently.

"Visiting someone," Clay replied.

Randy's eyes narrowed. "Who? There isn't anyone here who you need to see."

"My brother," Allie said then. "If you have to know, he's going to see Mark."

"Well," Randy started in the same tone and then stopped. He continued in a much quieter tone. "Don't seem much point to that, sorry to say."

"I don't agree," Clay said firmly.

Allie looked over at him in alarm. "Remember."

Clay nodded but didn't say anything else.

"The two of you are in cahoots, aren't you?" Randy asked, a quiet edge to his voice as he jerked his head in Allie's direction.

Clay wasn't sure what the other man was implying, but he kept his voice neutral. "Allie has a right to speak up around here. This is her home."

"And we're only the hired help," Randy shot back. "You best remember that."

Clay flinched. The other man wasn't saying anything Clay didn't know, but he didn't like to hear it.

"You might as well spit it out," Clay said then, knowing there was more poison to come from the man.

Randy nodded and lifted the finger he had pointed at Clay earlier. "You are the one to blame. Always have been. The boss here took you in when he didn't need to all those years ago. Not all of us in the bunkhouse thought it was a good idea. But he did it—out of the goodness of his heart. And what did you do? You brought this ranch to its knees. Clean wiped the Nelsons out. There's nothing left out there. And me? I lost my job because of you and haven't found another once since."

Clay had been told by the social worker who brought him to the ranch that everyone was on board with the decision, but Clay had wondered at the time if that were true. He wasn't going to apologize, though, so if that was what the other man was waiting for, they would be standing here for a long time.

"It wasn't just me—" Randy started in louder now that Clay was silent.

"Who wants bacon?" Allie called out and interrupted the other man. Clay could have kissed her. She was the peacemaker. Everyone paused and assured her that they did want a few slices.

Mr. Nelson walked to the table and sat down in a chair. Then he looked at Randy and motioned him to the table, as well. "Is this about your cousin? Is that what has you stomping around?"

"For starters," Randy admitted as he joined the other man. He took his hat off and slapped it on the side of his leg to dislodge the few flakes of snow that hadn't melted yet. Then he set the Stetson on a side chair.

"Sam Collins is his cousin," Mr. Nelson announced to Clay and then pulled out a chair at the table for Clay. "You remember him?"

Clay nodded. He'd never forget the clerk at that gas station who had spoken out against him at his trial.

"He's never gotten over the shooting that happened that night," Randy said accusingly as he sat there. "Now he won't take a job in any service station. Too afraid of being robbed again. Can't seem to get any other kind of a job, either. Not even pizza delivery. He moved back to his parents' old house. Nobody had lived in it for years. Had to take the boards off the windows. All he's got for money is the rent I pay for staying with him in the house."

"I remember you talking about your cousin." Clay didn't move closer to the table like the other two men had. "Always sounded like you got along together fine."

"We did. I mean, we do," Randy said, moving his hat from the chair to his knee. Maybe because he was getting warmer, the red in his face had lessened. "But my cousin can't get by without what little I pay him in rent, and I don't want to spend my life living with him. I feel like we're still kids together. The time comes when a man's got to have a place to call his own. A home, you know. Some place where he could set up a family."

Randy's face flushed a deep red. "You know how it is. A woman would refuse to even date a man with no job and nothing but a room in his cousin's house."

"Ah," Clay said. Now he understood.

"Come to think of it, I don't suppose you would know about that," Randy said. "The dating I mean."

Clay shrugged. "There are guys in prison who have women who write to them and propose. We're better than a dating service."

Randy shook his head but gave a wry chuckle. "You're a regular a comedian, aren't you? Or are you saying I should go rob a bank to improve my chances with women?"

"I'm just saying you shouldn't give up," Clay said, and then he looked over at Allie. "Isn't that right?"

Allie smiled. "Leave me out of this one."

Clay imagined she was smiling straight at him. She always had appreciated his joking around. It suddenly struck him that he was as bad off as poor Randy here, wishing for what he didn't have.

"You won't think this is so funny when you lose your job and it happens to you," Randy said to Clay then, back to being glum.

"I didn't mean to make light of it," Clay said, sobering. "I know a man needs a job."

"He sure does," Randy said, giving Clay a defiant look before turning toward Mr. Nelson. His voice lost any belligerence it had and became subservient as he addressed the older man. "Just want you to know that if you need a ranch hand, you don't need to rely on Clay there. My job taking care of those daffodils for the church is just until Easter. They don't pay much. It's not even really a job. I think they just have me doing it so they can give me some money, and I'll take it. But it's something so I can take partial wages until you get the ranch going again. I can still pay some rent to Sam if I live in the bunkhouse. We'll work it out."

Clay supposed he shouldn't be surprised that one of the old ranch hands would be circling his new position like a hungry vulture waiting for its prey to stumble and die. Clay knew how to stop that, though. "I'm not getting any wages."

Randy seemed taken back at that announcement. "Are they holding your money back until harvest or something?"

Clay shook his head as he walked over to the table. He still didn't sit down. "It's called victim reparations. I don't get paid—ever."

Randy looked like he was taking a minute to digest that information.

"So, if you want the job," Clay said softly, "it's all yours."

Randy didn't answer.

Clay walked over to the stove and held out his hand to Allie. "Can I help?"

She looked up at him in surprise before giving him the platter of eggs and bacon to take over to the table. A dish towel had been put under the plate like a pot holder, and he welcomed the warmth in his hands as he carried the food.

"I'll bring the coffee," Allie said as she lifted up the plate of toast, as well.

Clay nodded.

"Thanks for helping," Allie murmured as they walked together.

Randy frowned over at Clay. "You wear an apron these days?"

Clay didn't say anything as he started walking to the table. "I sure do if I can find one. Nothing wrong with a man helping in the kitchen. Especially if he wants to eat."

Randy scowled even deeper.

Clay and Allie set their platters on the table and then each sat down.

Allie had to admit she'd been as surprised at Clay's actions as Randy had been. Cooking was still considered women's work in this ranching area. She didn't remember Clay ever offering to help with kitchen chores when he'd been here before. Maybe he had learned a thing or two in prison.

"Let's pray before we get to the eggs and bacon," her father said then as a fully dressed Jeremy raced to the table and found his chair. Allie noted he'd found the blue shirt he'd been looking for. She looked closer and could see the cat hair on it.

Allie saw her father reach out his hand to her and then Jeremy. The boy held out his hand to Randy.

"After Grandpa prays," Allie whispered to Jeremy, "you'll need to go wash your hands. One of the rules of having a pet is to wash your hands before you eat anything."

Jeremy nodded.

"We hold hands as we pray," Allie then turned to her side and murmured to Clay. When he'd been here before, the ranch hands had their meals out in the bunkhouse. Her father had said it was too much work for Allie at her age to cook for eight working men in addition to the family. They had put in a full kitchen out there, and one of the older men had fixed the meals.

She offered Clay her hand.

For a minute, Allie thought he wasn't going to take it.

"I hope it doesn't offend you if we pray," she whispered, feeling awkward with her hand still stretched out. She sometimes neglected going to church when she was working in Jackson Hole, but she never did in Dry Creek. She knew prayer worked; her mother had taught her that. She was grateful she could pray with her family.

"I wouldn't say it offends me." Clay finally reached out, as well. "I'm used to doing for myself so I sure don't count on prayers to do much good, but I don't mind folks asking for help."

Before she knew it, he had her hand securely tucked inside one of his. She could feel the cold from him still even though he'd been inside for a while now.

"I think one hand is enough, though," Clay said quietly with a smile at Randy. "No offense if I don't take yours."

"None taken," Randy said with some relief in his voice.

"We need to pray for the mama kitty," Jeremy said as he looked up at his grandfather with trust in his eyes.

"So she knows I'm her friend and will feed her. I think she's still a little scared."

Allie smiled at her nephew. "You'll need to be patient with her. Is she drinking the milk Grandpa gave you for her?"

Jeremy nodded.

Her father's prayer was simple, and it calmed her. As she sat with her eyes closed and listened to him ask for God's blessing on those animals he'd just bought, she prayed for her own strength. She could not blame her father for wanting his ranch to be active again. It's just that she was paying those mortgage payments and she didn't know how she'd stretch things to include more.

"And we thank You for Your bounty to us." Her father's voice interrupted her thoughts.

"Amen." Allie joined him in saying the word.

The smell of bacon and fried eggs hung in the air until breakfast was finished.

"I appreciate the meal," Clay said as he pushed back his chair and rose. "I'd like to take a look around the barn and see what's what, though, before too much time passes."

"You'll want to look at the bunkhouse, too," Mr. Nelson said, looking up to meet Clay's eyes. "It'll make you want to sleep in the house tonight. You can take Mark's old room. Jeremy's using it now, but he can sleep on the couch. I didn't get anything out there straightened up."

"The bunkhouse is fine for me," Clay said as he walked over to the rack and lifted the sheepskin coat off it. "It looks like this storm isn't going away, so I'd like to get settled in out there anyway."

Allie watched as he stood there a moment. Then he turned toward her and her father.

"I never did hear who this sheepskin coat belongs to," Clay said.

Allie noticed he didn't ask outright, but he was clearly curious.

"Oh, I forgot," Mr. Nelson said. "I was supposed to tell you that the coat belonged to Mrs. Hargrove's first husband. He's been dead for a long time now, and she thought you might need a warm coat. Told me to have it sent over with the pickup. You know Mrs. Hargrove, don't you? Well, a few years ago she married my cousin, Charley Nelson, but she keeps her old name."

"She didn't want to confuse all the little kids in Dry Creek," Allie added. "She'll always be Mrs. Hargrove to them."

"She's a good woman all right," Clay agreed as he stood looking at the coat in his hands. "She wrote to me in prison, and I appreciate that. Which is all the more reason for me to borrow something else to wear while I clean out the barn. I'll save the coat to wear to church tomorrow."

"It'd look nice with a good tie," Allie teased.

Clay grinned back at her. "Ties are not real popular in prison. Neither are belts or shoelaces. I do have a good shirt, though."

Allie couldn't manage a smile in return. She suddenly didn't like the thought of Clay being in a prison. There was nothing amusing about that.

"We have some things in the spare closet," she said as she led Clay into the hallway.

Allie remembered that her mother had always complained that the hallway was too small and too dark. They'd done what they could by painting the walls a mint green that her mother claimed would remind everyone of spring. Several pencil drawings were framed and lined up between two doorways. She noticed Clay studying the artwork, but he didn't say anything.

"Some cousin drew them," she finally mumbled as she slid the closet doors open and reached inside. "My mother liked them."

"They're good," Clay said sincerely.

"Here are a couple of the extra work coats." Allie held up a red parka and a brown wool coat. Both were a little ragged. She held the parka higher. "Mark wore this one in high school. Said it was warm enough for skiing—not that he ever got a chance to go. My dad uses it some now."

Allie almost put the jacket back in the closet. It wasn't fair that her brother never even had a chance to ski down a mountain.

Clay reached for the jacket, though, and she let it go.

"Let's see if it fits," he said. "It looks like the bigger of the two, but—"

Clay started to shrug his shoulders into it. He didn't have it all the way on when Allie heard the sound of fabric tearing.

"Oops," she said as Clay froze in position.

"Here, let me see what's wrong," Allie said as she hung the brown coat back on a hook in the closet. The light in the hallway might be dim, but she could see a pucker in the back of the red parka, and she reached her hand out to feel along the seam of the coat.

"It's the lining, I think," Allie said as she lifted the

back of the coat up as far as she could. That left a broad expanse of gray plaid flannel shirt covering Clay's back. Frayed threads from a tear in the red nylon lining of the coat stuck to the shirt. Allie laid one hand on Clay's back to steady herself while she picked the few threads off Clay's shirt. It was a mistake. The heat coming from him made her pull her hand away.

Suddenly, the hallway seemed even darker than it had been. It was all in her mind, she told herself. She was more than eight inches from Clay West's back, and she needed to collect her wits.

"I'll be able to mend that for you," Allie said, hoping her voice didn't give away her agitation. She supposed she was having a temporary flashback to her teenage years. She certainly felt like the love-struck sixteen-year-old girl who had a crush on Clay.

"You've grown," she said without thinking as she smoothed the coat down over his back. Even with all of the padding in the coat, she could feel the strength of his muscles. She let her hands drop when she realized she was almost caressing him.

He turned around. She hoped he didn't see the pink in her face.

"You don't need to fix the coat on my account," Clay said, his voice low and uneven. "I just need it to clean the barn. The tear isn't very big."

Allie thought Clay sounded rattled. She hoped he hadn't wondered what she was doing leaving her palm against his back like that. She didn't know if she could explain it.

"You'll need a scarf, too," she said, leaving the closet

door open. "On the hook to the right. There are a bunch of them."

She could see Clay nod.

Allie hurried back into the kitchen. Randy was standing beside the table.

"I'll be going," the ranch hand said when he saw her. "Thanks for breakfast."

"Come back later if you want to work a few hours today," Allie said impulsively. "We'll have work for a couple of days next week, too. We're going to need help getting the barn and corrals ready for all the animals. An extra pair of hands will help. Especially with Sunday coming up tomorrow. It won't be long, but we can pay an hourly wage."

"Great," Randy said, a smile splitting his face. "I'll go back to my cousin's and get some work clothes. I have a few other things to take care of for the church, but I'll be back by noon."

Randy had his hand on the outside door as Clay walked back into the kitchen from the hallway. He had a mud-colored wool scarf twisted around his neck.

Clay walked out of the door behind Randy and closed it. Allie could still see his shape through the screen door, and she watched him head toward the bunkhouse.

"I wonder if he realizes that he picked that pink scarf," her father said, a smile on his face. "At least the wool was pink before you dyed it. I believe you knitted that the winter when you were twelve."

Allie nodded and scrunched up her nose. "That was when I decided pink was for girls and I wanted to be more…" She shrugged.

"You wanted to be one of the guys." Her father supplied the rest of her words.

"It seemed to work back then," Allie said.

It was odd that Clay had chosen that scarf. She generally kept it as far back in the closet as she could. It was the ugliest scarf she'd ever seen.

"And now?" her father asked quietly.

Allie looked up in surprise. Her father never wanted to talk about feelings and things like that. She wondered suddenly if he had seen her standing in the hallway with her hand on Clay's back. She'd no sooner asked herself if that could have happened before she decided it was meaningless anyway. It wasn't like they had kissed or anything.

"I could wear pink now," Allie answered her father.

He nodded. "That's what I thought."

She didn't say anything else as she put on her own coat and scarf. "I best go help. Keep an eye on Jeremy."

"We'll come out in an hour or so," her father added.

"Randy might be back by then," Allie said as she headed for the door. "You and Jeremy might as well spend the morning inside. The boy doesn't need all this cold."

Her father nodded. She couldn't help but wonder if he was giving her some time alone with Clay.

Her father's color was beginning to look normal again. The temperatures were too low for him out there, so she hoped he would be content to stay with Jeremy.

Chapter Six

The sky was still overcast when Clay walked out of the house and headed to the bunkhouse. He noticed a small drift building in front of the pickup as he walked by. Damp air chilled him as he breathed it in, but the cold helped settle him. He told himself he needed to call a halt to the feelings he was starting to have. The one thing Randy had gotten right this morning was that they were both workers on this ranch. Allie was the owner's daughter. He and Allie had always had a certain something between them, but that didn't mean she was interested in him as anything more than a ranch hand.

The snow was deep on the steps to the bunkhouse, and Clay used his boots to open up a wide pathway. When he tried to open the door, it would not budge. The knob turned, but the door was stuck.

"I'm guessing the latch is frozen. Ice," Clay muttered to himself. Nothing happened easily around here, and that was fine with him.

He put his shoulder to the door and pushed. It opened. Light came into the bunkhouse through the side windows. He barely noticed the layer of dust on the plank floor of the long room. Everything was brown in the shadows. Seven metal cots lined the north wall, nails sticking out of the raw wood boards above each short headboard. An old shirt that used to be white and was now gray hung from one of the nails, and the other homemade hooks looked ready to hold more belongings. The cots were still neatly made with the top of the white sheets folded back over khaki blankets. There were no pillows.

Clay eyed the last bunk in the lineup. That one had been his. No nails had been hammered into the wood above that cot, which made him realize that his cot had been added later than the others. He had squeezed the other ranch hands when he moved in. None of them had said anything, though. He wondered now what other cues he'd missed back then.

Like with the other cots, the top blanket on his went to the floor on both sides, so he couldn't see under it. He did wonder briefly if his old suitcase was still there. No one had mentioned his belongings when they sent him off to jail. He had never heard what had happened to that suitcase. Someone had probably thrown it out by now. It had been with him for all twelve of his years in the foster care system, but it didn't look like much so he didn't think anyone would hesitate to toss it. It had been where he'd kept his drawings, though.

By now he could see through the window that Allie was walking over here, picking up her feet in the packed snow like she was walking through a layer of thick sand. That meant the snow must be melting a little. Clay would look under his old cot, but he didn't want to be going through those drawings when she was around. Too many of his drawings had been of her. The thought of her seeing them made him hope someone had thrown that suitcase away without bothering to open it. Not that there was anything improper in the drawings; they were just starry-eyed. As he remembered, he'd even drawn roses around the border of one of her portraits.

He shook his head just thinking about it. He supposed every man had a sentimental streak when he was young. That didn't mean he wanted anyone to know about it, though.

Clay moved deeper into the room. A rock fireplace dominated the wall by the outside door. There were still ashes in the grate and a glass canning jar on the simple pine mantel. Three brown leather sofas were gathered in front of the fireplace. A scarred coffee table stood in the middle of them, and a pole lamp stood to the side.

Clay remembered some good times, sitting around that fireplace in the evenings with the other ranch hands. Sometimes the cook would make them all cocoa when a blizzard was howling outside.

He continued gazing around and saw the door to the left that opened up into what everyone had called the new kitchen when he'd been here. It had been added to the bunkhouse a few months before he got there. A new large bathroom had been added, as well. He walked over and looked into the kitchen. Black-and-white linoleum covered the floor. A long counter lined the wall across from the door, its length interrupted by the double sink in the middle. The dark green countertop was tile. The cabinets had been painted white. Two regular-sized refrigerators sat to the left of the door, and a double-oven gas stove was on the wall opposite.

Large square windows dominated the far white corner of the kitchen, and that's where the rectangular oak table sat, three chairs to each side and one on each end. In the winter, when the shades were rolled up, that was the warmest corner in the bunkhouse, including the sofas by the fireplace. A bookcase stood under the left window, not that there were many books. The ranch hands joked that the bookcase was nothing but a fancy display for the cook's philodendron plants. Clay and Mark used to sit in that corner, playing chess at the table and discussing the problems of the world.

Clay looked closer and remembered the Bible that stood in the bookcase. He and Mark had been doing something called the Easter Challenge that year. The church had invited everyone to read the Gospel of Luke.

Clay went over and slipped the Bible off the shelf. Mark had his own Bible in the main house; this one had been left behind by some ranch hand Clay never knew. The gum wrapper he'd used to keep his place in the Bible was still there. As he recalled, neither he nor Mark had gotten very far in the story before that night interrupted both their lives.

Clay set the Bible back where it had been, noting for the first time that the shelf had rust rings where metal planters had sat for years. Someone must have eventually thrown the planters away.

He heard the door open in the other room, and he turned slightly.

Before long, Allie stood in the doorway of the kitchen. She had a loose knit scarf around her neck, the red of the scarf making her cheeks look even pinker than they did from the cold. Allie always had liked color.

She looked around and shook her head. "I thought we at least had some pictures on the walls out here. It's pretty dreary. We'll fix it up for you."

Clay shrugged. "I've lived with worse. It's okay."

He knew he'd said the wrong thing when he saw Allie's face crumple a little.

"We're not going to let you live in a place that's as bad as prison," Allie said, her voice firm. "You can stay in the house." She paused and added softly, "In Mark's old room."

Clay looked at her. He'd seen less resolute faces on men headed to solitary confinement. "There's no need for that. You've no reason to feel guilty."

Her eyes flashed at that. "The least we can do is see that you have a nice room. I figure other parolees get paid for the time that they work for someone."

"I wouldn't know," Clay said shortly.

"You might have ended up with a regular parole if it wasn't for my father," Allie said in a rush.

Clay was silent.

"It's the truth then?" Allie said as her shoulders slumped and she stared at the floor.

Clay hated seeing her look miserable. And it certainly wasn't justified. "I never qualified for parole."

Allie looked up at that.

"Before you can be considered for parole, you have to say you are sorry for what you did," Clay continued quietly. "I never did what they said I had so—"

Clay couldn't take his gaze off Allie. As he watched, her eyes grew round.

"You wouldn't admit it," she finally said. "Not even to get out of prison."

The silence between them stretched long.

Finally, Allie shifted her stance. More light was coming in the windows, and it sounded like the wind had died down outside. She had known Clay was proud and stubborn, but she almost couldn't believe what she was hearing.

"When would you have gotten out on parole?" she asked then. "If you had done what they asked?"

"Last year about this time," he said.

Allie nodded for lack of anything else to do. "Please, do take Mark's bedroom if you'd like. It's much warmer in the house."

Clay shrugged. "I'm guessing Mark's room has been kept for him, just the way he left it."

Allie nodded. Her father had insisted on that, and she had half agreed with him so neither one of them had disturbed it much. They even left his comb on his dresser and the books he was reading on his nightstand. She had changed the linens before Jeremy came, but no one else had stayed in the room in the past four years.

"Jeremy can sleep on the airbed in my dad's room," Allie continued. "He spends half of the night there anyway. He likes to sleep with his grandpa."

She could see Clay considering her words.

"Thank you," he finally said. "But I'd do better out here. I'm sure there's firewood out by the back door, and we'll be able to turn the water on today. Randy might want to stay in the bunkhouse, too. It'll be like old times."

He was trying too hard to convince her, Allie thought, but she wouldn't argue. "I'll take the bedding in and let that go through the washing machine while we're working in the barn. You'll have your meals with us no matter what."

Clay looked relieved when she accepted his decision. She supposed he might like the solitude of the bunkhouse after being in prison.

"I suppose we should see to the animals first," she finally said. "Once we have some hot water to work with, I'll run the mop over these floors, as well."

Clay nodded. "Let's go to the barn then."

Allie followed him as he walked out the door.

The number of things she was responsible for was growing, she told herself. She missed her mother. She had spent her childhood trying to control more than she could with her father and brother. She wasn't about to become involved with a man she could not trust.

Which reminded her of something.

"My father has a note for you," she said to Clay as they approached the barn. "He wanted me to be sure and take you back to the house before Randy got back. He thought the note might be private."

"Private?" Clay stopped and turned around. "For me?"

Allie nodded. "I didn't ask from whom."

Her father liked to be secretive, but she wished he had given her some clue. She could tell Clay looked worried. She wondered if there was any way the parole board had sent him a message telling him to come back. She knew she should want something like that to happen, but she didn't.

Clay was here, and he seemed to want to stay. At least, she thought so.

"We should get things set up in the barn first," Clay said. "Let's check on the pump. And we should turn the propane heater on here in the bunkhouse and in the tack room off the barn."

"I'd like to take another look at the Appaloosa horses, too," Allie said.

"I knew you couldn't resist those horses," Clay said, grinning. "They'll eat you out of house and home, but you're going to like having them here."

Allie didn't even bother to reply. She'd forgotten how well he'd known her when he lived on the ranch. It would be easy to step back into their old friendly ways. But that robbery had changed everything. She didn't know if she could ever trust him again.

Chapter Seven

Allie stepped into the barn before Clay. Sunshine streamed in through the windows and the air vents until there were rectangular blocks of light throughout the barn. The smell of sweet hay mingled with that of horse. None of the Appaloosas turned to look at Allie and Clay when they walked farther into the barn, but Allie noticed the goat, Billy Boy, stood next to the stallion and gave them a warning bleat.

"We're harmless," Allie said to the goat.

Billy Boy dipped his head, but didn't make another sound.

Allie let the silence surround her as she watched Clay walk toward the animals. When he came to one of the mares, he held his hand out.

"Easy now," he whispered as he ran his hand along the mare's spotted flank.

Allie could sense how much Clay liked being with the horse. Chocolate-brown splotches mixed with the light cream of the animal's coat.

Clay looked over the horses back to the water trough and turned to Allie. "Looks like the pump is working."

Allie nodded. She felt like she had come home in a way that she hadn't felt in years. The Nelson ranch had always had horses. Even though she didn't like the way her father had done things, she couldn't be sorry that these horses were here.

She walked over to a different mare from the one Clay had claimed. She made sure she was on the right side of the mare so the animal could see her out of the one eye that seemed to be working.

Allie ran her fingers across the sway in the back of the young mare. The horse backed away and nickered a little. Allie took her hands off the animal and waited until the mare came close again. Allie rested her hand on the mare's back this time without moving it. She could feel the nervous tension in the horse.

"Easy," she murmured as she started to stroke the horse again. A riot of gray spots covered the white coat of this one. She had always liked Appaloosas; they were like some impressionistic painting hanging in a museum. They used to be the horse favored by the Plains Native Americans, too, so they were in their share of famous artwork.

"Those spots on her look like smoke going up a chimney," Clay commented to Allie as he studied the horse she was working with. "Wonder what her name is."

"The only information in the paperwork about the horses are numbers," Allie answered. "The horses were stock, not pets. I doubt they have names."

"Even the goat has a name," Clay said. "I can't see calling the horses by numbers."

"They were part of a larger herd," Allie said. "No one names a hundred horses. But for these, it's going to change." Allie stroked the mare's neck. "Isn't that right, Zee Zee?"

Clay looked over at Allie in surprise. "I figured you'd go with something like Spot. You know, an animal's name. *Zee Zee* sounds like a rock star."

Allie pointed to the mare's neck. "Doesn't that cluster of spots form a *Z*?"

Clay nodded. "Close enough."

"Besides, she's a classy lady," Allie added as the mare finally turned to her and nuzzled her hand. "One who expects a little sugar now and then."

Clay was silent as Allie kept petting the mare's neck. Finally, she looked over at him. He was staring at her like he was puzzling over something.

"What?" she said.

"I always wondered what a classy lady would want," Clay said with a wry twist to his mouth. He had walked closer and no longer stood by the mare he'd singled out earlier.

Allie felt her mouth go dry. She worked so many hours in Jackson Hole that she didn't date. She was, however, used to men flirting with her. That seemed a perennial problem for any woman who worked in the ski resorts. She'd handle this the same way she would if she were on the job.

"What do ladies want?" Allie stopped stroking the horse. More sunshine was coming into the barn, but it was still dim enough for the barn to feel intimate. She waited an extra moment to be sure she had his attention. "Most of the ones I know want someone to clean up around the house."

Clay grinned. "I thought it was diamonds."

"That, too," Allie said, flashing him a cocky look. She was relieved he had been teasing.

"Well, that leaves me out," Clay said then as he started walking to the barn's door. The wood floor echoed with each step of his boots.

Allie fell into step with him as he passed. She wore tennis shoes and she made no sound.

She told herself she had handled that well. She supposed it was only natural that she and Clay would flirt with each other a little until they found their rhythm again. They had both grown up since they had been friends before. Their lives had changed. Yet some of their teasing still seemed to be in place.

As Clay reached for the barn door handle, Allie decided she might as well ask the question she wanted answered.

"But how about you?" she said. "What is it that you want? I mean, with your girlfriend."

He hadn't mentioned any woman, but Mark always said Clay had women coming on to him all the time. She'd spent her sixteenth year jealous of phantom girls who she never knew even existed. It wasn't wrong, she told herself, to want to know if her old friend had a connection with someone.

Clay stopped and considered a moment. Then he turned and looked directly at her. The dim light in the barn darkened the blue in his eyes. His lips quirked slightly, and he reached out to gently touch her cheek. She parted her lips as he trailed his finger down her cheek until it rested near her lips. He leaned downward in slow motion, and she arched up on her tiptoes.

He kissed her, and Allie felt the warmth of it curl inside her. It was the gentlest kiss she'd ever had, scarcely more than a brush of his lips, but she didn't want it to end.

Clay rested his forehead against hers for a few moments before eventually pulling away.

"All I want is for someone to trust me," he whispered. "To believe me and know what I say is true."

"Oh." Allie knew then that this had also been the saddest kiss she'd ever had.

"I'm not sure if I've met her yet or not," he whispered.

"I can't choose you over Mark." She felt a moment's anger that he would ask that of her, and then she remembered she had been the one to bring up the question.

"I'm sorry," she added.

"So am I," he answered.

He pulled away then, and they stood there looking at each other.

She knew without asking that he would not compromise on this point. They were on opposite sides here.

Clay finally moved to open the door, and they walked out of the barn. The midmorning sun had warmed everything outside. The snow was melting, and that made it even harder to put one foot in front of the other.

Sometimes, Allie told herself, a woman had to stick with her family even if her heart wished she could believe something improbable. That was part of being a grown-up. Things did not always go the way one wanted. That night could not have happened the way

Clay remembered. But he'd been tried and convicted of armed robbery. The court might have some doubt that Clay was the one who planned the holdup, but for the past four years, Allie had refused to believe her brother had been the one to do so. Clay had to be the one most at fault. If only Clay would admit it, she could forgive him.

Chapter Eight

The gray clouds were leaving and the sky was turning blue. Clay noticed the change as he walked toward the house. The morning was quiet. Allie stayed a few yards away from him. He didn't think it was deliberate, but it was there nonetheless. Each step he took was more difficult. The snow was turning to slush, and his feet were tired. In fact, everything about him felt a little worn down.

Clay wondered suddenly if his father had ever lied and confessed to something he hadn't done. Maybe to keep his mother happy. Living by the truth sometimes didn't seem worth what it cost a man. He and Allie had no chance. That moment in the barn had just proved it. How could he love a woman who thought he would lie about something important enough that her brother had almost been killed? And how could she love him when she thought he had done it?

Allie had been walking a little faster than he had, and he saw her take the few steps onto the porch leading to the door by herself. Clay hadn't seen the front of

the house clearly earlier. Now, he noticed the beige sid-
ing needed a coat of paint. These harsh winters were to
blame, he knew. But when he'd lived on the ranch, everything was kept in perfect condition. It was like the
Nelsons had just given up.

All of those years when he had been serving his time,
Clay had known that things would change on the ranch
after the night of the robbery. He'd expected Mr. Nelson would be testier than usual. And that Allie would
be sad. But he'd never expected the neglect that he'd
seen since he'd been back.

Allie stood in the doorway, holding the door open for
him, and he stepped through it into the warmth of the
kitchen. The rug was there and Clay stood on it, bend-
ing to scrape the snow off his boots. Allie did the same.

The smell of bacon still scented the air, but the table
had been cleared. The dishes had been washed and were
drying on a rack by the sink.

Mr. Nelson walked out of the hallway into the
kitchen.

"Good, you're back." He reached for the pocket in
his coveralls and pulled out a crumpled piece of gray
paper. "I keep forgetting. Mark wrote this. Gave it to
me a couple of weeks ago when I saw him."

The rancher held it out to Clay. "It's got your name on
it. It's not private or anything. Mark said I could read it."

"Let me get my boots off first," Clay said as he sat
down on the bench by the door and took them off. There
was no other way to keep from trailing wet snow around
the house. Only then did he stand back up.

"Thanks," Clay said as he walked across the floor
in his stocking feet and took the paper.

"Jeremy is in the back bedroom talking with that cat of his," Mr. Nelson announced. "Never knew he could jabber so much."

"Is the door closed?" Allie asked him. "So Jeremy can't hear us?"

The older man nodded.

Clay wondered what they were so worried about, but there was no time to ask before Allie started talking again.

"Well, what does it say?" Allie asked Clay like she'd never heard that Mark had left a message.

Clay walked over to the table and sat in one of the chairs before he unfolded the note. It was a lined paper, like those in school tablets. The letters were large and ragged—like a small child would write. But they were legible. Clay read the words aloud. "'Dear Clay, I need your help. My girlfriend won't talk to me. She broke up with me, but I think I can get her back if you help me. Be a good buddy. I think she'd be impressed if I do the wagon for Easter morning. The doctor said I can go if someone drives the thing for me. Remember I told you about that? It's a big deal around here. Her mother makes her go to church on Easter so I know she'll be there. I'll be some kind of hero that day. I'm going to ask her to go to dinner with me after church on Easter. How can she say no? I'll owe you one if you help me.'"

The note was signed "Mark."

There was a postscript. "Your brother—sort of. For real."

Clay was silent after he finished reading the words. He glanced over at Allie. She met his gaze.

"He could have asked me to help," she whispered.

She had her boots off, too, and walked over to sit in a chair at the table, as well.

"I would do anything for him," she added.

Clay felt relieved that she sat down beside him. But he shook his head slowly. "It's a guy thing. He can't ask his little sister to help get his girlfriend back. Besides, you used to tease him mercilessly about him dating someone."

Allie scowled at him, but she couldn't seem to stop her lips from curving up in a smile. "Well, he was too busy for all that. He wanted to go to college and he almost had that scholarship." She thought a moment. "He still has the scholarship, I think. They froze it for him in case—"

Clay wondered if he should feel so good just to be talking with her.

"He did have plans, didn't he?" Clay said, hoping to lighten her emotions. When he first heard about that scholarship, Clay remembered wondering how Mark could bear to leave the ranch. But he was set on college and then medical school. It was Allie who wanted to stay and work with the horses. Now it was questionable whether either one of them would have their dreams.

Mr. Nelson was still standing in the doorway, clearly lost in his own memories. "When he was a little boy, Mark always liked to get up at five o'clock on Easter morning and drive our old hay wagon down the street, leading everyone to that seven o'clock service behind the church. I used to let him sit on my lap and take the reins. People would just stand outside there and look up at the old cross. Mark was a good boy. And he loved Easter. Called it the best day of the year. I should have seen it coming, but I didn't know he realized the time of year. They don't give him a calendar. He wouldn't have known when Easter was coming, either, except last month he saw some decorations in the nurse's station and asked when the day was. He wanted me to tell Clay to get the wagon ready. You know people around here count on that tradition. That and the yellow daffodils—they make Easter morning."

"He still doesn't need Clay," Allie said quietly.

"He seems to think he does," Mr. Nelson replied. "He said Clay agreed to help him."

Mr. Nelson finally walked over and sat at the table also.

"I will do what I can," Clay told him. "But I haven't heard from him." The prison was pretty good about getting mail to the inmates, and he had heard regularly from Mrs. Hargrove. "Did he write and ask me to help with that? Maybe he expected you to mail the note he wrote." The older man shook his head. "Well, Mark and Hannah must have been off and on for some time now."

Mr. Nelson was silent for a minute longer. He studied the floor, seeming to be searching for an answer, and then looked up to meet his daughter's gaze.

"We have to tell him everything," Mr. Nelson finally said to Allie. "It won't make sense otherwise."

She nodded and looked at Clay, her eyes searching for something in his face. "But you have to keep what we tell you to yourself. We haven't told anyone around here. People know that Mark is improving and getting better every day, but they don't know the full situation. They think he's still just wiggling a few toes."

Allie stopped then as though she couldn't go on, but

she kept staring intently at Clay. "You have to promise to keep it a secret—at least until Mark says it's okay to say something. We don't know, but it could hurt him in his recovery if we're not careful. Like ripping off a bandage too soon. That's what the doctors say."

Clay nodded. "I'd never do anything to make his situation worse. I don't lie, but I can keep a secret."

Allie kept her eyes on Clay as though she was still taking his measure. Finally, she spoke. "Mark doesn't know how much time has passed since his accident. He thinks it's just now coming on to Easter. He must have asked you about helping with the Easter wagon that year before the accident."

"He did—" Clay said. "But that was back then."

They had been reading the Gospel of Luke for that challenge at the church. Mark said it would be great fun to bring the cross to the back of the church for the processional.

Clay was beginning to understand.

"Mark only knows what he's told," Allie continued as she paced the kitchen floor. Then she turned to her father. "We need to tell Mark he can't do it. Anybody in the church could say something to him. Surely, they will. And it's too many people to keep a secret. This coming Sunday is Palm Sunday. Then it's Easter. There's not time for Mark to be ready to do something like that."

Mr. Nelson shrugged. "The doctor thinks it will be good for Mark. He's figuring Clay can drive the wagon. People won't even necessarily know Mark is there. We'll have him so wrapped in blankets no one will see him. But Mark is expecting Clay to do this with him, and he wants to see Clay anyway. I'm thinking Clay can leave the wagon and drive Mark home after the service in that old red pickup. Mark won't even need to speak to anyone else."

"But what about Hannah?" Clay asked. "Is she on board? She's the one Mark wants to talk to. He's not going to be happy to make all of this effort if she isn't even there on Easter morning."

"Mark might do it for the church anyway," Allie said, but she didn't look convinced.

"Trust me, he'll want her to be there," Clay said. No wonder Mark asked him to help with this. Any guy would know what was important.

Mr. Nelson looked uncomfortable, and Allie didn't say anymore.

"She—ah—" Mr. Nelson stuttered. "Hannah's moved on with her life. I'm afraid she's given up on Mark. She hasn't been to see him since he's been re-gaining consciousness. She came a few times early on, but—"

Mr. Nelson let his words taper off.

"She might have come without us knowing," Allie interjected.

Clay recognized that look. She wasn't convinced.

"You want to think she would have come," Clay corrected Allie. She always saw the best in everyone. Well, except for him, Clay told himself.

Allie nodded.

"And he wants me to get her interested in him?" Clay asked. It suddenly hit him how big the problem was. "He doesn't know four years have passed since that night. Is that right?"

"He doesn't remember anything after Hannah broke up with him," Allie said. "Not even the robbery. Or where the two of you got that tequila."

Her father winced as he stood there. "The alcohol isn't important. You need to forget about that. It doesn't matter where they got that tequila."

"Nothing about the robbery?" Clay asked. "He's forgotten all that?"

"That's right," the older man said. "His mind is wiped clean of the memory. And the doctor said we shouldn't force Mark to remember. He needs to do it in his time."

"But he will remember?" Clay asked.

"We don't know," Mr. Nelson said. "He hasn't so far."

Clay let the words settle in. He hadn't even let himself hope yet that Mark would one day be able to set the record straight on that night. Now it appeared that it might not happen. Mark was the only other person who knew the truth. Clay realized for the first time that he likely would never be acknowledged as innocent. Allie would never know the truth of what happened.

"I'll do whatever I can to help," Clay said firmly. Now was not the time to worry about himself. Mark needed his help. "I can't make any guarantees about Hannah, though. I don't have much experience with women."

Allie lifted one eyebrow and smirked.

"What?" Clay remembered her wearing that same expression when her brother said something outrageous. She'd never given Clay that look before. "I told you before I didn't."

Her eyes were shaded and her voice smooth. "Don't expect me to believe that."

She'd never used that tone with Mark, either. There was nothing girlish about the sound. It was warm and feminine.

Clay's heart started beating faster, but his tongue was tied up in knots. What a tangle they were in. He could see Allie didn't like thinking of him with other women. He wondered where she thought he'd gotten any experience dating anyway. But she didn't like it. Allie's voice had almost sounded like she was flirting with him.

He must be hallucinating, he told himself. He thought she'd never warm to him.

The sound of the clock ticking was all that filled the silence. Allie thought it should be soothing, but it made her edgy. Her breath kept coming fast. She couldn't take her eyes off Clay. He seemed a little stunned as well, his blue eyes wary. The sun coming in the window at them showed the dark stubble on his face. She didn't want to keep staring, so she turned her head slightly. That's when she saw her father studying her like he was trying to puzzle something out. The last person in the world she wanted speculating about her feelings toward Clay was her father. When he caught her eye, though, he spoke.

"You still trying to figure out where that tequila came from?" he asked, his head tipped to one side.

Allie blinked. So that was what he was thinking about.

"You can't buy tequila in Dry Creek," Allie said. "I'm sure there are a few places in Miles City that carry it, but there's no need for you to concern yourself with it. Mark wouldn't have bought any tequila that night."

Allie knew her father was an alcoholic. Even if he had stopped drinking before her mother died, he still fixated on anything to do with alcohol. At least, Allie certainly hoped that was it and that he hadn't been trying to find a place to buy some alcohol.

The sound of an engine coming up their drive distracted everyone.

"That'll be Randy," Allie said. "One of you go meet him and I'll get dinner ready. We need to fix the corral fence first so the horses have room to move."

"I'll go out with Jeremy and check the chickens, too," her father said. "There won't be any eggs today, but I thought he'd like to know where the nests are."

"I'll take Randy to the bunkhouse," Clay offered. "That is, if he wants to stay tonight."

"It's up to him," Allie said as she walked over to the kitchen cabinets. "We'll only need his help for a few days, though, so he might not want to move anything out here."

Within minutes, Allie was alone in the kitchen. She had already put a roast in the oven, but she'd need to peel some potatoes and put together a salad. Before she started in with the food, though, there was something she had to do.

She opened all of the cabinets and took a slow look at what she could see. Then she got a step stool and stood closer to the shelves, moving the spice bottles and flour sacks to the side. Her mother had told her that she needed to do more than check behind the tall containers like those for vinegar or molasses. A bottle of alcohol, she'd said, could be placed on its side and hidden behind short items, too. Allie didn't expect to find anything, but she routinely checked every time she came home. She did it for her mother, who had told Allie that her father always hid his bottles in the kitchen cabinets.

Five minutes later, Allie found the bottle behind her mother's prized blue willow plates in one of the bottom cupboards. From the looks of the faded label, the bottle was likely from before her father had given up drinking. The cork hadn't been secure and a dark stain marked where the last of the bourbon had leaked out years ago. She gently lifted the bottle, knowing from the light weight that it was empty.

Both her parents had always said her father drank only whiskey. She realized then that if her father had been drinking bourbon back in those days, he might also have bought a bottle of tequila.

Allie carefully took all of the blue willow plates off their shelf. As she was growing up, they used these dishes only for holidays or sometimes Sunday dinners. In spite of everything, she smiled as she brought those dishes out. When she washed them as a girl, her mother would explain that the picture of the willow trees and bridge showed the tragic story of a young Chinese woman and the man she loved.

Allie had been enthralled with the story plates, as she called them, wondering at the strong love that would make the young couple risk their lives in hopes of being together.

Allie shook her head. She wondered if she'd have the courage to really love someone like that. To her, everything seemed murky. She wondered if she was right to ignore the tugging in her heart for Clay. He demanded she believe him; she refused to ignore what seemed to be true. They had less hope of being together than that poor Chinese couple on the plates.

After she had potatoes boiling and sourdough rolls heating in the oven, Allie washed the blue willow dishes and dried them. She told herself it was foolish to put them away without using them, so she set them on the table.

The kitchen was quiet. The sun was high in the sky, and the day was warm. She glanced out the window and saw a single set of footprints in the melting snow leading all the way to the barn. The footprints were disappearing into puddles.

Then she saw the barn door open. Allie watched as Jeremy stepped in Clay's larger footprints, even though the snow had mostly gone. She had done the same when she was a little girl walking behind her father.

She remembered then that there was a jar of homemade apple butter somewhere in the cupboard, and after she set some honey on the table, Allie turned back to look for it. She didn't know if Jeremy had ever had apple butter, but she knew Clay hadn't tasted it before coming to the ranch.

By the time she had drained the potatoes, Clay, Randy, her father and Jeremy had come inside.

"What's the occasion?" her father asked when he saw the table.

"I was looking down in the cupboards and saw mom's special dishes," Allie said. "Decided I might as well wash them and use them when we eat."

Allie watched her father's face as he unwound the

scarf from around his neck. One moment his face was relaxed, and the next, he'd gone pale. She saw the guilty look he gave the bottom cupboard. He didn't say anything, but she noticed he was trying to figure out what to do.

"I found it," Allie said then.

Her father's shoulders slumped. "I forgot it was there."

"Since when did you drink bourbon?" she asked, her voice tight.

He didn't answer right away, but he finally started. "After your mother died, there were a couple of years when I was drinking anything I could get my hands on, and a bar in Miles City was going out of business. They had a sale, and I bought a few bottles real cheap."

Allie smelled the roasted beef. Everything was dished up. The mashed potatoes. The gravy. The bread was ready to take from the oven. A bowl of green peas stood on the sideboard. But she had no appetite. She wondered if any of the men did, either. Clay was looking at her like he was trying to figure out what was wrong. Randy had a slight frown on his face. Jeremy was looking at the adults as though he knew something was amiss.

Allie turned to her father. "Was one of those bottles tequila?"

He was silent for a long moment. "I never liked the stuff."

Allie knew what that meant. "So the bottle was almost full when Mark found it."

It wasn't Clay who had given Mark the alcohol, Allie realized.

"I'm sorry I didn't believe you when you said that the bottle wasn't yours," she said to Clay. She felt ashamed. "I will do what I can to set the record straight."

"How would you do that?" Clay asked quietly.

"If you're still going to say something in church tomorrow, I'll stand by you on the question of where the alcohol came from," Allie said.

Her father made a sound of protest, but when she looked over at him, he shook his head. "I'm sorry. I didn't want to admit I still had a problem with alcohol. I'd promised your mother I was giving the stuff up and then—"

"I don't need to mention the alcohol tomorrow," Clay said. "And Randy won't say anything, will you?"

The ranch hand shook his head. "That's right. I won't."

Allie looked at Clay incredulously. "I thought that the whole point of saying something tomorrow is that you want people to believe you. This is your chance."

"Having your father confess about the alcohol won't make anyone believe I had nothing to do with the robbery," Clay said.

Allie wondered if Clay meant she wouldn't believe it, but she wasn't going to ask. She had been hoping it would be enough for him if she agreed with him that he hadn't provided the alcohol. She saw now that it wouldn't be enough for either one of them. But she couldn't wear blinders, no matter how much she wished for it to be true that Clay was innocent.

"Isn't it enough if you are just forgiven?" she asked him. "The church will do that much."

He didn't answer her, but she could see from the

faces of all the men that forgiveness wasn't enough for a proud man.

"We may as well eat then," she said.

Clay helped her put the food on the table like he had done for breakfast, but he didn't talk, and when it came time to say the blessing for the meal, no one held hands.

Father, forgive us, Allie added silently to her father's prayer. *Help us to understand each other.* She looked across the table at Clay. *And accept each other.*

Chapter Nine

The sun rose bright the next morning, the light shining through the blinds. Clay opened his eyes a little and squinted. The linoleum on the floor was cold, and he felt his hand resting against it. He was puzzled a moment and then remembered he was in the bunkhouse. He'd moved the mattress from his bunk bed to the kitchen floor in the middle of the night because Randy snored. Which probably wasn't the real problem, Clay told himself. He'd listened to dozens of men snoring at night in prison and it hadn't stopped him from sleeping. No, what kept Clay awake was that Randy talked in his sleep.

Clay groaned as he rolled over so he could see the small clock he'd plugged in last night. It was a little before six o'clock. Church was at ten o'clock, and there were chores to do before he got ready.

He had asked Allie for a box of cold cereal last night, and she'd given him that and a small carton of milk. He didn't want her to have to get up early on Sunday morning to cook him and Randy breakfast.

Clay heard a noise by the doorway and looked over to see Randy. The ranch hand was wrapped in a blanket, and his hair looked like he'd spent the night wrestling with someone.

"Who is Lois?" Clay asked as he lay there.

Randy glared. "What do you mean?"

"You were talking about her last night in your sleep," Clay said with a yawn. "I thought she might be someone special. You know, your mother or someone."

"Lois isn't my mother," Randy snapped.

"Well, then—" Clay started to continue.

"She's none of your business," Randy said then, with enough fire in his voice that Clay decided she was someone important.

"Sorry," Clay murmured. "I won't mention her again."

"See that you don't," Randy said as he walked over to the refrigerator. "Did you get us orange juice?"

"Milk and cold cereal," Clay said as he sat up on the mattress. "That's all."

Randy grunted at that news and stomped back into the other room.

Clay decided it was a poor morning when he and Randy Collins had nothing better to do than feel sorry for themselves, but that's the kind of day it was shaping up to be.

"We need to get some more wood to build another fire," Randy called from the other room. "We could freeze to death in here. Besides, we'll want hot water for when we shave."

"It's not that cold," Clay said as he stood up. They'd had a fire last night, and the water from the tap was warm. He kept a blanket around him and thought he was doing pretty well until he put his feet on the freezing floor.

"I'll get some wood in a minute," he called out to Randy. "You get some of the kindling going."

Clay opened the back door just enough to pull in some logs. Fortunately, they were dry since it hadn't snowed last night.

"I'll heat a pot of water on the stove for shaving," Clay called out, as well.

It wouldn't be the first time Clay had gone to church with a dark shadow from not shaving, but he figured it was best that he look as sharp as he could this morning. People were sure to take a good look at the ex-con who was out on parole. He didn't want to give them any reason to doubt the account he was going to give of the robbery.

"You're welcome to use my aftershave," Randy called. "It's on the shelf in the bathroom. Sort of pine smelling."

"Thanks," Clay called back. He couldn't remember Randy ever offering to share something with him, and it felt good. Maybe the other man knew it would be hard for Clay to walk into the sanctuary this morning wearing old jeans and a shirt that was frayed around the bottom.

"I'll give you a ride to church, if you want," Clay offered in return. "Mr. Nelson told me I could use the red pickup."

As he got dressed, Clay mused on how people were basically good. Randy might be a little testy when talking about his Lois, but he was all right. They'd cleaned the bunkhouse yesterday afternoon, and Randy had accepted the Nelsons' invitation to stay a few nights.

Clay fed the horses while Randy tended to the chickens and the pig. They both ended up feeding the goat. Mostly because the animal was unpredictable. It took one man to feed him and another to be sure the goat behaved. Everyone was fed and watered, though, by a little before nine o'clock, which left both men time to polish their shoes and be ready to leave for church on time. Clay put the sheepskin coat on. If he kept that on, no one would notice his clothes. And, he had to admit that he smelled good with that pine aftershave of Randy's.

"People are going to think we're a forest," Clay said as he and Randy gathered up their things for church.

"Better that we smell of forest than of old goat," Randy said with a grin.

Clay answered with a chuckle. He patted the pocket of his coat where he still had about twenty dollars. He'd like to put something in the offering plate just to prove that he could. At the last minute he went to the shelf in the kitchen and picked up the old Bible sitting there. He'd take that, too.

Clay heard the door to the main house open. Mr. Nelson, Allie and the boy were heading out, and he knew that meant it was time for him and Randy to get going, as well.

"This old thing gets around," Randy said as he climbed into the passenger seat of the pickup. "Remember when we used to load it with a few bales of hay and take it out to the horses?"

Clay nodded. "Those were the good old days."

He got inside and put the key in the ignition. "The heater doesn't work very well."

"It's okay," Randy said.

Clay studied the fields as he drove down the gravel road. When he'd come in earlier, it was all dark. But now he could see the gray dirt showing through patches of melting snow. Brown tufts of weeds and rocks were sprinkled over the land.

Clay passed several pickups heading into Dry Creek.

"What's up with the traffic?" he asked Randy.

The other man shrugged. "Guess word is out that you're going to speak."

Clay gasped and turned to him in shock. "I'm just going to make a small announcement during prayer time. Did you tell everyone I was going to speak?"

"Watch the road," Randy said when Clay stared at him.

Clay's hands tightened on the steering wheel as he turned back. Then he slowed the pickup. They were past the café and the hardware store.

"Well, people want to hear it, whatever it is." Randy's voice was confident. "I've heard them talking."

"Where?" Clay looked over at the ranch hand. "I just got back here. No one even knows I'm here."

Randy snorted at that. "You woke half the town up driving through it yesterday morning. It didn't take much for them to tell the other half of the town that you'd come back."

Clay wished he'd stayed home. Or, well, at the bunkhouse. It was too late, of course, to go back. He'd already pulled the pickup to a stop on the side of the road next to the church. A woman in a hat had smiled at him.

And he saw Mrs. Hargrove climbing the center stairs with her husband, Charley.

"They have pretty good coffee inside," Randy said as though he could tell Clay was reluctant to keep going. "Sometimes doughnuts, too."

Clay figured he was trapped, so he reached over and opened the door of the pickup. There was a strong wind as he stepped down, and he reached up to keep his hat in place. When he looked back at the church, he saw Allie and Jeremy walking up the steps. Allie was wearing a gray wool coat, and the wind was swirling two tails of a long bright scarf around her neck. Red was mixing with gold and orange. Allie's hair was uncovered, and strands of it flew with the scarf. She held Jeremy by the hand, and the boy squealed with pleasure in the wind.

Clay sensed someone standing beside him and looked over to see Randy staring, too.

"Who would have thought," the ranch hand said. "She used to be a scruffy-looking tomboy."

"She was always beautiful," Clay said quietly as he started to walk toward the church.

Randy grunted as he followed. "By the way, that's the other foster kid over there."

Randy gestured with his head, and Clay saw the teenager standing by a pickup on the other side of the church. The youngster was dressed in a black hoodie and jeans. Most of the teenage boys around Dry Creek wore plaid shirts and blue jeans, so Clay figured the boy was proving he was different. Or maybe that's all he had. Clay recognized the vehicle as belonging to the Redfern ranch, so he guessed not as much had changed around here as he thought. The men who worked there used that old blue thing to feed the hay in the winter and come to church on Sundays.

Clay saw the boy watching him, so he wondered if he knew who Clay was.

"Hi, there," Clay called to him with a nod of the head.

Clay got a glare in response. That's when he noticed the nose ring on the teenager. The kid shifted his legs then, and Clay saw a crease in his jeans near his right ankle. The boy had a knife sheath snug to his calf. Whether it was empty or not, Clay couldn't tell.

"What's his name?" Clay asked Randy quietly so that the boy wouldn't hear.

"Henry," Randy said as he started taking the steps up to the church. "They call him Hen for short."

Clay kept his head down until they both stepped into the entry to the sanctuary. The sound of the wind was cut off suddenly, and the air was warm inside. He wasn't sure, but he thought the sounds of people talking quieted considerably while he stood there. About half of the people were making their way to the pews, and the other half were standing by the coat racks.

The church looked the same as he remembered. A polished mahogany cross hung from the front of the room. A row of square windows, filled with stained glass, went down both sides of the church. Two rows of pews, with a carpeted pathway, went down the length of the sanctuary. A wood pulpit stood on a slight rise in the front.

He recognized many of the faces, but he had a hard time thinking of the matching names. Most of the women wore dark slacks and sweaters. The men wore cotton shirts and ties. No one wore a suit.

He saw Allie's bright scarf out of the side of one eye and turned his head. Mr. Nelson, Allie and Jeremy were settling into one of the pews on the right side. Allie had her head bent down, talking with Jeremy, and the next thing he noticed the boy was slipping out of the pew and walking toward him.

"Aunt Allie said you was to come sit with us," Jeremy whispered as he put a hand out to Clay. Then he reached the other hand out to Randy.

Clay looked at Allie, but she was facing toward the front and didn't even see him. He wondered if Allie had really made the invitation or if Jeremy just wanted some company.

Randy shrugged and started allowing the boy to lead him, so Clay did the same. No one seemed to think anything was unusual as Jeremy guided Clay into the pew, not even when Clay ended up sitting next to Allie.

Clay saw a pink flush on Allie's face as he looked over at her. She must be embarrassed. Then he remembered what a small-town church was like. The people there probably all thought that he and Allie had some kind of understanding.

The thought settled well with him.

"Morning," he whispered as he leaned over slightly. Allie smiled back.

Mrs. Hargrove started playing the piano, and the few stragglers hurried to find seats. By the time the older woman had finished the song, the pastor was behind the pulpit and ready with a hymn for them all to sing.

The last chords had scarcely faded away when the pastor asked Charley Nelson to come up to the pulpit and give the announcements. "We have a special guest with us today," Charley began, looking every inch an old-time rancher, with his white shirt accented by a silver bolo tie and his worn jeans sporting a silver belt buckle.

Clay's arm brushed against Allie and he could feel her tense up as Charley spoke.

"Clay West wants to say a few words to us," Charley said as he stepped away from the pulpit to make room for him.

"I'll pray for you," Allie whispered as Clay stood up.

He looked down at her and nodded. He supposed it would make her feel better to pray. Then he made his way past Jeremy and Randy and walked to the front.

Clay stood behind the pulpit and swallowed. He looked around. He saw Sheriff Wall sitting there with his wife and kids. The man had a good poker face. Clay couldn't tell what he thought. He saw Mrs. Hargrove in her usual seat close to the piano. She was beaming at him, but then she had experience encouraging nervous speakers given all the kindergarteners she'd helped say their lines at Christmas pageants.

He saw some of the wranglers from the Elkton ranch and Mr. and Mrs. Redfern. He slowly looked from face to face, seeing curiosity in most of them and condemnation in a few.

"I suppose you know my story," Clay began. "I've been in prison for four years now, and Mr. Nelson has helped set me up with a parole. I thank him for that. It's important to me that you know I didn't plan that robbery, though. I don't steal. I don't lie." Clay didn't want to talk about Mark's part in that night, so he found he didn't have much more to say. "Since I'm going to be around here, I wanted you to know. That's all."

Clay didn't even need to see the faces out in the pews. He could almost feel their shock. Jaws were slack, and he could hear whispers. Maybe he had been too outspoken. He did notice a couple of the older men glaring at him.

"We forgive you," one of the women in the front row called out. Clay couldn't remember her name, but he saw a few heads nodding in relief. The older men weren't among them, though.

"I don't need your forgiveness," Clay said and walked back down the aisle.

He didn't get to the door before Charley had regained the pulpit and called out, "Wait."

Clay turned to look at the other man.

"I need to make the announcement for the Easter sunrise service," Charley said, his eyes trained on Clay. "We'll meet at the edge of town by the stop sign at seven o'clock and form a processional to the area behind the church. My wife tells me our daffodils should be in full bloom by then. We'll keep the tarps on until that Sunday. The weather looks like we'll have some cold snaps, but they're set to bloom like always. God is faithful to us."

Charley paused, and Clay figured the announcement was over. He turned to finish his walk to the door when Charley spoke again.

"We're hoping you will help with the processional," Charley said, still looking directly at Clay. "As a tribute to your friend Mark Nelson."

Clay felt firmly caught. He wondered if Charley knew

that Mr. Nelson had already asked him to do just that. Whether he had or not, there could be only one answer.

"I'll do it," Clay said, his voice heavy.

Mr. Nelson stood up then from where he sat in the pew. "Mark is going to be there, too. Clay is going to make that happen."

A rush of exclamations greeted that news along with a few hands clapping. This announcement was something they understood.

Clay saw the concerned look on Allie's face. She had wanted to keep Mark's presence quiet. But there was no way to unsay those words.

Clay needed to escape into the fresh air. He was done for now. He opened the door and stepped outside onto the cement steps. He felt like he could finally breathe again as he leaned back against the doors. He noticed then that the two doors didn't meet well in the middle.

From where Clay stood, he could still hear the voice of the pastor asking everyone to open their Bibles to the Gospel of Luke. They were going to talk about Palm Sunday, he said, and what it meant to have faith.

Clay looked straight ahead and saw Hen, the foster kid, sitting in the Redfern pickup with a knowing smirk on his face.

Clay had planned to go and sit in the pickup until the sermon was over, but he didn't want to set a bad example for that kid. At least that's what he told himself as he found himself standing by the door.

Clay figured maybe the kid would come up and listen with him, but he didn't. Eventually, Clay forgot about anyone else as he concentrated on the words. After the pastor finished, Clay decided he'd go home tonight and read the whole Gospel of Luke just as he and Mark had set out to do four years ago.

Clay had barely managed to make it down the steps before the doors to the church were thrown open and Jeremy raced down them, as well.

"We're staying for dinner," the boy announced joyfully when he got to the bottom and stared up at Clay. "Mrs. Hargrove invited us. She's making tamales."

"Is that right?" Clay asked as he knelt down to Jeremy's height. The boy was jumping around in excitement. "Have you ever eaten a tamale?"

The boy nodded vigorously and then turned to point up the stairs. "Auntie will tell you."

Clay looked up and saw Allie standing at the top of the steps. Her coat was open, flapping slightly in the wind. Her head was bowed so she could see him, and she looked dismayed.

Clay stood back up. He didn't want to upset anyone. Things here in Dry Creek weren't what he expected, though. He wondered if he'd been too quick to judge people before. Maybe they hadn't been as set against him as he had thought.

Allie caught her breath. Clay looked like he was trying for a quick getaway when Jeremy had caught him. She had no idea what he was planning to do now. She noticed Clay was smiling at her nephew, though.

"Mrs. Hargrove gets her tamales from the sheriff's wife," Allie said. "They are really very good. Chicken and beef ones. And some special spicy ones she ordered with you in mind."

"I like hot food," Clay said.

Allie nodded. "Mrs. Hargrove knows. Extra chili peppers."

Clay smiled, and she watched his face transform itself. He appeared years younger, the way he used to look years ago when they had a new colt born on the place and he'd been happy.

Allie heard the door open behind her, and she turned to see who else was leaving the church before the coffee was served. It was Mrs. Hargrove. The older woman stepped to the far right on the stairs so that she could grab the handrail. She carefully started to step down, and Allie rushed over to take her other arm. Fortunately, the short piece of walkway in front of the church and the whole stairway were always shoveled off before services. So by now, the steps were free of ice and they were dry.

When Allie and the older woman reached the bottom of the stairs, Mrs. Hargrove held out her arms, and Clay stepped into them eagerly. Allie watched the two of them hug each other tight. They made a strange sight, a white-haired farm woman and a young man with a prison haircut, but there was no doubt of their affection for each other.

She heard Mrs. Hargrove repeatedly whisper, "Welcome home."

Allie was stricken with remorse as she contrasted Mrs. Hargrove's greeting with the one Clay had received at the Nelson ranch. Maybe guilt and judgment weren't as important as love and forgiveness. Her only saving grace, Allie thought, was that no one else in Dry Creek had idolized Clay like she had. He had further to fall in her estimate than in anyone else's.

Still, she wished she had welcomed him home.

Chapter Ten

A little while later, Allie was in Mrs. Hargrove's kitchen and the other woman was taking a pan of Spanish rice out of the oven. The air was warm and smelled of cooked beef. Wide windows on the left of the room looked out to the yard. A small wooden table stood next to old-fashioned white cabinets. A bowl of lettuce salad sat on the counter, bright red tomatoes and green cucumbers peeking out between the leaves. A small meat loaf sat cooling on one of the stove burners. A huge platter of tamales sat on another burner.

"There's ice in the top freezer to fill the glasses," Mr. Hargrove said as she moved around the kitchen. She wore a large ivory apron with large pockets that covered most of her green-checked gingham housedress. She'd changed after she came in the door after church, saying she didn't want to get any spots on her new wool suit.

It was the suit more than anything that told Allie the older woman saw this as an important day. Most of Mrs. Hargrove's Sunday clothes were simple polyester dresses in navy or gray. The wool suit was a beautiful pale pink with dark rose piping around the edge of the collar.

"You looked particularly nice this morning," Allie said as she reached into the freezer and pulled out a tray of ice cubes.

"I ordered the suit from a catalog," the older woman said as she stopped with a small frown on her face. "My daughter, Doris June, suggested it. You don't think it looks too…" She spread her hands as though she couldn't find the word she wanted.

"It was perfect." Allie used a plastic tong to put ice cubes in the dinner glasses.

Mrs. Hargrove nodded in relief, the tight gray curls on her head bouncing as she moved her head. "It's not every day that Clay West comes back home."

Clay and the other men were out in the garage looking at a small saddle Charley had stored from the days when his son was Jeremy's age.

Allie stopped what she was doing. "You think Clay's innocent then?"

Mrs. Hargrove did not answer right away. She was scooping some cooked corn into a serving bowl.

Allie had turned back to the drinks when the older woman answered.

"I'm not sure it matters anymore if Clay is guilty or not," Mrs. Hargrove said. "He served time in prison. He's a good man. You only have to look him in the eyes to know that he's going to try hard to live a worthwhile life. Anyone can make a mistake."

"It seems to matter to him if people think he's innocent or not," Allie said.

The other woman nodded. "Men can be that way. I'm

reminded of the Prodigal Son. All the father wanted to do when his son came back was celebrate. Sometimes people forget that with God, guilt isn't permanent. Forgiveness can make us new."

Allie hoped that would be enough for Clay. And for her.

The sound of the door opening in the living room was followed by the thump of many boots.

"They're back," Mrs. Hargrove said as she picked up the platter of tamales. "They'll be ready to eat."

By now, Allie had a tray of ice-filled glasses, and she lifted it so she could follow Mrs. Hargrove into the dining room.

Sunshine filled the dining room. White net curtains hung at the wide windows along the side of the large wood dining table. A couple of ferns hung from hooks in the tall sills of the windows.

"Auntie, Auntie." Allie heard Jeremy's call before she saw him come running into the dining room.

"Unka Clay is teachin' me ta ride a horse," the boy almost shouted, he was so excited.

Allie almost dropped one of the glasses. She set the glass down on the table before she walked over to her nephew.

By that time, the men had come into the dining room, too. They all had sheepish looks on their faces.

"I made a mistake," Clay confessed. He still had his Stetson and his coat on, so Allie figured he'd only managed to scrape the snow off his boots. "It's all my fault."

"Jeremy," Mrs. Hargrove called. "Why don't you come in the kitchen with me and see if we can find you a cookie. Do you like cookies?"

"Yes, ma'am," the boy said with a grin, happily following the older woman into the other room.

"Now, it wasn't all Clay's fault," Allie's father said to her when the kitchen door was closed.

Charley and Randy stood there looking uncomfortable, but they were quiet.

"We were looking at that saddle Charley's son used when he was a little tyke," Clay began. His eyes met hers, but they were stormy with distress. "Jeremy was all excited about learning to ride a horse and I forgot—I said his father would be pleased that he wanted to ride."

Allie's jaw dropped open.

"We never mention his father," she whispered.

"I know," Clay said. "That's why I said I meant his uncle. His uncle would be pleased. He seemed to accept that. Then he wanted to know who his uncle was. Then—"

Clay turned to look at her father, and Allie followed his gaze.

"Don't look at me," her father said. "Jeremy already knows I'm his grandpa. I can't be his uncle, too. He's a bright boy. He'd figure that one out. So I'm the one who told him Clay was his uncle."

Allie shook her head. "I can't believe this."

"Well, it's sort of true," her father explained. "Clay was a foster son in our family and Mark looks to him as a brother. Clay's the closest thing to an uncle that the boy has. His mother is an only child, and you're a girl."

"Okay," Allie said as she nodded. "I guess I can see that."

"A fatherless boy needs an uncle," her father said. "In some villages in Africa, an uncle can be nothing more than a family friend," Clay said. "It's an honorary title. I'd like to think I'm that at least."

Allie met Clay's eyes. His hat shaded his face, but she could see he was sincere and nervous. Suddenly, he seemed to remember his Stetson, and he swept it off his head, leaving his hair a little mussed.

"You're going to have to keep your promises to Jeremy," Allie said fiercely. She wasn't so sure it mattered who the boy's uncle was as long as the man was dependable. "I won't stand by and let you disappoint him."

"I never lie," Clay said calmly.

"He's too young to ride a horse," Allie said.

Clay looked at Randy then.

"I figure we'll start him on the goat," Clay confessed. "We've already explained that there will be a training period before he actually sits on a real horse."

Allie was silent as she looked at the men.

"We figured it was the goat or the pig," Randy said then, his voice hesitant. "And that pig is too small."

Suddenly, Allie started to giggle.

"Those poor animals have no idea what they are getting into," Allie finally managed to say. By now, everyone was chuckling.

"The boy will do fine," Charley said then. "My pa taught me how to ride on a sawhorse in the barn. A ranch boy has to be flexible. I've heard of small boys learning to ride on large calves."

Mrs. Hargrove opened the kitchen door and stuck her head back into the dining room. "All clear?"

"We're ready to eat," Charley said as he motioned everyone to have a seat.

Allie walked back to the kitchen to help Mrs. Hargrove bring the rest of the food to the table. She was surprised at how relaxed she felt today.

By the time they all were ready to push their chairs back from the table, Clay was full.

"That's the best meal I've had in ages," Clay said to Mrs. Hargrove. "I can't thank you enough. Are you sure I can't chop you some wood before we leave?"

"Absolutely not," the older woman said. Her face pinked in pleasure. "This is your welcome-home party. You're the guest of honor."

Clay blinked away a sudden tear. This woman had stood by him all the years he'd been away, and it touched him. Fortunately, no one seemed to notice his sudden need to blink.

"I have something to show you," Mrs. Hargrove said then as she slid her chair back from the table. "The dishes can wait."

"I'm more than happy to take care of those dishes for you," Charley said as he pushed his chair back, too. "I figure me and Jeremy can manage to wash everything up fine. How about that, pardner?"

Jeremy nodded his head vigorously.

"I'll give you a hand, too," Randy said as he rose with them.

Clay looked up at the ranch hand in surprise.

"What?" Randy said with a grin. "It's not like I'm wearing an apron or anything."

"Still," Clay muttered. The whole world was shifting. "You have something in the kitchen? A cake or something?"

Mrs. Hargrove chuckled. "It's peach pie, and we're

going to serve it after the dishes are done. But before anyone leaves the table, I have an announcement for you."

The older woman reached into the big pocket in her apron and pulled out a glossy flier and a newspaper article. The flier was folded into thirds, and she held it up like it was something special. The article stayed in her other hand.

"I suppose you're wondering about the artwork you sent me over the years," Mrs. Hargrove said, with a smile for Clay.

"It was just a few sketches," Clay said.

The older woman nodded. "I usually have them hanging on the walls around the dining room. Your agent contacted me, though, and we talked. He was looking for sketches he could enter for an art showing at the Charlie Russell museum in Great Falls."

Clay swallowed back an exclamation of surprise.

"I gave him what he is calling the Dry Creek collection," Mrs. Hargrove continued. "The showing was last week and this—" she waved the newspaper article "—is the review. The art critics are saying you have a bold new look. They call you the next major Western artist."

Clay was speechless. He looked around and saw that everyone at the table seemed at a loss for words, as well.

"That's nice," Clay finally managed to say.

Mrs. Hargrove beamed even more. "They say there were offers for the collection of sketches starting at twenty thousand dollars. That is for the ten sketches."

"You need to sell," Clay advised with a gasp. "Quick, before they change their minds."

"I wouldn't sell those sketches for anything," the

older woman said firmly. "They have sentimental value. I did decide to get them insured, though."

"But—" Clay said, and then stopped. His mouth was hanging open, he knew, but he couldn't seem to collect his thoughts enough to close it.

"I did also say I would ask if you have other collections," Mrs. Hargrove continued. "I talked to your agent, and he'll handle the business side of things. I figure you must have other sketches that can be grouped together. Do you have any other sketches with you?"

"In my old suitcase," Clay said. "It's still under my bunk. I checked it last night before I went to bed. I have dozens of sketches of—"

Suddenly, Clay stopped. He blinked and looked around. He was too rattled by Mrs. Hargrove's news to be thinking straight. "They wouldn't work, though."

"Why not?" Charley asked, his tone suggesting Clay was not making the right choice. "I bet you could get tens of thousands of dollars for something. The time is right."

"They're private sketches," Clay finally said.

"What of?" Mr. Nelson asked. "It didn't seem like you were old enough when you were here to have much that was private."

Everyone looked at Clay as though trying to picture his secrets. He resisted the urge to squirm in his chair. He figured there was no hope of hiding anything. "I drew a few pictures of Allie."

He looked down at the table.

"Was she…?" Randy looked around and whispered, "You know…naked?"

Clay snapped his head back up. "Of course not."

His face was red and he couldn't look over at Allie, although he wanted to know how she was taking all of this.

"Well, what was Allie doing?" Mrs. Hargrove asked then. She, at least, seemed reasonable.

"She was looking out the window," Clay said. "One was her riding her horse. A couple of her with the new colts. One of her all dressed up for church. A few of her in the kitchen."

There was silence as everyone seemed to absorb this.

"You sketched me?" Allie finally asked, her voice one of awe. "I never thought you even noticed me."

"I noticed," Clay said.

"Well, are you willing to give them over to those collectors?" Charley asked. "I think you could get a pretty penny for them."

"It's up to Allie," Clay said, looking at her directly for the first time since the conversation had started.

"I'd be honored," she said.

Clay nodded.

"I'll let that agent of yours know," Mrs. Hargrove said. "He said he could come by Dry Creek tomorrow."

Clay started to agree, and then he remembered. "I'm going to go see Mark tomorrow."

"We can work it out," Mrs. Hargrove said. "Maybe I'll tell him to come Wednesday morning. Would that give you enough time?"

Clay was struck with uncertainty. "The paper I used might have gone bad sitting in that suitcase all these years. I can't promise anything until I see the sketches." He looked at Allie. "You'll have to give me your approval, too, before we close any deals."

Allie nodded.

"What suitcase is that?" Mrs. Hargrove asked.

Clay shrugged. "Just a case that was in the trunk of the car when my parents had their accident all those years ago. It was empty, but the policeman gave it to me days later. I took it to my first foster home and kept it all the way through until I brought it here."

"I remember you had it when you came to the ranch," Allie confirmed.

"It's under my bunk now," Clay added. "Full of this and that from my years bouncing around from place to place. None of it worth anything."

"It's certainly worth something now," Mrs. Hargrove said gently.

Everyone was silent.

"Well, I think that this all calls for peach pie," Mrs. Hargrove finally said. "With ice cream."

Clay sat back in his chair. If it wasn't for the strength of the spindles in the chair, he would be slumped down. He wondered if he was opening a door to something wonderful or something terrifying. It wasn't just the events with the sketches that had surprised him. He was almost as astonished at the ease with which Jeremy had adopted him as his honorary uncle.

He didn't know what more to say about either one of those things. Fortunately, no words were needed because Charley brought in the pie.

Chapter Eleven

Allie was anxious to get home with her father and Jeremy. Clay followed in the pickup while she drove her father's SUV. Randy was spending the afternoon in Dry Creek with his cousin. The snow had melted along the road except for a few small white patches. Gray clouds were gathering in the north, and she realized they might have more snow tonight. Spring wasn't coming to Dry Creek on its regular schedule this year.

She had to admit that it had felt good to drive into the ranch property and see the horses out in the corral. From a distance, no one would know that any of the Appaloosas were blind. Their coats were beautiful in the afternoon sunlight, muscles rippling as they trotted around the enclosure. She wished she had a camera.

Clay stopped the old red pickup next to the parked SUV and stepped out of the driver's door. He walked along the side of the pickup and reached over to pull the small saddle out of the back of the vehicle.

"I'll take this to the tack room," Clay said.

Allie and her father had both doors of the SUV open, and Jeremy climbed out the passenger side.

"My saddle," Jeremy said with pride as he raced over to the pickup.

"It sure is, partner," Clay told the boy.

Allie watched the man and the boy walk through the yard to the barn.

She looked over and saw her father studying them, too. "Not a better man around to teach that boy to ride than Clay West," he said.

Allie nodded. "I always hoped Mark would do it, though."

"I'm not sure Mark will ever be able to ride again," her father said. "He's better, but I just don't know."

Allie reached over and put her hand on her father's arm. "We'll take things day by day."

He grinned. "Mark will be happy if he can just ride in that wagon on Easter morning."

Allie gave a brief nod. "I'm going to go ask Clay to bring those sketches into the kitchen. Do you really think some collector will pay money for them?"

Her father shrugged. "That's what Mrs. Hargrove says, and she's not one to overstate things."

"You don't think they would sell for more than twenty thousand dollars?" Allie asked in astonishment, but by then her father was already walking up the steps.

He turned back when he got to the door, though. "You should read the article in that art magazine. They sure thought Clay's sketches were something. Said he had expressive lines—whatever that means."

Allie walked over to the barn and stood in the open door. She had dress boots on, so she didn't have to be too cautious with the soles, although she didn't want to do them any damage. She didn't mind standing in the doorway, though. She could hear Jeremy chatting in the tack room and smiled. He usually took a long time to warm up to strangers, but he liked Clay.

Clay stepped out of the room where the saddles were stored, and Allie felt her heart skip a beat. The sun streamed in behind him from the high window in the room. His hat was tipped back enough that she could see the smile around his eyes.

"We got Jeremy's saddle hung up," Clay announced as he started walking toward the door. Her nephew marched along beside him.

"I figure we can take a lesson after nap time," Clay added.

Jeremy looked up as though he was going to protest, but he didn't.

"Cowboys need their sleep," Clay announced.

Allie grinned. She had never gotten Jeremy to agree to lie down and sleep a bit in the afternoon, not even when she knew he took naps when he was home with his mother.

"We might as well throw in a glass of milk while we're at it," Allie said as the man and boy came closer.

Clay winked at her. "I explained that riding a horse is a privilege and requires some extra preparation like naps and doing chores."

"You'll make a good…uncle," Allie stumbled. She'd been about to say *father*. She'd never thought that about Clay before, though. She'd known he was handsome and exciting. But she'd never considered how much he had to give to a family.

She suddenly realized she had been selfish all those years ago. She had been delighted when her father signed up to get a foster kid, and she had just assumed it would be a good arrangement for whoever came to the ranch. But she hadn't thought about it once after Clay was here. She didn't remember ever asking if he was happy on the ranch.

It was too late to ask now, though, she told herself as she started up the steps to the house. Clay and Jeremy were clomping along behind her talking about why that pig in the barn was so small.

"I never knew about your suitcase," Allie turned to say as she reached the door. "I should have looked around in the bunkhouse to gather up your things. I could have sent everything to you. It was yours."

Clay shrugged as he swung the door open for her. "They wouldn't have let me keep my stuff anyway in prison. Against the rules."

"Then I could have put the suitcase someplace safer," she said as she stepped into the kitchen. "No one has lived in the bunkhouse for several years now. Someone could have walked off with it and we would never have known."

"The case is pretty shabby. I don't think anyone would want it," Clay said as he stood in the doorway.

"Still," Allie said.

"I could bring the sketches inside so you can look at them," Clay said as he continued standing in the doorway. "That would probably be more comfortable than looking at them in the bunkhouse. We didn't leave the heat on when we left this morning."

"We have plenty of propane for the heater," Allie

said. "I don't want you and Randy freezing out there just to save a few pennies."

"We probably only have one cold snap left," Clay said. "Then everything will be warming up. I'll go get the sketches then while you get Jeremy set for his nap."

Allie nodded. He stepped back out of the house, and Allie stood there with her nephew. She wondered if Clay had liked living in the bunkhouse. She remembered some of the older ranch hands complaining about the cold nights out there, but she had not worried about it back then. The main house had been cold, too, in the winter. She was beginning to feel, though, as if her family had failed Clay in some way over the years.

Clay might not be as innocent as he said he had been on that night, but she had to admit that she and her family were not blameless, either. The truth was that she needed to consider that Clay might be telling the truth. Had she been wrong about her brother?

Clay was glad he was alone in the bunkhouse when he pulled that old suitcase out from under the bed. A thick layer of dust lay on top of the brown-checked hard shell. The whole thing wasn't much bigger than a duffel bag. He'd always thought it might have belonged to his mother because it had carried the faint smell of lavender, and he had believed a perfume bottle had been broken in it at some time. Thinking she liked lavender helped Clay form a picture of his mother. He always thought she'd been a pretty lady. He had no pictures of either of his parents, though.

A gold catch closed the case, and he pressed on its sides to make it snap open. The dust went flying as the suitcase vibrated sharply. He lifted the lid and peered inside. The stained gold lining was frayed in places. He had an old T-shirt laid out on top of everything. He took that out and set it on his bed. A brown bag of marbles nestled in a corner of the suitcase. He had collected a few cat's-eye marbles when he was seven or so. And there was a broken watch that had been a gift to him from a social worker once. That was the Christmas when he was between foster homes and had been in some kind of an institution. He'd been surprised and grateful for the timepiece. It was one of the few presents he'd gotten that hadn't come from a charity gift drive.

Ah, there it was, Clay thought as he found the sturdy folder. He'd used those in high school. This one must be the sketches, he thought. He was half-afraid to open the thing up and look. He remembered each of the drawings he had made of Allie, but he wasn't sure if his mind had persuaded him over the years that they were better than they really were. He'd thought at the time that they were fine drawings, very fine. But he had not known much about art then. At least in prison he'd been able to borrow a few art books from the library.

Suddenly, Clay decided he'd take the folder into the house and open it with Allie. He wanted to be able to judge if she actually wanted the sketches even seen by anyone else. Once they sold the sketches, Clay wouldn't be able to control where they were shown.

Clay noticed the silence in the air as he walked toward the main house. He was so used to the constant low hum of noise in prison that he needed to remind himself that this quiet was normal. Nothing was wrong.

The sun was shining, the sky was blue and the clouds were low in the east.

A quick knock at the door gained Clay an invitation to come inside.

Allie had changed back into her jeans and sweater while he'd been in the bunkhouse. She hadn't taken the makeup off her face, though, and he enjoyed seeing her more polished look. He liked seeing Allie dressed up for the day. She had tiny pearls earrings on, as well.

"We can sit over here," Allie said as she walked to the wall and flipped a switch so the hanging fixture over the table lit up. "My father is lying down with Jeremy to help him go to sleep, but he'll be out in a few minutes. Jeremy runs around with all this energy, but if we can convince him to lie down he nods off pretty quickly."

"We'll wait for your dad then," Clay said as he set the folder down. The table's surface was a polished oak that was worn. There was a burn scar to the right of the center. A pair of salt and pepper shakers stood in the middle of the table.

Allie pulled out a chair and he did, too.

"Before we even look at the sketches," Clay said as he settled himself on the hardback furniture, "I want to be sure that you know I'm okay if you'd rather not have anything done with them. The drawings are of you. You own them as much as I do."

Allie sat down and didn't even hesitate. "But if they can help you—"

Clay shook his head. "I'll get by. I can draw new sketches. This collector's thing might be a two-second wonder anyway. Nothing says it will last."

Allie leaned forward. "But that's all the more reason

to use whatever sketches you have. If you wait to draw new ones, you might miss the opportunity."

Clay had never been able to resist the sincere look in Allie's green eyes. Her whole face beamed when she was doing something she believed in. She'd pulled her auburn hair back in a clip, but several strands hung free.

"If anyone pays for the sketches," Clay said, "the money will go to you."

"No," Allie gasped. Her eyes went dark, and she looked upset. "It's your work."

"It's your face," he countered.

"But I couldn't take it," she said, shaking her head. Even more hair fell from the clip, but she didn't push it back. She just kept staring at him. "You're already working here for free."

"Room and board," Clay said with a grin. "And I plan to eat a lot."

He meant to lighten the mood, but she just sat there shaking her head.

"The ranch needs the money," Clay finally coaxed her softly. "More than I do right now."

"I'll take care of the ranch," Allie protested. "I've been doing it for years. We get by."

"If you have the money, you could spend more time here," he said softly. He wondered then if that's why he wanted her to have it. He had visions of days spent with her as they worked with those horses. They used to make a good team doing that.

Allie didn't answer for several moments, but when she did her voice sounded resolute. "No. It's your fresh start. It's only fair that anything that comes goes to you. You're a—"

Allie stopped and didn't continue.

"A foster kid?" Clay asked bitterly. "An ex-con?"

"I was going to say you're a good man," Allie said quietly. "But you're also too generous."

Clay was speechless. No one had ever accused him of being good before.

A soft footfall sounded in the hall, and Mr. Nelson stepped out of the shadows into the kitchen.

"He's finally sleeping," the older man whispered. "Had quite a time getting him to close his eyes."

Mr. Nelson drew up a chair and sat down, leaning his elbows on the table. He took a deep breath and then looked directly at Clay. "The boy asked me if an uncle can become a dad."

"What?" Clay sat back like he'd been shot.

"He likes having an uncle," Mr. Nelson said. "Only one day and he's taken with it. But he must want a dad, too."

"But he's never said anything," Allie protested. "At least not that I've heard. Maybe he talks to Hannah about it, though."

They were all silent.

"I'm sure this is all very difficult for Hannah," the older man finally said. "She's never even mentioned to me that she's dating anyone. As far as I know, she's still mourning her life with Mark."

"But Mark's not dead," Clay protested.

"He was in a coma for years," Mr. Nelson said. "No wonder she doesn't say anything to Jeremy. You'd have to explain to him then that he couldn't even talk to his father."

"He's a bright boy," Allie said. "It's not surprising that he's starting to question things."

They were all quiet and Clay sat there, still stunned that he was a little boy's uncle, if not by blood then by choice. He didn't like to picture the hard bumps Jeremy would encounter in the coming years. Even if he ever did learn that Mark was his father, what would that mean? Clay wasn't sure if Mark would ever be able to fill that father's role for Jeremy. And Clay might be around the ranch for only the year he was assigned. If he wasn't there to watch Jeremy grow up, either, then he wanted the boy to know he had someone in his corner.

"The money can go to Jeremy," Clay said, catching Allie's eye. "If you don't want it, we can set up a college fund for the boy." Allie didn't say anything for a minute, so he continued. "I want him to know he has a family who will look out for him."

"You'd do that?" Allie asked. She blinked them back, but Clay could see she had tears in her eyes.

He didn't trust himself to speak, so he nodded.

They sat there in silence until Mr. Nelson stood up. "I'm going to put some coffee on. Anyone else want some?"

Allie and Clay both nodded.

"We should look at the sketches before getting our coffee, though," Allie said. "We don't want to spill on them."

Clay opened the folder.

"Ah." Allie sighed when Clay lifted out the first sketch.

He smiled. It was the drawing of Allie looking out her bedroom window. Black ink strokes outlined everything. She was looking up at the night sky, her face filled with longing.

"I called that one *Wishing on a Star*," Clay noted.

"It's perfect," Allie said. "That shows exactly how I felt. I was so full of longing to experience life. To go places and see things. I thought I would burst."

Clay held up another sketch.

"Here's one of you cooking in the kitchen," Clay said.

He remembered seeing her that day. She was so intent on cracking the eggs that she was biting down on her bottom lip slightly. Her hair had more red in it back then, and the morning light made her curls shine.

"You have me in my mother's apron," Allie said.

Clay nodded and took another sketch out of the folder.

"And my horse," Allie exclaimed. She had almost the same expression on her face now as she'd had back then. "I loved my Peony. She died not long after you left."

Clay stopped midreach. "I'm sorry."

Allie nodded. "It was a hard time for me. I felt like I'd lost my best friend."

Clay didn't dare ask if it was the horse or him that she had missed so much. He did notice that she put her finger on the sketch and traced the horse, though.

"Maybe we should keep that one back," Clay suggested. "You might want to have it."

Allie looked up and smiled. "I would. Thanks."

Clay nodded. Whenever Allie smiled, her whole face lit up. He'd always thought that was one reason he sketched her. She was so alive. Now, seeing her pleasure in the sketches, though, he wondered if he hadn't made them for this very moment. When Allie smiled at him like that, everything was right in his world.

He wondered suddenly why there was no give in him when it came to his insistence that Allie believe what he said about the robbery. He knew he was innocent. Would it be enough if he just started now and worked forward, ignoring what she thought he had done on that night so long ago? He wasn't sure.

"Ready for coffee?" Mr. Nelson asked from where he stood by the counter. "We'll want to look at the sketches later, too. Maybe Mark would enjoy seeing them. Did you ever show any of them to him?"

"No." Clay started gathering up the drawings. "I'm not sure how he'd like them. So much time has passed and, well, wouldn't Mark notice that Allie looks different today than she did back then?"

Clay looked over at Allie for an answer.

"He's never said anything to me about that," she said. "Maybe he can't remember what I used to look like. I've seen him about once a month all this time. The doctors have always told us that we shouldn't mention how much time has passed to Mark. But I wonder if he knows."

Clay thought Allie looked worried.

"I'm sure everything will be fine," Clay said.

"It has to be," Allie added.

Clay nodded. He would just as soon stay back at the ranch tomorrow and work with the horses. He knew that wasn't going to happen, though. He had to go visit with Mark. But what if seeing him brought that robbery back to Mark's mind?

Chapter Twelve

Allie dressed with care the following morning. The sky was overcast, and very little light came inside her bedroom even though it was seven o'clock already. She felt self-conscious after the conversation yesterday suggesting Mark might wonder why she looked different from how she had at sixteen. She had deliberately kept her hair styled the same for the past half-dozen years because she thought Mark would find it familiar in his coma. She meant it to be comforting, not to deceive him about the passage of time.

She took the stairs down to the kitchen, intending to make some eggs and toast to go with the coffee. She glanced out the window and saw that Randy's brown pickup had been moved from where it was yesterday. She thought she'd heard him drive in last night. He'd be ready for work this morning. The lights were on in the bunkhouse, so she assumed Clay and Randy were getting ready for the day.

While the eggs finished cooking, Allie changed the page on the calendar hanging on the wall. She remembered she'd had to do the same thing the last time she'd been back at the ranch. Her father just let the days flow over him.

Jeremy and her father came into the kitchen, and she dished up breakfast for them.

"We're going to start working on the hay wagon today," her father said as he settled himself and Jeremy on their chairs. The table was already set with dishes and silverware. "I've talked to Clay. He has some ideas. We'll make sure the wagon's ready for Sunday."

"You're still set on doing this Easter processional?" Allie asked as she set the platters in the center of the table.

Her father nodded as he held out his hands to Jeremy and to Allie. "Now that Clay is here we should have no problem."

Allie didn't answer.

"Well?" her father said.

"I'll stop at the hardware store in Dry Creek on our way to the nursing home," Allie said as she took her father's hand. "We'll all need new hats this year."

One of the traditions with the processional was for those riding on the wagon to all wear new white Stetsons. Mark would enjoy having his hat early.

Allie bowed her head as her father started to pray aloud. She let his words of gratefulness speak for her. Her family had endured its share of hard times, but her parents had both believed in being thankful for what God had provided.

They finished eating and she had the table cleared when she heard footsteps on the porch.

She opened the door after the knock and saw Clay

standing there. He wore the sheepskin coat and his black Stetson. The temperature outside was low enough that a cloud of white air showed when he spoke.

"Ready to go?" Clay was hunched slightly like he was cold.

"We can take my dad's SUV," she said as she stepped out of the door, her purse slung over her shoulder. "I suppose you want to drive?"

The freezing air hit her when she moved past the doorway.

He grinned. "You know I do. But I'd rather take that old pickup if you don't mind. Your dad should have his vehicle in case he needs to go someplace."

Allie nodded as she closed the door behind her. "You're right. My little car isn't much good on country roads in the winter, so he wouldn't want to drive that for any distance."

She remembered how much Clay enjoyed driving that old pickup around. A person would have thought it was a sports car rather than a worn-down ranching vehicle. Clay had volunteered to haul bales out to the horses for the night feeding many times just so he could get behind the wheel. Her father had already mentioned that he'd hired one of the Elkton wranglers to drive the pickup over to the prison in Deer Lodge and leave it there for when Clay was released.

Clay backed up so she could climb into the pickup without having to cross the puddle that had formed beside the cab. Allie's teeth shivered as they drove off the ranch and headed down the gravel road into Dry Creek.

"I can't wait to see Mark," Clay said after a few miles.

Allie nodded. "He will look different. Just so you're prepared. He's thinner now. He lost most of his muscles. They have him doing rehab work, but he still looks like a starving man."

"I wouldn't expect him to win a beauty contest," Clay said. "Is he strong, though? Should I shake his hand? Hug him? Or do I keep my distance? I can do whatever is best for him."

Allie relaxed. Clay was asking the right kind of questions. He knew her brother would need special care. "I'm sure he'd appreciate a handshake."

They spent the rest of the ride into Dry Creek reminiscing about their days on the ranch with Mark. Allie had forgotten half of the things that Clay remembered. They made her smile. Those had been good times.

"I thought we'd stop at the hardware store," Allie said when they were at the outskirts of the small town. "We always get—"

"White hats!" Clay finished for her in excitement. "I remember Mark talking about that. He called them the Nelson Easter bonnets."

"My mom and I got them, too," Allie said with a grin. "That's why he used to joke about them. Sometimes Mom would put a flower in the band around her Stetson. We used to wear these pretty Easter dresses, but she said we needed to have a rancher's hat to show where we came from."

Allie wished it was that easy now to be sure of where she belonged and what direction her life should take. Ever since Clay had come back, things had seemed unsettled.

* * *

Clay opened the door to the hardware store for Allie and stood to the side while she entered. He could hear the deep-toned chorus of welcome from what he figured was the group of men sitting around that potbelly stove in the middle of the store. Clay had never sat with the men there; Mr. Nelson had invited him once when they were in town, but Clay had preferred to slip over to the café with Allie and get a soda.

When Allie had stepped into the store, he followed her, closing the door behind him. A large store window looked out to the street. A cashier's counter was on the left, and he saw that the pastor, Matthew Curtis, stood there tallying up something in a ledger. Rows of shelves held the merchandise.

"Good to have you stop by, Clay," the pastor said with a smile.

Time had passed. Since Clay had been sent to prison, the man's dark hair had gained a few gray streaks. Laugh lines showed by his eyes. But his welcome was as warm as ever.

"Thanks," Clay said. He remembered Allie telling him once that the pastor worked part-time in the hardware store so he could put money aside for the college funds for his twin boys. The boys had to be past that stage now, though. Or, close to it.

"We came for hats," Clay finally said as he glanced over to where Allie was chatting with a half-dozen old, grizzled ranchers. They were sitting in an assortment of hard-backed chairs that were ringed around that potbellied stove. He could tell by the looks on their faces that they adored Allie. She was no doubt talking crops and horses with them like she'd done since she was a kid.

"Easter hats?" the pastor asked as he walked over to a shelf on the back wall.

"Yes," Clay said as he stood still.

He thought he was doing fine until Allie looked back at him and frowned slightly. "Come on over and say hi to everyone."

He could spot a phony smile a hundred feet away, and he was much closer than that to those old ranchers. If they tried to smile any harder, he was afraid they'd strain something.

The only sound in the place as Clay walked over was the creak in the ladder as the pastor climbed up to bring down the hats.

Finally, one of the ranchers slowly rose to his feet. "The wife tells me you're reformed now. Some kind of an artist."

The man didn't sound impressed, and he didn't offer to shake hands.

"I draw a bit," Clay admitted. He didn't hold out his hand, either.

"Learn that in the joint?" another man asked. He didn't show any inclination to stand.

The rest of the men sat there looking at him suspiciously. The smiles were gone. Clay was relieved for that at least.

"I expect you learned more than how to draw when you were in prison," the man continued. "Or maybe you taught the boys there something, what with your history and all."

"What do you mean by that?" Clay asked.

The other man didn't answer, but Clay noted that Allie's face had reddened. She was embarrassed. He supposed he shouldn't blame her. No one liked to hang out with a foster kid turned ex-con.

He could hear the pastor climbing back down the ladder.

"I got an assortment of sizes to try on," he said cheerfully.

Clay turned and saw the pastor carrying an armload of white Stetson hats over to the counter. He looked like he hadn't heard the accusation hanging in the air.

"Thank you," Allie said with relief in her voice as she gestured for Clay to meet her over at the counter. "We'll be quick about it. We need the smallest one you have for my nephew. Then we'll take three in a size seven and—" She looked at Clay. "Do you know the size you need? There's a tag inside the hat you have on that probably says."

"It's seven and five-eighths." Clay didn't need to remove his hat. When a man didn't own much, he usually knew what he had.

The pastor pulled a hat off the top of the stack and put it with the others he'd already set aside. Then he put them all in a beige plastic bag with a sales slip.

Clay felt self-conscious because he knew the ranchers were listening to everything he and Allie said. But none of the men voiced any opinions. He supposed they thought even troublemakers were entitled to wear a new hat.

Clay followed Allie's lead and they were soon out of the hardware store with five brand-new Stetson hats in their possession. The bright white felt in the hats was accented with bands of brass-tipped leather cords.

"They look great," Clay said when they climbed back into the pickup. He set the bag with the hats on the seat between them. "I've never had such a good-looking Stetson."

He hated to see Allie subdued like this when she'd been looking forward to something as simple as a new Easter bonnet. "You'll look great in your new hat, too."

She smiled at him, but it was a halfhearted gesture.

The drive to the nursing home outside Miles City was quiet. The land was flat, and they didn't see many vehicles on the freeway. The sky had darkened, and Clay suspected it would snow before the day was over.

"They don't mean to be unfair," Allie said at one point. "Back at the hardware store."

"It's okay," Clay assured her. He shouldn't be disappointed. A few people in Dry Creek had been happy to see him. That would have to be enough. "Some people don't understand."

"They're good men usually," she added.

"I know," Clay said, and he meant it. Those men would do almost anything for a neighbor in trouble. But he was an outsider to them, and he always had been. They probably didn't like seeing him with Allie either, and he didn't blame them. No woman needed to be tagged as a friend to an ex-con.

Of course, saying anything like that to Allie would only get her hackles up. So, he asked Allie about her life in Jackson Hole, and they talked a little of happier things.

Clay had driven through Miles City before he saw

the sign for the nursing home. He turned off the free-way and slowed down to enter the lane leading to the long frame building. Clay could tell from the soft gray paint and white trim that someone had tried to make the structure look inviting. There was a large yard at the front of the home, but the grass was dead and patches of snow were scattered around.

"All of the rooms have windows at least," Allie said as Clay parked the pickup. "Mark is on the west side, so he sees the sun go down every day."

Clay tried to look positively at everything. He knew from prison how important seeing the sun was, but he also knew that having a view was seldom enough to make up for being confined for whatever reason. He wondered if Mark felt trapped in this place. Or was he so sick that he didn't care?

Allie brought in one of the size seven Stetsons for Mark. They left the rest of the hats in that bag in the pickup.

Clay stopped when they came to the steps going into the building. He turned to Allie. "Do I look okay?"

She must have known what he was asking because she studied him. "Smile when you see him. You look younger when you do that. And keep your hat on if you can. That hides your eyes a little."

He grinned. "What's wrong with my eyes?"

"They've seen a lot of life," Allie replied. "It shows."

"I'd seen a lot of things before I met Mark, too." Clay turned and opened the main door to the place. "My eyes have always looked like this."

Clay noticed it was not silent as they walked down

the corridors. People were talking in hushed tones, but it all added up to a medium hum that didn't stop.

"Here it is," Allie said when they came to one of the small rooms. She looked up at Clay. "I'll go in first and let him know you're with me."

"That's probably best." Clay tried to rein in his excitement. He knew Mark wouldn't be able to handle an exuberant greeting from him so, regardless of the joy he felt inside, he took a deep breath and told himself to calm down.

Clay heard the surprised cry inside the room as Mark realized Allie was there.

After a couple of minutes, Allie came back to the door. She had a huge grin on her face and tears falling down her cheeks. "Come in."

Clay stepped inside and saw his old friend. "Mark."

Despite the warnings he'd had, Clay was shocked. His friend was gaunt. He looked worse than men who'd been in solitary confinement for a month. Mark had grown a few inches taller since Clay had seen him last, but he probably weighed forty pounds less. His skin was slightly yellow. His black hair was poorly cut, and he'd nicked himself shaving. He wore blue-and-white-striped pajamas. His brown eyes were shining, though, as he looked at Clay.

"It's about time," Mark said as he took a feeble step toward Clay. "I'm not contagious, you know. People don't need to worry about seeing me. I just had a—" Mark got a confused look on his face as he hesitated "—an accident, I guess."

"You've had a hard time," Clay agreed softly as he walked farther into the room.

Mark stared at Clay for a few seconds. "I need to lie back down."

Clay nodded.

"Come sit and talk to me, though," Mark said as he lay down on the hospital bed. "I want you to tell me how everyone is." He paused and then grinned. "Especially Hannah. I guess she's still mad at me."

Clay took his time walking over to the one chair beside the bed. He didn't know what to say.

It was silent for a moment and then Mark turned to Allie, who stood by the door. "Can you get us some sodas from the machine at the end of the hall?"

She looked at Clay before nodding and leaving.

"You can tell me about it now," Mark said after Allie was gone. "Hannah hasn't come by. I tried to call her number, and the phone was disconnected. I know Sammy Yates would like to ask her out, so I don't want him making moves on her while I am laid up in here. I want to take her to the prom, and I haven't had a chance to even ask her."

Clay swallowed. "There's no hurry. You've got time."

"You haven't seen them together?" Mark asked anxiously.

"No." Clay was glad he could answer that at least.

Mark seemed worn out from the conversation and lay on his bed for some time just looking over at Clay.

"Have you been working out?" Mark finally asked, studying Clay.

"Just hanging out," Clay said as he tried to look a little less bulky in the heavy coat he wore.

Mark kept eyeing him, though.

"You're different," he said quietly. "You look—" Mark seemed to search for the word "—settled."

Clay sat up at that. "What do you mean?"

"Have you finished reading the Gospel of Luke?" Mark asked. "I've been wanting to talk to you about it. I keep going over it again and again. It was a good challenge from the church. I think it's true, you know."

"I read it yesterday." Clay had lain on the mattress on the kitchen floor in the bunkhouse last night and couldn't sleep, so he pulled the Bible off the low shelf. The account of Jesus had drawn him in, and he hadn't been able to stop reading until he finished.

"I'm glad we're doing the Easter processional," Mark said. His voice was getting weaker, and he had to pause between the words. "You're still in on that, aren't you?"

"Yes, I'm in," Clay said.

"It's important to me to be there," Mark said, slower yet. Each word seemed an effort now. "I never understood about Easter until now."

Clay saw the truth on his friend's face. Mark knew something about the Easter story that he didn't. "I'll see that you get there."

Allie came back then with three cans of cola.

"I need to take a nap now," Mark whispered. "But I'll see you early on Sunday. Real early. We have to be there for the Resurrection."

Clay nodded, and Allie quietly set one of the cans of soda on Mark's nightstand. He'd already closed his eyes.

"See that Hannah doesn't go out with anyone else," Mark whispered as Clay walked to the door.

Clay turned around, and Mark had opened his eyes again.

"You just rest now," Clay said softly. "Don't worry about a thing."

Clay left the room with Allie.

They were silent as they walked through the corridors and exited the building. Snow began to fall as Clay started to drive back to Dry Creek.

"Are you okay?" he asked Allie after a few miles. She'd been quiet.

She nodded. "He's come so far, but he has a long way still to go. I just feel bad for him."

"Is there a reason the doctors don't tell him how long he's been out of it?" Clay asked.

"They say it's better for him if he figures it out for himself," Allie said. "They keep him away from mirrors and calendars. They say that when he's ready to absorb the information, his mind will let him know it."

They drove awhile in companionable silence.

"Do you know about Hannah?" Clay finally asked. "Does she still have any feelings for Mark?"

"I don't know. She never says. She did go to see Mark a lot when he was first in the coma, but after Jeremy was born she didn't go as often. Of course, it was probably hard with the baby. Then I think she gave up. All I know is that she finished a nursing program and has signed up for some kind of specialized training. She's taking the course now back east. That's why Jeremy is here with us for a couple of weeks."

"She's not engaged, though?" Clay persisted.

Allie hesitated. "She hasn't said anything. Jeremy has talked about a man his mother knows, though—Sammy something. Jeremy doesn't seem to like the man, but I don't know what Hannah has planned."

"Not Sammy Yates?" Clay protested in alarm.

Allie frowned. "I think so. I didn't know much about him, but he was in school with Mark and Hannah."

"Well, that's not good," Clay said.

"What's wrong with Sammy?"

"He's stealing Mark's girl."

"But—" Allie started and then stopped. "Does it matter now?"

There seemed to be no answer for that, and they continued the drive in thoughtful silence. Clay noticed the wind starting to blow as they got near Dry Creek.

"We should stop at the café and get something to go," Allie said as they came to the first building in the small town. The sky had darkened by now, and it was clear a storm was coming. "It's past noon and they will have already eaten at the ranch. Not that they won't all have room for a hamburger, too. We'll want to be able to get right to work and make sure everything is closed up tight in the barn before this storm hits."

The strip of asphalt running through the small town widened a bit in front of the café. Cement steps led up to the door, and red-and-white-checked curtains fluttered over the glass-paned windows on each side of the entry. Three other mud-spattered pickups were parked next to the café, and Clay slipped his vehicle into place at the end of the line.

When he stepped out of the pickup, Clay was grateful for the sheepskin coat that he still wore. He opened one of the front flaps and wrapped that around a shivering Allie as they hurried over to the stairs. The rush of the wind made them laugh as they pushed against it all the way. Finally, Clay opened the door and they tumbled into the café, breathless and still laughing.

"It's getting fierce out there," a pleasant-looking waitress with red hair said as she paused in her path across the café, a full coffeepot in her hand. "Have a seat anywhere and I'll get to you after I refill the cups over there."

She inclined her head to where four of the ranchers sat. Clay recognized them from this morning at the hardware store. He nodded in their direction, but none of them nodded back.

Clay decided to ignore them. Life was too short to butt heads against everyone who had an inclination to suspect other people of everything they might have done in life.

Clay followed Allie to one of the side tables. Before he sat down, he took his coat off and laid it over one of the empty chairs at their table. He liked the cozy warmth inside the café.

The woman came back quickly with an order pad in one hand and a pencil in the other. "Sorry about that."

"Not a problem, Lois," Allie said.

So this was Lois, Clay thought in delight. Her hair was too bright to be natural, but her smile looked 100 percent genuine. She had pretty amber eyes and well-defined cheekbones. He'd guess she was about forty years old, so she'd be a few years younger than Randy. He looked at her hands and didn't see any kind of a ring. Her white apron was neat, and it covered a blue T-shirt and basic jeans.

He'd known Allie was giving the order while he studied Lois, but he was suddenly aware of an ominous silence and looked over at Allie.

She was not happy with him. Her lips were pursed and only relaxed slightly when she spoke. "I've been asking how you want your hamburger."

"Well-done with grilled onions if you have them," he said, looking up at Lois.

"Not a problem," the waitress confirmed as she added a note to her order pad. "Now for the pie. We have apple, cherry and a lime chiffon that I made. I make a different chiffon pie every day. The apple and cherry are excellent, too. We have them delivered from a bakery in Miles City."

"We'll get five pieces of pie then," Allie said. "I'll take apple for my dad and nephew. A cherry for me. Clay, what do you want?"

Her eyes glowered at him, but he answered politely. "I'd love a slice of cherry, too."

"And Randy?" Allie asked.

"Randy Collins?" Lois echoed the question. Clay was gratified to see her face brightened up even more than what looked like her usual good cheer. "He always gets a slice of chiffon. Lemon, raspberry. Like I said it's lime today, and I know he'd order that if he were here."

Clay grinned. The Randy he used to know would rather eat sawdust than something as girlie as chiffon pie. In fact, Clay distinctly remembered Randy chastising him for eating cherry pie. That's when the other man had explained that a wrangler ate only apple pie unless it was Thanksgiving. On that day it was permissible to have a slice of pumpkin, as well.

Clay chuckled, and both women looked at him askance.

"Everyone will love a piece of pie," he said. The words were meaningless, but at least no one looked at him funny any longer. "In fact, give me an extra slice of apple."

Fifteen minutes later, Clay and Allie were leaving the café, carrying white bags of takeout. The wind was whipping around even stronger, so Clay walked close enough to shelter Allie from some of the worst of it.

He opened the door for Allie, and she climbed into the pickup. He handed her all of the food, and she set it on the floor at her feet. Then Clay shut the door and fought his way around to the driver's side.

He was freezing by the time he opened his door and got inside.

"I hope this blizzard goes away before Sunday," Clay said as he blew on his hands for a few seconds to warm them before he put them on the cold steering wheel. "Mark couldn't be out in a storm like this one."

"It won't last that many days," Allie said. "According to the weather forecast it'll be gone by Wednesday."

"Good." Clay's meeting with his new art agent had been set for seven o'clock Wednesday morning at this café.

Clay turned the key and started the pickup. Then he backed out and got started on the road to the Nelson ranch. The smell of the hamburgers had him pressing a little harder on the gas pedal.

They had gone a few miles when Allie looked over at him. He was just beginning to wonder why she was so quiet when she spoke.

"I saw you checking out Lois," Allie announced haughtily. "She just moved here a few months ago. She's pretty, don't you think?"

Clay smiled. Allie was trying to pretend she didn't care, but she did look put out about it, which gave him more hope than it probably should have.

"Just doing a favor for someone," Clay replied mildly.

Allie snorted. "Don't expect me to believe that. You don't even know anyone around here in need of a favor except me and Mark and Dad and—" She stopped and her eyes got wide. "Randy?"

Clay nodded with a grin.

Allie hooted in laughter. "I wondered what was up when she said Randy was ordering all that chiffon pie. He's more a meat-and-potatoes kind of guy. And I don't think he even likes lime."

"I'm sure he doesn't," Clay agreed. "That's why I asked for the extra slice of apple pie. He'd be feeling pretty low if everyone else was having apple and cherry and he was stuck looking at his piece of lime chiffon."

Allie nodded, her eyes still dancing with merriment.

Clay saw her smile periodically as they finished the trip to the ranch. He was glad to know she was still a romantic at heart. She was probably picturing Randy and Lois getting together at some point. It took a real man to eat chiffon pie to prove his love, Clay told himself.

He sat there a moment before the realization struck him like a bolt out of the sky that he wasn't sure he'd be willing to eat chiffon pie. Was he too set in his ways for love? Was he asking too much of Allie to insist she believe that he was telling the truth about his innocence in that robbery four years ago? Would it be enough if he put the past behind them and just moved on from here? Or would her unwillingness to believe him on that one point always be with them? Agreeing on chiffon pie wasn't the same as agreeing on a matter of truth.

Maybe he didn't have what it took for love. Maybe he was like those daffodils that were starting to bloom around the church. They would be dying without that tarp. Unfortunately, there were no plastic wraps for people's emotions.

He was surprised to realize he would be disappointed if the sunrise service didn't happen. He planned to read the Gospel of Luke again tonight. He wasn't sure he understood everything. And what he did understand seemed impossible to him.

He thought of Mark and their old pledge to study up on the Gospel of Luke. He'd read it through several times already, but he'd go slower with it tonight and see if he could find any clues on how to know what were the right things to say to Mark.

Chapter Thirteen

"**W**e need some work on that wagon," Randy said as Clay stepped inside the barn. Allie had gone into the main house with the take-out bags, but Clay knew he would enjoy his food more if he checked on the progress out here first.

Clay walked over to where Randy was standing by the Easter wagon. Rickety gray planks leaned inward as they formed the two sides of the wagon. The back was open. The bed was made of the same kind of wood, but seemed to be in better shape. Long gaps showed where the wood had splintered away, and rusty nails held the whole thing together.

"There's some plywood up in the hayloft," Clay said. "Maybe we could use that to shore up this thing."

The wind was blowing flakes of snow into the barn through the opening that led out to the attached corral. There was a sliding door that could be closed, but no one had done it yet. The horses were bunched together near the barn wall, but so far they hadn't come back into the barn. Clay didn't blame them for preferring to stay outside as long as possible.

"I hope the blizzard is gone by the time we have to drive this wagon into Dry Creek," Randy said as he squatted down to point out some boards low on one side. "It could fall apart from the rattling."

"We'll get at it in a bit," Clay said. "But Allie brought everyone hamburgers and pie at the café in Dry Creek, and we'll want to eat that while it's warm."

"Sounds really good," Randy said as he straightened. "Mr. Nelson made up some soup and sandwiches earlier, but I'm hungry already."

"I figured as much," Clay said.

The two of them went into the house and washed up. Allie already had on the table the hamburgers in their wrappers and the pieces of pie in the plastic containers the café had given them. Mr. Nelson and Jeremy were finishing playing a game of some kind and were at the table shortly after Clay and Randy got there.

"I hear you like chiffon pie," Clay said innocently as he and Randy sat at the table.

Allie grinned as she sat down to join them. "Lime," she added.

Randy nodded grimly. "How many pieces of that were left?"

"You wanted more?" Clay asked in astonishment. Maybe he had misjudged the wrangler. "Of chiffon?"

Randy shook his head and leaned forward with his elbows on the table. "I just want to know how many pieces of her pie are left. There are a couple of the guys at the Elkton Ranch that go in and buy a piece of her chiffon pie every day. They even bought some of her kiwi chiffon! They've started getting it to go so I know they don't eat it, but they have no business making time with Lois that way. They stand and flirt with her while she dishes up the pie."

Clay couldn't help but grin. "I didn't see any ring on her finger. I guess they figure she's not spoken for yet."

"I'm working on it," Randy said testily, glowering at him. "I figure she'd want to know me some before she'll agree to go out with me."

"That's a good plan," Allie said soothingly. "Be friends first."

Clay didn't comment. That wasn't how a man went about all of this—not if he had competition for the lady of his heart.

"But those Elkton guys are crowding me," Randy said. "I want a spectacular first date, and I'm not ready for it yet."

"Maybe they just like pie," Clay offered.

"It's chiffon," Randy protested. "Nothing but air and some frilly stuff. Those guys don't like it. It's a woman's pie."

By that time, Allie had the hamburgers passed around. Mr. Nelson said the blessing and everyone started to eat. It was silent until Allie started to give out the slices of pie.

"That green one must be mine," Randy said, his voice sounding dejected while his eyes watched the slice of apple pie that was making its way over to Mr. Nelson. Randy didn't say anything, but a deep sigh rose from his chest.

"Don't worry," Allie said to Randy. "Clay has you covered on this one."

Then she handed him the piece of apple pie. "He insisted we get this extra for you."

Randy's face brightened immediately, and he looked over at Clay. "I owe you for this one, buddy."

Clay nodded but didn't say anything.

"Seriously," Randy continued. "I could have been nicer to you when you got here, and for you to do this— I'm insisting I pay you back some way."

"That's not necessary," Clay said.

Clay looked out the closest window. He wondered if Randy was suggesting they become friends. He didn't know what to say about that so he concentrated on the view from the window instead. Snow was falling in earnest now, large wet flakes coming down. "We better get going if we want to get those animals taken care of."

Allie was the first one out to the barn, and she reveled in the silence when she stepped inside the small door that was across from the house. The horses had made their way inside and were waiting by the feed trough. She'd stored the cortisone drops for their eyes in the tack room, so she figured she'd get those dispensed before she worried about getting another hay bale down from the loft.

She realized she was mighty cheerful considering a storm was coming their way. She had to admit she liked having chores to do again. Halfway through the barn, she heard a squeal and a series of rapid footsteps.

"Julie," she said as she squatted down to meet the miniature pig that was barreling toward her. When the animal got to her, its squeals intensified.

"Sorry," Allie said. "I didn't bring a treat for you."

She patted the pig on the head like she would a dog. It didn't seem to satisfy the animal much, though, because it kept making a racket.

The stallion suddenly neighed and stomped its foot. The pig looked up and stopped making noise at that signal. Allie smiled. It seemed the animals had things figured out among themselves.

The air blowing into the barn from the opening to the corral was getting colder, and Allie could see that the horses were wet. She walked to the tack room and brought back some of the old towels she kept out here for the very purpose of rubbing animals down when that happened. By the time she'd finished with the rubdowns, Clay was there to bring the hay down from the loft.

"Give them enough hay to get them to morning," Allie said as Clay was climbing the ladder. "That way we don't have to come out later."

"I'll do that," Clay said. "But I want to work on this wagon some this afternoon. I need to sort through the leather harnesses, too."

Allie nodded. She was grateful Clay was putting all he had into this Easter processional. She knew he was doing it for Mark, but she hoped it would also ease some of the tension between Clay and the older ranchers around here. She'd been upset when she'd seen how unfriendly they had been to Clay. Every man had a right to a second chance.

After Clay threw a couple of hay bales from the loft to the feed trough, he climbed down the ladder with a small bag of oats over his shoulder for the goat.

"You're going to have to earn this," Clay said to the brown-haired goat. Then he put some out for it.

Allie smiled. Her father used to say a man could tell which wranglers would make good ranchers by whether or not they talked to the animals in their care.

"Don't spend so much time out here that you forget about getting your sketches ready for that agent of yours," Allie cautioned. Clay might enjoy the animals, but it sounded like his future was brighter with his artwork.

"I've got time for it all," Clay said as Randy came inside the barn to join them.

Allie nodded. She hoped Clay was right. It would likely snow all day tomorrow, but the next day Clay would meet with his art agent. She kept wanting to take another look at the collection of sketches he had done of her. She still couldn't believe what she saw. It was like he'd seen her emotions in all her everyday tasks. It might be strange to think of others looking at those drawings and seeing her emotions, but it also made her feel good, like she would be connected with all of those people in some way.

She wondered suddenly what would happen if the agent didn't like the way she looked.

"Are you doing some new sketches?" Allie asked Clay. "Maybe you should. For your meeting."

She'd feel better if the agent has something to choose from.

Clay nodded. "Last night I did some sketches of the stallion and the goat. I want to get a few more of the horses tomorrow."

"Good," Allie said. She didn't want Clay's success as an artist to rest on drawings of her. He would be safer to focus on the horses. Everyone loved pictures of animals.

Chapter Fourteen

Early Wednesday morning, Clay woke up and saw a layer of snow on the sills of the bunkhouse windows. He relied on the yard light to show the white flakes since the sun had not risen yet. Clay looked at the illuminated hands on the alarm clock he'd left by his mattress and saw that it was a little after five o'clock.

He didn't need to get up for an hour, he told himself as he pulled the covers tighter around his shoulders. He was comfortable as long as he stayed where he was. The floor under his mattress was freezing, and he had no desire to put his feet on it. He smiled as he remembered that Randy had vowed last night that he was getting up before Clay this morning to build a blaze in the fireplace. It was his way of paying Clay back for that piece of pie.

In Clay's opinion, no heat felt as homey as that coming from a nice fire.

"Randy," Clay called out.

"I'm getting up," the wrangler answered back with a yawn in his voice.

Clay must have slid back into sleep because the next thing he knew the air in the bunkhouse was tolerable and the red rooster was crowing. Clay could hear someone moving around in the other room, so he looked at the alarm clock and saw it was six o'clock. He had an hour to get himself into Dry Creek for the meeting with the art agent.

Clay dressed with care, and before it was time for him to leave, there was a knock on the bunkhouse door. Allie had come over with some hot sausage biscuits wrapped in tinfoil.

"You can come to the house to get yours," Allie said to Randy before holding out the biscuits to Clay. "But it's a long drive to Dry Creek, and I want you to know I'm praying for you and your meeting."

Randy nodded. "Break a leg."

"I think that's for actors," Clay said as he looked at them both. He wasn't used to support like this.

"You might see me in Dry Creek," Randy said. "I need to go in and check on those daffodils. I'll feed the animals here first, but I won't get in your way with your meeting."

Randy made the motion for zipping his lips. "I won't interrupt at all."

"I don't think we need to be that quiet." Clay hated to pull himself away from this cozy scene, but he wanted to leave plenty of time to get to the café before that art agent. The café opened at seven o'clock, so he needed to leave soon.

"I might need to go to Dry Creek, too," Allie said then. She looked a little shy. "I won't say anything, either."

"You can say anything you want," Clay assured her.

"Can I get a ride with you?" Allie asked Randy.

The man nodded, and the arrangements were all made.

The red pickup was cold when Clay climbed inside, but he set the hat bag on the floor of the passenger side. His was the only hat inside that bag, and he would have been tempted to pull it out and wear it for his meeting. But while it would look great for Easter morning, it seemed too dressed up for a Wednesday. Clay didn't want to look like he was putting on airs.

He drove in darkness, but the sun was beginning to rise when he pulled into Dry Creek. He saw the lights go on in the café and noticed three other pickups were already gathered around the place. One of the vehicles was from the Redfern ranch, and it looked like someone was sitting in it, no doubt keeping warm until he could order a cup of coffee.

The light that went on must have been the signal that the café was ready for business because the door to the hardware store opened and five stocky ranchers came out and walked across the street. Clay waited a minute to follow them into the café.

Black-and-white squares covered the floor. Red stools stood at the counter. A pie stand on the counter held a fluffy pink pie. Clay liked this place, he thought as he settled himself at a table. Before he knew it, Lois brought around the coffeepot and poured him a cup.

"Can I get you something more?" she asked. The smell of bacon came from the back of the café, and he saw that those old ranchers had their menus in hand. "We've got buttermilk pancakes. Eggs any way you like them."

"Maybe later," Clay said and then asked, "What kind of chiffon pie do you have today?"

She beamed. "We don't serve pie until lunch, but it will be strawberry chiffon. I put it out early just because it's so pretty."

"I might get a piece to go later," Clay said. "My buddy Randy sure does like your pies."

She positively glowed at that.

"Some of the recipes are mine," Lois confided, her voice low. "I'm thinking of entering them in a dessert contest. The prize is a trip to Seattle to see the Space Needle. For two."

"For two," Clay repeated, trying to sound casual. "Who is the fortunate person who gets to go with you if you win?"

"Probably my mother," she said. "But it's too soon to know if I have a chance of winning."

"There's always a chance," Clay said. Even for Randy, he added silently to himself.

Clay looked over and noticed that the five ranchers were sending unfriendly looks his way. He figured they didn't want him holding up the waitress. Lois must have thought the same because she walked over and refilled their coffee cups while she noted what they wanted to eat.

It wasn't much longer before Clay's agent walked into the café, full of apologies for setting the meeting so early on a cold morning.

"You can't control the weather," Clay assured the man with a smile. "And I'm always up by now. A rancher does his best work in the early part of the day."

"I'm glad," the agent said. "I have to catch a plane later."

Clay forgot about everyone else as he opened his folder and started to show his agent the sketches of Allie. The man examined each drawing intently with a series of appreciative murmurs.

"These are excellent," the agent said at the end. "Just what you need."

"I have a few others." Clay pulled out the three drawings he had made of the horses and the goat.

The agent gave a warm chuckle when he looked at those. "Can you draw more of these?"

Clay nodded. He was on the verge of asking the agent a question when he heard the café door open with a bang. Angry footsteps sounded. Clay looked up and saw Randy standing in the open doorway with Allie trying to make her way around him.

"Where is that kid?" Randy bellowed, his voice rattling the dishes on the table. The cook even came out of the back where the grill was.

Randy didn't seem to require an answer because he kept looking all around the café as though there might be a hiding place he hadn't noticed before. It was clear he'd dig anyone out of that place if he saw it.

"What is it?" Lois finally asked, her voice quaking with nerves.

Randy seemed to realize where he was then. He ducked his head.

"Nothing for you to worry about." Randy's voice was soft. "I'm looking for that foster kid."

The ranchers all stood up at that, all five pairs of boots hitting the floor at the same time.

"The new foster kid or the old one?" one of the ranchers asked, his eyes going over to where Clay still sat.

"What's happened?" another rancher asked. He was halfway to Randy by the time he finished his question.

"Someone cut all the tarps on the daffodils," Randy said, his voice outraged. "At the church! Those flowers are all frozen solid now. It's a desecration."

Randy stood there, his shoulders squared with righteous indignation. Clay wanted to say something to calm the situation, but no words came. This was the kind of fury that had led to the townspeople condemning him four years ago.

Clay looked down in time to see Allie slip around Randy.

"Now, there's no need to jump to conclusions," Allie commanded as she stood in front of the ranchers. She stretched her arms over the door as though to slow down a stampede. She'd known these men all her life, and she knew they were fair-minded if they understood a situation. "It's not as bad as it seems."

"Not as bad?" Randy turned to her in loud protest.

"It could have been an accident," Allie continued in desperation. She could see by their faces that those ranchers were ready to haul Clay back to jail.

"Those tarps were deliberately cut," Randy said firmly.

Allie noticed that even Randy swung his head until he was looking squarely at Clay. Surely they could not suspect him. "Clay didn't even—"

"Of course not," one of the ranchers said. "But he's still got his nose out of joint. Admitted as much in church before he stomped out last Sunday."

"He was only trying to tell everyone what happened," Allie said. The ranchers turned to look at her now. She put a bright smile on her face in hopes that would convince them to leave Clay alone.

It didn't work that way.

"I hope you ain't sweet on him," one of the men said instead as he shook his head with a hangdog expression on his face. "He led your brother into a life of crime and almost got him killed. It's no good if you take up with him, too."

The other ranchers nodded. Allie noted they didn't even need to discuss it among themselves. They had condemned Clay once again for the past.

The whole thing was making her mad. And here Clay was with his agent, someone he wanted to impress.

"As a matter of fact," Allie said crisply, "I've been sweet on Clay West since the day I first met him."

The entire café was silent. Allie herself was dumbfounded. The words had come out of her without any thought. The ranchers just stood there with their jaws dropped and their eyes wide. Even Clay stared at her.

"I mean," she stammered. "I think we need to reconsider. I think Clay is innocent. That's all."

"Innocent of what?" one of the ranchers asked.

Allie flushed red at his words. "We all know he didn't cut those tarps. He's a good man. We need to look elsewhere for someone to blame."

The café seemed to have grown overly hot in the time Allie stood there with the door open. Which was impossible, of course, but her neck sure did feel warm. She stepped inside and let the door close behind her.

She didn't want to look at Clay, but she did anyway. He was sitting there with a frown on his face. Not that she knew what that meant. Was he happy that she'd made a fool of herself telling everyone that she liked him? Or was he just pleased that she had finally stood up for him in this town?

A tiny doubt sneaked into her thoughts. Was she willing to declare him not guilty of that robbery years ago or was she just saying he couldn't have cut those tarps? She had nothing but emotions to guide her either way.

"It has to be the new foster kid then," Randy said, breaking the silence. "And I think he's around here somewhere. I saw that pickup he drives outside."

The ranchers started to head toward the door, and Allie stepped out of their way. Clay and Randy followed the other men outside. She had no choice but to follow, as well.

Chapter Fifteen

Clay knew what it was like to be a foster kid who was blamed for everything that happened for miles around. That teenager, Hen, probably wasn't guilty of this, and Clay couldn't stand by while a mob of angry men confronted him. If they badgered the boy, Clay didn't know what would happen.

Unfortunately, they didn't need to go far to find Hen. He was standing against the panel of the truck he drove, wearing ragged black jeans and a black parka. His legs crossed at the ankles and his arms crossed in front of him. He was the picture of defiance, right down to the dangling earring that shone in the rising sun and the lit cigarette between his lips.

"Where's your knife?" Randy demanded as he faced off with the teenager.

"What's it to you?" Hen answered back with a snarl in his voice.

"Somebody used something sharp to cut through those tarps by the church," Randy said. "It would take a knife."

"That was a dumb idea anyway," Hen said. "What kind of church worries about having flowers for Easter?"

Allie gasped but didn't say anything.

Clay felt unqualified to answer that question, although he had learned a thing or two from all his readings of the Gospel of Luke.

"The church needs your respect," Clay finally said. "You're better off to confess now if you cut those tarps."

Hen didn't look convinced, but he did move his glare from Randy to Clay.

"You're one to talk," Hen said to Clay as he flicked the ash from the end of his cigarette. "Heard you're a jailbird. Real bad guy."

Clay was glad the agent had stayed inside, although the fact that Clay had served time was not a secret.

"Look, just show us the inside of your pickup," Randy demanded. "We want to see if you have a knife on you."

Hen smirked and stepped away from the pickup. "Be my guest."

Clay watched the teenager as Randy, Allie and the ranchers searched the vehicle. Hen stood away from them, glaring as he followed their movements. Hen was trying to look tough, but Clay thought he saw a twitch in the teenager's face.

"The pickup's clean," Randy announced when they'd finished. He looked at Hen speculatively then. "Take that coat off and let's see if it's tucked in there."

"Man, its cold out here," Hen complained, but he unzipped the parka and took it off. Randy quickly felt the seams and pockets of the coat. Then he handed it back to Hen. "It's clean."

One of the ranchers asked Hen to turn around before he put his coat back on so he could see if he had a knife hidden anywhere.

"He's clean," the rancher agreed.

The rest of the men looked defeated, but Clay wasn't convinced Hen was as innocent as he was pretending to be. The ranchers, Randy and Allie started to walk across the street to the church. Clay kept standing where he was.

When the others were far enough away that they couldn't hear, Clay leaned over to Hen. "Pull up your right pant leg."

Hen looked scared for the first time this morning. "You got no call to—"

"Pull it up," Clay repeated.

The teenager still didn't, so Clay reached down and tugged the jeans up enough that the knife's sheath was visible.

"They were just some stupid flowers," Hen said. "It wasn't like I killed anybody."

Clay was silent.

"What are you going to do?" Hen finally asked defiantly.

"I'm not going to do anything," Clay said. "You are. You're going to go over to the church and tell everyone what you did. Then you're going to apologize and ask them to forgive you. Then you're going to do everything you can to make up for what you did."

"Humph," Hen said. "Why should I do that? They didn't even see my knife."

"I saw it," Clay said. "And if you want to keep yourself out of jail, you'll do as I say."

"Like you're such an expert," Hen muttered.

Clay laughed at that. "Frankly, in this situation, I am just about as expert as you'll find. Now let's go."

He was surprised at how easily the boy went with him.

Allie almost cried when she saw the shredded tarps behind the church. Generations ago, the congregation had chosen this side of the building for the Easter sunrise service because the cemetery stood here. They wanted to share the Resurrection joy of the morning with their beloved ones who lay in this sacred ground. Allie herself always stopped to pray at her mother's grave on Easter morning.

And now the area where the daffodils had been planted looked devastated. The gravestones were damp. The air was cold. Heavy plastic was lying on top of green shoots, all pushed to the ground by what looked like tire marks.

"Look what they did!" Randy said as he used his arm to sweep the scene of destruction. "There's no way to save any of the flowers for Easter morning."

Allie looked over at the faces of the five ranchers who had followed Randy over here. They were among the churchgoers who had made the decision to hold the Easter sunrise service here years ago. Half of them had wives or children buried in this cemetery. They understood the joy of Resurrection Sunday. They knew faith held families together, and this was their one day to celebrate that fact. The daffodils were their gift to God in thanks for what He'd given them. One of the men had plowed the land last fall so it would be ready for planting. Another had come with his two grandsons to put the stakes in to hold up the tarps. Yet another had taken care of buying the daffodil bulbs.

Now they were shocked and angry.

All of their eyes turned to look as Clay and that boy, Hen, came walking around the side of the church to where they stood.

The storm wasn't the only thing responsible for the chill that hung in the air. No one greeted the newcomers. The silence was long and tense.

Finally, Clay spoke. "Hen, here, has something to say."

The teenager swallowed. His face was pale. Allie could see he was terrified.

"It's time to tell the truth," Clay said to the boy. "It might be hard, but a man isn't much if he can't be honest. It's what makes you who you are."

Allie blinked. *Oh, my,* she thought. She suddenly understood why it was so important to Clay that people believe him when he said he didn't plan that robbery. He believed with all his heart that everything that he was demanded he be truthful.

She stared at him. He was so focused on the boy that he didn't see her, but Allie knew she needed to sit down with him later today and tell him that she believed him. She had no choice. She could see that Clay wouldn't lie. She let the knowledge sink into her heart. That meant robbing the gas station had been all Mark's doing. And Clay had been sent to prison for something he hadn't done.

She heard Hen clear his throat. "I—I'm the one who did this."

Hen held up a knife he had gotten from somewhere. "I'm guilty."

The ranchers stared at the boy, unmoved by his confession.

"But why?" one of them finally asked. "Why would you do this?"

"I—" the boy started and then stopped to look at Clay.

"Go on," Clay encouraged him. "You're not done here yet, so you may as well answer the question."

"Everyone was so perfect inside there," Hen said as he jerked his head in the direction of the church. "There's no one like me there. So I just did it. I'm sorry."

The boy's words had been raw when he spoke them, his voice low and hoarse. Allie thought he might be on the verge of tears.

She wasn't sure how the ranchers managed to communicate, but she saw them shift as one and she knew that a decision had been made.

"I've failed at more things than you can possibly know, boy," one of the ranchers said. "I've been an alcoholic. A liar. I'm not as perfect as you might think."

"I have a terrible temper," another one offered. "Ask anyone. I do battle with myself almost every day."

"I cheated on my wife," another one said. "It was many years ago—before I became a Christian—but I thank God every day that she forgave me. I don't stack up better than any man."

"Elmer and me," one of the last two men said as nodded to the man beside him, "we've been swindled so bad we almost lost everything. One of those pyramid schemes with a buy-in that was supposed to pay off big-time. Greed, you know. That's our downfall."

Elmer nodded. "None of us are perfect in that church. We're all just forgiven. God loves us and He loves you."

Tears were streaming down the boy's face by now. Allie could see he was touched and embarrassed by his emotions.

"I'm sorry for what I did," Hen mumbled.

The ranchers nodded in unison.

"And—" Clay prompted the boy.

"And I plan to do anything I can to make things better," Hen pledged.

Allie had tears in her eyes, too. She wished the community had gathered around Clay all those years ago like they were doing with this boy. "I plan to make things better, too," Allie said as she went over and stood by Clay.

She watched him, standing there looking satisfied that Hen had confessed and been forgiven.

"You're a good man," she said to Clay, soft enough that only he could hear.

He seemed startled at her words, turning to study her.

"Everyone knows that," she added, feeling self-conscious. "Even if they haven't admitted it yet."

A slow grin spread across his face. "I'm just glad that you know it."

Allie smiled back. "Me, too."

She hadn't felt so happy in years. And then she remembered the daffodils. Easter wasn't going to be the same in Dry Creek without the daffodils.

Chapter Sixteen

Clay went out to the barn the next morning. He'd told Hen to meet him there. The day was warmer than the day before. The storm was over. There was no way to physically replace the daffodils that had been destroyed, but Clay knew they could go all out and paint the wagon with pictures of daffodils. Traditionally, the wagon carried a large cross, and Clay figured they could make a plywood backdrop to put behind the cross that would show a field of daffodils.

Clay had brought down the yellow and green paints from the hayloft and had already painted a small section of daffodils. He planned to have Hen paint the yellow and recruit Jeremy to paint the leaves.

Allie came by before Hen arrived.

Clay saw her standing just inside the barn. She'd been quiet, and Clay wanted to take time to enjoy looking at her before she made herself known. The sun shone through the strands of her hair, giving her a coppery look. She looked nervous, but not scared. Clay refused to think of her leaving in a little over a week, but he knew she planned to go back to her job in Jackson Hole.

Clay hoped in a few months he'd be making enough money with his sketches that they could at least make plans for a future where Allie stayed on the ranch she loved. He didn't know how to even talk to her about that, though, so he just watched her from a distance.

She stepped closer and quietly cleared her throat. He looked up.

"I want you to know I believe you about that robbery," she said without any drama. "I'm sorry I held on to my anger. I think that's what stopped me from seeing that you wouldn't lie."

Clay leaned back on his heels. He had squatted down to draw some more daffodils on the front of the wagon. He had hoped for years to someday hear Allie say she believed him, but now that she was saying it, he realized how unfair he'd been.

"I'm sorry I've been pressing you to take my side," he said as he stood up. "I'm willing to compromise. We can just start from now and move forward. You don't have to believe I'm innocent."

He wiped his hands on the cloth he used to clean up any paint splatters.

He appreciated that Allie was willing to say she believed his side of the story. But hearing all of those old ranchers confess their faults to Hen yesterday made Clay wonder if he wasn't too proud of being truthful. Quite often people saw the same situation from different perspectives. He didn't need to always have everyone agree with him.

Allie frowned. "Okay."

Clay saw he'd only confused her. He stepped closer and opened his arms wide. "Come here."

Allie stepped into his arms, and he was centered. "What I'm trying to say is that I don't want anything to come between us again. Not who's guilty or innocent. Right or wrong. Rich or poor."

Allie leaned back and eyed him wryly. "Rich or poor? I'm guessing we don't have to worry about the rich side of that one."

"We'll get by," Clay said confidently. He hadn't told Allie yet that his agent was getting bids already for a series of sketches on the goat and horse. Of course, nothing was certain yet. The bids could evaporate. The truth was, he had nothing to offer Allie yet. He was a broken-down ex-con with a future that could go up in smoke.

"So we're still friends?" Allie asked hopefully.

That stopped Clay. He felt like he was on a precipice with her. But she seemed to be on firm ground. He saw now that she had spoken out to shore up what she thought of as a good friendship. She didn't look like she wanted anything more.

"Yeah, sure," Clay said.

Suddenly, Clay envied Randy his ability to buy all those slices of chiffon pie. He wished there was a similar way for him to show Allie that he wanted more than friendship.

Clay had let the moment pass, and he realized he might as well get back to the wagon. Allie had already started looking around to check on the animals.

"Wondering where the goat is?" he asked as he picked up the marker he was using to outline the floral motif on the wagon.

Allie nodded. "Remember that man Stan said we shouldn't turn our backs on him?"

"The goat only gets mad if we're working with the horses," Clay replied. "Besides, I put him in the stall over there by the pig."

Allie stayed to work with the Appaloosas. Clay knew she had a good eye for telling which two horses would work best together when harnessed to the wagon.

When Hen showed up, he went right to work. Clay was a little surprised the teenager took to the task with reasonable enthusiasm.

"Sheriff Wall talk to you?" he asked the boy after a while.

Hen nodded.

"I remember a couple of problems I had with him when I was here before," Clay remarked. "He can be a powerful motivator."

"You ain't kidding," Hen said and looked over his shoulder toward the barn door as though he was making sure the sheriff wasn't there. "He said he was going to keep an eye on me, and I'm thinking maybe he's with the Mafia or something."

"I don't think they have the Mafia around here," Clay said, trying to control his laugh.

"Well, he sure sounds like he could do something if he doesn't like what he sees," Hen said.

Clay let his laugh roll out.

"He'll get the church talking to you is what he'll do," Clay said.

Hen grinned wryly at that. "Those old men are pretty tough customers."

Clay nodded. He figured Hen had gotten the lay of

the land. He would do fine as long as he was in Dry Creek. That fact gave Clay a good feeling. Maybe if things had been different when he'd been here, he would have done well, too. He had realized by now that if he and Mark had taken the church's challenge more seriously back then and had read the Gospel of Luke, they might have stayed in the bunkhouse that night talking theology instead of driving all over the country looking for more beer.

He couldn't wait to see Mark and find out what he thought about that Gospel. It sure was a fascinating account, Clay told himself. He'd read it several times by now. He didn't see how it related to him, but Mark might know.

Clay's alarm clock woke him at four o'clock on Easter morning. The night was dark. Everything was planned down to the minute, though, and he needed to get up. Allie was waking about now, too. She was going to drive to the nursing home and bring Mark back to Dry Creek. Randy and Clay were going to get the wagon and horses to the church. Mr. Nelson and Jeremy would drive in later in the old red pickup. That would be where Mark would wait until everything was set to go.

Clay was drinking a second cup of coffee when Allie knocked on the bunkhouse door. He opened it, and she presented him with a bag from the hardware store.

"For Hen," she said as he looked inside the bag and saw the white Stetson sitting there.

"He's worked hard lately, and I thought he might like to share in the Nelson family Easter hat tradition," Allie said.

"He'll like it very much," Clay said. He should have thought of doing this himself.

"I need to be going to get Mark," Allie said. "I'll meet you at the church around six thirty."

Clay nodded and she was gone.

The barn was cold and the metal snaps on the harness colder still. Clay wrapped the leather inside his coat a bit before he put it on the two horses. Allie had chosen the stallion and the tallest of the mares to pull the wagon. Randy helped get the horses in position, and Clay draped the harnesses around them. The goat nearly started attacking until Randy showed the animal where to stand beside the stallion.

The rooster started crowing about the time Hen showed up. The teenager's hair was tousled and his eyes sleepy. He had his faded black jeans and the black parka on. But someone had found him a white cotton shirt, and the collar was crisp. For the boy, this was as dressed up as he was likely to get.

"Happy Easter morning," Clay said as he held the bag out to Hen.

"For me?" the teenager asked in disbelief.

Clay nodded and Hen opened the bag.

"Ah!" the teenager said with a triumphant shout. He took the white Stetson out of the bag and put it on his head. "I'm a regular Dry Creeker now."

Clay and Randy were both grinning, too.

"You sure are," Clay said as he stepped up to the seat on the wagon. Randy told Hen he could ride in the pickup with him. It was too dark outside still for the team to make their way down the roads, so Randy was going to drive his pickup in front of them and light the way.

Clay had stacked as many wool blankets as he could in the back of the wagon. He'd need them to keep Mark warm. The tall wooden cross that they would eventually set up in the back was waiting at the church. They would add that to the wagon later, just before they did their procession through town.

The road was bumpier behind a horse team than in a pickup. Clay discovered that as he made slow progress toward Dry Creek. Mr. Nelson had told him it would take some time, and the older man was right.

Clay rather appreciated the quiet of the drive, though. He'd read the crucifixion account in the Gospel of Luke again last night. He could picture it better driving through the cold damp morning than lying in bed at night. He still didn't find a way to connect to the story, though. Everything seemed to have happened so long ago to people so very different from him.

They arrived at the church before the sun started to rise. That had been Clay's plan. He wanted the wagon to be a surprise to the people of Dry Creek. Hen had worked hard on painting the flowers.

Clay looked at where all of the daffodils had been planted. The plastic was cleared and the dead stalks raked up. Randy showed Clay where the cross was kept, and they both tied it into place on the back of the wagon.

They were finished with everything when Mr. Nelson drove up in the old red pickup.

"Where's Jeremy?" Clay asked as the rancher stepped out of the vehicle.

"Mrs. Hargrove offered to feed him breakfast," the

older man said. "I decided there was no reason for him to sit out here in the cold when he could be eating her cinnamon rolls. Besides…" The man's voice trailed off.

Clay understood. Mark would wonder at a small boy being tended by his father. Clay didn't have much time to consider things, though, because Allie drove up in her father's SUV. Mark had his face almost pressed to the window, he looked so eager.

There was room for only one vehicle behind the church, so Mr. Nelson went to greet his son and help him move to the red pickup. Clay climbed in behind the wheel after Mark was settled in the passenger seat.

"Warm enough?" Clay asked as he adjusted the knob to the heater.

Mark nodded as he looked around the vehicle. "I just can't believe I'm here in this old pickup with you. We had some great times, didn't we?"

Mark didn't seem to need an answer to his question. He ran his hands over the dashboard and fiddled with the radio. A scratchy sound came on.

"Someone fixed the radio?" Mark asked in surprise. "I was intending to do that."

"Must have been your dad," Clay answered.

Mark frowned then. "That crack wasn't there before." He pointed to the left side of the windshield.

Clay was becoming uncomfortable. He hadn't expected Mark to be so aware of things. How were they ever going to keep it a secret from him that he'd lost four years of his life?

Then Clay saw that Mark was looking behind him.

"What happened to my rifle?" Mark asked, frowning. "I always keep it in the rack behind us."

Clay guessed the rifle was buried in the sheriff's department somewhere as evidence of the armed robbery. Or did the authorities return those items to Mr. Nelson? Clay had no clue. He could not even think of a plausible thing to say to Mark that was the truth.

"We're going to need to get out there on the wagon," Clay said instead as his hand reached for the door handle.

Allie walked with them over to the wagon. She hadn't intended to go, but Clay realized he might need help. He hoped Mark would forget about his missing rifle, but he had a feeling his friend was thinking about something.

"Come with us," he mouthed to Allie.

Clay and Allie set Mark between them on the wagon seat. He was wrapped in a half-dozen blankets, and his face was glowing with excitement. Hen stepped into the back of the wagon, behind the painted plywood. He was to keep that and the cross steady.

"We're doing it," Mark leaned over and said to Clay.

Clay nodded.

"I've been praying for this day ever since I started reading the Gospel of Luke again," Mark said. "I believe it all."

Clay was silent. Finally, he said, "It's a compelling story. But it happened so long ago."

Mark snorted. "It could have happened yesterday. Jesus comes down to earth. Everything goes crazy. Then a bunch of people get together and convict an innocent man—"

The words hit Clay like a bullet. All of the pieces fell into place. He'd never considered it that way. If anyone understood what had happened to him, it was Jesus. He might have lived thousands of years ago, but he knew what it was like to be innocent and have everyone look at him like he was guilty.

"We need to pull out," Mr. Nelson called, and Clay picked up the reins.

The sun was starting to rise by the time Clay got the wagon to the start mark outside the small town. Almost a hundred people were huddled together at the stop sign that marked the beginning of the procession.

Clay heard a collective gasp of delight when he pulled the wagon close enough for people to see all the flowers painted on the sides.

"Hallelujah!" someone shouted. "We have our daffodils."

"Praise God," another said.

Clay figured it was a happy group that fell into step behind the wagon. He drove slowly. The goat did his job, guiding the stallion as they moved forward.

Prayer started to bubble up inside Clay as he drove.

"I think Jesus knows me," he whispered to Mark as they rolled along.

Mark squeezed his hand. "He does."

"I heard that," Allie chimed in quietly from where she sat. "I'm so glad you realize that."

"Sometimes it takes me a while," Clay said as he glanced back at the tall cross standing there. He knew without thinking about it that he was never going to be the same.

"Some things take me some time, too," Mark said quietly.

Clay didn't say anything.

"That rifle—" Mark started and looked over at Clay. "Did that night happen? Did I leave you pumping gas and take that rifle into that gas station?"

The people walking behind them had started to sing a hymn, and the words wrapped around Clay with comfort.

"We can talk about it later," Clay said. "Don't strain to remember."

He didn't know how Mark would feel when he realized the enormity of what they had done.

Clay pulled the wagon into place behind the church, and everyone sitting there climbed down. Allie helped Mark into the shelter of the red pickup. By now, the sun had turned golden as it rose in the east. The stones in the cemetery were bathed in light, and Clay saw others looking to the graveyard, as well.

Allie walked over and stood beside him as he eyed the small crosses on the burial ground. The hymnal being sung changed, and Clay heard words about Jesus conquering death. He understood now why the people of Dry Creek celebrated Easter morning with as much joy as they could muster and why they did so in the presence of their departed loved ones.

Clay listened to the pastor's Easter sermon, the peace inside him growing.

When the service was over and everyone else had gone inside to have coffee, Clay stood with Allie back by the wagon. He could see in her eyes that she had questions for him.

"I need some time," he told her. "I'm not the man today that I will be in a few weeks. I plan to talk with the pastor and get my life on track with God. I'm not going to ask you to wait for me, but when you come back next time from Jackson Hole, I want to talk to you about the future."

Allie looked at him soberly. "The future or our future?"

"Ours," he said. "I hope."

"I don't need to wait," she said softly.

"Oh." That didn't sound promising to Clay. "I wanted to have a chance to show you I can be better. You deserve a good husband and…"

He didn't know what else to say. Life didn't always give second chances. He looked down at Allie and stood silent. He'd endured loneliness for most of his life. He could handle it again.

Allie looked up at him. She'd dreamed about Clay for over four years. When she'd known him earlier her feelings had been more a teenage crush than anything. Getting to know him now, though, she could see the solid foundation of his character. He was a good man. He was her man.

"The answer is already yes," Allie whispered. "If you need time to think about it, that's fine, but don't expect me to change my mind."

Allie watched the sun rise again in Clay's eyes. He reached up and traced her cheek with an expression of wonder on his face.

"I never thought," he murmured.

She reached her own hand up to touch his cheek.

"I love you," he said simply.

Allie knew he did. Clay never lied.

"You're going to make me cry," she said.

"That won't do," Clay said with a smile as he dipped his head toward her.

The kiss was her undoing. A flash of sweet promise sizzled through her as his lips explored her.

"I love you, too," she said.

It wasn't until they parted that they noticed half the people in the church were watching them from the building's back window.

"Oh, oh," she said.

Clay gripped her shoulder in support.

Then she saw the people act in unison, all giving her an exuberant thumbs-up signal.

"I think that's your welcome home." She smiled as she turned to Clay.

She knew then that, as long as she lived, she would never forget the look of wonder on Clay's face.

Epilogue

In June of that same year

Sunshine streamed in through the side windows, but Allie stood in the shadows at the back of the Dry Creek church. She clutched a bouquet of pink roses in one hand and held her father's arm with the other. She hoped no one could see how nervous she was. All she could do was stare ahead at Clay as he stood in the charcoal-gray suit he'd bought especially for today. He was hundreds of feet away, but she could feel his gaze warming her. Suddenly, she was calm.

She and Clay had wanted a simple wedding, but the women of the church asked to be part of the celebration, and now everything shone. Rose bouquets lined the aisle and gave a sweet scent to the air. Two of the town's best seamstresses had made Allie's white silk dress. Another had made a short veil for her head. Every pew was filled with neighbors and friends, all of them attired in their Sunday-best clothes.

Allie and Clay had finished their marriage counseling with the pastor weeks ago, and he had pronounced them a good match. Now he looked over at Clay with approval and nodded.

That was the signal for Doris June Hargrove to stand and walk up to the piano.

Allie took a deep breath and turned.

"It's almost time," she whispered to her father.

He nodded before glancing back at the church door furtively.

"They're not coming," Allie said.

Everyone had thought her brother's old girlfriend, Hannah, would relent and allow Allie's nephew to attend the wedding.

"She's got to talk to Mark eventually," her father muttered.

"Hannah says not," Allie countered. A curt note had come from a lawyer last week; Hannah had been informed of the change in Mark's condition and he had tried to contact her, asking to meet his son, but she never answered any of Mark's messages.

Allie didn't know what to do. Mark had regained his memory and told all of the people in Dry Creek what had really happened the night of the robbery. He knew Jeremy was his son. But Hannah kept refusing to see him or to let him see Jeremy.

Allie told herself there was nothing she could do about it today.

The music to the wedding march started. Allie and her father began to walk forward.

From then on, Allie couldn't think of anyone but Clay. His voice when he spoke his vows made her shiver. She couldn't believe she had wanted to send this man away when he appeared back at the ranch in March.

When Clay finished his vows, he added something they hadn't rehearsed.

"Allie Nelson, I will love you until the day I die," he said with such sincerity that Allie heard a flutter of sighs in the pews behind her.

"And I will love you," Allie said, blinking back tears.

Clay kissed her then, fierce and hard like he was sealing a bargain.

The pastor cleared his throat indulgently. "We're not quite to that part of the ceremony yet."

A ripple of soft chuckles came from the pews.

"We don't mind doing it twice," Clay said with a grin.

Allie said her vows, her voice not wavering once.

"And now," the pastor said, "I pronounce you man and wife." He turned to Clay. "You can now officially kiss your bride."

Allie felt the warmth of that kiss right down to her toes. She was happy and knew Clay was, too.

* * * * *

Lois Richer loves traveling, swimming and quilting, but mostly she loves writing stories that show God's boundless love for His precious children. As she says, "His love never changes or gives up. It's always waiting for me. My stories feature imperfect characters learning that love doesn't mean attaining perfection. Love is about keeping on keeping on." You can contact Lois via email, loisricher@gmail.com, or on Facebook (loisricherauthor).

Books by Lois Richer

Love Inspired

The Calhoun Cowboys

Hoping for a Father
Home to Heal
Christmas in a Snowstorm
A Plan for Her Future

Rocky Mountain Haven

Meant-to-Be Baby
Mistletoe Twins
Rocky Mountain Daddy
Rocky Mountain Memories

Visit the Author Profile page at LoveInspired.com for more titles.

THE COWBOY'S
EASTER FAMILY WISH

Lois Richer

Whatever your hands find to do,
do it with all your might.
—*Ecclesiastes* 9:10

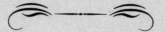

Chapter One

"That's not Dad's peanut butter." Eight-year-old Noah looked shocked by his own blurted words. He quickly ducked his chin into his chest.

"We could try it." Fully aware of how much the busy Tucson grocery store aggravated her son's autism, Maddie McGregor hesitantly suggested, "You might like this kind."

"I like Dad's kind. So do twenty million other people according to ads." Noah always recited facts he'd memorized. "Dad's rule was, buy the bestseller." And he always quoted his father's rules.

Noah's hands were fluttering, a sign of his mounting agitation. Changing peanut butter brands right now wasn't worth it. Maddie set the jar back on the shelf reluctantly. She was giving in to Noah's rules. She'd vowed to stop doing that. But it had been a long day and giving in was easier than dealing with his upset behavior for the rest of the evening.

"Twenty million people could be wrong." His expression said arguing was futile. "Okay, you choose."

She almost groaned when Noah selected the same oily brand his father had preferred. So much for her goal to break free of the past.

"You should give the other kind a try," a male voice suggested. "It's the one with the nut on top and if you're going to eat nut butter, you need many nuts."

"Many nuts eating nuts. Ha!" Noah's burble of laughter erupted, then died away.

Maddie turned to find a pair of twinkling blue eyes studying her from an angular sun-tanned face atop a lean, lanky cowboy. Her first thought was how carefree he looked. Her second turned to envy of his confident, relaxed stance. He looked so comfortable in his world.

When she noted a fan of tiny creases beside his eyes her envy died. He, like everyone else, no doubt had some story of past pain. She wondered half-absently what that story was before noticing the man's short cropped hair was the same shade of gold as a tropical sandy beach she'd once dreamed of visiting. And his shoulders—well, that broad width was the perfect place for a girl to rest her head.

Not *this* girl, of course, but—Maddie's cheeks burned as she visualized her late husband Liam's berating if he knew her shameful thoughts.

Forget him. You're breaking free of the past, remember?

But how to do that when her self-confidence was nil?

"I'm a peanut butter expert, ma'am." The stranger's smile coaxed her to respond to his joke. "Trust me, that brand tastes way better than the one the boy and twenty million others mistakenly prefer."

"Noah." Maddie's heart winced when her son's

brown eyes flickered to the man, then skittered away, his face closing into its usual disinterested mask.

"Sorry?" The peanut butter expert arched an eyebrow.

"His name is Noah." Maddie hoped the stranger wouldn't comment on her son's now swaying body.

"Noah—like the guy with the ark," the man remarked. Something in his teasing tone caught Noah's attention, Maddie noticed. "You have lots of animals?" he continued.

"A dog. Her name is Cocoa." The swift response surprised Maddie.

"Why Cocoa?" The man looked interested, not merely polite.

"'Cause she's a chocolate lab," Noah clarified. "Dogs should be named by their features. It's not a rule but—"

"It's a good idea," the stranger finished with a nod.

"Yeah." Noah's eyes widened with surprise at his agreement.

Maddie stared at her child. Noah didn't talk or interact with strangers. Not ever.

"Chocolate labs are the best." The man thrust out his hand. "I'm Jesse Parker."

Though Noah hesitated, he couldn't ignore the gesture. His father had drummed politeness into him, one of his many unbreakable rules. Sure enough, Noah finally thrust out his small hand.

"Glad to meet, you, Noah, owner of Cocoa." Jesse's blue gaze slid to her. "And your lovely mother is?"

"Maddie McGregor." She liked the way Jesse included her.

"Maddie McGregor." He said it slowly, his forehead

furrowed as if he was reaching for a stray thought. Then those blue eyes widened. "Not the amazingly talented quilter named Maddie McGregor who works for my grandmother at Quilt Essentials?"

Amazing? Talented? No one had ever called her that before.

"Grandmother—?" Maddie tried to put it together while distracted by his good looks. "Oh." Suddenly it made sense. "You're Emma's grandson."

"The best one of the bunch." He preened, then laughed. "You look shocked."

"No, I—that is, I wasn't expecting…" Thrown by his mischievous wink, Maddie gulped.

"Ninety-five percent of all children think their grandparents love them the best," said Noah, who didn't have any grandparents.

"In my case it's true." Jesse grinned.

"Emma always speaks of you as if you're four," Maddie blurted. Her cheeks burned when Jesse's hoot of amusement rippled to the ceiling. She almost checked over one shoulder before correcting the impulse.

It's been more than a year since Liam's death. He's gone. You're free now. Free.

"I guess I act that age sometimes," Jesse joked, and laughed again.

All down the grocery store aisle, heads turned to study him, and Maddie knew why. His laugh revealed the same zest for life that his grandmother possessed, the kind that beckoned you to join in. Maddie was pretty sure Jesse would be fun to be around.

Not that she was looking for fun. She was too old,

too world-weary, too responsible for that kind of girlish silliness. Still, Jesse intrigued her.

"We have to go." Noah frowned at her.

Maddie studied him in confusion. Noah never volunteered conversation when strangers were present. Even more unusual, his agitated arm movements had ceased.

"What's the rush?" Jesse asked.

"Ice cream." While Noah pointed into the cart, Maddie wondered why her son was apparently unruffled when speaking to this stranger. But it didn't matter. Better to leave now, before something else upset Noah. Because something always did.

"Nice to meet you, Jesse. Thanks for the advice." In an act of defiance, she grabbed the jar of peanut butter Jesse had recommended and put it in her cart. *Baby steps to independence*, she thought defiantly.

"Uh, Maddie?" Jesse's amused voice stopped her in her tracks. She couldn't help contrasting his tone with a memory of Liam's beguiling-when-it-wanted-to-be voice that could also cut like a sword.

Immediately, her tension returned. Schooling her face into impassivity, she glanced at Jesse. "Yes?"

"I've been trying to reach my grandmother by phone with no success." His sincere friendliness chased away her tension. "I've stopped by her house a couple of times, but she doesn't answer."

"No, she wouldn't." Maddie almost groaned as Noah mumbled statistics about meeting strangers. Hopefully, Jesse hadn't noticed her discomfiture.

"Why wouldn't Gran answer?" Even Jesse's frown didn't spoil his good looks.

"She's not home." Noah's quick response surprised Maddie.

"Where is she?" Jesse glanced from him to her.

"Away." Noah's vacant stare returned, but his hands stayed by his sides, calm for now.

"Emma's at a women's retreat in the mountains of New Mexico." Maddie was puzzled by Noah's seeming tranquility. Prolonged grocery store visits usually upset him.

"She likes it there." Though Noah appeared inattentive, he was obviously keeping track of the conversation.

"Emma goes every January," Maddie clarified. "She's due back tomorrow, but you can't reach her cell because she always shuts it off for the retreat."

"I forgot about her yearly retreat." Jesse looked so disappointed Maddie felt a twinge of pity when he added, "I wanted to surprise her, but I guess the surprise is on me."

"She's supposed to call me at work tomorrow morning." Maddie couldn't stop herself from offering to help. "Do you have a number I could give her to reach you?"

"No. I don't have a cell phone."

Maddie blinked. She'd thought Liam's refusal to own a smartphone made them virtually the only ones left behind in this age of technology. Of course, now that she was a widow she could have bought her own, but hadn't yet because of inner doubts about mastering it. Battling doubts had become an ongoing war for her mind.

"The FCC says to keep cell phones one inch from the body." Noah's speech ended as abruptly as it had begun.

"Oka-a-ay." Jesse, eyes wide, dragged out the word, then glanced at Maddie. "I let my contract expire when I left Colorado. I've been on the move for several months, so I haven't really needed a cell phone."

The way his voice tightened when he said that made her wonder if he'd left Colorado under unhappy circumstances. Funny, Emma hadn't mentioned anything.

"Well, when I see your grandmother I won't tell her you're in town, so you can still surprise her," Maddie promised.

"Scientific studies say unexpected pleasure is more rewarding. Emma will probably like your surprise." Noah frowned at Maddie. "Ice cream?"

"Yes, we're leaving." She laid her arm protectively across his shoulders, expecting him to jerk away, and not caring. Her action was meant as a motherly defence against Jesse's searching scrutiny of her child. She hated when people gawked at Noah, then labeled him weird.

"Nice to meet you, Noah and Maddie," Jesse said.

Nice? Maddie almost laughed at the pale, insipid little word that didn't describe this encounter at all.

"Bye, Jesse." Maddie walked with Noah toward the cashier while sorting through what she'd learned about him during her three-year tenure at Quilt Essentials.

Details were scant. Though Emma constantly raved about Jesse; how loving and generous he was, how good-natured his big heart, how his love for God embraced everyone he met, the one thing she hadn't mentioned was Jesse's good looks. But then Emma was all about a person's heart, not their looks. Perhaps that's why Emma had never asked Maddie about the puckered red scar that ran from her left earlobe down her neck, the scar that made her so self-conscious.

Emma's friendship had been the lifeline Maddie had

clung to—that and her own prayers that God would help her survive her marriage. Emma's quilt shop was a refuge where Maddie could bury her unhappiness in the comforting textures and glorious colors of fabrics, and let her inner soul come alive in a quilt. That very first day, Quilt Essentials had become Maddie's sanctuary and Emma the best friend she'd ever had.

Now Maddie pulled out her credit card to pay for her purchases, savoring thoughts of a relaxing evening ahead. Her hobby ranch on the outskirts of Tucson was mostly cactus and desert, but the charming, newly renovated house was all hers, the place where she could be and do what she wanted. And what Maddie wanted was to make Broken Arrow Ranch into the kind of home where Noah could enjoy a happy, carefree childhood while she taught herself to be strong and confident.

So far Maddie wasn't succeeding at either. No matter how she prayed, she couldn't shed the memory of Liam's voice constantly berating her. As for independence—well, learning to stand on your own two feet after a lifetime of having someone tell you what to do was a lot harder than she'd imagined. But she couldn't, wouldn't give up, though Noah resisted every change she tried to make.

Some days Maddie almost lost hope that she would ever feel worthy of God's love, that Noah would make friends, relax and have fun like an ordinary kid. But she didn't often pray about it anymore, because she figured Liam was right; God probably wouldn't answer the prayers of someone as unimportant as Maddie McGregor.

They were storing their groceries in the trunk of

Maddie's red SUV when Noah said, "Tomorrow's Martin Luther King Day lunch. I hafta bring food to school."

"Why didn't you tell me while we were in the store?" Maddie masked her exasperation.

"Forgot." Noah shrugged. "Doesn't matter. Ninety-nine percent of the other kids will bring stuff."

"I'm sure your teacher expects one hundred percent participation." She closed the trunk with a sigh. "Come on. Let's go find something."

"You want to talk to that guy again." Noah's lecture tone reminded her of Liam. "Sometimes strangers form lasting relationships after their first meeting."

"Lasting relation—what?" Maddie gaped at him.

"Dad would be mad that you like Jesse." Noah's dark-eyed gaze met and held hers.

"Honey, your father is gone." *Where did he get these statistics?*

"He'd hate Jesse." Noah kicked a pebble on the pavement. "Dad never liked his kind."

"What kind?" Maddie asked. *The happy kind? The kind of person who doesn't automatically find fault?* "Jesse seems nice. And he's Emma's grandson," she reminded Noah.

"Emma's nice. But Dad wouldn't like Jesse."

"Maybe, maybe not. But that's no reason for *you* to dislike him." Maddie refused to pursue this. They both needed a break from the past. "Let's quickly get whatever you need so we can get home before the frozen stuff melts." As they walked across the lot and in through the automatic doors, she asked, "You didn't get a note from your teacher?"

"Lost it." He wouldn't look at her.

"Noah," Maddie chided, then let it go. He was always ultra responsible. Maybe losing the note was his way of avoiding the interaction of lunch. He wasn't exactly the social type. "What exactly did your teacher say?"

"Memorize six lines of Mr. King's speech and bring a food treat that will remind others of it," Noah recited in a high-pitched, singsong tone.

Maddie hid her smile. His imitation of his teacher, Mrs. Perkins, was uncanny. "Have you memorized a portion of the speech?"

"The 'I have a dream' part." Noah's chest swelled as he precisely delivered the beginning lines of the famous speech. Then his pride visibly deflated. "I don't know any food to go with that."

"I do." Jesse stood nearby, his wonderful smile flashing. "Sorry, didn't mean to eavesdrop, but those lines always remind me of Gran's I Have a Dream snack."

"What's an I Have a Dream snack?" Noah asked, seemingly interested.

"It's pretty easy, Ark Man." Jesse grinned, and to Maddie's surprise, Noah didn't decry the nickname.

"Ark Man?" She wrinkled her nose.

"Like Noah in the Bible, Mom. 'Cause I have Cocoa. An' there's a roadrunner that goes past our place, too," he told Jesse with an eagerness she hadn't seen—maybe ever? "An' sometimes coyotes howl. An' Mom feeds hummingbirds."

"Wow." Jesse looked impressed.

"So I guess I kind of am Ark Man?" he said, obviously seeking confirmation.

"Absolutely." Jesse held up his hand to high-five, and Noah matched it. Both of them wore goofy grins.

Maddie stared at her introverted kid. This change—because of Jesse?

"So, to make these treats you need big marshmallows and some caramels," Jesse continued.

"I'll find some." Noah raced away before Maddie could stop him.

"I'm sorry. I'm interfering without even asking you," Jesse said after a quick glance at her. "I'll go get him."

"Please don't. It's the first time Noah's been that excited about anything since…ever." Without thinking, Maddie put her hand on Jesse's arm to stop him, then jerked it away when her brain repeated Noah's strangers-forming-a-relationship fact.

No relationship for her. Never going to get hurt again.

"I warn you. If this recipe of Emma's involves baking, it will be a failure."

"It will?" A puzzled look darkened his blue-eyed gaze. "But it's simple."

"Maybe, but I can't do simple baking," Maddie admitted. "Actually, I can't do complicated either," she added, eyes downcast in a rush of shame. "I'm not a good cook."

"She's not," Noah agreed solemnly, having returned with a huge bag of marshmallows. "Ninety-nine point nine percent of her cooking burns."

"Noah!" Maddie exclaimed in embarrassment.

"Fortunately, this recipe requires no cooking. Just melting." Jesse glanced at the marshmallows, then raised an eyebrow at Noah. "Caramels?"

"Couldn't find any." Noah looked dejected. "I guess we can't make the snacks."

"You can always make I Have a Dream snacks, Ark

Man. One hundred percent of the time." Jesse's firm tone had the strangest effect on Noah.

"Okay." His boyish shoulders went back and his face got a determined look that Maddie had not seen before. "How?"

"We find caramels because they're the best part. And we need cream." Jesse beckoned. "Come on, you and I will check it out. They have to have them somewhere. Every self-respecting grocery store carries caramels."

"I didn't know that." Noah tucked the information away.

A bemused Maddie trailed behind the pair, accepting the pint of cream Jesse handed her as she worried about where this was going to lead. To disaster probably, and not only for Noah. Melting meant heat, which meant burning, which meant...

"Here we go. Crazy section to stock caramels in." Jesse plopped two packages into Noah's arms. "Let's make sure we've got enough for seconds."

"I'm not allowed seconds of sweets. It's a rule." The non-challenging way Noah said that made Maddie wince. What normal eight-year-old didn't automatically reach for seconds when candy was involved?

Just another thing she planned to change. Help Noah shed his stringent list of rules and become a regular kid. *Check.*

"Let's take three." She snatched another bag of caramels from the shelf. "Just in case they turn out okay."

Which they won't. She repressed the memory of that scoffing voice.

"I like your spunk, mother of Ark Man." Jesse grinned at her. "We need dry chow mein noodles, too."

He laughed at their surprised expressions. "You'll see. It's delicious."

With noodles in hand, Maddie paid for their loot then led the way out of the store, wondering if sharing a sweet snack with his classmates would finally gain Noah acceptance from the other kids. He'd been an outcast for so long, mostly because of Liam's rules.

After her husband's death Maddie had blown a good part of her budget to change Noah's world. She'd located a private school that specialized in his issues and whose uniforms didn't make him look weird. She had his home haircut professionally restyled and enrolled him in a swimming class because he seemed to excel at that one sport. Yet despite all that, Noah still clung to his father's rules, which frustrated Maddie no end.

"Now you have everything you need, Ark Man. You and your mom can melt the caramels with a little cream, dip in the marshmallows, then roll them in the noodles. My job is done, so I'll be on my way. See you." Jesse waved and turned away.

He thought she could do this on her own?

"Wait," Maddie called out in panic. "Could you—uh, come to the house and show us exactly how to make them? Please? I'd ask Emma, but she's away."

She sounded desperate. Well, she was!

But she was asking for Noah's sake, because she wanted him to know what it was like to be the one to bring a special treat, to be in the limelight in a good way. Just once she wanted Noah to be envied by other kids instead of being mocked.

And maybe you're asking because you like the way Jesse didn't make fun of you for not being able to cook.

Her son frowned in confusion. "Mom?" he whispered. "Stranger rule?"

Liam's rules had taught Noah fear, and Maddie saw it now in his brown eyes. She was usually wary of strangers, too. But funnily enough, not with Jesse.

Why was that?

"Um, maybe I shouldn't go to your place," Jesse said, his gaze on Noah. "I could just—"

"Please come," she invited, discounting her inhibitions. "I'd really like to make this treat."

"I guess, if you're sure?" After a moment's pause Jesse added, "Since Gran's away I haven't got anything special on tonight. Maybe after we're finished I could use your phone to call Wranglers Ranch about a job?"

"Sure. Tanner Johns owns Wranglers. His wife, Sophie, is a friend of mine. Actually, we're neighbors." Maddie stashed the second set of groceries in her vehicle. "If you help us, I'll put in a good word for you in exchange."

Maybe she wasn't being totally straightforward by not telling Jesse that his grandmother was an ardent supporter of Wranglers Ranch and its outreach mission for troubled kids, or that Emma's referral would probably be far more valuable than hers. But Maddie needed Jesse's help. For Noah. So she waited on pins and needles.

"Okay, it's a deal." Jesse motioned to a battered brown half-ton truck that sat at the far end of the parking lot. "That's mine. How far is your place?"

"About ten minutes outside the city. We live on Broken Arrow Ranch. You can follow us there." Maddie waited with bated breath until he nodded. As he walked away she was surprised to see him clap a black Stetson on his head. Where had that come from?

You were too busy gawking at his hunky face to notice his hat.

"I guess Jesse's nice. But Dad's rule…" Noah's confused voice died away.

"Jesse is Emma's grandson. He's like a friend." She was doing this for Noah. She'd do anything to help him.

You're making another mistake, Madelyn.

That voice killed the confidence she'd had in her hasty invitation, until she remembered her last talk with her boss.

Maddie, you went from being a child to being a wife and then a mom. Now you need to take the time to figure out who Maddie is. Not Maddie, Liam's wife, or Maddie, Noah's Mom, but Maddie, the beloved child of God. The first step is to learn to trust your Heavenly Father.

Okay then. She'd take this step, and maybe if she trusted God enough, He'd show her the next one, the step that would help Noah heal.

"Jesse calls me Ark Man," Noah mused aloud.

"Is that okay?" she asked.

"I guess." A tiny smile curved his lips. "I never had a nickname before."

Because Liam hadn't allowed them.

"It makes you feel kind of special," Noah said thoughtfully.

Maddie pulled into her yard with a sense of wonder. Because of Jesse, her son the rule-keeper was changing. Was this the beginning of the breakthrough she'd been praying for?

What else could happen?

* * *

Jesse was simply going to show Maddie and her kid how to make the treats his gran had taught him to make when he was Noah's age.

He was *not* going to get involved. So what could happen?

As he climbed out of his truck his stomach issued a loud and angry protest at its empty state. He stomped his boots free of the dust to cover the rumblings. He'd been counting on one of Gran's delicious meals to satiate his hunger. Clearly, that wasn't going to happen, but maybe Maddie wouldn't mind if he gobbled up a few of her treats.

Jesse could tell by the look on the kid's face when Maddie invited him inside that Noah minded him being there. Obviously, he'd heard many warnings to be careful of strangers. Not a bad thing, Jesse decided.

"This is a beautiful spread." He glanced around appreciatively. "The untouched desert is fascinating."

"I think so, too." Maddie looked surprised by his comment. "I often sit on the porch with my coffee in the morning and just enjoy it. I love the peace."

Meaning she hadn't had a lot of peace in her life? Curiosity about this woman mushroomed as Jesse took the grocery bags from her.

"The mountains make a great backdrop," Maddie said, as she unlocked the door and pushed it open. "Although coming from Colorado, you probably think ours are puny."

"No such—oof." Jesse struggled to keep his balance as a chocolate lab jumped up at him. "Pleased to meet you, Cocoa." He chuckled as the dog licked his hands.

"Oh, I'm so sorry. Down, Cocoa." Maddie tugged at the animal's collar, dragging the dog away from Jesse. "Take her outside, Noah."

Jesse noted the boy's frown as his glance moved from her face to his, his eyes dark and stormy.

"Now, please, son," Maddie said.

After a moment Noah nodded and clipped the lead on the dog's collar.

"Hang on tight, Ark Man," Jesse advised, as he plopped the grocery bags on the counter. "That's a strong animal you're taking out of the ark."

Noah almost cracked a smile as he half walked, half dragged Cocoa outside.

"She's a bit of a handful for him, but I'm hoping they'll soon get used to each other." Maddie smiled at Jesse's questioning look. "Cocoa was my Christmas gift to Noah."

"Nice gift." *Her* Christmas gift, not *our* gift, he noted. So where was the kid's father?

"If you want to wash before we make the treats, the bathroom's just down the hall," Maddie offered.

"Thanks." Jesse walked past her, noticing that aside from the caramels and marshmallows, there were no frivolous purchases. Fruit, vegetables, bread, frozen dinners, peanut butter and milk. The basics. No cookies, no chips, no junk food at all, except for the caramels and marshmallows. Poor Noah.

She pressed the answering machine and listened to Noah's teacher while she unpacked and stored her groceries.

Jesse took his time scrubbing up. When he returned to the kitchen, Maddie was telling Noah to leave the dog outdoors. On the deck outside, Cocoa was busy chowing down. Every so often she gave a guttural woof, glanced around, then returned to eating.

"Cocoa likes it better out there than inside the ark."

Jesse did a double take. Noah's face looked blank, but a tiny smile twitched at the corner of his lips. He chuckled. The stiff-necked kid had actually made a joke.

"So how do we make these treats?" With an apron wrapped around her narrow waist, Maddie stood primly poised behind the breakfast bar, hands folded, waiting for directions.

Jesse got trapped admiring the way her chin-length black hair glistened like an ebony frame around her oval face with its huge green eyes. Her lashes, long and lush, helped accentuate the smooth angles and curves of her sculpted cheeks, complimented by a pert nose and full lips. Maddie wasn't tall, yet when Noah was near she somehow seemed stronger, invincible.

Jesse also glimpsed in Noah's mother an innocence, a delicate fragility. For as long as he could remember he'd had this weird ability to see beneath the mask others presented. That proficiency now told him that Maddie had suffered, but somehow Jesse knew that though bent like a reed in the wind, she had not been broken by her suffering. Instead, the tentative way she smiled at him added to his hunch that hardship had left Maddie McGregor stronger, still genuine and sincere, uncorrupted.

Exactly the opposite of his own world-weariness.

"Is something wrong, Jesse?" Her considerate tone pulled him back from the cliff of his sad memories.

Who *was* Maddie McGregor?

"I shouldn't have pushed you to do this tonight.

You've been traveling." She offered him a sympathetic smile. "I'm sure you're tired. Maybe it would be better—"

"I'm fine." He noticed Noah sitting on the other side of the breakfast bar, watching them with those dark see-all eyes. "Gonna help, Ark Man? It's for your class, isn't it?"

Silent, Noah slid off his stool and joined his mother.

"First we need a heavy saucepan half full of water," Jesse explained. "Once the water's hot we can set another smaller pan inside it to melt the caramels."

Without a word, Maddie produced a pair of saucepans, half-filled the larger one with water and set it to heat on the expansive gas range.

"Okay?" she asked, a nervous edge to her voice.

"Great." Jesse smiled to reassure her. "Let's start unwrapping those caramels and putting them in this smaller pan."

"How many?" Noah deftly slid a candy out of its covering, but made no attempt to eat it.

"How many kids in your class?" Jesse hid his surprise when Noah said eleven. "Small class."

"He attends a private school," Maddie explained.

"Okay, so eleven kids, multiplied by at least three treats for each. Let's make fifty." Jesse grinned at their surprise. "One of these is never enough, you'll see. Plus they are small. Oh. I forgot to ask if you have toothpicks." He noticed Maddie's forehead crease in a frown. "Something we could use as skewers?" he prodded.

"I don't think so," she murmured.

"Does that mean we can't make them?" Noah looked worried.

"We can still make them, but it's much easier if we have something we can poke through the marshmallow to dip into the melted caramels, and leave in so we can stand it up." Jesse wasn't sure why, but suddenly it seemed very important that he help this woman and her child make his gran's treat. "I could run back into town—"

"Dad got sticks for my science project. There were some left." Noah's eagerness made Jesse smile.

"Honey, I have no idea where those might be." Maddie's cheeks grew pink. She did not look at her son. "When we moved here we had so much stuff and—"

"And you wanted to get rid of Dad's stuff," Noah's harsh voice accused. "Waste not, want not. That was his rule."

"Yes, it was." Maddie's voice dropped to a whisper.

Jesse hated the way her lovely face closed up, like a daisy when the sun went behind a cloud. He had to do something.

"Can you call your dad and ask him if he knows where they might be?" he suggested.

The room went utterly still.

"He's dead." Noah's voice broke. He glared at his mother. "You hated his rules, but I don't." Then he raced from the room.

Jesse had vowed not to get personally involved in a kid's life again, not after the fiasco in Colorado. Why hadn't he stayed out of his grandmother's favorite grocery store tonight? Why hadn't he avoided this woman and her troubled kid, simply swallowed his impulse to help?

Most of all, what was he supposed to do now to stem

the tears tumbling down Maddie's white cheeks as she stared after Noah?

Lord, You know how I've failed others. You know I've vowed not to get involved again, to never again risk failing a child.

So, God, what am I doing here with this woman and her troubled son?

Chapter Two

Weeping in front of a stranger?

Liam would—*Forget him!*

"I'm sorry." Maddie swiped a hand across her wet face. "Noah is still struggling to deal with his father's death."

"How long has it been?" Jesse asked quietly.

For the first time since she'd met him, Maddie tried to recall Emma's words about her grandson. Why had he offered to help them, strangers he didn't even know?

"Liam died of a heart attack just over a year ago."

"A heart attack?"

She saw Jesse's eyes flare with surprise and felt compelled to explain. "I'm twenty-seven. Liam was eighteen years older than me."

"His death must have been very hard on both you and Noah," Jesse said in the gentlest tone. "So after he died, you moved here?"

"We were renting a house that belonged to the church Liam pastored. We had to move because they needed the house for their new minister." Maddie wasn't about to admit just how eagerly she'd left that unhappy place. "Noah and I rented for a while, then moved to Broken Arrow Ranch last summer."

"I see." Jesse nodded. "That's a lot of change for any kid to handle."

She immediately bristled, then realized Jesse wasn't criticizing, simply stating facts. And yet she still asked, "Do you think I was wrong to move here?"

"Are you kidding?" Jesse chuckled. "It was dusk when we drove up, so I didn't get the full impact, but what I did glimpse of your spread was impressive. I doubt anyone would fault you for wanting to live here."

"I love it," she whispered, but she didn't tell him it was because the ranch represented freedom. Maddie glanced out the window as she explained the rest of her story. "Broken Arrow belonged to an elderly couple. They'd just completed interior renovations when the husband got sick. When they decided to move closer to medical care, Emma and Tanner both suggested I buy this place."

"Tanner—of Wranglers Ranch?" Jesse interjected.

"Yes. I think he and Sophie wanted to make sure they got a good neighbor. They helped us move here. But I'm not sure they've benefited much. I've had to call Tanner for help with a mouse—twice." Maddie chuckled. "The upside for us is that Sophie's a caterer. She often invites us over to try her new recipes and they are always delicious. I think I got the better deal when it comes to neighbors."

"Ah." His eyes twinkled with fun. "They get a good neighbor and you get good food. You're a smart lady."

"Not that smart." Maddie frowned. "What do we do for skewers?"

"Why is making this so important to you?" Jesse asked curiously. "It's just candy."

She glanced at the doorway through which her son had disappeared a few moments earlier, then answered in a hushed tone. "It's not just candy to me. It's a chance for Noah."

"To do what?" Jesse scanned the caramels and marshmallows. "This isn't the stuff heroes are made of."

"It could be." Maddie wasn't above begging when it was for Noah. "Please, Jesse, show us how to make these treats."

She held her breath. Emma said Maddie was God's child. Surely He would help her convince Jesse to help them?

Jesse had never been able to turn down anyone who asked him for help, and despite his recent vow to remain uninvolved, he couldn't do it this time, either. Calling himself an idiot, he began unwrapping more candy, adding to the contents in the saucepan, which he noted was gleaming and without a scratch.

She was a mom with a kid of, what? Seven? Eight? But apparently she'd barely used these like-new saucepans.

Jesse glanced around. Come to think of it, the furniture looked brand-new, too. Nicely tailored, not fussy, definitely comfortable, with quilts scattered here and there. Precise, finely patterned quilts with detailed stitching... Everything looked unused.

Also, everything was in its place. There wasn't a

speck of dust or a mess anywhere, no toy tossed here or a shirt discarded there. To Jesse, eldest of four rambunctious kids, this didn't look like the home of a dog and a young boy. It was too—*restrained.* As if it hadn't yet become home.

Two pictures hung on the wall. One was a very large portrait of Noah staring at a birthday cake with eight burning candles. The second was a smaller photo of him and Maddie standing by a flowering cactus. There were no snapshots or precious photos of the late husband and father. Questions multiplied inside Jesse's head.

"What can we substitute for the skewers?" Maddie asked, drawing him from his introspection.

"Forks, I guess. You don't have regular toothpicks? Because they would work," he said, as he added a small dollop of cream to the melting candy.

"No, I'm pretty sure I don't—oh, wait." With a smile as big as Texas Maddie flung open a cabinet and lifted out a massive cellophane-covered basket. "This was a housewarming gift from your grandmother. I guess she thought we'd be camping out or something, because she put in a bunch of disposable things. Maybe there's something we could use in here."

She pawed her way through the crackling cellophane, pulling out items and discarding them on the stone countertop in her search for toothpicks.

"Well?" Jesse waited, content to watch this beautiful woman.

"Nothing." Maddie's tone deflated when she came to the bottom of the basket.

"These might work." He selected and rotated a box.

"What are they?" She leaned across him to read the

label. "Oh. Stir sticks." She turned away, then stopped and turned back, eyes glowing as she took the package and tore it open. "Stir sticks!" she repeated, her grin wide as she held up a handful.

"Wooden ones, which are perfect, though I'm surprised my tasteful grandmother chose such lurid colors." He plunged the tip of one purple-and-green-striped stick into a marshmallow and grinned right back at her. "Hey, Ark Man," he called. "We're making the treats. You better come help us so you'll be able to tell the other kids how to make 'em."

Jesse hadn't given a thought to calling Noah until he glanced at Maddie and suddenly realized he should have let her do that. He opened his mouth to apologize, but she stopped him with a tearful look.

"Thank you," she whispered, just before her son appeared. "We found stir sticks for the I Have a Dream treats, Noah. Emma sent them in that basket of stuff."

"Huh." Noah watched Jesse, who drew his attention to the melting caramels. The boy spread the crisp noodles on a sheet of wax paper as directed, then mimicked Jesse's action, dipping a skewered marshmallow into the melted candy, rolling it in the noodles and standing it in a glass to set.

"Wait," Jesse ordered, when they'd made a total of three treats. Mother and son turned questioning gazes on him. "There's no point in making any more unless they taste okay. Go ahead," he urged Noah. "Do a taste test."

Noah glanced at his mom, who nodded. With exaggerated slowness he lifted one of the sticks from the glass and tried to bite the caramel. Of course the marshmallow moved, escaping his teeth. Jesse couldn't control his amusement, until Noah set the stick down, his face a wounded mask.

"This is what you looked like." Jesse made a fool of himself trying to coax a laugh from Noah and his mother and finally succeeded. "Now this is the proper way to eat them, or at least it's how I've always eaten them." He popped an entire marshmallow into his mouth, closed his eyes and chewed. "Mmm. I'd forgotten how good these were." He savored the taste.

Maddie reached for the last one. She put it in her mouth hesitantly, but then her eyes widened as she chewed.

"Noah," she said, wonder coloring her musical voice. "Taste it. They're delicious."

"Sweets are bad for you," Noah recited. "A third of all children starting school have tooth decay."

"It's okay to have a treat now and then," she told him.

Jesse could see how hard the boy was finding it to taste the candy. Those rules again. Someone had sure brainwashed him.

"Too many sweets are bad for you," he agreed. "But you're not going to have too many. Are you, Ark Man?"

After a moment, Noah shook his head, picked up his skewer and studied it with a critical eye. "I like triangles," he said firmly. "They're the best. These are circles."

Jesse blinked. "Uh, I don't know how to make them into triangles."

"It doesn't matter." Maddie intervened with a smile. "Just try it, Noah," she encouraged. "Circles are good, too. Think about apples and oranges."

"I like triangles." But he did slide the covered marshmallow into his mouth. The myriad of expressions that chased across his face was a delight Jesse was glad he was there to witness.

"So tell me, Ark Man, are circles okay?"

Still chewing, Noah nodded vigorously.

"And do you think three each will be enough for your classmates?"

He shook his head in a very firm no.

"Then let's get busy," Jesse urged.

They worked together in a relay. With delicate precision Noah speared the marshmallows, then handed the skewers to Jesse for dipping. He passed them on to Maddie to roll in the noodles. Halfway through they changed positions, so Maddie could dip and Noah could roll. And somewhere in the midst of the laughing and giggling and sneaky licks of a finger, Noah became an ordinary kid making a treat in the kitchen.

When Jesse glanced at Maddie he found her watching him, appreciation shining from the depths of her gorgeous green eyes. He couldn't look away, but she did, quickly, as if she was embarrassed.

"We've used all the marshmallows, so I guess it's time to clean up, and you need to get ready for bed." Maddie mussed Noah's too-perfect hair and pressed a kiss on his head. "How shall we keep these overnight, Jesse?"

"Just leave them. They'll dry out and firm up a bit. Then you can lay them in a box or container for school tomorrow." He was embarrassed by his stomach's loud rumble.

"Didn't you eat dinner?" Noah paused in his cleanup of the leftover noodle bits.

"I didn't." Jesse shrugged. "That's why I went to the grocery store. It's Gran's favorite. When she wasn't at home, I hoped I'd find her there and that maybe she'd have dinner with me when she was finished shopping. Or maybe make me dinner." He shook his head. "Doesn't matter. I'll get something to eat on my way back to my campsite."

"You're camping?" Noah's bored look vanished, replaced by excitement.

"Ever since I left Colorado, Ark Man."

"In a tent? With a campfire? And cookouts?" Awe filled Noah's voice.

"All of the above," Jesse agreed.

"Cool." The word whooshed out of Noah as if he could only imagine such a life.

"It is fun, except when it rains or there are mosquitos. Thankfully, the desert has little of either right now." Jesse turned to Maddie. "I've taken some time away from work to see this country," he explained.

"What is your work?" she asked.

"I'm—I was a youth pastor." He could almost feel her draw back when he said the word *pastor*. "I, ah, needed a break."

"I see." Maddie's face tightened into a mask. She abruptly turned her focus on Noah. "Get ready for bed, please."

"Eight o'clock is bedtime," Noah explained with a sigh. "It's the rule." He hesitated. "Will I see you again, Jesse?"

"I hope so, Ark Man. I intend to apply for a job at

Wranglers Ranch. That's right next door, your mom says." He smiled at the boy, but Noah was deep in thought.

"You're a minister," he said quietly, then glanced up. "Like my dad was?"

"Not anymore." Jesse felt funny saying that, as if God had somehow rescinded the call He'd made on his life so many years ago. "For now I'm going to try being a ranch hand." *Until I figure out what God's doing and what I'm supposed to do.*

"My dad said that when you work for God you can't quit," Noah said firmly. "He said that God wouldn't let him quit. He said it was a pastor's rule."

"For him, sweetie. It was a rule for *him*." Maddie nudged his thin shoulder. "Now thank Jesse for showing us how to make the treats."

Noah obediently thanked him, but it was clear that though he left without further protest, the question of Jesse's unemployment was not settled.

"I should get going, too," he said.

"Please stay and share a cup of tea, maybe a sandwich?" Maddie stood at the counter, hands knotted as if she was nervous. Her black cap of hair gleamed under the lights. "I'm no cook, but I owe you at least that much."

"You don't owe me anything. But I wouldn't say no to a cup of tea. Or a sandwich," he added, when his stomach complained again.

"I can do a sandwich." Maddie's face looked like the sun had come out, so brilliant was her smile. She put the kettle on, then pulled open the fridge. "What would you like?"

"Anything is fine. Thank you." He hoped she'd offer a thick slice of roast beef with hot mustard on fresh French bread. Or maybe—

"Is peanut butter okay?" Maddie stood in front of her fridge, clutching an almost empty jar of peanut butter, the same wimpy brand Noah preferred. "I could mix it with honey," she offered.

"Great." Jesse sat at the counter and accepted the sandwich when she served it, biting into it with relish, smiling and nodding as he chewed. "It's good."

"I should have made you something nice. I wish I could. You deserve it." She sat one stool away from him, elbows propped on the counter, inhaling the steam from her tea. "Here I have this designer kitchen that most women dream of, and I'm a useless cook."

That sounded like something someone had called her.

"Why don't you take cooking lessons?" he asked, after swallowing the sticky mass. "Gran made my mom take them."

"Really?" Maddie looked as if she'd never heard of such a thing.

"Sure. When my parents lived here there was a cooking school called Alberto's Mama. That's where my mom went to learn to cook before she had me." He grinned. "Gran insisted it was a necessity and my dad was happy to pay when he started tasting Alberto's Mama's recipes. Was your husband a cook?" He pretended to ask out of idle curiosity.

Immediately, Maddie went tense. Her fingers tightened around her cup and her cheeks lost the delightful pink that had bloomed there. "Gourmet," she murmured.

And that only made you feel worse.

Jesse's heart hurt at the wounded look on her face. "I'm sure you have talents in other areas."

She laughed, head thrown back, throat bare. It was the way Maddie should always laugh—full-bodied and freely expressing her emotions, Jesse thought. Not like that timid, fearful mouse he'd glimpsed a few moments ago.

"I don't have many talents, but I can make a pretty good quilt," she agreed with a cheeky grin, then quickly sobered. "Though some say that's a pointless and dying art."

"Since when is giving comfort pointless?" Jesse was angry that someone had so cruelly disparaged her gift. "When I was a kid I used to go with Gran to take her quilts to the cancer ward and to the homeless shelters. People loved her gifts because the quilts made them feel special and cherished, as if they mattered. That feeling is an amazing gift to give someone. It takes real talent. Cooking is just following directions."

Jesse hadn't meant to sound off, but when he noticed Maddie's spine straighten he was glad he had, now certain of his original assessment that someone hadn't properly valued this woman. He got caught up in speculating who that was, but his thoughts were interrupted by a call from the bedroom.

"Excuse me." Maddie disappeared into Noah's room with a smile, but when she emerged moments later her green eyes swirled with uneasiness.

"Everything okay with the Ark Man?" he asked.

"Noah's fine." Maddie frowned. "Why do you call him that?"

"Ark Man?" He shrugged. "Noah seems all about formalism, rules, that kind of thing. I've found—I used to find," he corrected, "—that sometimes a nickname helps break through the mask most overly responsible kids wear. I can stop if you want."

"Please don't." There was something about Maddie now—a tightness that echoed the tension on her pretty face. "Noah likes that nickname."

Jesse couldn't define the vibe he was getting, but that openness he'd so admired about her earlier had disappeared. He had the impression it had to do with him having been a minister—like her husband.

"Noah would like to speak to you for a minute."

"Sure." He walked toward the room Maddie indicated, and stepped inside, surprised by the plain simplicity of it. No superhero posters, no toys scattered around, no video games or computer. No distractions. Just one small bedside photo of a man with dark hair graying at the temples and a severe-looking face. Noah's father, Jesse guessed. "Hey. Ready for bed, huh?"

"Yes." Noah lay tucked in his bed, covered to his chin in a gorgeous gray quilt with puffy, silver-white clouds delicately dotting the surface. Somehow Jesse knew Maddie had made it. "Thank you for helping my mom and me make the treats, Jesse."

"You're very welcome. I hope you enjoy them." Jesse could tell the boy wanted to ask something, so even though Maddie stood behind him, ready to escort him out, he waited.

"Sometime…" Noah paused, glanced at his mother, then let the words spill out. "If it's not too much trouble, could you maybe show me your tent and campfire and—everything?"

"Sure." There was such a longing in the boy's request that Jesse couldn't let it be. "We'll make s'mores," he promised.

"Some mores?" Noah frowned. "What's that?"

"S'mores." He grinned. "Did you like the I Have a Dream snacks?"

"Oh, yes." Noah licked his lips with relish.

"Then you'll like s'mores," Jesse promised with a chuckle. "After I talk to the people at Wranglers and find out if I can get a job, I'll check with your mom and we'll set up a time for you to visit my campsite. Okay?"

"Thank you very much." Noah's eyes shone.

"You're welcome. Good night, Ark Man."

"Good night, PBX." A sly smile lit his face.

"Pardon?" Jesse couldn't figure out what the letters meant, but the boy wore a smug look. "What's a PBX?"

"Peanut butter expert." Noah grinned when Jesse laughed. Then he suddenly looked worried. "Is it okay?"

"It's an excellent nickname. Thank you, Ark Man. Sleep well."

Noah nodded, snuggled his head against the pillow and closed his eyes.

Jesse followed Maddie to the living room and sat in the chair she indicated, still chuckling.

"PBX. What a kid." He caught her studying him. "By the way, if his quilt is an example of what you can create with mere fabric," he said, "I'm in awe. Forget learning to cook. Your work is spectacular."

"Thank you." She actually blushed at the compliment. "It couldn't be bright and colorful, so I did the next best thing. Noah seems to like it."

"Why couldn't it be bright?" Jesse was curious about her response. "Are colors against Noah's rules?"

"No." She gave him a quick glance, then shifted her gaze to somewhere beyond his shoulder. "Noah is autistic. Too many bright colors or vivid patterns create heightened stimulation and that stresses him. So I tried to make his room calm but still attractive, a place where he can rest, concentrate, be at peace."

"Looks to me like you succeeded. With him, too. He's a great kid."

"Thank you." Maddie twiddled her fingers together, then looked directly at him. "I guess you know a lot about kids, having been a youth pastor."

"I don't know as much as I should," Jesse said bitterly, his joy in Noah's excitement evaporating. If he was going to hang with her son, Maddie deserved to know the truth. "One of the kids in my group committed suicide and I'm to blame."

"Why?" Her soft question wasn't perfunctory. She leaned forward, her eyes wide with interest, as she waited for his response.

"Because I couldn't stop him." How it hurt to admit that.

"I don't understand." Maddie frowned. "Were you there at the time?"

"No. Scott was at home, in his room, when he took an overdose of pills." Jesse gave the details clearly and concisely, his guilt burgeoning with each word. "His parents found him in the morning, lifelessly clutching a note that said he was being bullied and wanted to make it stop." Waves of self-recrimination returned.

"Oh, no." Her whisper of empathy helped him continue.

"I was Scott's friend as well as his youth pastor. I saw him at least three times a week. I took him for a soda that very afternoon." He shook his head. "Why didn't I know? Why didn't I see something?"

"I'm so sorry, Jesse." Maddie's sympathy brought him back to the present.

"Thanks. I had to tell you."

"You did?" Her green gaze widened. "Why?"

"In case you don't want me to be around Noah." To his utter shock and dismay, Maddie began to laugh. "What's so funny?"

"You." She shook her head. "Jesse, do you have any idea how I've longed for my son to break free of his autism long enough to find joy in kid things?"

He shook his head.

"Only since he was diagnosed, when he was three," she told him, her tone fierce. "Tonight, for the first time in eons, I watched Noah become engaged and interested, really interested, in something."

"It was just candy."

"*Just* candy?" Maddie chuckled. "Noah doesn't eat candy. Ever. He only talks about candy, repeatedly reciting his father's rule about its unhealthiness. Tonight, somehow, you got him to not only make candy but eat it *and* enjoy it. That's huge."

"I'm glad if he did." Jesse grinned. "Even if it wasn't triangles."

"He has a thing about triangles. But that isn't all you

did." Maddie's lashes were suddenly wet as a tear rolled down her cheek. When she looked at him, deep love for her precious boy lay vulnerably revealed. "You talked to him, not at him. You treated him as if he's normal kid."

"Well, he is. Isn't he?" Jesse frowned at her.

"Noah has…issues other kids don't have. He's very reclusive. He doesn't interact easily and yet tonight you discovered interests in him that I never even imagined. Nicknames. Camping." She shook her head, a rueful look on her face. "How could I not have known Noah was interested in camping? Liam was right. Sometimes I am just plain dumb."

"Liam being…?" Jesse had to ask, though he was pretty sure he already knew who this denigrating person was.

"Liam was my husband. That's his picture by Noah's bed." A rueful smile lifted the edges of her lips. "You probably wonder how I could have married a man so much older than me."

That question along with a hundred more about this amazing woman had burned through his brain, but Jesse remained silent, letting her speak on her own terms.

"Everyone wants to know that and the answer is…" she paused, her face tightening "…escape. You told me about your past, so I'll share some of mine." She took a deep breath. "My father was abusive when he got drunk. I spent my childhood and youth avoiding him, hiding out at a friend's, keeping his secret, trying to finish my studies so I could graduate and leave."

"But you should have—"

"Told someone?" A half smile that held no mirth lifted her lips. "I did once and paid for it dearly. I knew that if I told again, I would only get hurt that much more. I wasn't that stupid," she added, almost defiantly.

"So Liam came along," Jesse murmured, knowing exactly where this was going.

"He stopped by initially to invite my father to his church, and then he just kept coming back. I could tell he was interested in me, but I never took it seriously. I didn't know anything about men. I was so naive." She looked embarrassed and…ashamed? "One day my dad came home in a foul mood. He'd lost his job and he was drunk. Very drunk. And I was his punching bag."

Anger burned inside Jesse for the girl she'd been, alone, unprotected and unloved. But he held his tongue, letting her vent, because he'd learned the abused often needed to verbalize their pain.

"I endured as long as I could, but later, when he zonked out, I saw my chance and I ran away. I was huddled on a park bench when Liam found me. He bought me some new clothes to replace my torn ones, fed me and then he proposed." Again that unamused smile. "He was my way out and I grabbed at the chance."

"That was the night you got the scar." Jesse didn't need to see her nod or the way she lifted her hand to touch the puckered skin to know the truth. "I don't blame you for seizing the opportunity."

He hesitated. He'd vowed not to get personally involved again, but he couldn't just up and leave her like this, stuck in what sounded like a miserable past.

"It wasn't a good marriage," Maddie whispered, her voice forlorn. "I didn't know anything about being a wife, let alone a pastor's wife. I couldn't cook and the child I bore was what Liam called defective. My fault. I was a failure."

"How could Noah's autism possibly be your fault?" Jesse demanded. "And he is *not* defective," he hissed through clenched teeth.

"Thank you for saying that." She offered him the saddest of smiles. "To be fair, my husband was much older and not used to children. Noah had colic. He cried a lot and that got on Liam's nerves. I guess that's why he stopped asking me to be involved in the church, and left me to tend our son. As Noah got older and other problems emerged, Liam decided the way to control Noah's outbursts was to instill in him a set of unbreakable rules."

"Ah," Jesse said, understanding. "Noah learned he could please his father if he obeyed all the rules."

"Exactly." Maddie grew thoughtful. "I'm not exactly sure why, but now Liam's gone and Noah still clings to those rules, even though his dad is no longer here to approve. I'm trying to break his reliance on them by showing him that rules are only a guide."

"And that maybe some of those rules are wrong?" Jesse added very quietly.

"Yes." She lifted her head and thrust out her chin. "That's why what you did for him tonight is so amazing. Jesse, I have never seen Noah so eager about anything. I'd really appreciate it if you could take him to see your campsite. I don't want to inconvenience you, but if he's truly interested in camping, perhaps I can find a way to build on that."

"I don't know exactly how long I'll be in Tucson." Jesse was cautious, aware that it would be all too easy to get involved with this pretty mom and her needy child. "But I'll certainly show him my campsite and cook him some s'mores, as I promised."

"Thank you. I appreciate it." She grinned cheekily. "Emma was right about you. You really are something." Then she sobered. "May I speak plainly?"

"Of course." He wondered what was coming.

"I want—in fact, I crave—your help with Noah. But I don't want there to be any mistakes between us to spoil things."

"Okay." Where was this going?

"Please be clear that I am not looking for anything more, Jesse."

"Pardon?" He watched her face flush and her hands knot as she said it, but Maddie's intense gaze held his.

"I'm not looking for a husband or a father for my son. I was not a good wife. I did not love my husband the right way. I was a failure and one mistake was more than enough." Maddie paused, then offered, "I'm not interested in romance. But I surely could use a friend."

"You've got one." Relieved, Jesse relaxed. "I feel the same. My fiancée recently dumped me. It's been painful to discover that the woman I thought I'd love forever was not the person I believed her to be, and that I wasn't the one she really wanted. She preferred my best friend. I still feel stupid, and I sure don't want to go through that again, you know?"

He gulped, then expelled a rush of relief when Maddie nodded in understanding.

"I don't think I'm meant to be anyone's mate." Jesse figured he might as well be blunt. "But friendship is something I think we could share. To help Noah." He held out his hand. "So hello, friend Maddie."

"Hello, friend Jesse." Her slim fingers slid into his and gripped with a firmness he hadn't expected. "Whatever I can help *you* with, just ask."

"A recommendation to Wranglers Ranch?" he suggested, as he drew his hand away, surprised that the warmth of her gentle touch lingered on his skin.

Maddie smiled, picked up the phone and dialed.

"Tanner, this is Maddie. We're good, thanks. How's baby Carter?" She chuckled at the response. "Poor you. Call me to babysit anytime. Listen, Tanner, I have a friend who's looking for a job. I think he'd be perfect for Wranglers Ranch. His name is Jesse. He's Emma's grandson... Okay, I will. Bye." She ended the call. "Stop by Wranglers anytime tomorrow."

Jesse's jaw dropped. "Just like that?"

"I told you there were advantages to living next door to Tanner and Sophie."

"Thank you," he said, and he meant it.

"You're welcome." When she checked her watch Jesse took that as his cue to leave.

"I should go. Thank you for a fun evening, Maddie. I enjoyed myself." He rose and walked to the door, aware of her slight figure padding barefoot behind him. He pushed open the screen door and caught his breath.

The desert beyond lay in darkness save for an array of solar lights.

"It looks like someone painted a giant stained-glass butterfly." He turned to look at her. "You?"

Maddie nodded, a satisfied smile tipping up her rosy lips.

"How?" Jesse couldn't imagine the hours it must have taken to place each lamp just so in order to create this intricate design.

"I used a quilt pattern. Noah helped me get the wings right." Her green eyes peered into the distance but Jesse was fairly certain she wasn't staring at the lights because after a moment she said in a whisper-soft voice, "I dreamed of creating it a long time ago." Her gaze slid to study him. "Maybe this is the year for my dreams to come true. First we moved to my ranch, then my butterfly became reality and now you're here helping Noah."

My ranch. *My* butterfly. Something about the way she said it got Jesse pondering what other dreams this woman held tucked deep inside.

"Will you be able to find your way to your campsite from here?"

Maddie looked so concerned that he hurried to remind her that he and his parents had once lived in Tucson.

"I'm glad you came back, Jesse."

"So am I." He walked toward his truck and was about to climb in when her quiet call stopped him.

"Jesse?"

"Yes?" He paused and peered toward her slim figure, saw her hands grip the balustrade as she tilted forward.

"Thank you very much." The soft words brimmed with intensity.

He waved, then got into his truck and drove away, wondering why he knew that quiet expression of gratitude came from her heart.

Maddie McGregor was a puzzle. She seemed young and innocent, and yet was apparently the product of a miserable childhood and a wretched marriage. Gutsy but somehow vulnerable. Nightshade and sunshine. She had a home taken straight from the pages of a magazine, but apart from a couple of quilts tossed over the sofa, it looked too neat to be truly lived in. In fact, aside from her quilts, there wasn't much in that house that said anything about Maddie McGregor.

That whimsical butterfly, however, said a lot. And that intrigued him.

When Gran came home Jesse intended to spend an evening plying her with questions about his new friend.

But as he lay in his tent, he had to remind himself to stop thinking about sweet Maddie McGregor.

You can't get involved. Nobody else gets hurt, remember?

Chapter Three

"Jesse." Tanner Johns shook his hand heartily. "You're Maddie's friend."

Relief suffused Jesse. After the fiasco in his Colorado church there hadn't been many who'd wanted to call him friend.

"And you're Emma's grandson." Tanner grinned. "Welcome to Wranglers Ranch."

"Thanks." A little taken aback by the warmth of his greeting, Jesse figured the cowboy must not know about his past. Tanner's next words disproved that.

"I was really sorry to hear about the death of that boy in your youth group." His voice dropped. "It's so hard to know what goes on inside a kid's head. Thank God He knows."

"Yeah." Jesse gulped. *He knew, so why didn't He stop Scott?*

"So you're taking a break from your ministry." Obviously unaware of Jesse's revolving faith questions, Tanner tilted back on his boot heels, his voice thoughtful. "Sometimes it's good to reassess if you're where God wants you."

"I guess Gran told you—" He stopped because Tanner was shaking his head.

"When it comes to kids' work I keep my ear to the ground so I can pray for all of us who are working with these precious souls." He grinned. "A friend of mine told me about your program in Colorado. Said you did amazing work. When he heard you'd resigned, he emailed me, ordered me to offer you a job if you happened by the area to visit Emma."

"That's kind of him," Jesse murmured.

"He's a man I trust, but he's not the only one singing your praises. Your grandmother has lots of stories about you, too. One day I'd like to see all those rodeo trophies you've collected, cowboy." Tanner chuckled at his grimace. "Okay, I'll drop it. Don't want to make you blush."

"Thanks," Jesse said with relief.

"Come on. I'll show you around." As they walked, Tanner explained that the focus of Wranglers was to reach kids through acceptance. "The man who owned this ranch, Burt, led me to God here, and many after me. His dream was for Wranglers Ranch to become a sanctuary, a kind of camp for kids. When he passed away he left this spread to me to make his dream come true. I started working with street kids because I was one once and I knew the impact this place could have. God's kind of expanded my puny efforts. Now we host church groups, kids from social agencies, kids involved with the justice system, kids who just stop by to see what's going on and sick kids, to name a few."

"Wow." Jesse was awed by such an expansive ministry.

"We use equine-assisted learning programs," Tanner explained. "We try hard to reach every kid for God, but, like you, we do lose some. Not every kid who comes to Wranglers Ranch is ready or willing to turn his life around."

"All we can do is shed some light on the path," Jesse agreed. "They have to choose it."

"That's why my friend was so impressed with your work. He said you made sure your kids understood what making the choice to be a child of God entails." Tanner then pointed out the horses in the paddocks, the land that stretched to the Catalina Mountains and the hands whom he credited for keeping his ranch functioning. "Wranglers Ranch is all about spreading the love of God. We use every resource we have to do that."

That simple explanation of such a far-reaching ministry sent Jesse's admiration for this man soaring and upped his desire to be part of it, a small part, anyway. But how to do it without getting personally involved?

"My friend said you have your degree in counseling." Tanner lifted one eyebrow.

"I went to college before I attended seminary," Jesse said.

"Actually, you started college on the expedited track when you were fourteen," Tanner corrected, a smile flickering at the corner of his mouth. "And left several years later with your master's degree in counseling."

"Yeah, I was kind of a misfit." It seemed Tanner had collected a lot of information about him, but Jesse wasn't going to add to it. It had taken forever to shed the geek label he'd carried in those days. He sure didn't want it back now.

"I'm not asking because I want you to do any counseling, Jesse." Tanner's quiet voice belied his probing look. "That's not what we do here."

"Then...?" He was mystified as to what his job might be.

"No counseling, but I sure wouldn't mind having someone with your credentials on-site." Tanner tilted his head to one side. "You're what—twenty-seven?"

Jesse nodded.

"You have education and life experience. You've worked with kids a lot so you have an advantage in spotting the kid who's good at hiding his feelings but desperately needs an outlet. You're probably more able than any of us here to spot the kid who's walking a tightrope of despair. That's what I want at Wranglers Ranch," Tanner said thoughtfully. "We need someone who'll catch the kid we've missed or the one whose needs haven't been properly addressed."

"I didn't manage that so well in Colorado," Jesse admitted, the shame of it rushing up inside.

"You didn't see your youth group kids' struggles?" Tanner's eyes widened in disbelief.

"Yes, of course, but—"

"You didn't go out of your way to talk to each of them privately, take them for coffee, spend extra time praying for them?" Tanner's probing was relentless. "Come on, Jesse. Tell me you didn't do everything you could to help each one of them."

"Yes, I did." Guilt ate like acid inside him. "But in

the end it didn't make any difference, because I failed to save Scott."

"How do you know you didn't make any difference?" Tanner touched his shoulder, his voice quiet. "But whether you did or didn't isn't the point. We're called to show God's love. He takes it from there."

"I guess." Yet no matter how many months had passed, Jesse still couldn't wrap his mind around why it had happened.

"If you're still interested, here's the job. Work as a ranch hand. Offer as much love and caring as you can to every kid that comes to Wranglers Ranch, while keeping your eyes peeled for problems. If you find something that needs changing, you tell me." Tanner studied him, waiting.

"I see." Could he do this and still remain detached? Jesse wondered.

"At Wranglers we don't counsel anyone," Tanner enunciated. "Our job is first and foremost to befriend every kid who comes here, to make them feel this is a safe place and that we're here to help. Together we try to reach every child who shows up."

So maybe he could still be a kind of youth pastor, just in a different way, without letting himself get too personally involved with any of the kids. Was that what God wanted?

"I'd like to be a part of Wranglers Ranch." Jesse held out his hand. "Thank you, Tanner."

"Today's Friday. Start on Monday?" Tanner smiled at his nod as he shook hands. "Noah says you're camping out."

"For now." Jesse chuckled. "I had the impression

Noah wouldn't mind joining me. He got this look on his face—I gather he's never camped before."

"No. His father wouldn't have allowed that." Tanner's expression grew solemn. "Maddie sometimes helps Sophie with our new baby, Carter, and Noah visits our kids a lot, so I've gotten to know the McGregor family fairly well since they moved in next door. Noah struggles to deal with his father's death and his list of unbreakable rules."

"Maddie told you about it?" Jesse blinked in surprise when Tanner shook his head.

"I've never heard Maddie talk about her husband except to say he died." The rancher inclined his head. "I did attend Liam's church once, years ago."

"And?" Jesse could hardly control his curiosity about sweet Maddie's former husband.

"Liam McGregor was much older than her, a stern man whom I thought was overly focused on details instead of God's love. I wouldn't say Liam found joy in his faith, more like it was his duty." Concern lay etched in the fine lines around Tanner's eyes. "His legacy of rule-keeping isn't helping Noah."

"Noah seems almost…" Jesse hesitated "…emotionally backward?"

"He's been diagnosed as a very high functioning autistic. After Liam's death, Maddie moved him from public school into a private setting to challenge him and to help his social awkwardness." Tanner's gaze turned assessing. "Noah probably feels like you did when you were so far ahead of other kids your age."

"Then I feel sorry for him." Jesse winced at the cascade of memories. "Social ineptitude leaves you out of the group, on your own and desperate for a friend. Except you don't know how to make them, and if you do, it's hard to discern which one is a real friend. You can't reach out, or you're afraid to in case others make fun of you. It's a lonely place and depression can easily creep in."

"And autism makes it ten times harder. I knew you'd be an asset here." Tanner looked pleased by his evaluation. "Wranglers Ranch is hosting Noah's class in a beginners' riding group next week. Both Maddie and Noah's teacher hope that working with the horses will help all of the kids relax their barriers, form some social bonds and develop a team spirit."

"A few riding classes are going to do all that?" Jesse asked skeptically.

"You've worked with horses. Didn't you ever feel the animals were a kindred spirit?" Tanner asked.

"My own horse, yes." Jesse smiled in remembrance. "In fact Coal Tar seemed to sense exactly what I needed him to do before I asked, but I raised him, worked with him for years."

"Here at Wranglers Ranch our animals are mostly abused stock that we've rescued. Maybe that makes them extra sensitive, but I think you'll soon see that as the kids work with their horses week after week, a bond develops. A kind of mutual trust." Tanner's self-deprecating shrug said a lot. "We've seen it happen over and over. Time at Wranglers Ranch with our horses always brings a change in the kids. You'll see it, too, Jesse."

"I'm looking forward to it." And he was. Meantime maybe he could learn more about his new friend. "Maddie seems very attuned to Noah."

"Her son is her whole world," Tanner agreed quietly. "Everything she does is for him, which is great but…"

"But?"

"But I wish she'd take more time to replenish her own well. Sophie and I keep hoping she'll accept your grandmother's offer of a partnership in her quilting store," Tanner said quietly.

"I guess that would help Gran, but maybe Maddie can't afford it or isn't well versed enough in business," Jesse suggested.

"She is on both scores." Tanner smiled. "Maddie told us she purchased her ranch with part of a sizable life insurance policy she received after Liam's death, so she can certainly afford to buy the business. But the best part is the way she feels about quilts. She loves anything to do with them. She seems to come alive when she's working with fabric, as if the texture and pattern allow her to express feelings she usually keeps tucked inside."

"So what's the problem?" Jesse felt he was missing something. "Why hasn't she bought Gran's business already? I think Gran would sell."

"I believe Maddie refuses to buy out Emma because she lacks confidence in herself. From what she's said, I think she believes she isn't capable, and that simply isn't true. She's a very capable woman. I saw that when she was buying and moving to the ranch."

"Really?" Jesse was intrigued.

"Maddie had organized everything ahead of time. She prepared the house so the movers knew exactly where every box went. By the end of moving day, she had everything unpacked and in place, which I find as-tonishing." He grimaced.

"Why?" What was this about? Jesse wondered.

"Because it was nothing like that when I helped Sophie and the kids move here after we were married. We still haven't unpacked some of her bags and boxes." His pained look said it all. "Maddie is detail-oriented, has foresight and considers everything from many angles."

"So?" Jesse waited, curious to hear the rest.

"I think Maddie McGregor lacks confidence because she hasn't ever had anyone to champion her, urge her to reach out of her comfort zone and support her efforts. In fact, judging by what I've garnered, I think she's been put down and deprecated."

Tanner didn't say it, but Jesse had the distinct impression he was referring to Maddie's former husband. The gourmet cook, he remembered, recalling Maddie's downcast face when she'd said that.

His new boss changed the subject by moving on to discuss hours, wages, staff meetings and a myriad of other employment details that Jesse only half heard because his mind was busy trying to put together a puzzle called Maddie.

As if he'd conjured her, she drove up at the end of his interview, as he was walking to his truck—which, he noticed with disgust, had a flat tire. She climbed out of her car and hurried toward him, her green eyes dark and shadowed.

"Hi," he said, a bubble of joy building inside his chest. "How are you?"

"I'm fine, but I need to talk to you, Jesse." Maddie looked serious. "About Emma."

His heart squeezed so tight he could hardly breathe.

"What's wrong?" he asked, forcing the words out through his blocked throat.

"She's in hospital in Las Cruces." Maddie paused.

"What happened?" Panic gripped him.

"She was in a car accident. Among other injuries, including a fractured wrist, her hip was damaged. She's undergoing hip replacement surgery as we speak." Maddie's fingers rested on his arm, as if to comfort him as she continued.

"And?" Jesse steeled himself to hear the rest.

"Her friend Eunice, her passenger, was not badly hurt. She's the one who called your parents. Apparently they're flying in to see Emma. They asked Eunice to notify me at the shop, hoping I'd heard from you, since they knew you intended to stop in Tucson to visit her."

"Is Gran going to be all right?" The very thought of not having Emma there when he needed her sent a wave of devastation through Jesse. He gulped hard, lifted his head and found compassion in Maddie's gaze. "I can't lose her," he whispered brokenly.

"You're not going to lose her, Jesse." Maddie touched his cheek, forcing him to keep looking at her. "This is Emma, remember? She's very strong. You know she has a to-do list as long as my arm?" When he nodded, Maddie smiled. "Then you also know she's not going anywhere until that list is finished. Right?"

"Yes." He exhaled and smiled at her. "Thank you, Maddie."

"I'm praying for Emma." Her worried look returned. "But I'm very concerned about Quilt Essentials. Should I close the doors?"

"But…you've been running it for her. Can't you keep doing that?" Jesse asked.

"I've only ever taken over for a couple of days. Hip replacements have a long recovery time." Maddie looked scared at the prospect of handling the business on her own.

He didn't know why, maybe it was from talking to Tanner, but somehow Jesse had the utmost confidence in Maddie. "You can do it."

"How do you know that?" Her eyes widened in surprise.

"Gran trusted you enough to leave you in charge while she went away, and I don't think it was the first time," he added, feeling more certain by the moment.

"I've often managed the store if she had to be away for a few days, but—"

"Then just keep doing what you've always done." He smiled at her. "She'll come back to find you've made her business better than ever." He searched for a way to chase the doubt from those turbulent green eyes. "My grandmother believes in you, Maddie. So do I."

"You barely know me. But thank you for saying that." Her eyes glowed for a moment, then darkened again, her apprehension returning. "Except I don't think running Quilt Essentials will be that simple and I don't think I can do it for very long, though I guess I could handle it for a few more days. At least until things get sorted out. But we can talk about that later." She looked as if she was mentally gathering her strength. "You need to get to the airport now."

"I'll drive there." He made a face. "After I fix my flat tire."

"A flat can wait. It's more important that you ensure Emma's fine, get anything she needs, and speak to your parents." Maddie's hesitation hinted there was something she hadn't yet explained.

"Okay." Jesse tensed as he waited for whatever came next.

"If you leave right away you can return tonight and move into Emma's house. Somebody has to stay there and take care of her babies." Maddie looked as if there was nothing the least bit unusual in that comment.

"Babies?" Jesse felt as if he'd missed an important kernel of information. "What babies?"

"The rescued animals." Maddie's green eyes widened again. "You don't know?"

"Uh-uh." Though he was impatient to get to Gran, Jesse knew he needed to hear this.

"Ever since her dog Buddy died, Emma's cared for rescued animals, ones that need more attention than the animal shelter can provide." Maddie shook her head to stop his protest. "Not medical care. She cares for the ones who need coddling or watching."

"Who looked after them while she was away?" Jesse asked.

"She hired someone to come in," Maddie explained. "Emma was returning home today because the caregiver flies out tonight to be with her pregnant daughter. Since Emma won't be coming home for a while, somebody has to take her place to care for the puppies."

"How many?" Jesse asked curiously.

"Nine. Newborns. Their mother died and they were left alone for at least a day before they were rescued. Emma took them in because they need feeding every few hours and lots of cuddling. The shelter couldn't manage that twenty-four hours a day." Maddie paused, then chided, "Are you following me, Jesse?"

"Yes. But I want to spend the weekend at the hospital with Gran." Talk about a change in plans. More than ever he wondered what God was doing. "Isn't there someone else?"

"I asked, but the shelter doesn't have anyone. They're really short of help right now. Emma was their last hope to save those puppies." Maddie frowned. "They're not very healthy. They need regular feedings."

"I must get to Gran." Jesse was desperate to reassure himself that his grandmother would still be around to cheer and advise. He needed her sage advice and her tough love to help him find his way back to the faith that seemed so wobbly.

"I'll drive you to the airport," Maddie said. "But can you return tonight to care for the puppies? I can handle their six o'clock feeding, but not the night ones."

Of course she couldn't. Maddie was already going above and beyond by keeping Emma's store going. Jesse couldn't ask her to relocate to Gran's home with Noah, let alone get up at night with needy dogs.

"I'll deal with the puppies, but first I must see Gran." *Why Gran, God?*

"I suggest you leave your truck here. I'll drive you to the airport. I've reserved you a ticket." She smiled at his surprise. "Emma has a friend in the travel business."

"Thank you." He glanced at his truck. "I could drive myself—"

"Parking is really bad because of all the renovations they're doing," she said with a shake of her head. "It's better if I drop you off. You have to make this flight because it's the last flight of the day to Las Cruces. If you miss it you'll have to wait until tomorrow to see Emma."

"Okay." With no other option, Jesse made sure he had his wallet in his pocket, grabbed a jacket from the truck and climbed into her vehicle.

Moments later Maddie was weaving her way through traffic that seemed unusually heavy until Jesse spotted a road sign proclaiming this the first day of the Tucson gem show. That explained the excess of vehicles.

"You don't have to talk to me. Go ahead and pray for Emma." Maddie tossed him a sideways smile, then concentrated on merging onto Valencia Road toward the airport. "You're a pastor. I know you want to pray."

Yes, he did *want* to. But what had once come so easily was no longer so simple. What if, once again, God didn't answer as he hoped? Unable to even consider losing Gran, Jesse glanced out the window as he recalled familiar landmarks.

"How did your talk with Tanner go?" Maddie asked after some time had passed.

"As of Monday I'm newly employed at Wranglers Ranch."

"Good for you. I'm sure you'll enjoy it." Her smile eased the awkwardness of his inability to pray. "Tanner and Sophie are great."

"Sophie sure is an amazing cook." He patted his stomach. "She served chicken pot pie and blackberry cobbler for lunch. Delicious."

"I'm jealous. I had a peanut butter sandwich." Maddie laughed at his grimace. "Did you meet Wyatt and Ellie?"

"That would be Wranglers' veterinarian and his wife, the camp nurse," he said after a moment's thought. "I did. And the foreman, Lefty, and a bunch of others. Everyone seems very pleasant."

Another stretch of silence. Jesse couldn't think how to fill it.

"Oh, I almost forgot. I thought you might like a coffee, so I stopped for two on my way to Wranglers Ranch. That one's yours." Maddie indicated a cardboard cup in the holder with white writing on the lid. "Double cream, right? Like you had in your tea last night?"

"Thank you. It's exactly what I need." He sipped his coffee. Noting the excellent flavor, he checked the label, then let out a low whistle. "You must like coffee a lot. This place is the crème de la crème for serious coffeephiles."

Did her green eyes brighten? Her cheeks certainly turned a deeper shade of pink.

"Yes, well, I have a bit of an addiction to coffee," she confessed, her face averted.

It wasn't just because Maddie was lovely and gentle and sweet that he enjoyed getting to know her. It was all that and something more, something Jesse couldn't explain. He wasn't looking for a romantic relationship or any kind of involvement. But he *was* looking forward to broadening their friendship.

"I don't think addictions can be quantified as *a bit*," he teased, and laughed at her wince. "Fess up, lady. You've got a big obsession for coffee."

"I love coffee. Especially latte macchiatos. There. I said it. Are you happy?" Maddie being feisty was even more intriguing.

"Will you laugh if I tell you something?" Jesse asked sotto voce.

Her eyes widened when he leaned toward her. Her whole face was animated and her dark hair shimmered in the sunlight.

"I won't laugh, I promise. What is it?"

"After last night I was afraid you were a tea granny. You see, I only do tea with Gran or when there's no coffee." He couldn't suppress his burst of amusement at the relief flooding her face. He inhaled the aroma from his cup. "This makes the drive perfect."

But it wasn't just the coffee. Away from Noah, Maddie relaxed, laughed and smiled more. She'd removed the lid from her cup and Jesse smothered his grin when a sip left a puffy little cream mustache above her lips.

"You do realize that what you're drinking is not real coffee." Jesse enjoyed the way her green eyes expressed her mood. Right now they darkened with warning. "Latte macchiato means stained milk, so you're drinking mostly warm milk with a little espresso."

"It's *mostly* delicious and way better than that plain old regular double you're drinking." She defended herself with a mischievous grin.

"I'm looking forward to teaching you the delights of real coffee, Maddie McGregor." To that and a lot of other interactions.

She glanced at him, then concentrated on negotiating the car through the twists and turns of construction before finally pulling up in front of the departure doors.

"Thanks a lot for the ride," he said, before swallowing the last of his coffee.

"Please give Emma my love and tell her not to worry.

I'll do my very best at the store. She must concentrate on recovering." Maddie handed him a small flowered box he guessed was candy. "Please give her that and my love." Her amazing smile hit him like a jolt of electricity.

"Will do," he promised.

"When I pick you up tonight I want to hear all about her," she added. "Your return flight lands here at nine." The last sounded like a question.

"I'll be back," he promised. "But Maddie, you don't have to—"

A horn sounded loud and long behind them.

"I'll be here, Jesse," she promised, then shifted the car into gear, waiting for him to exit. "Your ticket's at the counter."

"Thank you, Maddie," he said, as he climbed out. "For everything."

She waved before driving away.

As they took off Jesse peered through the airplane window, watching the pink adobe houses that dotted the desert valley beneath dip away. He would enjoy coming back.

Because of Maddie?

You're not getting involved. Remember?

Maddie sat outside the airport terminal waiting for Jesse, wondering if it was too forward to have insisted on picking him up.

"That sign says we can only stay here five minutes," Noah warned. "Then we'll be breaking the rules."

"I don't think we'll have to wait—" She broke off, struggling to stem her excitement as Jesse emerged. "There he is."

Why excitement? He was just a friend.

"Didn't mean to keep you waiting." Jesse climbed inside her car and tossed a smile over one shoulder. "Hey, Ark Man."

"Hi, PBX." Noah lost his stressed look.

Jesse chortled as Maddie pulled into traffic. Then she asked, "How's Emma?"

"Spitting mad." He chuckled. "She just bought that car—eleven years ago," he added in a droll tone.

"I can almost hear her." Maddie giggled. "She always talks about Beastie the car as if it's brand-new. Not that it's nice to have your car demolished in an accident, but—"

"Oh, it's not just the car." Jesse grinned. "She's also mad that her passenger got hurt, even if it was only bumps and bruises."

"What happened, anyway?" Maddie sobered at the thought of Emma hurt.

"Drunk driver." Jesse squeezed his eyes closed for a moment. "She was very fortunate."

"I know Emma," Maddie said gently. "And I'm quite sure she didn't give good fortune the credit for her survival."

"No. She's certain God saved her life because He has things for her to do. She'll be back before we know it." The way Jesse looked at her now made Maddie squirm. "When Gran returns she's going to press you hard to buy Quilt Essentials. This accident made her realize she has a long list of things to accomplish. She feels she must sell the store to have time to do them."

"Oh, but I can't buy…" Panicked, Maddie kept her eyes forward and swallowed hard. "I'm not a businessperson, Jesse. I'm trying to help her out, but I don't know anything about actually running a business."

"Gran says you know more than she does about quilts," he responded.

"That's only because I had a grandmother who taught me every quilting thing she knew." Maddie felt a rush of warmth at the memories. "My mother died when I was eight. When he had a job my dad would leave me with my grandmother. We had the grandest times. I guess that's why I love quilting, because it takes me back to that joy."

"She's gone now?" Jesse asked quietly.

"Yes." The depth of that loss still got to Maddie sometimes.

"And your father?"

"He died, too." She couldn't help the harsh way it came out. "Right after I got married."

"So you had only your husband to lean on."

How to answer that?

"I have Noah now." Maddie glanced in her son's direction. "He and I lean on each other."

"That's good." Jesse chatted with Noah for the rest of the drive to Emma's tidy adobe house.

"I need to get Noah home, but first I'll show you what to do for the puppies." Maddie switched off her car and pushed open her door. "I warn you, they'll probably wake up to eat at least a couple of times tonight. It's a good thing you don't have to start at Wranglers Ranch for a few days."

She inhaled the scent of Emma's blooming rose garden as they walked toward the house, but quickly turned back when Noah called out. She was surprised to see his whitened face.

"Are you sick, honey?" she asked in concern, remembering he'd acted oddly the last time she'd brought him over to check on the dogs.

"Do I have to go in?" he asked.

"I don't want you sitting out here alone." Maddie opened his car door. "You can help us with the puppies."

Noah made a face then left the car to trail reluctantly behind them to the house. With a sigh of resignation, Maddie unlocked the door.

"What's wrong?" Jesse asked in a hushed tone when her son quickly veered toward the living room.

"Noah's never comfortable with anything that disrupts his usual patterns," she murmured as she switched on the lights. "I think the puppies scare him."

"Oh." Jesse studied Noah for a moment before asking, "Where are they?"

"In the laundry room." She raised her voice. "Come and help, Noah."

Glowering, the boy slowly walked toward her.

"I'm sure Jesse wants to rest, but if I show him what to do then he can get a few hours of sleep before the next feeding. If you help us, we'll finish quicker. Okay?" She waited for his reluctant nod. "Go with Jesse into the laundry room."

Noah still hung back, so after a moment Maddie drew him forward, trying to ease his nervousness as the tiny animals mewled around Jesse's feet.

"First we must change the papers." With Jesse's help she rolled up the floor covers and placed them in a bag, which Noah carried outside to the garbage. When he returned he had to be coaxed to help lay new ones, and would do so only after he'd folded them into triangles. Frustrated and weary, Maddie simply said, "Now we need to get their food ready."

She had done this only once, with the caregiver, but she pretended confidence as she demonstrated to Jesse how to prepare the formula the animal shelter had provided.

"Now for the fun part. Feeding." She smiled at her son. "Who's first?"

"Me." Jesse sat, leaned his back against the wall and cradled the tiniest furry body. "Hungry, are you, little one?" he cooed tenderly as he coaxed the puppy to latch on to the bottle. "That's right. Eat. But not too fast." He chuckled as the animal ignored his advice and greedily sucked the fluid.

"Your turn, son." Maddie touched Noah's shoulder, found it rigid. She didn't want to embarrass him, but—

"You gotta help me with these guys, Noah. After all, you're the Ark Man, in charge of animals." With his toe, Jesse nudged a pup closer to him. "Aren't they cute?"

Maddie had had little success involving Noah when they'd been here previously, but she persisted now because she so wanted him to have this experience.

"Come on, son. We'll do it together."

Attempts to engage Noah were not a success. He pulled away every time she tried to hand him a hungry pup. It was only when Jesse cupped his hands around Noah's and kept them there as Maddie set the next puny animal in them that her son finally cradled a puppy. His body stiffened at the touch of the claws, and he seemed frozen until Jesse began to speak in a calming, intimate tone.

"Good work, Ark Man," he murmured. "They're too little to hurt you, but they're hungry, so they claw to try to get the food faster. You have to hold their little feet so they can't scratch you."

Under Jesse's encouraging tutelage and effusive praise, Noah slowly relaxed and finally got the puppy drinking. Afraid she'd give away her delight at this big step in Noah's personal growth, Maddie left them to it while she retrieved the groceries she'd bought before she drove to the airport. She thought Jesse might want to have a warm drink before what she was certain would be a long night, so she set the kettle to boil and left a can of the hot cocoa mix that Emma preferred on the counter.

When Noah finally emerged from the laundry room, Maddie couldn't believe the transformation in her child. He looked—well, maybe not happy, but as if he'd overcome a barrier.

"They've all eaten, Mom," Noah told her. "I fed two."

"Well done." Maddie mouthed a thank-you to Jesse, who stood behind him.

"It's not bad once you get used to their claws," Noah mused.

"When we were here before you didn't even like them near you. What's different?" she asked curiously.

"Jesse said they'd die if we didn't help. He said God put people in charge of animals, so it's our job to help them." Noah's face scrunched up as he thought about it. "Jesse said the puppies make that noise 'cause their stomachs hurt 'cause they're hungry. I didn't want them to feel like my stomach does when it needs dinner."

"What kind of feeling is that?" Maddie asked. She'd never heard him speak so long.

To her surprise, Noah looked directly into her eyes. "Hurting."

"I see." A bit misty-eyed at this revelation from her often uncommunicative son, Maddie touched his shoulder. "I'm very proud of you for caring about the puppies, Noah."

"I'm the Ark Man, in charge of animals." His chest puffed out. He glanced at Jesse. "We're the caregivers."

"Yes, we are." Jesse held up his hand to high-five Noah, and after a moment the boy slowly returned the greeting. "We made up the middle-of-the-night feedings, too. Your very smart child figured I wouldn't have to stay up for so long if they were ready."

"Good thinking," she praised, privately noting that the former minister looked more tired than her young son. "I boiled the kettle if you want some cocoa. And there's a snack if you're hungry. I'm sure you know where everything is better than I do, so we'll get going home."

"That's nice of you." Jesse handed Noah a cookie, then bit into one himself. "Thank you."

"You'll set an alarm?" At his questioning look, she added, "So you won't sleep past the feeding time."

"I won't. I promise."

"Caregivers don't forget, right, Jes—I mean PBX?" Noah almost grinned.

"Never, Ark Man." He and Noah shared a look that brought a lump to Maddie's throat.

I don't know how Jesse's accomplished this, but please, don't let him leave just when Noah's finally beginning to come out of his shell.

Seeing the pair studying her with odd looks, she blushed, faked a cough, then said, "So we'll be off. Have a good rest, Jesse. I'll come and check on you and the puppies on my way to work tomorrow morning. Okay?"

Jesse nodded, but he didn't answer.

"Good night, then." She picked up her bag and shepherded Noah toward the door.

"Maddie?"

"Yes?" She stopped to face Jesse.

"Thank you. For everything. From me and from Gran, for the flowers you ordered for her, the encouraging note and for looking after her business. We appreciate it." Jesse's gentle blue eyes rested on her with an odd look that brought butterflies to Maddie's stomach.

He's just being friendly.

"Emma is our friend. So are you. Noah and I want to help both of you however we can." She said goodnight once more then ushered Noah out the door and into the car.

As she drove away she noted that Jesse remained in the doorway, backlit by the lamps she'd switched on earlier to make the house feel homey.

"Mom?"

"Yes, Noah?" Maddie knew what was coming.

"I really like Jesse."

"Me, too, son. He's a good friend."

"Do you think Dad would be mad that I like him?" Worry seeped through Noah's quiet voice.

"What do you think?" Maddie temporized, having no ready answer.

Silence stretched for a long while.

"I think that if Dad knew Jesse, he would like him." Noah's voice gained confidence as he spoke. "Jesse talks about God all the time, about what He wants us to do and what Jesus would do. That's kind of like Dad, isn't it?"

Jesse was *nothing* like Liam. But Maddie didn't say that. Noah had taken an important step, made a new friend. Now, thanks to that dratted list of rules, he was having second thoughts.

"Is it wrong to be friends with Jesse, Mom?" His doubts made her rush to respond.

"No, son. Being friends with Jesse certainly isn't wrong." She hated feeling so defensive, then suddenly remembered a Bible verse from long ago. "The Bible says God directs our paths. I think God brought Jesse into our lives and He wouldn't do that if it was wrong, would He?"

"No. I remember Dad said God never does wrong things." Noah heaved a sigh. "That's good. Because I really like Jesse."

"Why?" Maddie asked, curious as to how Jesse had been able to reach Noah when many others had failed.

"He doesn't make me feel weird. Maybe I am kinda weird," Noah admitted thoughtfully. "But when I'm with Jesse I feel like he's okay with me being weird and then that helps me be okay with it, too."

Acceptance. That's exactly what Jesse had offered her, as well, Maddie mused as she drove onto her land. It was the one thing her father and Liam had never offered, the one thing she so desperately craved. To be accepted for who she was, faults and all.

To feel worthy of being loved.

When Noah was in bed, Maddie sat on her deck, staring into the desert as she organized her schedule in her mind. She was the longest-serving employee at Quilt Essentials. Emma had left her in charge, so keeping the store running was up to her. There were many things to think about.

Immediately, her body tightened with tension and fear took hold. What if she messed up? What if she did something so wrong that it cost Emma a lot of money to fix? What if Jesse was sorry he'd said he trusted her?

You need a protector, Madelyn. You're not smart enough to be trusted with anything important.

While she stared into the night sky, Liam's denigrations played over and over, until fear held her firmly in its grip.

"I can't do it, God. Liam was right. I *don't* know how to run a business," she confessed, pouring out her deepest heart, as Emma always urged. "I'm not good at being responsible."

She'll come back to find you've made her business better than ever. Gran trusted you enough to leave you in charge while she went away. My grandmother believes in you, Maddie. So do I.

Maddie stared at her solar butterfly for a long time. Then she took a deep breath and slowly exhaled, pushing out doubt and drawing in courage. Gaining confidence was her goal. Okay, this was the time to prove herself. With God's help, she *would* do this and finally repay sweet, generous Emma for all those times she'd listened and encouraged when Maddie had so desperately needed a friend.

Somehow it was reassuring to know that her new friend Jesse would also be there for her if she asked. But Maddie would do that only if she absolutely had to, because her days of being weak and needy were over. Hadn't she put away the romantic, girlish dreams she'd clung to all those years she'd been married to Liam?

She *was* learning to be independent and that meant remembering Jesse could only ever be a friend.

Maddie was never going to let anyone get close enough to hurt her again.

Chapter Four

Jesse groggily pushed his way out of a solar-butterfly-filled dream to answer the impatient summons of his grandmother's doorbell.

"Coming," he called, as he dragged himself up from the sofa where he'd spent the night. He needed a shower, a shave and a change of clothes, but because the doorbell kept up its persistent ringing he yanked open the front door, desperate for silence to quell the pounding in his head.

"Good morning." A vibrant Maddie stood on the doorstep, black hair gleaming in the brilliant sun. She wore a bright pink cardigan over a demure sundress splashed with tropical flowers.

"Morning." Next to Maddie's beauty Jesse felt like scum.

"I'm sorry to wake you. It's just that I need to be at work and I figured you'd need a ride to your truck and… Are you all right, Jesse?" Her glance revealed her concern.

"I'm fine. I had a restless night and fell asleep on the

sofa." He translated her frown. "Don't worry. The puppies were fed, three times."

"Oh. Good." She stood there, gripping the handles of her green bag, obviously waiting for…?

"Sorry. I'm still a bit muzzy." He opened the door wide. "Come in."

"Thanks." Maddie's cheeky grin made him feel much better. "I'll put on some coffee if you'll change the puppies' papers."

"Mmm…" He licked his lips. "Did I mention I think you're an amazing woman? And that I love coffee?"

"I understand." She laughed, more of a carefree giggle really, but it suited her. "Strong double-creamed coffee coming right up."

"Thank you," he whispered, then paused as a new thought crossed his mind.

"Something wrong?" Maddie set her bag on the hall table.

"You, uh, said you didn't cook." Jesse didn't want to hurt her feelings, but he needed coffee to get him going in the morning and he sure didn't want to have to drink slough water. He kept his head averted. "So can you…?"

Hmm, not the most delicate approach.

"Can I make decent coffee?" Maddie said for him. He lifted his head and found her green eyes laughing at him. "Yes. I had to learn because Liam didn't drink coffee."

"And you're—ah, how shall I say it?" He widened his eyes.

"I can make coffee, Jesse. Very good coffee." Her narrowed gaze dared him to argue. Then she laughed. "Have to because I'm addicted to the stuff, remember?"

"I said you were amazing, right? And very talented?" He winked at her, closed the door and led the way to the kitchen.

Maddie opened a cupboard, selected a fresh container of coffee and opened it. Jesse paused for a moment to inhale the aroma of the fragrant grounds before he entered the laundry room to the whine of the puppies.

Thoughts of a hot, steamy cup of java kept him going as he restored the room to a semblance of cleanliness. He was about to snitch a cup of brew to sip before he mixed the formulas when Maddie appeared with a trayful of bottles and a very large steaming mug.

"I'm not the only coffee addict, am I?" she teased.

"Nope. Thank you." Jesse sipped the perfectly creamed coffee and allowed it to slide down his throat, hoping it would zip directly to his bloodstream. Then he set the cup aside, scooped up a puppy and began the now familiar ritual of feeding one hungry mouth after another.

"Even though you don't have triangles on the floor, I'll help you." Maddie giggled, then pulled a stool from the hallway and perched on it.

"But your dress—" he warned.

"Will be fine." She smiled at him, took a drink from her own steaming mug, then spread a large towel in her lap and lifted a puppy.

Jesse found something sweetly intimate about sitting here with Maddie in the early morning, tending to the puppies and sipping coffee together. It made him recall those daydreams he'd once had, silly imaginings of sharing his life with Eve. In fact, she was probably doing that right now. Only she was sharing with Rob, his best friend and the music minister in what Jesse had once called his home church. A lump lodged in his throat.

Lord, how could I have been so wrong about everything?

"Jesse?" Maddie's hand on his shoulder jerked him back to the present.

He pushed away the feelings of betrayal and teased, "Still here. Did you think I'd fallen asleep?"

"No. But the puppy has and there's another waiting to take his place. Drink your coffee. It'll wake you up while I fetch you another dog."

She scooped the puppy out of his hand before he could object, and by the time he'd taken a small glug of coffee, she replaced it with another starving mouth and a fresh bottle.

With careful manipulation Jesse managed to wedge the pup and bottle in one arm so he could use his free hand to hold his cup, as he struggled to clear his brain of dreams that could never be.

Eve and I weren't perfect together because she never believed in me. Not really. Otherwise she'd never have blamed me for not helping Scott. How could she have thought I was working with him to feed my ego?

But she was right. I am to blame.

"So what do you have planned for today?" Maddie's gentle query brought reality's return as she selected another pup and began feeding it.

"Get my truck tire fixed." Jesse discovered that as long as he kept his eyes on Maddie, the day seemed full of potential. "It's very good coffee. Thank you."

"You're welcome." She smiled and that simple stretch

of her pink lips lifted the heaviness from his heart. "I wish I didn't have to ask you to look after these fellows, but I didn't know who else…"

"It's fine. I'll catch some sleep later."

"What were you thinking about just now, Jesse?" she said in a very quiet voice. "Or should I ask whom?"

Normally he'd have brushed off the question or made some goofy response, but the compassion on Maddie's sweet face wouldn't permit a response that was less than honest. This must be why Emma loved Maddie, because of her caring concern, even for him, someone she barely knew.

"You don't have to tell me," she said in a self-conscious tone. "It's just that you've heard so much about my pitiful life that—"

"Your life isn't pitiful," he said sternly. "It's full of quilting and Wranglers Ranch and Gran's store and your child. By the way, where is the Ark Man this morning?"

"Noah's having breakfast at Wranglers. Sophie's making his favorite—waffles made in triangles, with blackberry syrup." Maddie arched her eyebrows. "You don't want to tell me your thoughts."

"It's kind of you to ask, but…" Though moved by her offer, Jesse didn't want to drag her down with his sad history.

"You don't think I'd understand." Maddie's whole face expressed her hurt before she ducked her head.

"No." He hated that he'd offended her. "It's me. I don't like to talk about my past."

"Me, neither." Her focus rested on something beyond the laundry room. "I'm trying to concentrate on the future, on my new life."

"As a widow, you mean?" He didn't quite understand why, but Maddie had suddenly tensed, as if whatever was in her past was painful.

"More as a new person, an independent person who is strong enough to build a good life for herself and her son." She frowned. "I'm trying to forget my past but—sometimes it seems like there are things you'll never be able to forget. Do you know what I mean?"

"Yes." He nodded. "In a way I suppose I'm trying to do the same."

"To forget the boy who died." Maddie said it gently, as if she thought the words would hurt him, but it wasn't the words that hurt Jesse. It was knowing he'd failed Scott. She handed him a puppy and a bottle and said, "You need a fresh group of kids to work with."

"No!" The word exploded out of him. Maddie blinked in surprise.

"Then why work at Wranglers Ranch?" While she waited for his response Maddie started feeding another dog.

"My parents raised four sons. My brothers are still there, ranching with Dad." Jesse didn't know why he was telling her this. He'd never shared a lot of personal details with anyone. "I was kind of an oddball kid. Never quite fit in. But then I had this…experience I guess you'd call it."

"Oh." Maddie blinked but said nothing more as she waited for him to explain.

"I'd been riding the hills and I stopped to rest the horse. I was lying on the grass, watching the clouds float past. Ever done that?" Would she understand? Jesse had never shared these memories with anyone, including his former fiancée. Because he'd somehow known that Eve wasn't the type of woman to lie on the grass and daydream about clouds.

And you think Maddie is? Because of that butterfly?

"I know exactly what you mean. I used to do that, too. Only I made up stories about the clouds." Maddie's eyes sparkled. "One was a prince swooping in to carry me away. Another was a house that was a real home. I'd always see a cloud that made me wish for a big happy family." She looked down, her lashes covering her expressive eyes. "Mostly I dreamed of freedom. Silly things like that."

Freedom? That tweaked Jesse's curiosity about the lovely Maddie, but he forced his brain back on the topic.

"Well anyway, I was lying there, watching the clouds, and all at once I just knew that God wanted me to work with kids." Jesse clamped his lips together. It sounded puerile put like that.

"How wonderful to know your purpose with such assurance." Maddie's voice echoed her wide-eyed admiration. "Amazing."

"It was, kind of." A rush of relief whooshed out of him. She understood.

"So you became a youth pastor? I know you'd be good at that because you have such a way with Noah."

"He's a great kid." Jesse felt a bubble of pleasure in having shared something so personal with Maddie. "Well, that's the last pup." He grinned as he offered her a hand up. "I promised Gran I'd take care of her babies, so when she emails you to ask, and she will, you can reassure her that they're being well cared for."

"You're doing a great job." Maddie's fingers clung

to his for a moment as she rose unsteadily. "Thanks. My foot went to sleep."

"Better now?"

"Yes. I need to get to work." She tossed the towel into a nearby hamper before smoothing a hand over her dress. "If you're ready, I'll drive you to Wranglers Ranch now to get your truck."

"Maddie, you don't have to worry about me." A little spot inside him warmed at her thoughtfulness. "I'll call a cab. I don't want to make you late for work."

"I won't be if we leave soon. A taxi from here will cost you a fortune." Her forehead pleated in a frown as she checked the plain, cheap watch around her wrist, her concern about arriving late at Quilt Essentials evident.

"What if I tag along with you to Quilt Essentials?" A frown appeared on her pretty face, then melted into an expression he didn't understand. "No?"

"Of course that's fine. I'm sure you want to check that I'm doing everything right while your grandmother is away." Though Maddie said it evenly there was a hint of hurt underlying her comment.

"No, no. That isn't what I meant." Why hadn't he thought before he spoke? "I meant I could be there if you need me to do anything. Then, and feel free to say no if you want to, I thought maybe I could borrow your car to get to the ranch. I promise I'd have it back to you quickly. That way you wouldn't have to waste time driving me around."

She didn't look convinced.

"I really would like to help if I can, Maddie," Jesse insisted. "You've done a lot for me. I don't know anything about running Gran's store, and fortunately, I don't have to, because you're the one she entrusted that to. But if I can do anything to make it easier, I'd like to."

Maddie remained silent, her face unreadable.

"On second thought, my plan probably isn't that great. I'll rent a vehicle until I get my truck fixed."

"I think your idea is very generous and I'm happy to lend my car. But could we please leave soon?" Maddie checked her watch once more, frowned and shook her wrist. "This has stopped again." She walked into the kitchen and gasped at the time on the wall clock. "I have to leave!"

"Let's go." Jesse closed the laundry room, grabbed his keys and his wallet and led the way to the front door. "By the time I get back the dogs will be ready for another feeding. I'll do that, then go check out the truck. Will you need your car before two?"

"I have to pick up Noah at Wranglers at three thirty and take him to swimming lessons. He's having a special one on one lesson." She led the way to her car, got into the driver's seat and, when his belt was fastened, drove toward his grandmother's store. "We have a quilt shop hop running this week, so it's going to be a busy day. I hope no one calls in sick."

"A quilt shop hop? Is that a dance or something?" Her musical laughter made him think of butterflies and rainbows and possibilities.

"A shop hop is a kind of tour of quilt shops in the area," Maddie explained. "Guests bring in a passport that we stamp, and when they have it filled with stamps from different stores, they can enter it for a quilting cruise."

"A *quilting* cruise?" For a moment he thought she was joking, but her face said she was quite serious.

"I talked Emma into joining the other shops for that promotion. It's such good advertising. We've had a number of sign-ups for workshops when quilters stop by for the stamp and see what we have to offer." Maddie bit her lip. "Now I wish I'd kept silent. It makes for a lot of extra work."

"That's good, isn't it? You want more customers," Jesse reminded her. "That's another reason you should buy out Gran. She depended on word-of-mouth advertising, but you're up on current methods of merchandising that make it more fun for the clients. I noticed there's now a web page for Quilt Essentials. You set it up, didn't you, Maddie?"

"Yes. In high school I learned I have a knack for computer stuff. But—"

He chortled at her flushed face, amused by her embarrassment.

"You're a businesswoman." Jesse said it intentionally, hoping she'd realize what was so plain to him. "It's obvious why Gran thinks you'd make an excellent owner for her shop."

"Well, I love working there, but I can't own Quilt Essentials. It's too complicated and I'm not good at complicated."

Jesse thought of Noah's quilt and wanted to say, "Seriously?" But Maddie pulled into a parking spot beside the store and thrust the lever into Park. She turned to face him.

"I will do the very best I can to keep the store running while she's recovering. I promise you that. Now I must get to work."

Maddie gathered up her bag, a lunch container and a

change of footwear, orange strappy sandals that showed a daring side to this modest mom, before exiting the car. He walked with her to the front door.

"I'll wait until you see if there's something you need help with," he said as she unlocked the door. "You're positive you want to let me borrow your car?"

"I'm positive." Her smile reassured him.

"Then thank you very much." Jesse watched her welcome two other employees, then explain about Emma's accident.

"I hope we can surprise her with what we accomplish by the time she comes back to Quilt Essentials," she said to the group, then introduced him.

Jesse shook their hands and tried to ignore their curious glances from Maddie to him.

"I'm sorry to rush, ladies, but we must restock the batiks before we get a rush of clients. Davina, can you get started shelving that new shipment?" She turned from the younger woman to the older one. "Anna, would you cut some more fat quarters from that new Kaffe Fassett fabric collection?" When Anna nodded, Maddie smiled, then added, "I'm going across to the warehouse to bring over some more kits. After Valentine's Day, if not before, I'll change the window to an Easter display. Easter's not that far away."

Valentine's? Easter? This was January!

Jesse almost laughed as the women moved to carry out Maddie's directions. He trailed behind her, out the door and across the parking lot to a space he knew Emma had purchased two years ago for storage. When Maddie noticed him following, she blinked.

"Oh, the car keys," she said with an embarrassed

look. "I'm sorry. I forgot. We'll have to go back to the store."

"First let's get whatever you need here," he said, and held out his arms. "Load me up. I'm good at carrying."

"Thank you." With a distracted smile Maddie selected a number of kits to fill a big cart sitting nearby. "We can sell more than that," she murmured thoughtfully. Jesse knew she wasn't talking to him as she selected another twenty premade quilt kits. "When our picnic basket project finishes next week, these will go like crazy." She dragged a second cart forward and filled it, too. "That's enough for now."

Jesse touched her arm, stopping her from manhandling the carts out the door.

"I'm here to help, remember?" He eased them forward, hooked one to the other, then paused to smile at her. "You know what, Maddie? Whoever told you you're not smart enough to run a business is just plain stupid. You're quick, you're intelligent and you know your market. All you lack is a little faith in the abilities God's given you."

"I—"

"You've got what it takes to make Gran's store better than it's ever been, and I'm going to keep telling you that until you believe it." He grunted as he shoved the carts ahead of him. "Now will you please show me how to steer this thing so I don't run down someone in the parking lot?"

Maddie studied him for a moment, then grinned. "You have to take off the brake," she explained with a chuckle. Something he couldn't describe flickered in her green eyes. "Thanks for the encouragement, Jesse."

"You're welcome." He made a production of getting the supplies into the store, but privately he thought he'd never had more fun. Maddie blushed at his outrageous teasing, peeked to see if the other two women noticed and told him to hush a couple of times. When everything was inside and the carts returned, he held out his palm. "Keys, please."

Maddie handed them over.

"You're absolutely sure you're okay with me driving your car?" he said seriously.

"I'm very okay with it," she told him. "Unless you're not back by three o'clock."

"I'll be here," he promised. "Have fun, ladies," he called.

Jesse drove away, surprised to note when he turned the corner to leave the lot that Maddie was still standing in the doorway where he'd left her, staring after him.

"Probably worried about me wrecking her car," he muttered.

But he knew that wasn't true. Maddie wasn't just beautiful. She was intelligent and kind and very generous. Who, he wanted to know, had tried to make her think she was less than that?

He needed to know so that he could be a good friend.

"You can't work if you're feeling ill, Jayne. I'll cover your shift." *How?* Maddie didn't say that into the phone. Instead she said, "I hope you feel better soon."

A moment later she hung up, focused on finding a way to deal with this newest problem. Staffing was by far her most difficult issue in managing Emma's shop. Customers kept her busy for the next few hours, so that when she finally glanced at the clock on the wall she was stunned to notice it was ten to three. She would be able to pick up Noah by using the time as her lunch break, but there was no way she could be absent for the extra hour and a half needed for her son's swimming lesson.

I'm trying to help Emma, God. I'm trying to trust You. Can't You help me?

A customer interrupted her prayer and Maddie became engrossed in showing the woman how to rate the color values of various fabrics for her new quilt project. Only when that client left the shop did Maddie notice Jesse standing near the door, watching her.

"Hi." Why was she so glad to see him? She waited behind the counter as he approached her. "I didn't notice you come in."

"I'm not surprised. You were completely focused on helping your customer." He checked his watch. "When do you need to pick up Noah?"

"Now." She snatched her bag from under the counter, told her second in command that she was leaving and hurried toward the door which Jesse held open. "Thanks."

"Mind if I tag along?" he asked.

"Sure." Though Maddie was surprised by his request, she didn't have time to question it. He'd parked directly in front of the store so it took mere seconds to get in, buckle her seat belt and back out. "I can hardly wait to email Emma that the store is busy. We even had to find extra room for a class today and then it was bedlam."

"Bedlam? In a quilt store?" He looked unconvinced.

"Utter bedlam," Maddie assured him with a grin.

"After a class, people always seem inspired and eager to shop for their next project. It's a good thing we have the new spring stock arriving every day because we need it. Some of the kids' lines—" Realizing she was babbling, she broke off to focus on her driving. "Sorry. I get carried away sometimes."

"It's nice to listen to you talk about your work," Jesse said. "You get this fervor in your voice that says you enjoy what you do."

"I do," she assured him. "Who wouldn't love working in such a wonderfully creative atmosphere?"

"Then why don't you buy out Emma? Or at least go into a partnership with her?" Jesse's warm gaze studied her. "You're obviously a natural."

"Are we back on that again?" She shot him an arched look.

"Why not? It's a valid question," he retorted.

"It's true that I love fabrics and quilting. And I love sharing what I know." Maddie allowed herself to dream, just for a second, that she owned Quilt Essentials. Then she quickly shook her head. "But I wouldn't be a success at running the store."

Jesse frowned. "Why not? You managed today."

"A few days don't make me qualified to run a business."

"But you've run it on several occasions when Gran was away, right? You didn't have any problems, did you?" The intensity of his stare made her nervous.

"No, but I always knew she was coming back. Emma does the ordering. She has a personal relationship with our suppliers and she's developed a good rapport to get just the right blend of stock. I don't have connections like that." Maddie glanced at the clock and hoped Noah was busy with his video game and hadn't noticed she was running behind. She felt guilty, because she usually prayed he'd spend less time with the machine and more time interacting with people, and today it was her fault he wasn't.

"You build connections by being in business," Jesse countered.

"Besides that, Emma keeps a running mental tally of what we've sold each day. I'm not that clever with numbers."

"You mean…" Jesse thought for a minute. "Like, you haven't balanced the cash register these past few days?"

"Yes, of course I have." Maddie felt indignant at his implication. "We balance to the penny. Every day. It's mostly credit card receipts, anyway, so it's not hard."

"Then what do you mean, you're not good with numbers?" he asked.

"It takes a lot more than balancing a till to run a business." Maddie could tell he wasn't going to stop asking questions, so she began enumerating. "There's stock to purchase—not too much and hopefully not the wrong kind because we could get stuck with poor choices that don't sell and then we'd lose money." She glanced at him as she continued.

"Okay." His face encouraged her to continue.

"You also have to know the trends, keep in touch with what's happening in the quilting world, innovations, et cetera. There are wages to pay, overhead, taxes, lawyers, accountants and staff schedules." She was out of breath. "Running a business is complicated."

"So you've thought it through pretty thoroughly."

Jesse pinned her with a look. "Emma has a bookkeeper to help her. No reason you couldn't do the same. I think you're pretending to have a lot less skill than you do. Or that you've listened to someone who wanted you to think that."

Maddie frowned. What did he mean? Had Emma said something—but no, she knew her friend would guard whatever secrets she'd been told, although Maddie had never disclosed details of her troubled marriage. She'd been too ashamed.

"I think you'd make a very good business owner, Maddie. But I guess if you don't want to do it..." Jesse shrugged.

"It's not that. I'd love to buy Quilt Essentials and have my own business." Maddie couldn't stop the passionate words from blurting out. "It would be something of my own, something that *I* could make work, could build on."

A way to prove I'm not the airhead Liam always said I was.

But that negative thought drowned under the plethora of ideas filling her mind. If she let them, the ideas would grow into fantastic dreams, but Maddie seldom allowed those dreams to progress. She stopped them now, as she always did, because she'd learned that there was no point in dreaming.

"So why don't you do it?" Jesse asked. "Where's your faith?"

"I'm afraid faith isn't something I have much of," she admitted, with a quick glance over her shoulder before she turned. "It's hard to trust God when it feels like He doesn't answer."

She expected Jesse to counter her comment with something ministerly, to tell her that God always answered, or some similar response. To her surprise he remained silent, his face thoughtful as he stared through the windshield. She wondered if he'd ever experienced the same unanswered doubts as she had.

Jesse Parker's faith is none of your business, an inner voice chided. Maddie swallowed a rush of shame that her thoughts were getting so personal about this man she barely knew. A glance at the clock made her catch her breath.

"You cannot be late," she muttered to herself, forced to brake because of the driver in front.

"A few minutes won't make that much difference," Jesse said. He took a second look at her, frowned and asked, "Will it?"

"Yes." She didn't intend to explain, but he kept looking at her so she finally said, "Noah's autism makes him very conscientious about scheduling. It upsets him when there are unplanned changes in his day. In his mind there's an order for everything and disrupting that order throws him off-kilter. He gets angry and uncomfortable."

"Ah. That explains his adherence to his father's rules." That thoughtful look again filled Jesse's face.

"Today's going to really throw him off because not only am I late picking him up, but I'll have to cancel his swimming lesson," she said with a frown as she turned toward Wranglers Ranch.

"Why?"

"One of Emma's staff phoned in sick. Two are on

holiday and one is off on maternity leave. We're really shorthanded. I'll have to fill in the late afternoon shift."

"Added on to the day you've already worked?" Jesse frowned when she nodded. "I guess you can do that once in a while in a pinch, but it sounds to me like Quilt Essentials needs to hire more staff."

"We do. Emma was going to work on that when she returned. Now it will have to wait." Maddie couldn't get near Wranglers' main house where she thought Noah would be. She had to take another spot farther away. She could see Noah leaning against the fence, fidgeting, head down, shoulders hunched in the bustling midst of other more exuberant kids who were probably either beginning or ending a camp. He didn't even notice she'd arrived. "Oh dear."

She'd barely slid her fingers around the door handle to open it when Jesse touched her arm. "Maddie?"

"Yes?" She didn't want to stop and talk, but good manners prevented her from ignoring him.

"I could take Noah to his lesson, and back to Emma's house afterward," he offered. "I'd feed him supper so you wouldn't have to worry about getting back for that."

She wanted to say yes so badly. But Jesse was a stranger and Noah struggled with the unfamiliar.

"I don't think he'd go for it," she said, forcing a smile as she declined. "But thank you for offering. Excuse me. I need to get him."

Maddie hurried toward her son, her heart aching at his obvious confusion. She called his name when she got closer, but he didn't look up. When she arrived she didn't hug him as most parents would have. She wanted to, so desperately, but she knew Noah would shrink back. Physical contact wasn't something he needed as much as she did. In fact, touching made him antsier, so aside from a morning and evening hug, Maddie controlled her longing to hold him close.

"You weren't here." Noah's whisper barely penetrated the din around them.

"I know. I'm sorry I was late. Jayne called in sick at the last minute." Maddie shepherded him toward the car.

"Will she be okay?" Noah asked. When she nodded and opened the back car door, he stepped inside, pausing halfway when he saw Jesse. "Oh."

"I came along for the ride." Jesse flashed his Hollywood grin at Noah. "What's up, Doc?"

There was a pause. Noah frowned. "Huh?"

Maddie knew he didn't understand Jesse's colloquialism.

"Jesse means how's it going." She shot an apologetic look at her passenger, then when Noah didn't respond, clarified further. "He's asking how you are, honey."

"That isn't what he said." Noah buckled his seat belt as he thought about it, then responded. "I am well, thank you."

"Oh. Good." Jesse blinked at the very formal response.

"Noah, I'm sorry, but you're going to have to miss swimming today." Maddie drove between the ranch gates and into traffic, dreading upsetting him.

"I don't have an excuse to miss my lesson, so that would be rude." Noah's face tightened as he repeated another of his father's rules. "You never miss an appointment unless you're sick or in an accident."

"This is something like that. Jayne is sick and that

means I have to cover her shift, so I can't take you to the pool today," she reiterated. "I'm so sorry, son."

"But I have my suit and towel and my goggles in my backpack. I'm ready." Noah began to fuss with his hands, agitated by the alteration in routine, as she'd known he would be. "I have to go."

"We can't today."

For the hundredth time Maddie asked God why her son had to have autism. It kept him from enjoying so much in life. Liam's rules only added to the burden of worry that deprived Noah even more, rules now so ingrained she wondered if her son could ever be free of them.

"Hey, Ark Man, I have an idea. Could I take you to your swimming lesson? That way your mom could fill in for Jayne." Jesse ignored the swift shake of her head and continued speaking. "I used to be a pretty good swimmer, you know. I even got my lifeguard badge."

Maddie so wished he hadn't said that. Noah often spoke of becoming a lifeguard, but that was so he could be in charge and make sure everyone followed the rules.

"I don't think—" She was about to brush off Jesse when Noah spoke.

"That's a good plan. He could take me, Mom. Then I wouldn't have to break my appointment." He sounded so serious.

"Well, Mom?" Jesse quirked an eyebrow. "What do you say? Tanner drove my truck to Emma's store, so Noah and I could go in it. You'd have your car, so you could take your time at work and join us at Emma's house when you're free. Noah could help me feed the puppies again, too. I would appreciate the assistance."

Maddie was about to refuse, until Jesse added that last bit. She recalled last night and the way he'd gotten Noah engaged in the puppies. She glanced at the youth pastor and quickly looked away. It was hard to concentrate on her driving with Jesse so attentive, as if he valued whatever she had to say. Recently she'd wondered if Noah needed some separation from her. Maybe it would be a good thing for him to spend time with a man like Jesse, who didn't stint on encouragement and praise.

"It's up to Noah. Is that what you want to do, son?" She glanced at him in the rearview mirror, saw his forehead pleat as he thought it through.

"I would like to go swimming," Noah said. Then added, "And after I will help Jesse with the puppies, because I think he needs help. And so do the puppies."

Maddie wanted to squeal with delight. Noah had actually thought about someone else's needs outside of his own tightly contained world.

"Then I say thank you very much, Jesse." Maddie pulled into her parking spot at the store and switched off the car. "We appreciate it."

"No biggie." He climbed out and extended a hand to Noah, who hesitated a moment before grasping it and exiting the vehicle. "Friends help friends."

Maddie had certainly never had a friend like Jesse. What a relief that he wasn't looking for more than that, because she was never going to be vulnerable again.

"Have fun." She ruffled Noah's hair, then pulled a twenty-dollar bill out of her pocket and held it toward Jesse. "For pizza," she explained, confused when he frowned and pushed it away.

"You helped me. Now it's my turn to help you. Because we're friends. Okay?"

Maddie couldn't stop her heart from skipping a beat at his cheerful smile. In fact, she couldn't stop staring at him at all. All she could do was nod her head.

"You're a very nice friend to have, Jesse."

Chapter Five

Jesse hid a smile as Noah struggled to follow every one of his swim teacher's directions. The kid had grit. When the lesson was finished, Jesse added his praise to the teacher's, commending the boy on his determination.

"You're going to be a strong swimmer," he added as he drove to Emma's.

"I'm going to be a lifeguard." Noah stared straight ahead.

"How come?" Surprised by the resolve in his voice, Jesse waited for the answer.

"So I can make people obey the rules," Noah explained in a tight little voice.

"Why is that so important?" Jesse puzzled over his inner yen to help Maddie's son. He couldn't figure out whether that desire stemmed from his lifelong need to offer help when he could, or if it was because Noah was Maddie's son and she was his friend.

"Sinning is bad." It sounded as if Noah had heard those words many times before. "My dad said keeping the rules helps us not to sin."

"I guess keeping rules sometimes helps do that." Feeling as if he was about to tiptoe through a morass of theology, Jesse tried to explain his view. "I think not sinning has more to do with loving God and wanting to live the way He wants than it does with just keeping rules."

"My dad said you show you love God by keeping His rules." Noah frowned. "You think like my mom."

"I do? How does your mom think?" Jesse kept his eyes on his driving to hide his curiosity about that answer.

"She doesn't think rules are important." Again this sounded like something Noah was quoting.

"She doesn't?" Jesse gaped. "Are you telling me your mom doesn't think it's important if you make your bed or clean up your room or feed your dog?"

"Those aren't important rules." Disdain oozed from Noah's voice.

"They kind of are," Jesse countered as he drove into Emma's driveway. "Your dog would die if she didn't get food. If you don't make your bed you don't rest very well. And if you don't clean up your room, how can your laundry get done?"

He switched off the car, waiting for his passenger to digest that.

"I already do all those things." Noah unbuckled his seat belt. "Anyway, a messy room isn't a sin. Hurting someone is."

"Maybe a messy room hurts your mom." Jesse got out and held open Noah's door. "You don't want to do that."

The boy's jaw set in a stubborn line that Jesse struggled to understand. They walked toward the house, where Noah waited while Jesse unlocked the door. Something was going on.

"Because she already hurt a lot after your dad died, right?" Jesse hinted, unable to decipher the tension on the boy's face.

Noah shrugged, as if Maddie's suffering didn't matter. He set his backpack on the foyer bench, then motioned toward the laundry room. "Are we feeding the puppies now?"

"Judging by all the racket they're making, we'd better." Funny how Noah's impassive face lit up when he talked about those puppies. "You like feeding them now, don't you?"

"Uh-huh." Noah turned on the tap until hot water steamed out. Then he half-filled a pan with it.

"But you didn't before. Why now?" The kid behind that blank expression intrigued Jesse.

"'Cause they need me." Noah didn't even spare him a glance as he retrieved a tray of dog bottles from the fridge, opened the laundry room door and set them on the dryer.

Jesse set the pan of water beside the tray and placed the bottles in the water.

Without being asked Noah began to deftly replace the soiled papers with clean ones folded precisely in triangles. "I like triangles."

"I know." Jesse helped him, silently folding each paper in exactly the same way, waiting because he sensed that there was more this child needed to say.

"I'm important to the puppies."

Meaning Noah didn't feel important to anyone else?
But Maddie loved her son and she showed it. Puz-

zled, Jesse followed Noah as they took out the garbage. When they returned to the laundry room, he was surprised by the sound of the boy's soft chuckles.

"Look at them. They're greedy." When Jesse didn't immediately sit on one of the stools, Noah frowned. "Aren't you going to help me?"

"Of course." Breaking free of his thoughts, he picked up a dog, sat down and began feeding it the warmed milk. "Noah, what did you mean? You're important to Cocoa. She needs you."

"Cocoa doesn't need *me*, she just needs somebody to give her food and water." After that astute assessment, Noah began humming as his thumb rubbed rhythmically against the puppy's shiny coat.

"Cocoa is new to you and your ranch. It takes time to get to know each other. But your mom needs you. You must know that." Jesse took a chance and spoke his thoughts. "Both she and Cocoa would probably like it a lot if you hugged them, like you're hugging that puppy."

"Really? Why?" Noah lifted his head to stare, as though he'd never thought of such a thing.

"People and dogs like contact. Cocoa would like to be petted, have her tummy rubbed, given doggy treats. She wants you to pay attention to her, to need her. I'm sure your mom would like a hug, too. Everyone wants to feel like they matter to someone. Don't you?" Jesse wasn't sure where the words came from. He never was. He only knew something inside him compelled him to speak.

"I guess." Noah's glance slid to the puppy Jesse held. "Did you used to have a dog?"

"I've had several." Jesse let him remove the full pup. Oddly, Noah didn't hand him another animal to feed, but kept on feeding them himself. "One of them was named King, a black Labrador. He loved carrots."

"Carrots?" Noah's laughter echoed in the room. "I don't think Cocoa likes carrots."

"Maybe she hasn't tasted them yet." He watched Noah continue feeding, moving easily from one pup to the next until all the animals were fed. "You're very good with these guys."

"They don't understand what happened." Noah studied the animals now crowded together in a ball to nap. He slid his fingers over the satiny coats. "They're alone and they're scared." After a long silence, he added, "Sometimes I get like that."

"Me, too," Jesse admitted very softly.

"You get scared?" Noah's head jerked up. He frowned at Jesse's nod. "Why?"

"Everyone gets scared when they don't know what to expect. It doesn't matter if you're a kid, an adult or a puppy." Though Noah kept his gaze on the small animal cradled in his palms, Jesse knew he was listening. "When I get scared I pray."

"Why?" Noah's voice was almost inaudible.

"Because God doesn't want me to be afraid."

"Why?"

"You ask tough questions, Ark Man," he teased, then shrugged. "God doesn't want me to be afraid because it shows I don't trust Him to take care of me." Jesse could see by Noah's face that he needed to clarify. "It's like you and the puppies. At first they were probably afraid of you, but then they learned that they could trust you."

"But why does God want me to trust Him?"

"Because He's our father. He's going to take care of

us, so He doesn't want us to fuss about everything." Jesse found a parallel. "Just like your mom wouldn't like it if you were always bugging her about having enough food to make supper."

Okay, given Maddie's less than stellar cooking skills, maybe that wasn't the perfect example. Noah's wrinkled nose said he was thinking the same thing.

"Your mother doesn't want you to fuss about having enough groceries because she already knows you need food to eat. She wants you to trust her to make sure you'll have it." Jesse rose, but kept his eye on the little boy.

"Dad always said Mom would forget her head." Noah put down the puppy and followed him from the room.

"I don't think that's true." Jesse couldn't let that negative comment pass without a challenge. "From what I've seen, your mother is very careful about remembering everything."

Noah didn't look convinced.

"She remembered my truck had a flat tire and loaned me her car so I could get it fixed," Jesse explained. "She remembered to make me promise I'd have her car back in time to take you for your swimming lesson, even though she's managing Emma's store."

"She doesn't usually forget swimming," Noah admitted.

"Because you're the most important thing to your mom. She would never forget anything to do with you." Jesse knew that was true. "She loves you too much for that."

Deep in thought, Noah left to wash his hands. By the time he returned to the kitchen Jesse was scouring his grandmother's stock of groceries.

"What are you looking for?" Noah followed every movement with his big knowing eyes.

"One last ingredient—ah." Jesse triumphantly located a can of pineapple in the back of Emma's pantry.

"What's that for?" Noah asked.

"Pizza. Want to help make it?" Jesse almost laughed out loud at the look of shock on the boy's thin face.

"We eat pizza at a restaurant. I don't think you can make pizza at home." There was a warning in Noah's serious response.

"Homemade pizza is the best, son." Jesse grinned at him. "And my pizza is way better than any a restaurant makes. Want to help me?"

"I don't know how." There was that worry again.

"I'll show you." He winked, striving for some lightness.

"I'm not allowed to use the stove." Noah frowned. "That's a big rule."

"I'll do the oven part. You and I can make the pizza and when your mom comes to pick you up, we'll surprise her with our creation." Jesse wondered if the boy's father had ever taught him to consider his mother. "Having something hot and ready to eat will be nice for her after working so hard, don't you think?"

"I guess." Noah wore a confused look. "What do we do first?"

"The crust." Jesse grinned. "Gran keeps some of that made up in the freezer, so all we have to do is get the other stuff ready while we wait for it to thaw. How would you like to grate some cheese?"

"I don't know—"

"I'll show you," Jesse interrupted, grabbing a grater

and then a hunk of mozzarella cheese. "Just like this, only watch your fingers. I don't like fingernails in my pizza," he joked.

Noah didn't crack a smile as, after a pause, he settled into the task. With serious concentration he carefully grasped the cheese and touched it lightly against the grater. When nothing happened he frowned and began to set it down.

"Push a little harder. You can't hurt it," Jesse encouraged.

Though clearly uncomfortable, Noah tried again and quickly got the hang of it. He created a huge pile of shredded cheese, far too much for one pizza, but the boy's satisfaction at completing the job was obvious.

"Good work," Jesse praised, when the last bit of cheese was gone.

"I liked doing that." Noah looked surprised, but Jesse didn't give him time to dwell on it.

"Now we need to chop up some meat for our pizza. Want to do that?"

"With a knife?" Noah's forehead pleated at his nod. "Knives are a major cause of household accidents. What if—"

"I'll show you how I do it." Jesse picked up a small knife and demonstrated how to cut a crisscross pattern on the slices of ham. "We don't want big chunks," he added, then held out the knife. "Here."

"Okay." Noah exhaled heavily as if preparing to do battle. He accepted the knife tentatively, then with great precision began cutting the meat. "I like triangles," he said firmly.

"Triangles are perfect." The more Jesse worked with

this child, the more confused he became. Aside from gesticulating wildly when he was upset or frustrated, Noah did not usually exhibit the deep withdrawal he'd seen among the autistic children he'd studied during his college years. Noah was certainly high functioning and he didn't usually rage or have tantrums, so why had his father insisted on so many rules?

"Is that enough for the pizza?" At his nod, Noah set the knife down with relief. "I didn't get cut."

"No, because you were careful. Nice triangles." Jesse decided to voice a question that had been rolling through his brain. "Noah, do you have medication you need to take?"

Surprisingly, the boy made direct eye contact. "I'm not sick."

"No, of course you're not." Jesse backtracked, scrounging for a change of topic. "Is that your mom's car I hear?"

While Noah went to open the door for her, Jesse flattened the dough onto a pizza pan and tried to think it through. Maddie was a wonderful mother. She left nothing to chance. She'd said Noah was diagnosed at three. She would have had the diagnosis confirmed. She'd certainly know every detail in regard to her son's behavior. Hadn't his father?

"Hi, honey." The sound of her musical voice sent a rush of excitement through Jesse. "How was swimming?"

"Good. We're making pizza." A flicker of pride filled Noah's words.

"Really? You're *making* pizza?" She appeared in the kitchen doorway and stared.

"Jesse is." Noah shoved his hands in his pockets. "I helped. I used a knife to cut triangles."

"Your favorite. Wow." Maddie sent Jesse a grateful look before she crouched in front of her son. "What else did you do?"

"Cut up cheese with no fingernails." In spite of his flat tone, Noah's eyes sparkled. "And we fed the puppies."

"You've certainly had a busy time." Maddie brushed her hand over his head as if she couldn't help herself. Her eyes glowed with love. "Thank you for helping. But we'd better leave now so Jesse can enjoy his pizza."

Noah frowned. "But—"

"You can't go," Jesse interrupted. "The pizza is for all of us. It's our dinner. Noah and I made it to share with you."

"But you've already done so much," she protested. "I don't want to impose—"

"You aren't. There's more than enough pizza." He held her gaze. "Besides, I think Noah should taste what he helped make."

"Would you like to stay for pizza?" Obviously uncertain, Maddie looked at Noah, who didn't return her look. But the up and down jerk of his head was hard to misunderstand.

"Okay then," she said with a chuckle. "Thank you, Jesse. We'd love to stay for pizza."

While the pie baked Jesse squeezed some lemons for lemonade to go with it. Noah got involved on his laptop, so Jesse handed Maddie a cup of fresh coffee. He noted the way she arched her back to stretch it. And closed her eyes for a moment, as if searching for a second wind before facing the duties ahead.

"Busy day?" he asked.

"Very."

"That's good, isn't it?" He was confused.

"Oh yes. It's just that restocking isn't the easiest task." Maddie winced as she tilted her head to one side.

"Why is that?"

"Some of the shelves are too high and there aren't enough." She savored her coffee for a moment, then continued. "Emma's been talking of having someone build a better shelving system, but I guess that will be on hold for a while now."

"Not necessarily." Since Maddie was running his grandmother's business, Jesse figured he owed her any assistance he could offer. At least that's the excuse he gave himself. "I could build some shelves for you. I built those for Gran." He inclined his head toward the oak bookshelves he'd made several years ago to form the reading nook Emma had wanted.

"They're lovely, but I wouldn't want to interfere. Besides, it's your grandmother's business and she should be the one to decide..." Maddie's refusal died away when he shook his head at her.

"You got her email this morning, right? The one where Gran said to do whatever you needed to in order to make Quilt Essentials more functional? Besides, I'd like to help." He added ice cubes to the pitcher of lemonade and set it on the table. Then he grabbed a pad of paper and a pencil from Emma's kitchen desk. "Describe your shelves."

After a pause Maddie slowly began to explain her idea for a display unit. Her excitement grew and she talked faster and faster. Hiding his smile, Jesse sketched quickly, trying to turn her words into a picture.

"So this unit has four sides, all accessible?"

"Exactly." Her eyes sparkled. "I could really use it to display fabrics for the Easter quilt classes we'll be starting soon."

"What's an Easter quilt?" Jesse asked.

"A quilt that depicts the story of Easter in frames, kind of like stained glass windows. We've had a lot of interest in it ever since I hung the prototype." Her cheeks flushed and she tilted her head as if embarrassed. "I never thought anyone would want a class. I only wanted to make something to show potential for a new line of fabrics."

"Are you talking about the picture quilt I saw in the stockroom window, the one with the yellow trim? It had an empty tomb for the centerpiece?" Jesse gaped when she nodded. "You *made* that, pattern and all?"

"Well…yes." Maddie shifted uneasily under his stare. "It wasn't hard."

"It looks as if it has tons of pieces." The intricacy of that work had made Jesse assume it was a commercial quilt, sent from one of Gran's suppliers. "Are you sure you can teach someone to make that in—" he checked the calendar on the wall above the desk "—what? Eight classes? Easter's just over eight weeks away."

"You don't think I can do it." Her face fell and she resumed her familiar habit of knotting her fingers in her lap, her voice hesitant. "Maybe it is too big for a short class. I showed two of the other employees how to make it and they managed, but if you think—"

"What do I know about quilting? You have to teach it, Maddie," he said quickly, having just realized how he'd negated her ability. "Every quilter in town will sign up."

"I don't know. There are twelve panels," she mused aloud. "They'd have to complete more than one a week to finish in time."

Jesse mentally kicked himself. Thanks to him Maddie was now doubting herself. He started backtracking.

"Aren't some panels easier than others?" he asked. "So if they did two panels a week they'd have lots of time."

"That's what I thought, but maybe that's pushing it. I don't want anyone disappointed. It would reflect badly on Emma's business." Maddie sniffed suddenly. "I'm no cook, but is something burning?"

Muttering an unflattering expletive about himself, Jesse raced to the stove and threw open the door, lifted out the pizza and switched off the oven.

"Is it burned?" Noah studied the pie critically, a certain resignation in his voice, as if he was used to eating scorched food, but had been hoping to escape that fate.

"Just one teensy part and I'll cut that off." His pride smarting, Jesse snatched the pizza cutter and swiftly rolled it to make eight big slices. "See, Noah. Triangles. Now let's see if it's any good," he invited.

"If not you might want to join my cooking lessons," Maddie teased, eyes sparkling again. "My first one is tomorrow evening."

"You're going to do it?" Jesse was surprised she'd have enough time. But then Maddie seemed to make time for the important things.

"I have to do something," she said with a mischievous grin. "Otherwise Noah's going to be a beanpole. He's always hungry and he's growing so fast."

When they'd gathered around the table, Jesse offered a quick thanks for the food, then served mother and son before selecting the burned section for himself. He caught Maddie watching him with an amused look and before he knew it she'd switched their plates.

"Hey!"

"The cook should always eat the best part." She winked at Noah. "It's a rule, right?"

He said nothing, his mouth full of pizza, his cheeks dotted with red tomato sauce.

"Bon appétit," Maddie said, before taking a dainty bite of her food.

Jesse waited with eager expectation, charmed by her altering expression as the flavors hit her tongue. She reminded him of a connoisseur, savoring the full nuance of the spices in the tomato sauce combined with the meat and pineapple.

"This must have taken forever to make," she said after she'd swallowed. "It's really amazing pizza."

"It took very little time, but that's because Gran had the dough for the crust in the freezer." Jesse served her another slice and grinned when she didn't refuse. "The topping is pretty easy. Anybody could do it."

"Maybe I'll learn how to make pizza at my cooking lessons." Maddie sipped her lemonade. "Thank you, Jesse. When I learn how to cook, I'll return the favor and make you a meal."

"I look forward to it." They ate the rest with sporadic conversation.

Jesse wanted to ask her about Noah's diagnosis, medication, everything. He'd hoped to find an explanation for the whole rules thing. But he barely knew Noah or Maddie. He might feel there was an unexplained reason behind Noah's reliance on those rules, but he could hardly pry into their business.

"You aren't camping anymore?" His pizza gone, Noah selected one of Emma's cookies, then re-formed the soft round shape into a triangle. When it was the way he wanted, he smiled before popping it into his mouth.

"No, but my stuff's still at the campground. I guess I'd better go get it." He shrugged. "I don't need to camp when I can stay here."

"But don't you want to camp anymore?" An intense longing shone in Noah's dark gaze.

"Camping's okay for a while," Jesse explained. "But it's nice to have a house you don't have to bend over to get into." The boy's keen interest gave him an idea. "Would you like to come with me to take down the tent?"

"Yes." Noah checked his response by looking at Maddie. "Can I? Please?"

"When?" she asked in a thoughtful voice.

"Next Saturday afternoon?" Jesse chose the date specifically because he knew she'd be working. "Noah and I can have a campfire, cook our lunch and then take everything down. After all," he cajoled, "I did promise him."

"Yes, you did." Maddie smiled at her son. "That's very nice of you, Jesse. Thank you."

"And mores," Noah reminded him. "You said we'd have mores."

"S'mores," Jesse corrected, repressing his urge to smile. He didn't want the boy to feel he was being mocked. "We'll have those for dessert. What's a campfire without s'mores?"

"Yeah." Though he obviously had no idea what they were, Noah's grin stretched from one cheek to the other.

"We'll help you feed the puppies and then we'd better get home. Church is tomorrow." Maddie rose and began collecting plates.

Sensing an opportunity, Jesse asked Noah to tend to the puppies, so he wouldn't overhear their conversation. When the boy was in the laundry room Jesse began probing.

"Maddie, I don't want to be nosy, but I wondered if Noah is on any type of medication for his autism?" he asked, as they loaded the dishwasher together. "I worked with autistic kids in college one summer and most of them had a prescription."

"A lot of autistic kids do." She turned her scarred face away from him, her voice soft but with an edge. "Noah doesn't."

"Oh. Okay. Good." He didn't want to press the issue because it felt like Maddie was withdrawing. Then suddenly, she turned and faced him.

"On his first day in kindergarten Noah acted up. He didn't understand why he couldn't keep coloring. Liam was embarrassed, said he was being disobedient, so he asked the doctor to prescribe something. After my husband died I told the doctors I wanted Noah off all medication that wasn't absolutely essential." Her voice was tight, as if she'd had to defend her decision and didn't want to be reminded of that. "It made him so groggy. He wasn't Noah anymore. Liam wanted obedience, compliance. I just wanted Noah to come back. When he was on the medication his eyes were so empty."

"And?" he asked and watched as she chewed her bottom lip for a moment while staring at him.

"It didn't seem to affect him," she added in a murmur. "He's doing well in his new school. Do you think I was wrong?"

"I'm not a doctor, Maddie, so I can't say. But I do believe God gives mothers great intuition about their kids." Jesse hated the pain etched in her lovely eyes, but he felt compelled to ask the questions whirling inside his head. "I guess you could always have him tested again. When was the last time you did that?"

"Before he started at his new school and then again before Christmas." Her voice dropped. "I track him pretty closely because I missed his first diagnosis." Her voice dropped. "I wasn't, um, well." Her head lifted, eyes glittering with tears of agony. "I had a miscarriage."

"I'm so sorry, Maddie." Why hadn't he kept his mouth shut? He was causing her even more pain.

"She was the prettiest little girl. Even though she was so small, I could see her beauty. I called her Lila." Maddie swiped away a tear. "Liam said it was God's will that she died, but I couldn't understand that. Why would God want my baby to die?" The last word came out on a sob. Unfortunately, Noah arrived just in time to hear it.

"Mom?" With a frown he stared at her, then at Jesse. "What's wrong?"

"Nothing, honey. I got a little dust in my eye, but it's gone now." Maddie forced a smile, hiding her sorrow as she no doubt had many times before. "Do you have homework?"

"Did it." He grinned. "Jesse helped me while we waited for the pizza dough to thaw out."

"Was it art class again?" There was a hesitant note in Maddie's voice that Jesse didn't understand. Noah did, though, and he wore an earsplitting grin as he nodded.

"Farm animals," he said, clearly enjoying it when she groaned.

"It seems I owe you yet another thank-you, Jesse. Even double thanks."

"For helping draw animals?" He shrugged. "No problem."

"It is to me." Maddie's chagrin was obvious. "I can't draw anything but stickmen and even they look odd."

"But you do quilts good." Noah awkwardly hugged her side, bumping against her hip like an awkward calf before he moved away, head bent, so he didn't see the surprise and pleasure filling his mother's face at the unexpected contact.

But Jesse did.

"Thank you, son." Maddie's eyes welled, but she dabbed away the tears. "That's very kind of you to say. Now you'd better grab your backpack so we can get home. And don't forget to thank Jesse."

Noah did thank him. Effusively. And reminded him of his promise for next Saturday.

"It's a date," Jesse agreed.

"Thank you so much," Maddie said with a big smile. "For everything. It's been like old times to have supper at Emma's." Her face clouded. "I'm just sorry she's not here to share it."

"According to my parents, with the progress she's making she will be soon. And then Noah and I will make her our special pizza." He ruffled the boy's hair, and though Noah ducked away, Jesse knew he didn't really mind.

"That sounds great." Maddie took Noah's hand. "Okay, we're off. Thanks again."

"See you Monday," he called.

She stopped, turned and stared at him with a frown.

"To build the shelves," he reminded her, then waved off her protests. "I'll be there first thing in the morning."

"Oh. Well, thank you. Again." She opened the door, but Noah slipped under her arm and raced back to Jesse.

"I think she liked the hug," he whispered, eyes downcast.

"I know she did. You could do it more often."

"Really?" Noah frowned, then shot him a quick grin before scurrying out the door.

Jesse watched them drive away. All in all, a very good evening, he decided. He'd found the answers he'd wanted. The boy's father had been a stickler for rules. But Jesse wasn't sure that would help him understand Noah any better. It had, however, whetted his appetite to know more about sweet Maddie. In fact, his questions about her were growing exponentially.

If he pressed her too hard for more information about Noah, she'd probably blame herself again. That was the last thing Jesse wanted to see happen.

Funny how Maddie's emotional state was becoming so important to him.

Chapter Six

"It's very kind of you to build the shelves." Maddie stood in the middle of the store, arms loaded with bolts of colorful fabric, looking remarkably unruffled amid what seemed to Jesse to be pure chaos. "Especially after working all day at Wranglers."

"No problem. I just wish I could have made it Monday instead of making you wait till Thursday." He glanced around. "Can I come and go using the back door? I'll leave the saws out there."

"Sounds fine." Her smile was distracted. "Today's our afternoon piecing class, so for the next few hours we'll mostly be in the workroom. Excuse me, I'd better get this fabric cut."

He nodded, fascinated to watch her work. Each client got Maddie's complete attention. She listened to what they said then offered advice and suggestions that made each encounter very personal. Every single customer left smiling.

Jesse broke free of his musings and left after Maddie shot him a curious look. As he paused to check on the puppies sleeping in their box in the shaded truck, the door opened and the echo of laughter and happy chatter burst toward him. He smiled at the sounds of fun that emanated from Quilt Essentials as he unloaded wood, rechecked his measurements and began constructing. Gran would love to be here, though her emails said without words that she had all she could handle with her recovery.

"Thank You God for Maddie," he whispered.

As Jesse sawed and hammered in the back parking lot, he enjoyed the lovely breeze that kept his shady spot from becoming too hot. He'd just finished assembling the base for the unit when Maddie appeared.

"Coffee time." She held out a big steaming mug, then frowned. "You're welcome to drink it inside if you want."

"Thanks, but it's such a gorgeous day that it's a pleasure to be outdoors." He accepted a napkin holding two cookies, then sat on the tailgate of his truck, surprised when she joined him. "Your class sounds like a lot of fun."

"They always are," she agreed with a smile. "Though it gets a little hectic trying to make sure everyone's following directions, especially when it's first-timers trying our Bargello pattern."

"I'm not even going to ask you to explain that." Jesse grinned at her, enjoying the relaxed sense of camaraderie. "I should be ready to start putting pieces for the new unit in place soon, if that's okay."

"It's great. There's no class tonight." She studied his first-stage construction. "It looks exactly as I wanted. Have you always known how to build?"

"Dad started us young. When you live on a ranch that's miles from town you have to be able to repair and reuse what you have as well as make what you need." He shrugged. "I'm nowhere near as good a carpenter as he is but I try."

"And your brothers—are they good carpenters?" She looked startled when he made a face. "I'll take that as a no."

"Mac prefers the rodeo. Dan prefers breeding his Black Angus cattle and Rich…" Jesse wasn't exactly sure how to say this to her. "Rich prefers the ladies."

"Your face is red," she said with a chuckle.

"Rich is kind of embarrassing sometimes." He ducked his head and drank his coffee.

"After you left your church—you didn't want to stay and ranch with your family?" Maddie's long black lashes hid her eyes, but he could hear the questions in her voice.

"I wanted to leave Colorado as fast as I could." He tired to hide his frustration.

"Because?" She did look at him then.

"Because I knew I was to blame for that death. I knew I hadn't done enough to save Scott." He debated saying the next part, but something in him needed to verbalize his miasma of feelings. "But if I was to blame, so was God."

Maddie didn't gasp, stare at him or call him sacrilegious as his former fiancée had. Instead she seemed to be considering his words.

"Because He didn't stop it from happening, you mean?" she finally asked.

"Yes." Jesse felt great relief that she understood

without more explanation, but he also hated that such thoughts had ever taken root in his head. Maybe Eve was right. Maybe being blamed was his punishment for questioning God.

"I felt the same way when Noah was diagnosed." Maddie's retrospective tone broke into his thoughts. "I did everything I could to have a healthy baby. And yet Noah had problems. Liam said it was a genetic problem on my side, that it had to be because there weren't any autistics in his family." Her voice dropped to a whisper. "For years I couldn't understand why God had done that to me, punished me like that."

"Do you understand now?" Jesse asked curiously.

"Understand why Noah has problems?" She turned her head sideways to study him. "No. But thanks to Sophie I am beginning to accept that it doesn't matter, just as it doesn't matter why her daughter, Beth, has Down syndrome. Noah is who he is. What matters is loving both of them for who they are and helping them become all that they can be."

"Meaning?" In Maddie Jesse saw a maturity he hadn't anticipated. Though Noah was only eight, his mother seemed focused on his personal growth. From his youth group work Jesse knew some parents never understood their focus had to be on their kid.

"Liam wanted Noah to be a copy of himself. Top of the class, a leader, strong, competent." Her voice was soft, hesitant.

"And you don't?" Jesse's heart squeezed at her gentle smile when she shook her head.

"I want Noah to be Noah. I want him to experience the joys of life, to feel others' pain so he won't cause it.

I want him to grow up understanding that life isn't about being the smartest or the fastest or the richest." Her voice gathered strength as she spoke. "I am determined to help my son realize that when you give to others you are far richer than any money can make you. I want him to understand that a good friend will help and support you and that you can do the same for him. In other words, I want Noah to be the best he can be. Whatever that is."

"I think Noah got a wonderful mom when God chose you." Jesse's praise was genuine.

"Thanks." She blushed most charmingly. "It sounds grandiose and I'm not at all sure that I can do it. But that's my goal."

"But what about for you? What do you want for yourself?" he probed, thinking of Tanner's comments from the first day Jesse had gone to Wranglers Ranch.

"I don't need anything," she said, after a few moments had passed.

"That isn't what I meant. I was asking what Maddie McGregor dreams of for herself. What wonderful things do you want to be and do and say?" Jesse could tell by her nonplused mien that she'd long since put away her dreams. "You're young and strong. You're gifted with fabric. You're determined to learn what you don't know and you're great with people. So what do you see yourself doing in ten years, Maddie? Or when Noah grows up and is involved in his own busy life."

She stared at him for a long time. During those moments a hundred different reactions chased across her face: hope, optimism, possibilities. Then someone from inside the store called her name and the flare of excitement died as quickly as a fire doused with water.

"I'll just keep being plain old me, I guess." She scooted off the tailgate and picked up his empty cup.

Jesse couldn't let her go like that, couldn't let the first flicker of dreams he'd glimpsed in those green eyes die, so he waited until she had almost reached the corner of the building.

"I'd argue that word *plain*, Maddie," he said seriously. "But don't you want more? Don't you want to discover all the wonderful things God has planned for *you* to do with the rest of your life?"

She turned to look at him as if he'd suggested she make a quilt out of old shoes. Then she shrugged.

"I don't think God has planned much more for me than to be Noah's mom." Her voice was quiet, reflective. "Otherwise He'd have given me the qualifications to be something great. But that's okay, because being Noah's mom is a great enough job for me." She smiled at him before pointing out, "The puppies want feeding."

Then she turned and went inside the shop. Moments later a burst of laughter echoed from the building.

Oh, Maddie. Jesse's heart dropped to his feet as he lifted the dogs one by one and fed them with the bottles tucked into the cooler he'd brought. *You have so much to give and you don't even know it.*

Maybe he could show her that her dreams were achievable.

Except you're not getting involved, his brain reminded him.

So he wouldn't get involved, Jesse reasoned. He'd just use every opportunity he found to point out to Maddie that she already had the abilities she needed to reach for her dreams in spite of what her negative husband had drummed into her.

While he was here he'd do what he could to help. But when Gran returned and was settled at home, Jesse would leave Tucson and Maddie and Noah. Maybe by then he'd have found the answer to his question—why had God let Scott die?

"You look comfy, but I think those puppies are wearing you out." On Saturday evening Maddie studied Jesse, who sat flopped in a canvas chair beside a flickering campfire.

"I can't get used to the interrupted nights." He stifled his yawn. "But the dogs are growing. It won't last forever."

"I hope you last." She glanced to the side, where Noah was exploring Jesse's tent. "Thanks for putting off Noah until I could get here. I'm curious to see his reaction."

"Hard to tell, since he hasn't yet come out of the tent." For a moment Jesse wore a yearning look, as if he wanted to climb into that tent, crawl into his sleeping bag and dream. But then his blue eyes began to twinkle. He tossed his head back to shift his sandy hair out of his eyes. "You never said how your first cooking class went."

"I was afraid you'd ask." Maddie stopped her groan midway and made a face instead. "Horrible."

"What did you make?" Jesse looked so confident and strong, as if he never doubted himself.

"A boiled egg." She felt like a wimp. An incompetent wimp.

"How could a boiled egg..." She must have shown her distress because he stopped and shook his head. "Never mind."

"I dropped the first one on the floor." Maddie felt her cheeks burn with shame. "The second one I dropped into the pan. The white bubbled all over, so I only had a little ball of yolk left to put on my toast."

"Oh, dear." Jesse's shoulders hunched as he gave a sort of strangled cough.

"Stop laughing. It was awful." Maddie confessed the rest of her disastrous evening at the cooking school and her shame as the other students tried to help her. "Nobody else was as incompetent as me. But I'm going to do better," she said, thrusting up her chin.

"Of course you will. Cooking's just a matter of practice." Jesse could barely contain his amusement when Noah stuck his head between the tent flaps to say he wanted boiled eggs for breakfast.

"Not tomorrow, son. I need another lesson first."

"Prob'ly more than one." Noah's sigh said it all before he ducked back inside the tent. Jesse's chuckle drew heads from several other campsites.

"I'm laughing with you, not at you." His words did little to make her feel better. "You're a good sport, Maddie."

She gave him a dubious scowl.

"You're hungry. Let's cook some hot dogs." He called Noah to help him find sticks while Maddie unpacked the picnic basket he'd brought.

"We're ready," he said, when they returned with three sticks. With painstaking care, he explained to Noah how he'd sharpen the end so they could press on the meat. "Then you hold it very carefully over the fire. Don't let it get too near the flame or it will burn."

"Hey, maybe if we had hot dogs every night I wouldn't need cooking lessons," Maddie murmured. Noah looked ecstatic, but Jesse shook his head.

"You'd get bored with them after a while. Then they wouldn't be a treat anymore," he warned.

"I guess." With that way of escape blocked, Maddie focused on a new kind of cooking. She followed Jesse's instructions to the letter, but to her dismay lost the first two hot dogs to the fire. "I knew that would happen." Chagrined, she was ready to toss her stick and eat the wiener cold, but Jesse wouldn't let her.

"Maddie, you've got to stop thinking so negatively." He frowned at her. "Accidents happen to everybody."

"It didn't happen to you." She loved the calm, patient way he adjusted Noah's grip so he wouldn't suffer the same loss she had.

"I've done this before. Hundreds of times." Jesse handed her a loaded stick and made himself another. "But imagine if I were to make a quilt. There'd be lots of mistakes and you wouldn't think there was anything wrong with that because I've never made one before."

"Yes, but I can't—"

"Stop saying that. It's not that you can't cook," Jesse continued. "It's just that you've never learned. But you're smart. You *can* learn. You just have to be more positive."

"I do?" She stared at him, intrigued by the reassurance in his words.

"Of course. God doesn't create failures, Maddie. He knew all about us before we were even born and He

knows what we need to learn. He doesn't call us dumb."
Jesse lifted his head from his perusal of the fire. A lock
of sandy hair flopped over one eye, giving him a rakish
look she liked. "One of God's names is Jehovah Sham-
mah, which means 'the Lord is there.' As in, 'I'm here
to help you. Try again.'"

"I never thought of that." Feeling self-conscious,
Maddie thought the setting sun made the campsite seem
more intimate. "I've always felt like I've failed God."

"We all fail him." There was a smile in Jesse's voice.
"Fortunately, God gives do-overs."

"Yeah."

A lightness filled her heart until a quiet voice said,
"Burning."

Maddie lifted her head to see Noah's hot dog in
flames. She couldn't help laughing at her son's offended
look when the charred meat tumbled into the fire.

"I'm sorry, honey, but you and I are fiascos at this
camping thing."

"'Cause we need practice." Noah shot her a wily
grin. "Do-overs."

Surprised that he'd followed their conversation so
closely, she glanced at Jesse, who, with eyes twinkling,
handed her his own golden-roasted wiener in a thick
fluffy bun.

"Go for it," he said. Then he rose to get Noah a replacement hot dog. He'd barely threaded that onto Noah's stick when the puppies started crying.

Knowing Jesse must be hungry after hours of labor
at Emma's shop, Maddie handed him the hot dog. "Eat
it," she insisted. "Then you can roast me another after
I feed the puppies."

"That's not exactly learning the camping skill I was trying to teach," he chided, but when she wouldn't take it back he bit into it gratefully.

"I'll learn it another time. I promise I will not give up on this. Anyway, I doubt Noah would let me." She winked at him, ignoring the inner voice that chided her for such a brazen act, then began feeding a pup. It seemed only moments later that Noah reached out for the now satiated dog.

"Our turn." Jesse held out a steaming hot dog. "You eat. We'll finish feeding these guys then we'll make some s'mores." He nodded at Noah, who'd sunk onto a nearby log and was cooing gently at the puppy he was feeding. "Looks like he's become attached. You might have trouble giving them away."

"I hope not." She blinked. "I certainly can't keep nine puppies."

While Maddie savored the perfectly roasted hot dog, she studied Jesse and Noah. They teased each other about who was doing the best job feeding, and yet with every comment Jesse infused encouragement into his words. His calm certainty and compliments seemed to rejuvenate Noah, who didn't hang his head or avoid looking at Jesse. In fact, he became more engaged, especially when Jesse set the last dog back in the box and announced it was s'mores time.

She wanted to laugh as the two males soberly and with great ceremony arranged the supplies on the picnic table: graham wafers, huge fluffy marshmallows and four chocolate bars.

"Four?" she asked in surprise.

"I think we'll be having seconds, Mom." Noah gave

her a bold grin. "Maybe thirds." Then he frowned. "Okay?" His hesitation nearly broke her heart.

"Okay with me," she choked out. "As long as you don't make yourself sick, and as long as you don't do it every night."

Noah nodded happily then focused on Jesse who broke the bars into pieces before skewering a marshmallow on a stick.

"So we make s'mores by roasting the marshmallow golden brown, which isn't easy to do," he warned. "Because they catch fire if you're not careful."

"I'll be careful," Noah promised. "Then what?"

"Then we put the melted marshmallow on a cracker that has a piece of chocolate on it. We put another cracker on top and wait till the chocolate melts. And then we eat it. Watch," he invited, and demonstrated, patiently answering Noah's repeated question of—

"Is it ready yet?"

Finally, it was. Jesse put the treat together, then held it out to Noah. Surprisingly, the boy shook his head.

"You made it so you should eat it." Noah's dark eyes widened as Jesse took a bite, chewed thoroughly, then scooped the melting chocolate from the corner of his mouth with his tongue. "I wanna make my own. But I like triangles better than squares."

"We can make the cracker into a triangle but it'll be pretty small for these big marshmallows. Want to try?" Jesse experimented and ended up with a tiny morsel that made Maddie laugh. When she and Noah both lost their marshmallows to the fire he shrugged. "It happens. Try again."

They did try. Noah caught on right away and was

soon savoring his treat, edges reshaped into a triangle.
But Maddie's next two marshmallows turned to charred
cinders and fell into the coals before she finally toasted
one golden brown.

"Now that's edible." Jesse applauded.

The sickly sweet, sticky dessert wasn't her favorite,
but she enjoyed every morsel because Jesse was there,
making this a special occasion for Noah.

"One more?" Noah pleaded when Jesse began putting the s'more supplies away.

"Maddie?" Jesse waited for her nod of approval. "Go
ahead, son. You have just enough time," he told Noah.

"Huh?" Noah thrust the marshmallow on the stick.

"After we have s'mores I usually have a sing-along
around the campfire." Jesse studied the boy's blank
look. "You don't know what a sing-along is?"

"Singing?" He shrugged in disinterest then moved to
toast his marshmallow. He was savoring his final s'more
when Jesse lifted a guitar from his truck.

Noah froze. Maddie watched his eyes stretch wide.

"You play guitar? Cool," he breathed.

"You like guitars?" Jesse strummed a few chords.
"They're easy to learn to play." He demonstrated with
the first line of a popular church chorus. "See? It's not
hard. Want to try?"

Maddie held her breath. She'd never seen Noah so
captivated. He wore a rapt look as Jesse told him to sit
on the bench of the picnic table, placed the guitar in
his lap and set his hands on the instrument. Noah was
eight, and in all those years she'd never noticed his interest in a guitar or anything musical. How had Jesse
known how to reach him?

Though she fought to keep her face impassive, her heart thudded with joy as Jesse showed Noah how to play his first chord. A sandy-colored head huddled next to a dark brown one as Noah listened to Jesse's instructions and then, encouraged by the former youth minister, strummed a few tentative strokes across the strings. He beamed with delight at the sound.

"I played something!" His eyes glowed with pleasure.

"Of course you did." Jesse ruffled his hair. "You're a smart kid."

Before long Noah was playing a simple song and humming along. Curious about his reaction, Maddie finally asked, "Do you like the guitar?"

"Yes." Noah paused, and his face tightened. After several moments' thought he frowned then held out the guitar to Jesse. "Playing this is wrong. It's against the rules."

"It is?" Jesse carefully stored the guitar in the truck and returned. "God gave us music. How could it be wrong?"

Maddie wanted to hear the answer to that. Maybe it would shed light on what had troubled Noah since his father's death.

"It was such a lovely song," she said softly. "Why do you think it's wrong?"

"'Cause." All joy in the wonderful evening drained from his face, leaving his eyes dark and empty. "Dad said music should worship God in hymns. That wasn't a hymn." His voice dropped, anger threading through his words. "Those songs you're always singing are against the rules, too. Dad told you that."

As if she'd been singing something awful. Maddie's cheeks burned at the rebuke.

"You never obeyed Dad's rules. That's why he died." Noah dropped his head, shutting out everything, including Jesse's gentle explanation that there were many ways to worship God.

Maddie could see there was no use trying to reason with him. Noah had locked himself into his private world where rules controlled him and where no one else could enter.

"I'm sorry, but I think we'd better go home," she said to Jesse, and began packing up the picnic basket. "Thank you for a lovely evening. It was very kind of you to share your campsite with us."

She felt like crying as she urged Noah into the car. Tonight had been so wonderful, fun and carefree, almost like being a real family. Her heart ached for her son's pain and her own miserable past. Why couldn't they finally be free of Liam's rules?

"Thank you for coming." Jesse smiled, his demeanor absent of any chastisement or anger about their hurried exit. He bent his head to peer into the car at Noah in the backseat. "I'm glad you learned how to play a few notes," he said very quietly. "Playing my guitar is often the way I worship God when I can't think of the right words. Playing and singing something other than hymns isn't wrong. After all, King David made up his own songs. When he was a boy he played a lyre, which has strings kind of like a guitar. In the Bible it says he made up songs to sing to King Saul when he was upset."

"Really?" Noah's head lifted and his wide eyes fixed on Jesse's face.

Maddie felt her hurt and anger melt at the transformation she saw. Trust this wonderful man to know exactly how to reach her isolated son.

"When it comes to God, it all has to do with your heart. That's what He looks at." Jesse tilted toward her and said in a voice too low for Noah to hear, "Don't look so worried, Maddie. Questions are a natural part of a kid's life. He's just trying to sort out the truth. You've done a good job with him. He'll figure it out."

Her heart burst into its own song of thanks for this wonderful man who'd come into their lives and changed both of them, helping them slowly break free of their darkened past. She should have climbed in her car and driven away. She should have said thank-you and let it go.

Maddie did neither. Instead she tilted forward on her tiptoes and pressed a kiss against Jesse's cheek. When she pulled back his blue eyes were wide with surprise.

"Thank you," she whispered.

"For what?"

"For being such a good friend to us." Then she did get in her car, and quickly drove away before she did or said something she would regret.

But all the way home she couldn't quite suppress the song her heart sang, a thank-you song to God, for Jesse Parker.

Chapter Seven

"No, Gran. Maddie didn't say a thing about that, but I'll check it out for you."

On Monday afternoon Jesse pocketed his phone with a frown as he waited for Tanner's signal to lead the horses into the ring where Noah's class waited. He'd already noted Maddie among the group of interested parents watching their kids from the sidelines. He'd tied his three horses to the rails, purposely spacing them so, hopefully, he'd end up next to her.

Gran was worried about issues at Quilt Essentials but at the moment Maddie seemed focused on Noah.

"Hi, Jesse." The welcome in her voice and that smile of hers made his stomach clench. Funny the effect she always had on him. "You look as weary as Tanner has since their new baby arrived."

"Nah. He looks worse." Jesse chuckled when she rolled her eyes. "It was nice of him to let me bring the puppies to Wranglers so I can maintain the feedings." He paused when Lefty pointed Noah toward a horse named Amos, which he guessed Tanner had chosen especially because it was so gentle. Thing was, Amos was not one of the horses Jesse was in charge of. "Your son looks terrified."

"He is. He can't seem to get comfortable around animals. Except the puppies, and that's only because you helped him." She bit her lip. "His teacher and I had to do some sweet-talking to get him to come here. She said several of the other children are also hesitant to take part."

"Today will help ease their fears. Excuse me." At Tanner's signal, Jesse nodded and stepped away to begin working with the kids and horses he'd been assigned.

His three students were knowledgeable about horses and required little guidance. But through the next few minutes he kept watch over Noah, and when it became clear that the wrangler helping him wasn't making progress and that Maddie was getting more worried by the moment, Jesse had a quick word with Tanner. A few minutes later he changed places with Noah's wrangler, who gave him a smile of relief.

"Two of the three are petrified," he muttered before walking away.

"What's wrong, Noah?" Jesse asked after fruitless attempts to get the boy to relax. A sideways glance showed Maddie's smile was returning. She had that much confidence in him?

Focus on your job!

"I don't want to ride this dumb old horse." Noah's bottom lip jutted out in a fashion that said he would not be persuaded otherwise.

"Oh." Jesse rubbed his chin. "How come?" He kept his tone even, conversational. "Would you rather have a different horse than Amos?"

"No." Noah averted his dark brown eyes. "I don't like horses," he said firmly.

"Because you're afraid of them?" Jesse guessed, in a quiet tone so his classmates couldn't overhear.

Noah inclined his head just slightly.

"But you come to Wranglers Ranch all the time and there are always horses here."

"I don't go near them. Dad's rule was to stay away from animals. Horses are dangerous." Noah crossed his arms over his thin chest protectively.

"They can be if you don't know how to treat them, but that's why you're here. To learn." Jesse prayed for wisdom to coax away Noah's fear. "In the Bible David said, 'When I am afraid I will put my trust in You.' That's a good thing to do, don't you think?"

"I guess." The boy didn't look convinced.

"I hope you'll at least try to ride Amos." Jesse employed his most pitiful tone.

"Why?" Noah frowned at him.

"Because if you don't he's going to be very disappointed."

"Horses don't get disappointed. They don't have feelings." Noah scoffed.

"Are you kidding me? Horses are very sensitive. Trust me, when the other horses get their treat for doing a good job here today and Amos doesn't get his, he'll be very disappointed." Jesse sighed and shook his head. "I sure don't like to see that, because Amos is such a good horse. He wants to do his job, but you won't let him."

Confused, Noah glanced from Jesse to his mother, who nodded encouragingly.

"Couldn't you at least try? Just so Amos can get a

treat?" Jesse wheedled. "He's an old horse and he really loves his treats."

"Like s'mores?" Noah rolled his eyes.

"Nope. Horses can't eat chocolate." Jesse could see Noah was relenting, so he pretended nonchalance as he tilted back on his heels, stroked Amos's flank and pushed his point a little harder. "After this class each horse that works well gets half an apple and three carrots. Amos is real partial to apples. He can smell 'em from a long way away. Be a shame if he didn't get his apple, don't you think? But I guess if you're too scared to try…" He let that dangle.

"I don't want Amos to miss his apple." Noah glanced at the other kids. "I guess I could brush him like the others are doing."

"You could." Jesse pulled the currying tools out of a sack hanging over the rail. "Here you go. Nice and gentle, as if you were brushing your hair." He got Noah started, then turned to wink at Maddie, whose smile showed both concern and relief. "You're doing great," he praised, wondering why resurrecting Maddie's smile mattered so much.

His other two charges worked harmoniously, gibing each other as they groomed their mounts. All three kids seemed to grow increasingly more comfortable with their animals until Tanner blew his whistle signalling the end of that part of the lesson. Jesse could almost feel Noah's tension build.

"Don't worry," he murmured, resting his hand on the boy's shoulder. "We're just going to walk the horses around. So they get used to you." *And you to them.*

But when Noah didn't follow instructions, Jesse firmed up his directions.

"The rule is to lead your horse on the left side. Because it's the way Amos has learned, and doing things the same way makes it more comfortable for him," he added, forestalling the question forming on the boy's lips. "Keep Amos close to you and stay near his shoulder." He nodded when Noah stepped tentatively forward. "Good. But don't wrap the lead-rope around your wrist or arm. Hold it like this."

"He's too close." Noah jerked away, inadvertently tugging on the reins. Amos obligingly shifted sideways, which brought a yelp from the boy. "He's going to step on me!"

"No, he isn't. Listen to me, Noah." Jesse intervened, positioning himself between boy and animal. He crouched down to look into Noah's dark and fearful gaze. "Every horse learns the same set of rules. Amos knows all of them and he knows exactly what he's supposed to do when you pull on the reins. But if you don't follow the rules *he's* learned, he can't understand what you want. His rules are what tell him how he should behave."

"But—"

"You have to follow Amos's rules, Noah. Not yours." Jesse could see he wasn't making headway.

"It's the same as your rules, honey." Maddie's gentle voice from the sidelines brought calm to the tense atmosphere. "Your dad taught you not to lie. If he had suddenly asked you to lie, you'd be mixed up, wouldn't you? Because the rule you learned is no lying. This horse learned his horse rules and you have to follow them so you don't mix him up. Do you understand?"

Noah frowned, but his head jerked up and down.

"Listen to Jesse. If you do what he tells you, you'll

be fine. You can trust him, Noah," she whispered. Her wide-eyed gaze locked with Jesse's.

So she trusted him? Around horses at least.

The rest of the lesson passed without incident, but Noah did not relax, nor did he become more comfortable with his horse, though Jesse's other pupils seemed to gain confidence. By the time they were finished, Jesse felt drained and ineffective. He was here to work with these kids, but wasn't succeeding. *Lord, how in the world do I help Noah?*

When the class ended everyone went to sample Sophie's cookies and juice, but Jesse stayed with the horses, leading them toward the barn as he pondered his failure.

"Noah didn't do very well, did he?" Maddie trailed behind him, her voice soft, almost apologetic. "I'm sorry. I know you tried."

"It will take time. Noah hasn't been around animals that much." Jesse smiled at her. "He doesn't see them as much more than wild beasts."

"Liam's doing, I'm afraid." She walked beside him, her gaze on something distant. "He had this sermon he loved to preach about God giving subjugation of the animals to men. I used to wonder if perhaps…" Her voice died away.

"What?" Jesse's curiosity bloomed.

"Well, I wondered if he'd once been attacked and maybe become afraid," she murmured. "A parishioner offered to give Noah a puppy on his second birthday. Liam forbade it. He said God never meant for animals to be kept in a house."

So she'd bought the boy a dog for a Christmas gift hoping to normalize his childhood? Jesse handed over the horses to Lefty as he thought about that. He'd struggled hard to understand where Noah was coming from, yet he couldn't seem to get through to the boy. Again he considered asking Maddie to tell him more about Noah's father so he could figure out a way to counteract the kid's fears.

"Maybe you're right." He hesitated, then plunged ahead. "I'm really struggling to get a grip on what's going on in Noah's head, so I can help him enjoy the horses. Can you tell me anything else about your husband that might explain what he taught Noah?"

Maddie's face blanched. She gulped and blinked twice before clearing her throat. When she finally looked at him, Jesse was appalled by the dead look in her usually lively green eyes.

"Um, I don't know." There was a world of pain underlying that whispered response.

She's been through enough. Don't hurt her anymore, some voice inside his head ordered.

"Liam was very firm in his convictions." Her hesitant words warned Jesse that Maddie was about to say something important. "Sometimes that made him difficult to live with." She stared at the ground now, obviously feeling her way through a vortex of emotions. Then she lifted her head and looked directly at him. "I prayed all the time for God to help me be a good wife to Liam, but I wasn't. Why didn't God help, Jesse?"

He couldn't answer. Not because he didn't know all the right words a minister should offer a hurting soul. Not because he couldn't cite a hundred verses that were often used to do just that. And not because her anguish didn't touch his heart.

Because it did. Deeply.

But Jesse felt that anything he said would only trivialize her pain. He understood her feelings of abandonment, had suffered them himself. He still searched for his own understanding of God's ways and hadn't yet found an answer that satisfied his questions.

But he had to say something. He owed her that much.

"I don't know why, Maddie." Feeling utterly ineffectual, he mouthed the one truth he still clung to. "All I know is that God cares for us with a love we can't fathom. What He does, He does for our good and for His kingdom. Keep talking to Him. That's what's most important."

Did the hope that had flared in those expressive eyes dim? Jesse chafed against his feelings of failure and vowed to spend more time seeking God's answers so he could help Maddie and Noah.

And himself.

"I'd better go. Noah will be leaving with his class and I need to get back to the store." Her words reminded him of his grandmother's earlier call.

"You have to work late again?" He already knew the answer, but he waited for her nod. "Why?"

"One of our employees was admitted to hospital last night for an emergency appendectomy. She was supposed to work this evening. I need to cover her shift." Maddie's tired face told him she was not looking forward to her extended workday.

"Is there no one you could hire to cover her absence?" Emma had spoken of someone named Talia, but Jesse wasn't going to suggest her. Maddie was the manager, and in Emma's absence, hiring decisions were up to her. He wanted her to feel confident, not undermined, and she would feel weakened if she learned Emma had called him.

"We have a couple of staff who work extra hours when we need them. I suppose I could contact one to cover, but it means changing the schedules, and I don't like to do that without Emma's approval. It might increase her expenses and change the benefit structure her bookkeeper has in place." Maddie sighed. "I haven't had time to speak with her personally about it so I think I'll just fill in until I can okay it with Emma."

Maddie nibbled on her bottom lip. It was something she did whenever she was unsure of herself, and though Jesse found it endearing, he also agreed with Emma's comment that this was a time for Maddie to make a managerial decision.

"Can I say something?" he began, praying for wisdom and the right words. "Gran is depending on you to run the store. And you're doing a terrific job. But what will happen if you take on too much, wear yourself out or get sick and can't be there for Emma? Who will keep Quilt Essentials going?"

"I never thought of that." She frowned and her shoulders slumped, as if she'd done something wrong.

"Gran once told me that the hardest thing she had to learn about running her business was learning to delegate. She said she started out very hands-on, managing every detail, until she realized that her staff needed to feel included. She said she finally realized that the best way to ensure a business's success is to make sure your employees feel like it's their business, too, so they will keep it operating when you can't be there." He waited, trying to gauge Maddie's reaction.

As she thought it through, her face slowly cleared of the worry and apprehension that had filled it. Finally, her sunny smile broke through.

"Thank you, Jesse. You always seem to have the answers I need." Maddie pulled out her new cell phone.

Too bad he didn't have the answers *he* needed.

"Hi, Talia. This is Maddie McGregor. I'm wondering if you can work this evening and cover Abby's shifts until further notice. She's in hospital. You can?" Her face blazed with joy. "Thank you so much. I know we haven't often worked together, but I hope we can get to know each other much better over the next few weeks." She closed the phone with a huge sigh.

"Sounds like you have tonight off," he said with a smile, and checked his watch. "I don't. It's puppy feeding time. Then I'll load them up and get home. Emma's roses need watering and weeding."

"Noah and I could help," she offered. "He talks a lot about the puppies. I think he is beginning to love them."

"I wouldn't turn down an offer of help." Nor an evening spent with Maddie.

Jesse knew he was going to have to refocus and stop involving himself in her life, but he owed it to Gran to help her friends where he could. Didn't he?

And as a Wranglers employee he had to do his best with Noah, too. Even if he didn't have a clue how to do that.

"It's really nice of you to make us dinner again, Jesse." Maddie loaded the dishwasher with the few dishes they'd used. "I never imagined it was so easy to make soup."

"It was nice of you and Noah to help with the puppies' feedings, weeding and watering Emma's rose garden, and with chopping vegetables," Jesse replied with a grin. "As long as you have vegetables you can always make soup." He grimaced when Noah jumped three of his checkers and waited to be crowned.

"I'm good at this game." Noah's grin quickly faded. "But I'm not good with Amos." He turned his head to glance at her. "I shouldn't go to Wranglers Ranch with our class anymore. Right, Mom?"

"I don't know about that." Maddie pretended to think about it, wishing Jesse would jump in with some advice. But Noah was *her* son. It was up to her. "I don't think it's good to try something once and then quit. You need to give riding a fair chance."

"But I don't like it." He glowered at her.

"You didn't like the puppies at first, either," she reminded him quietly.

"Horses are different."

"Why?" She sat down at the table beside him, nursing her cup of tea.

"I dunno." Noah skipped his man across the board to win the game. "Do you want to play again?"

"No, thanks. Losing twice is enough." Jesse finished his own drink. "It's a gorgeous evening. Why don't we sit on Gran's deck?"

Maddie quelled a frisson of delight at the thought of spending more time with this man she admired so much.

"With your guitar?" Noah wore a hungry look.

"Yep. Is that okay?" he asked, pausing for Noah's nod before he lifted the instrument from its case.

Maddie thought it was very okay. She loved hearing Jesse's voice lift in the praise songs he favored.

"I guess." Noah followed them to the deck. He soon became riveted by Jesse's hand movements as he strummed the strings. The song that followed was a tender, poignant song of thanks to God for His wonderful goodness.

Maddie sat in stunned silence when Noah closed his eyes and let his head move to the rhythm of the music. Beat for beat her son's small fingers began to mimic Jesse's, sliding up and down the pretend neck of a guitar as if he, too, were playing. How could she have let Liam teach that worship such as this was wrong?

Maddie fell into her own meditation on the goodness of God, marveling at the sense of connection she'd only ever heard about but now glimpsed thanks to Jesse's music. His words voiced a complete confidence in God—a confidence that she didn't share.

But she yearned to. If only she could figure out how to find this sense of reverence when she was alone and feeling defeated...

"I guess that's enough for tonight," Jesse murmured some time later.

Feeling refreshed and renewed in spirit, Maddie blinked back to reality. Her glance at Noah showed that he, too, seemed less tense. Jesse's song had done that for both of them.

"I could feel the music," Noah exclaimed.

"Really? Show me." Jesse handed him the guitar.

After two false starts, Noah pursed his lips.

"Close your eyes now and try again," Jesse suggested.

Noah began again. In a jerky rhythm at first, but then evening out, her son reproduced the same haunting melody Jesse had played, but with a wistful edge. The night seemed to fall silent around them and even the stars seemed entranced by the boy's efforts. Maddie's heart squeezed with pride as he caressed the strings, coaxing every note until the last one died away into the darkness.

"That was wonderful, honey," she whispered, dashing away her tears because tears bothered him. Jesse had done this. For them. "So beautiful. How did you do it?"

"I dunno." Noah's face showed his own disbelief. "I just did what Jesse did and the song came."

"God's given you a gift for music, Noah," Jesse said, his voice filled with admiration. "I've never before met anyone who could pick up a tune after hearing it once or twice, let alone on an instrument they didn't know. You must develop your talent, practice and get better."

"Like it says on the barn at Wranglers, right?" Noah grinned. "Fan Into Flame the Gift That is Within You."

"Exactly." Jesse's gaze met Maddie's. "Each of us has a unique talent from God. Yours might be making music. I think your mom's gift is quilting and a heart for people."

It was so wonderful to be noticed, to be appreciated. What an amazing, caring man he was to take such an interest in them.

"Don't lock away your gift because of rules, Noah."

"You mean I should disobey my dad?" In a flash her son's expression changed to one of confusion. He glanced at Maddie with disapproval. "Like Mom did?"

"I don't think your dad knew you had this gift, Noah." A smile played across the former youth pastor's lips. "If he had I'm sure he would never have said what he did about music. I'm sure that if your dad knew that you could make the kind of worship music that helps people talk to God then he would want you to play it as often as you could. I think he'd understand and I think God understands about guitar music, too, because you're using it to praise Him and that's never wrong."

Frowning, Noah handed over the guitar. "I'm gonna feed the puppies again before we go home."

Maddie watched him leave the deck, her heart full of thanksgiving for the world that had been opened to him tonight.

"You're crying. Why?" Jesse murmured, taking the chair next to hers that Noah had vacated, and sliding his hand over hers.

"Because for the first time Noah's questioning his rules." Maddie was so moved she could hardly express herself. "Thanks to you."

"Don't get too excited." Jesse patted her hand and let it go but the warmth of his touch remained. "Kids are changeable. By tomorrow he'll probably revert to what's ingrained inside him. I think it's going to take a while for him to move beyond what he's learned."

"You're probably right." The weight of parenthood settled heavily on her. Why had God let Liam, a minister, be so wrong? The same old question still had no answer, but just for tonight Maddie was going to cling to her faith that God was changing things for her and Noah. "I'd better get home. I have a big day tomorrow."

"Bigger than usual?" He gave her a questioning look when she nodded. "Why?"

"Emma's latest order of quilting supplies came in today. It's a lot of stuff and we've had a ton of requests for it all, so it will sell. But there are so many new items that I'll have to reorganize everything in the notions corner." She grimaced. "Even then I don't know if it will all fit."

"Couldn't you do a revolving thing like you did with that fabric?" he suggested.

"I'm not sure I know how that would work in such a small space, and I don't like to make too many changes without Emma's input," Maddie admitted.

"You're the manager. You'll think of a way to make the store work better." He grinned at her heavy sigh. "Maybe I could stop by tomorrow on my way home from work and help," he offered. "I'm on the early shift."

"That would be very kind, if you're sure you don't mind?" Why did her heart give this silly little hiccup at the thought of working with Jesse again?

"No problem." He seemed to hesitate.

"Was there something else?" she asked, curious about his silence.

"I was wondering if Noah could come back with me to Emma's after school sometimes." There was a hesitancy in his offer that she didn't understand. "Maybe he could help me with a few things."

"The dogs, you mean?"

"That and some ideas I have to make it easier for Gran to manage when she comes home. The steps up to this deck could be covered with a temporary ramp. That would make it easier for her to care for her roses. And maybe I can do something in her bathroom to simplify showering." Jesse was so thoughtful—about everyone. It was a trait Maddie greatly admired.

"Maybe Noah would enjoy helping you make Emma's home better. Let's ask him," she suggested, when he appeared. Jesse explained, then they waited for her son to decide.

"Okay, but..." Noah's eager look melted. "I dunno know how to build stuff."

"Well, of course you don't. You haven't learned. Yet." Jesse messed his hair, then laughed when Noah smoothed it. "We'll figure it out together."

"Tomorrow is swimming."

"You can't miss that," Jesse agreed. "Not when you're going to be a lifeguard." He grinned at Maddie. "So how about I pick up Noah, take him to his lesson and we come here after?"

"It's very kind of you. Thank you." She smiled at Noah. "We must get home now. Cocoa will want dinner."

"She's good at waiting," Noah said as they drove away. "I'm not."

Neither am I. Maddie chided herself for the excitement that thought brought her.

Funny how things seemed so much brighter with Jesse in the picture.

Chapter Eight

"Very clever solution. I knew you were made for Gran's business." Jesse grinned.

After a month of continued contact over coffee, snacks and sometimes dinner, he'd fallen into an easy friendship with Maddie that revolved around Noah, Emma's prolonged recovery and both their jobs. Already Jesse saw many changes in the woman who sat across from him on the patio at Wranglers Ranch. For one thing she no longer shrank from every challenge but was slowly growing more confident in her ability to handle whatever came up.

"I doubt my new thread display is that crucial to the business," Maddie chuckled. "But thanks to your support and Emma's, too, I am learning that I can handle things. I couldn't ask for a better boss. Did you know she put me on an email list for a daily Bible study?"

Maddie's smile brought sunshine to Jesse's world and cheered his spirit, keeping him from dwelling on his perpetual 'Why, God?' questions.

"You're both really great encouragers."

"It's not so much us as it is you," he said quietly, studying the steam that floated upward from his coffee cup before he lifted his head to look into her lovely eyes. It wasn't that Maddie hadn't been poised before, but now she didn't raise her hand to cover her scar when he studied her. "You're beginning to understand that God didn't create dummies."

Her eyes flared wide before she burst out laughing.

"What's so funny?"

"You." She shook her head. "You wouldn't say that if you'd seen my macaroni and cheese dish last week." She wrinkled her nose and squeezed her eyes closed. "Disgusting."

"The one you made last night wasn't bad," he replied. Then, when her eyes demanded truth, he added, "Except for the charred parts."

Maddie hooted with laughter again, drawing Sophie's attention. The woman left Noah's school group and walked toward them. "More coffee?" she asked, holding the pot.

"Thanks, Sophie, but I'd better not. I need to get back to work." Maddie glanced at her son, her face pensive. "I only stopped by this morning to see how he's doing at riding." She pursed her lips. "Not that well apparently."

The baby monitor on Sophie's hip gave a wail and she hurriedly said goodbye before striding toward the house.

"Seeing Sophie with baby Carter almost makes me wish I could start over with Noah. I'd do things so differently, insist on a more normal childhood for one thing." She blinked again quickly. "He's growing away from me, Jesse. And I don't know what to do about it."

"Keep showing him you love him," her friend advised.

"I'm doing that, of course, but what if that's not enough?" Worry crowded out her smile. "He keeps pushing me away and I don't understand why."

"He's struggling internally." But with what, exactly? That was Jesse's conundrum. "My guess is that it has to do with his father's rules. Breaking them causes him a lot of self-doubt and pain. Something makes Noah feel he must keep them, or else. Only we don't know what the 'or else' is."

"Those stupid rules!" She modulated her voice when heads turned to study them. "I wonder if Liam had any idea of the problems his rules would cause."

"Did they cause problems for you when you were married?" Jesse hungered to know more details of Maddie's past and what had formed her into this amazingly strong woman.

"Yes, they caused problems for me." Her shoulders drooped. "I felt like I was in prison, that I couldn't be genuine. I had to become some caricature so that I fit all Liam's stipulations. Not that I ever knew who the real me was." She made a face. "I guess that's why working at Emma's was such a blessing. After our first meeting I was able to relax and enjoy my time with the fabrics and people. That meant a lot."

"And Liam didn't object?"

"I guess he thought I might as well earn some money, since I was hopeless at being a minister's wife." She shrugged. "I could only work while Noah was at school, but those precious hours were like my weekly vacation."

"Emma is blessed to have you." Jesse had noted several times that whenever her husband's name came up, Maddie tensed. "I know this might hurt you but I have to ask." He exhaled, then posed the question. "Is there some reason Noah might blame you for his dad's death?"

"Me?" She frowned, slowly shook her head. "Is that what he said? I can't imagine why."

"He didn't say it. Maybe I misunderstood. Forget it." Jesse brushed it off, not wanting to cause her any more distress. "His class is finished and the bus for the next one is pulling in. I'd better go." He swallowed the last of his coffee and rose. "Pray for me, will you, Maddie? My students in this group are really a challenge."

"Worse than Noah's class?" she teased.

"Noah's a piece of cake. A triangle-shaped piece." He grinned. How did this woman always manage to lighten his heart? "I could use a success story."

"Every child you work with is a success in the making, Jesse. Just be patient. God's on their case." She gave him a saucy grin. "It feels nice for *me* to encourage *you* for a change."

"I'll take all the encouragement you want to give," Jesse said, and meant it. He loved working on Wranglers Ranch, but his limited success with the kids was frustrating.

And yet, what else could he do? He could not, would not risk giving the wrong answers and being blamed for another tragedy, and he didn't know what else God wanted from him. It was like being in some kind of limbo.

"I promise I will pray for you. Now I must go." Maddie rose gracefully, her lovely green sundress a perfect foil for her dark hair and alabaster skin. "I'm going to try making spaghetti and meatballs tonight. Dare to join us?"

"Love to. It's my favorite."

"Apparently it's hard to burn. Or so the teacher says, although I'm not sure he knows just how skilled I am at doing that." She made a funny face, waggled her fingers, then walked toward her car.

Jesse watched her go with mixed emotions. That self-deprecating comment said a lot about Maddie. She was a very giving person, but she fought such a dark cloud of doubt. It sounded to him as if her husband had never praised her, never saw the wonderful woman she was. Liam McGregor must have been blind.

"See you after school, Jesse." Noah stood behind him, backpack in hand, ready to leave with his class.

"The puppies and I will be waiting as usual." Jesse grinned. "Bye." He watched Noah leave, a solitary figure, head bent, eyes fixed downward.

Why can't I help him, Lord? his heart asked, as the same old feelings of helplessness welled. *Show me what You want me to do.*

Maybe God was busy today, because Jesse wasn't struck with any ideas, and he had little success relating to the rest of his charges. The second lesson of the day ended with him feeling utterly frustrated. These kids needed him and he wanted so desperately to ask and probe and find out what was bothering them and try to help. Yet he was afraid lest he give the wrong response and cause irreparable harm.

Afraid? He'd never felt that so strongly before and he didn't like the sense of helplessness it provoked.

Jesse was also a bit envious of Maddie's progress

in her spiritual journey. She was beginning to bloom, slowly gaining confidence in herself, figuring out her personal worth, while he couldn't find the niche where he belonged. Counseling, encouraging, mentoring—it was what he wanted to do, what he *needed* to do. But how to do it without messing up?

Jesse heaved a sigh. God knew he wanted to serve, but he was also leery about getting too involved. Why didn't He reveal how Jesse could get past that? Frustrated, he got busy cleaning and storing tackle until Tanner called his name.

"That redheaded kid in Noah's class that you were working with? Kendal? What are your thoughts on him?" the rancher asked.

"Off the cuff?" Jesse waited for Tanner's nod. "He's bored and spoiled. There are too many people in his world devoting too much time to him and he couldn't care less. He's a bully and his curiosity about horses is less than minimal," he said honestly.

"Blunt and not flattering, but I agree. That's why it seemed odd when I overheard him getting a stern lecture from Noah about handling the puppies gently." Tanner scratched his chin, then shoved back his Stetson. "And Kendal took it, probably because Noah wouldn't allow him to touch them unless he did it without hurting them." Tanner grinned. "Bit of an eye opener about both of them, don't you think?"

"Never thought Kendal would take directions from anyone." Jesse frowned. "Never thought Noah would give them either."

"Be interesting to see what comes of that relationship." Tanner nodded and walked away.

Jesse completed the rest of his work with his thoughts on Maddie's son. Music and puppies; those were Noah's interests. They seemed to give him a sense of accomplishment and belonging. Apparently Kendal liked the puppies. Could music reach him, too?

As Jesse waited for Noah to arrive from school, ideas began to bloom, ways to engage the kids who came here because they sought something to make them feel better about themselves.

Is that what I'm here to do?

Fanciful ideas filled his mind. Jesse wasn't totally sure if it was God's or his own interests that prompted them. Either way, he was intrigued. It wasn't the ministry he'd had before, but at least he would be doing something for these kids. Maybe then he wouldn't feel so...useless?

"You want to start a Wranglers Ranch band?" Maddie wasn't sure she understood what Jesse was proposing, but she wanted to hear more.

"I think I do." After a very good spaghetti dinner, Jesse walked beside her through the desert near her home, appreciating its tranquil beauty in the twilight.

Noah stayed ahead, checking out the profusion of cactus blooms. When he did speak it was to Jesse. He gave only monosyllabic answers to Maddie's conversation, and she struggled to crush the building fear that she was losing him.

Stop being afraid. God didn't make you a mother to take away your needy son. He wants you to help Noah grow. At least, that's what Emma's email had advised this morning.

"But how and what will a band do for the kids?" Remembering how Noah had been touched by Jesse's music increased Maddie's curiosity.

"I'm not sure. The idea is still in the germination stage. But I've seen music reach into a heart when nothing else could." Jesse's introspective voice was so quiet she had to lean near to hear it.

"Okay, so a band. Instruments?" Her brain immediately skipped to ways to make his idea happen.

"I don't know." Jesse sounded tense. "I don't know how it would work. Anyway, Tanner would have to approve the plan first."

"I don't think Tanner's approval will be a problem. He's all for anything that will help Wranglers Ranch reach kids." She paused, halted him with a hand on his arm, and when he looked at her questioningly, asked, "What's really bothering you, Jesse?"

"I'm a youth pastor, Maddie. I am—at least I thought I was—supposed to minister to kids."

"And a band isn't a ministry?" she challenged, then softly murmured, "Or is it a ministry you don't want? Maybe you feel it's not on the same level as being a youth leader."

He frowned at her so fiercely that she wondered for a moment if she should retract her comment.

"You're calling me a snob." Jesse didn't look pleased, but he didn't immediately dismiss the notion, either. He threaded his fingers in hers and gently pulled so she'd resume their walk. "Maybe I am, but it's because I never had any doubts that youth ministry was where God wanted me. Then Scott died and, well, nothing makes sense anymore."

"Working at Wranglers Ranch is working with youth," Maddie reminded him, loving the warmth of his palm against hers.

"I know, but—" he glanced sideways at her "—I never thought of it as permanent. It's only a stopgap until I figure out where God wants me."

"Maybe the band idea is His way of showing you." She waited as he digested that possibility, letting her mind explore her own new idea. "Maybe He's showing me something, too."

"You've got that look," Jesse said, following Noah's lead along the path, which arced back toward her home.

"What look?" She met his gaze and blushed at the familiarity she saw there. Jesse was *such* a good friend. "You're not the only one who gets ideas."

"That's what scares me." He pretended fear. "It's not more shelving, is it?"

Maddie could no more have stopped her burst of laughter than she could squelch the spurt of joy that bubbled inside as she returned his grin. In front of them Noah turned to see what was going on. His gaze slid from their faces to their clasped hands. Immediately a frown tipped the corners of his mouth down, his disapproval obvious. Was that why she yanked her hand from Jesse's? Noah turned and walked on.

"It is shelves, isn't it?" Jesse sighed.

"No more shelving," she promised. "This is something different. I want Quilt Essentials to try something only I'm scared to tell Emma."

"Nobody is ever scared of my marshmallow-hearted grandmother." He frowned at her sober look. "What's this idea, Maddie?"

"There's a nursing home around the corner from the store." The idea grew clearer as she continued. "I met the administrator at church last Sunday and she told me that she missed Emma's weekly visits. Apparently, many of your gran's former quilting buddies are now in that home. The administrator said those ladies talk all the time about the quilting bees they used to hold, about their fond memories of sitting around a quilt frame, chatting as they worked together stitching. The administrator thinks it would lift their spirits tremendously if they had something like a quilting party to look forward to each week. But her staff don't have the time or knowledge to be in charge of such a project."

"And so Maddie McGregor, being the softie she is, came up with a plan." He chuckled at her glare. "You're just like Gran, you know. She told me you've taken over most of her charity projects, improved on a lot of them, especially the community garden for inner city kids." His eyes gleamed with unspoken support. "Gutsy move, lady, and very generous."

"My grandmother and I used to work in her garden together. It's no big deal," she demurred.

"It's a big deal for someone who used to be afraid of her own shadow," he teased. "Your confidence is growing and it's wonderful to see. Now tell me your plan and how I can help."

She loved his immediate offer of help without all the 'have you thought of this' and 'what about that' questions with which Liam had always squelched her ideas. Jesse trusted her knowledge and gave her credit for being able to think through her plan. Just another thing to admire about Jesse Parker.

"The goal is to get those ladies quilting. I can put together a quilt top for them to sew, but I'd need to get a frame to the home and set it up with the top, bottom and batting. Doable. But the biggest thing is, one of our staff would have to be present, at least for the first few meetings." She waited, and when he didn't speak, added, "That's going to increase the payroll."

"Well, yes, but it's also going to provide some good publicity while benefiting some lonely ladies. I say go for it."

Jesse's support was a boost to her confidence, but still Maddie hesitated. "It could turn out to be a flop," she warned. "And to do it without consulting Emma—"

"But Gran told me that as far as operations go, she wants you to go with your hunches, so she can concentrate on her recovery." Jesse's words made Maddie wonder how much he'd discussed her with Emma.

"Yes, but this isn't the same as her other projects."

"Of course it is." Jesse sounded impatient. "By now you know of the many things Emma does for the community, so you know they're not all done for profit. My grandmother genuinely cares about people." He brushed her cheek with his knuckles. "You have the same heart for people that she does, Maddie. So go with what your heart is telling you." His blue eyes softened and his voice dropped as he said, "Forget the past, forget Liam and his rules. Listen to the faith that tells you God is there, ready and waiting to guide and help you."

"I never thought of God waiting to help me personally. I guess I don't have the same faith that you do," she admitted in a low voice, so Noah wouldn't hear.

"Are you kidding me?" Jesse gaped. "You had the

faith to start the Easter quilt and believe your students would finish on time. You had the faith to start new projects, renovate the store, take cooking lessons and keep raising your son while filling in at Gran's community projects. Are you telling me you're not trusting God to help you with each of those things?"

"I guess," she said, slightly shocked to realize it was true. "I *have* been praying about a way to help those friends of Emma's."

"Now you've got your answer." God answering prayer was so ordinary to Jesse, but Maddie couldn't quite believe He'd do that for her.

"Can I ask you something?" She deliberately stopped a short distance from the house. Noah was sitting on the deck, playing with Cocoa for a change.

Jesse had helped them in so many ways. Could he help her with this?

"Ask anything." He studied her face as he waited.

"How do you know if you're good enough for God?" Seeing his confusion, she reworded it. "How can you tell if you qualify for God's love?"

"Everybody qualifies." He tilted his head to one side. "I'm not sure I understand."

"Well…" Maddie felt foolish, and yet she needed to know. "I wasn't a very good wife." Jesse's frown only added to her discomfort so she finally blurted, "I don't think I loved Liam the way I was supposed to. I don't think I'm a very good mother, either, because it seems like Noah hates me. So how can God love me?"

"God's love doesn't depend on what you do or feel." Jesse studied her with an intensity that made her shift nervously. "God loves you, Maddie McGregor, because

God is love. He created every single thing about you, from your gorgeous hair to your beautiful eyes to your wonderfully talented hands. So He doesn't think *Oh, this child of mine is worth loving, but this one is too bad or too silly or too dumb.* He knows exactly who and what we are and He loves us anyway."

"I don't understand that," she admitted sadly.

"Sure you do." He jerked a thumb over one shoulder. "When Noah was born did you think *How can I love this wrinkled, red-faced, squalling kid that smells?*" He laughed at her frown. "Of course you didn't. You didn't ask how or why you loved him or how he was going to earn your love. You looked at him and thought, *This is my precious boy and I love him.* Am I right?"

"Yes." She glanced at Noah and felt the same rush of love she'd felt the day he was born.

"So if you can feel that way about your child, don't you think the God of the universe who created us can feel the same love for us, only infinitely stronger?" His smile, calm, certain and so kind, reassured her. "See, Maddie, it's not about who we are. It's about who He is. And He is love."

"So it doesn't matter what I do?" she asked, still confused.

"Of course it matters. But what you do won't change whether or not He loves you. Malachi 3:6 says, 'I the Lord do not change.' James 1:17 says, 'Every good and perfect gift coming down from the Father of the heavenly lights who does not change like shifting shadows.' And of course you know John 3:16. 'For God so loved the world,'" Jesse began, then paused, one eyebrow arched, waiting for her to finish quoting the verse.

When she'd said the rest, Maddie began slowly walking again, her brain busy with all she'd heard.

"The best way to show our love for God is to trust that because He loves us, He will always do His best for us. Ask God for help when you need it, Maddie, and then believe He's there with you, leading you through the hard parts." Jesse's voice lowered as they neared Noah. "Remember, God is love. It has nothing to do with rules or payback or anything else."

"Thank you." Feeling as though a huge weight had slid off her shoulders, Maddie was able to smile at Noah even though he was glaring at her. "Something wrong, son?"

"What were you whispering about?" he demanded, his tone argumentative.

"God," Jesse said, before she could respond. "And His love for us."

"Dad said people talk about love too much. He said they should talk less and do more." Noah's chin thrust up as he stared down the youth pastor with a hint of belligerence.

Maddie bit her bottom lip at the jaded comment, but Jesse was nodding.

"That may be true, Noah. Many people do talk about love more than they actually love." He smiled, then shrugged. "But the thing is, if you don't tell someone you love them, how would they know? And if you don't keep saying it, they might believe you stopped. So it's good to talk about love and to be loving, too. Don't you think so?"

Noah frowned, obviously thinking about it. "I guess," he muttered.

"I'd better get home. Puppy time." Jesse made a face.

"Haven't you been able to cut down on their feedings?" Maddie asked curiously.

"Oh, yeah, but I've also learned that if I give them a good solid feed right before bedtime, they almost make it through the night and I get a longer sleep." Jesse's smug grin made her laugh.

"So no guitar tonight?" Noah sounded disappointed.

"Some other time maybe." Jesse smiled at him. "You should get your own guitar. Then you could play whenever you want. Thanks for dinner. Bye." He left a few minutes later.

After Noah was in bed, his face turned to the wall when she tried to kiss him good-night, Maddie found her favorite spot on her porch and fought to quell the hurt that burned inside while wondering what she'd done wrong. Jesse had said God knew her. But did she know Him?

As she watched the stars twinkle in the night sky, her mind tried to fathom God. He knew the solar system. He knew every single star, even the ones scientists were still discovering. He knew what was wrong with Noah. He knew her.

Which meant He also knew about the fondness growing in her heart for the only man she'd ever called friend. He knew how much she appreciated Jesse's encouragement, his support, his steady assurance that she could be and do the things she'd dreamed of. God knew how she spent her day dreaming about when she'd see Jesse again and share her day with him, how she valued the way he built her up instead of crushing her hopes.

So God must know Maddie no longer thought of the

future without Jesse in it. He must know she was falling in love with this wonderful man. He certainly knew that Jesse was a man worth loving.

But God also knew she was afraid to be vulnerable to love again. She'd raced into marriage with Liam to escape her father, had trusted too easily and gullibly believed that because Liam was a minister he would be a good husband. She'd been so wrong, made so many mistakes, chief among them that she hadn't loved her husband as she should have.

Jesse was nothing like Liam, of course, but she didn't know him that well, either. She didn't know his plans for the future or how he thought of her beyond friendship. She sure didn't know whether he shared this breathless feeling whenever they were together. She couldn't tell if he wanted to hold her hand as much as she loved him holding it, or whether he wanted to deepen their friendship as much as she did.

Once, Maddie had made a horrible mistake about love. She was not going to make it again.

"Show me how to be content with the precious time we spend together," she murmured. "I've made so many mistakes, done so many dumb things. I don't deserve to be loved either by You or someone as kind as Jesse. I know that. So help me be his very best friend. Help me help him find what You need him to see so he can be the pastor you want."

She sat long into the darkness, trying to think of a way she could help, but couldn't come up with a thing. But she wasn't going to give up. Somehow she would help him though because Jesse was worth caring about.

Chapter Nine

"You're not really into this, are you?" Kendal met Jesse's blink of surprise with a smirk. "I mean, helping us poor unfortunate dummies who don't know how to ride a horse—it's not really your favorite job."

"Why do you say that?" Stunned by the confrontation, Jesse swallowed, then did his job by pointing to the reins the boy had let dangle.

"Doesn't seem like you're here with us." Kendal picked up the reins. "You recite directions in a computer-type voice, like you don't care about us. You're just doing what they told you to do. We don't really matter to you."

Jesse opened his mouth to deny the accusation, but then he saw Noah watching and couldn't do it. Hadn't Tanner been working overtime to teach these kids truth? How could he slough off Kendal's indictment when it *was* the truth? He'd refused to allow himself to be engaged on a personal level so he *was* a fake, and kids could spot fakes a mile out, especially a whip-smart kid like Kendal.

What kind of emissary for God are you? Shame filled Jesse.

"You're right, Kendal. I wasn't here. I was thinking about something else. I'm sorry, guys. You now have my full attention. Let's get ready for your lesson." Jesse waited for the boys' nods. At his behest, Kendal finished checking that his saddle was secure on his horse. "Good work. Now can you get up on your own?"

"Sure." Kendal vaulted onto the horse, settled into the saddle, then peered down at him. "What were you thinking about?"

About to make some bland comment, Jesse caught the way Kendal glanced at Noah, as if to say, *Wait for it. He'll make something up.*

Jesse inhaled. "I've been thinking about starting a band, only I can't decide if anybody'd be interested." *Let's see what the kid made of that honest response.*

Kendal's usually bored stare snapped to life. "What kind of a band?"

"A kids' band. A Wranglers Ranch band." He glanced at Noah, who was making no effort to get on his horse. "Noah's interested in the guitar, I think, but I don't know if any other kids who come here can play an instrument. Maybe nobody wants to. Anyway, sorry. I should have been paying more attention to you guys."

"You didn't tell me you play the guitar." Kendal studied Noah with awe in his eyes.

"I'm just learning." Noah sounded panicked.

"He's good." Jesse kept talking as he maneuvered Amos so the stirrup was right in front of Noah. "He picks up a tune like nobody's business and he's hardly ever touched a guitar before." He kept heaping on praise as he lifted an unsuspecting Noah into the saddle.

"Jesse, I, uh, I don't like this." Noah sat stiffly, worriedly scanning the ground below.

"Hey, Noah? Can you show me how to play sometime?" Kendal nudged his horse to fall into the line of horses slowly plodding along.

"I dunno." Noah bobbled wildly on Amos, who knew exactly what was expected of him and followed the others around the ring.

He didn't say no.

"Anybody can learn an instrument." Jesse was secretly delighted that Noah didn't try to slide off the horse. Not that the boy was exactly participating. He sat stiffly, face frozen. "The thing is, it couldn't be a once-in-a-while thing. If you're in a band you have to be there for every practice and you have to work together. Bands take teamwork."

Tanner led the group through a walk and into a trot. Noah bounced wildly, clinging in terror to Amos's mane. When the horse moved into a slow canter, Noah rocked so violently Jesse grew concerned he would topple off so he jogged alongside.

"Don't pull on the reins like that," he said, and adjusted them. "You have to sit *in* the saddle, not on it. Keep your back straight. That's better. Relax, buddy. Amos knows what he's doing." He ran beside Amos, giving directions to both boys. Kendal quickly caught on, but Noah clung to his fear.

"I can't do it," he gasped, when they slowed to a walk.

"You can't if you keep being afraid." Jesse stopped him long enough to adjust his stirrups. "You have to think of Amos as part of you. You move with him by letting your hips shift, not by yanking on the reins or grabbing the saddle horn or bouncing around like a sack of potatoes. Ready to try again?"

"It's scary, Jesse." Noah's face lost all color as he gulped.

"It's only scary because you're not moving with your horse." He waited for a smile, but none was forthcoming. A flicker of inspiration flared. "There aren't always rules to guide you through the hard parts in life, Noah. Sometimes you just have to trust."

Two more rounds in the ring and Jesse was ready to give up, as feelings of failure engulfed him. Why couldn't he help Noah let go of his anxiety?

And then Kendal yelled, "If you can play a guitar you can ride that old horse, Noah."

Noah's smile barely flickered, but it was the signal Jesse needed.

"Close your eyes."

"Wh-what?" Noah looked at him as if he was crazy.

"Close your eyes and feel Amos moving, just like you felt the guitar music. Close them. Now!"

Noah glared at him, but finally squeezed his eyes shut, though his whole body was rigid with fear. With a touch, Jesse nudged Amos forward, holding his breath as the horse began to canter.

"Feel what Amos is doing," he ordered, but Noah seemed frozen. "*Feel* it." He waited, whispering a prayer.

And then something wondrous happened. Noah began to move with the horse, using his back and legs to control his movements instead of his hands. It took only a few minutes before he and Amos were smoothly circling the ring, horse and rider as one.

"Yes!" Jesse whispered, and fist-pumped to celebrate. He caught Tanner's grin and returned it.

"Way to go, Noah," Kendal cheered.

Noah opened his eyes, looking dazed but supremely happy. "I did it," he said with wonder as he reined in the horse.

"You sure did. That was perfect."

Jesse stood ready lest Noah freeze up again. Instead the boy nudged Amos's sides and directed him toward his spot at the rail.

"Very good work, guys. Both of you deserve those cookies today."

"And Amos?" Noah dismounted and stood studying the big animal. Then without warning he reached out and placed his hand flat against the horse's flank. "Will he get his treat?"

"Check my back pocket. I've got two sugar lumps there. You and Kendal each take one. Put it in your palm and hold it out. Your horses will take it from you." Seeing those dark eyes cloud again, Jesse touched the boy's shoulder. "Trust, Noah."

With a nod Noah looked at Kendal and together they held out their sugar lumps. Their horses delicately swooped up the treats, and then Amos nudged his head against Noah's, making the boy's dark eyes widen.

"That's how he says thank-you," Jesse explained with a chuckle.

"Oh." Noah nodded. "You're welcome, Amos. Thanks, Jesse." With a grin tossed over one shoulder, Noah headed toward the patio with Kendal, the two chatting like magpies.

"I don't know how you did that." Maddie stood under

a palo verde tree, tears streaming down her cheeks. "But thank you, Jesse. Thank you so much."

"I didn't know you were here." He pulled a tissue out of his pocket and handed it to her. "You better mop up those tears before Noah sees you. He'd be embarrassed to have his mom bawling with his new friend watching."

"He rode a horse and made a friend—a kid who's terrified of horses and doesn't make friends." Maggie's sunny smile peeked out as the hand holding the tissue waved in the air. "You did that, Jesse Parker. You. I'm so glad God sent you here especially for Noah. Thank you."

And then, before Jesse could say or do a thing, Maddie McGregor slipped between the fence rails, threw herself into his arms and pressed a kiss against his cheek. One of Jesse's hands held the horses' reins, but as if of its own volition the other wrapped around her narrow waist, drawing her close. His senses burst to life at the fragrance of lilies that always surrounded Maddie.

When her lips brushed his, his heart rate surged into the danger zone. How could he help but return her kiss? He couldn't. So he kissed her back, wishing it would go on forever—until a snicker behind him made him pull away. He turned to see Lefty grinning at them.

"I'll look after these fellas, Jesse," he said, his eyes twinkling as he gathered the horses' reins. "You just, uh, get on with what you were doing."

"Thanks." It was then Jesse realized that all the hands were watching them, smirks on every face. Funny, but he didn't care a hoot. Not if it meant getting kissed by Maddie. Still, he'd prefer to do that in private. "Have you got time for coffee?" he asked her.

"A quick one. I used my lunch hour to come here." She walked with him toward the main house. "Emma phoned. Apparently she's to be released the day before Palm Sunday. She wants to know if we can pick her up then."

"In three weeks? Seems a bit early to me." As he walked with her to the patio, Jesse forced himself to stop reliving that kiss. He fetched them both coffee and cookies, liking that Maddie chose a table away from the others that offered a modicum of privacy. Truth was, he liked an awful lot about this woman.

"She'll be home for Easter." Maddie sipped her coffee thoughtfully. "I think we should have the puppies gone before she comes home. They're getting so active. The last thing she needs is to trip over one."

"I've been working on that," he told her, loving the way she immediately thought of his gran's welfare. Maddie and her generous heart. "So far I've found homes for four of them. Five more to go."

"Good." Only Maddie didn't look that happy about the departure of the pups, and he knew why. She'd grown very fond of them. As had they all.

"My parents will probably visit Gran for Easter," he mused, then explained, "Easter was always a really big celebration in our house."

"Oh." Maddie look puzzled by that which made Jesse think her husband had probably overseen very solemn Easters, missing out on the precious joy of that blessed event.

"One reason is that when you live in Colorado, Easter signals spring and the end to winter and cold." He shivered, then grinned. "But mostly I loved Easter be-

cause in our church it was a whole weekend of cele-
brating Christ's death and His rising from the grave.
Potlucks, great services, youth get-togethers and the
most joyful music ever created. Easter is still my favorite time of the year."

They were interrupted by Kendal and Noah.

"Can me and Noah be in that band?" Kendal asked.
"I used to take saxophone lessons and I got pretty good."
His boast deflated when Jesse studied him. "Least, I
can play. Some of the other kids in our class play other
stuff, too. You should ask them to join."

Jesse glanced at Maddie, who smiled encouragement
at him. He took the plunge.

"Okay, but Tanner says you have to have a permis-
sion slip from your parents or guardians. And I say you
have to be here every Monday and Wednesday after
school for practice. You can ask others if they want to
join. We'll hold a meeting about it after class on Friday.
That's when we'll decide if we have enough people to
start Wranglers Ranch Band."

Kendal squealed, high-fived Noah, then at the honk
on the bus's horn, dragged him toward it, pausing only
in his chattering to announce the band start-up to every
kid they passed.

"You've certainly got them excited. Even Noah." She
checked her watch, frowned, then studied him. "Jesse,
can I ask another favor? Don't worry, it's not for Quilt
Essentials. It's for Noah. I want to buy him a guitar,
but I don't know anything about them. Would you—"

"I'll be happy to help you with that. When?" Privately, Jesse hoped getting a guitar might diffuse
some of the anger the kid directed at his mother, frosty

glares Maddie pretended not to notice but which always dimmed the light in her lovely eyes.

"Can we go today? After school?" Her face tightened for a moment before she gulped and shook her head as if to rid herself of anything negative. "Lately Noah barely speaks to me. I'm at a loss to figure out what's wrong, but maybe a guitar will help."

"Don't worry, he'll come around, Maddie. Just keep praying and trusting God," Jesse, urged, then wondered how he could give that advice when he couldn't seem to take it himself.

"I'm trying. I'm trusting you, too, Jesse. If anyone can reach Noah, you can. You already have." She wore the same wide smile he'd seen earlier when she'd embraced him. "I appreciate you so much."

"I appreciate you, too, Maddie." He fought an over-whelming urge to hug her, to kiss away the tiny fur-row of worry on her forehead when her gaze lingered on Noah's departing bus. "Especially the things you've done for Emma. Organizing that bus trip for her friends to visit her this week was very thoughtful and gracious of you."

"She sounded a little down, so I thought maybe a visit from familiar faces would help." Maddie frowned as she walked toward her vehicle. "I wish I'd been able to go with you to visit her last weekend, but it's been so crazy busy at the store. Still, I feel guilty—"

"No guilt." He tapped a forefinger against her lips. "Gran knows you're juggling a bunch of different balls. Truthfully, I think knowing you're right here to handle anything that Quilt Essentials needs has freed her to concentrate on her recuperation."

"I'm happy to help. She was my lifeline when—" Maddie pretended to cough, covering whatever she'd been about to say. When she resumed speaking she changed the subject. "So see you after school?"

"Yes. I'll bring Noah to the store and we'll go guitar shopping from there." He hated the worry lingering in the back of her eyes. She did so much for everyone else. *Please help heal her past and her relationship with Noah,* Jesse prayed.

With a swirl of emotions, he watched Maddie drive away. She was gorgeous inside and out. She gave unstintingly, without being asked, and she always made time for people. She was living the Christian life he espoused. Maddie McGregor was exactly the kind of generous, giving woman he'd once imagined would share his ministry. He knew he could count on her to be in his corner as she had been today, cheering him on, praising his efforts, encouraging him with her gentle soul that asked so little in return.

Jesse cared a lot for Maddie.

That realization stunned him for a moment. But then he pulled himself back to reality. He no longer had a ministry to share with her. He was a simple ranch hand who was as scared to risk himself with kids as Noah had been to ride a horse.

Except that Noah had got over it.

Shoving away those guilty feelings Jesse wondered; even if he let this attraction for Maddie proceed, what could he offer her? He had no ministry, no special call on his life. Not anymore. In fact, the brutal truth was that he secretly feared God had abandoned the call that Jesse had heard so long ago. Even if by God's grace he was given a new one, what if he messed up again? Would he shame and embarrass Maddie so badly that she'd dump him, as Eve had?

His brain told him no, but his heart burned as he imagined the devastation he'd feel if Maddie ever looked at him in disgust. He tried to envision his world if she wasn't there in his life every day, if he couldn't see her sweet smile nudging him to keep pushing on, if she didn't surprise him with a kiss or a half-burned meal or some new idea for the store that needed his help.

Maddie was moving beyond her painful past and learning to grow in God, to explore who He had created her to be as she lived out her faith. Jesse knew it wasn't easy for her, but she faced each obstacle, testing her newfound faith while expecting God to help.

If Maddie and Noah could trust God, why couldn't Jesse do the same?

She'd kissed Jesse!

Maddie spent the rest of the morning and part of the afternoon alternately appalled by her behavior and reliving the glory of those few blissful moments in Jesse's arms. It had felt so right to be there, to show him how much he meant to her. She'd ached to tell him she loved him.

And yet he'd said nothing about caring for her.

"I think you'll find adding the fabrics in these fat eighths will give a spectacular heritage look to your quilt," she told her customer as she tied a pretty blue bow to the handles of a white paper bag with Quilt Essentials embossed on it. "Enjoy."

"I will. Thank you." The woman hurried away, a smile on her face.

"Do all your customers leave looking so happy?" A smiling Jesse stood in front of the counter with Noah at his side.

"I hope so. Hi, Noah. Did Jesse tell you what we're doing this afternoon?" She glanced from her sulky son to Jesse and immediately her heart began that silly dance of joy. Just seeing him made her happy.

When Noah shook his head, she said, "We thought we'd go shopping for a guitar. That's if you're still interested in joining Jesse's band?"

"Yeah. Me and Kendal are joining." Noah's eyes widened as he gazed at Jesse. "Thank you."

"It was your mother's idea," Jesse told him, but to Maddie's extreme disappointment he ignored that and began peppering his mentor with a ton of questions that continued on the drive to the music store.

Once there Maddie again felt shut out as Noah walked through the store, more excited than she'd seen him for years. But it was Jesse he turned to, Jesse's opinion he sought, Jesse who received his thanks and praise.

Heart aching, Maddie told herself to ignore it. He was excited, that's all. He'd include her later. But even when, with Jesse's help, Noah finally settled on the guitar he wanted, even after she'd paid for it and they were on their way back to the store to retrieve Jesse's truck, Noah barely spoke to her. And then only to say thanks in a quick, abrupt way, because Jesse told him to.

This is so hard, God.

"You're welcome, Noah. I hope you have many years of enjoyment from it." Keeping her smile in place, she endured the searching look he gave her before he turned back to Jesse.

They drove to Emma's because Jesse wanted her help to choose the right pup to give to one of her staff at Quilt Essentials. They sat in Emma's backyard sharing a coffee and laughing together while Noah tried to tie a ribbon around the chosen pup's neck. But Maddie couldn't completely disguise the pain she felt when her son ignored her. Jesse, being who he was, saw that and offered some comfort. She loved him for it.

"He's going through a phase, Maddie. He'll get over it. Don't let it get to you. Just keep clinging to God." He slid an arm around her shoulder and squeezed as if to impart his strength to her.

"I'm trying, but it's not easy." She gulped to stem her tears. "I don't understand what I've done to make him so angry."

"It isn't you," Jesse assured her. "It's him. He's got a battle going on inside. I promise I'll try and help him figure it out."

"You're such a good friend." She gazed into his eyes. Didn't he feel anything more than friendship for her? "Thank you, Jesse."

"My pleasure." He checked his watch and rose, holding out a hand to help her up. "We'd better get that pup to the store before his new owner finishes her shift."

"Yes." Sad to end this time of sharing by giving away one of the animals that had brought and kept them together, Maddie grasped his hand and stood, noticing Noah's fierce frown as he studied the two of them and their joined hands. "Why don't you and Noah do that while I go home and start dinner? You're welcome to join us if you want to risk it," she said, hoping desperately that he would. She wasn't sure how much more of Noah's angry silence she could endure.

"What's on the menu for tonight?" Jesse asked keeping his expression bland.

"I have one more meal to make before Friday's class. Lasagna. I assembled everything this morning, so all I have to do is put it in the oven and make a salad." She frowned. "I think I did it right, but it will take an hour or so to cook, the recipe says."

"Good. That's just enough time for Noah and me to run our errand and then take Cocoa for a walk." Jesse winked at her. She knew he was trying to tell her he'd use the time to sound out her son.

"Sounds good." She dusted off her skirt. Tears welled as she picked up the puppy and brushed a kiss against its sweet nose. "Bye, sweetie."

"He's going to a good home." Jesse's whispered reassurance comforted her.

"I know." She handed the dog to Noah then touched his cheek, trying to remain impassive when he jerked away. "See you later, guys."

"You will," Jesse promised.

On the drive home and while she worked in the kitchen, Maddie sent up a steady barrage of prayer for help, understanding and wisdom. As she sat on the porch watching Jesse and Noah wander through her patch of desert, she whispered a second prayer.

"I love Jesse so much, God. Isn't there a way he could be more than just a friend? Could you make him love me?"

But after dinner, when Jesse had left and the sun was setting, doubt swept in. Emma's Bible study said that when you prayed for something, you were supposed to ask God with confidence that He would answer. Only Maddie didn't feel confident asking for Jesse's love. The Bible said wives were supposed to love their husbands. Liam had quoted the verses constantly to remind her of her duty.

Yet no matter how hard she'd tried, Maddie hadn't loved him. She'd disobeyed God's laws. How could she expect Him to trust her—a woman who'd blown her first marriage—with the love of a wonderful man like Jesse?

Chapter Ten

"What a gorgeous day to bring Gran home." Jesse's heart felt light as he drove Maddie's car to Las Cruces. One week to Easter. He could hardly wait to share this special season with her.

"I can't wait to see Emma again. I've missed her so much." Maddie sounded as eager to reunite with his grandmother as he felt.

Not that Emma hadn't kept in touch with them both. He and Maddie had shared his gran's pithy sayings and sage advice, which, though usually limited to emails or very short calls, were no less encouraging and appreciative of their efforts. Those glimpses had also shown Jesse the extent of Maddie's spiritual growth. Her direct questions to his gran revealed her ongoing struggle with letting go of past mistakes and feeling worthy, but also that she was growing in confidence in herself and her faith.

"Emma's emailed me at least twice a day since her surgery, but it's not the same as the heart-to-heart chats we've always had," he said thoughtfully. "I'm really looking forward to those."

"I hope she won't feel she has to get back to work right away." Maddie's smooth forehead pleated in a frown as she studied him. "Things are going smoothly at Quilt Essentials. I don't want her to rush her recovery."

"I think she'll be more than happy to leave it in your capable hands while she gets on with completing that to-do list of hers," Jesse told her, wondering if he should once again bring up the issue of Maddie buying Quilt Essentials. He knew his grandmother wanted that more now than she had before. If Maddie didn't buy, he had a sense Emma would put the business up for sale to someone else.

"I want to play Emma this song on my guitar. Listen, Jesse." Noah began strumming a haunting melody. The range tested his small fingers, but he kept going until the last note died away in eerie silence.

"That's really good, Noah. I bet your mom would like to hear it again later when the two of you are alone and there's no car noise." Jesse glanced at Maddie apologetically, trying to include her, but Noah merely grunted.

Jesse was having as little success reaching this kid as he was getting Kendal to explain the reason he kept acting up whenever the band met for practice. Though he'd thrown himself into the band, hoping to reach the kids with music, whatever ability he'd once possessed to communicate with youth seemed to have deserted him, making Jesse desperately yearn to get his gran's take on the situation. Maybe she could help him figure out exactly what he was doing wrong.

"We've arrived early. Emma won't be discharged till one. Why don't we stop for lunch?" he suggested.

"That sounds good." Maddie looked relieved. "We didn't have much breakfast this morning."

"Because it was burned." Noah's derisive tone matched the way he glared at his mother. "Never hurry when you're cooking. Dad's rule."

"I wouldn't have had to hurry so much if you hadn't spilled juice all over the kitchen floor," she murmured, then smiled as if to apologize. "But we made it and we're here in time so no big deal."

"It is so a big deal, because when you break the rules bad things happen," Noah sassed back. "Dad's rules—"

"How about if we declare today a rule-free day?" Jesse shot the boy a penetrating look meant to quell whatever criticism he was about to offer. "Let's enjoy this nice weather, each other and Gran's homecoming. Okay?" He kept a bead on Noah, trying to ensure that the kid understood he was serious about laying off these attacks on his mother.

"That's a good idea." Maddie pressed her back into the seat and cleared her throat. Jesse had a hunch she was in tears over Noah's crankiness, but he couldn't tell because of her sunglasses. "It was nice of you to have Emma's housekeeper come in to tidy up, Jesse, and I know she'll appreciate your thoughtfulness with the ramps. She'll certainly feel more secure with you there to call on if she has trouble."

"Well, I won't move in with her permanently, but I do want to make sure she's safe and capable of managing in her own home before I move back into my tent." He winked at her, just to watch the way she ducked her head in shy response. "And I'm doubly grateful you and Noah helped me get the last of the puppies to their new homes yesterday. The house seems empty without them, but we know they'll be well taken care of."

"It was hard to give them away. They were so cute." A smile of tenderness played across Maddie's pink lips. She was so lovely.

"We should have made sure the owners will take good care of them." Noah wore his usual frown.

"How?" Maddie asked. Jesse guessed from her tone that she'd already had this discussion with her son.

"You should have given them my rule list," Noah snapped.

"That wouldn't be right," Jesse said quickly, before Maddie could reply. "The dogs have new owners who will each make their own rules. We've done our part." Then, because Noah still looked worried, he added, "But maybe we could phone them in a week or so and ask how the puppies are doing."

"And if they're not good?" Noah's question made it clear that he expected problems.

"Well, of course we can offer to help, but I'm sure they'll be fine." The boy's increasing worries and insistence on his rules were getting to Jesse. By now he'd hoped to alleviate at least some of Noah's concerns. Instead they seemed to be growing. "Is this a good place to have lunch?" He pulled into the parking lot of a national restaurant chain.

"Do they make good food?" The boy's wrinkled nose gave his opinion without saying a word. "Dad's rule was to eat at home."

"I'm sure it's very good food, Noah," Maddie chided. "Jesse wouldn't have brought us here otherwise."

"I'll wash my hands really good. Do you know that if everyone washed their hands it would eliminate about a million deaths a year? Dad's rules—"

Jesse didn't hear the rest of it because he jumped out of the car, scooted around it, pulled open Maddie's door and held out his hand. "They have all-day breakfasts. I want waffles."

"With strawberries." She accepted his helping hand and didn't let go. "Thanks for driving. I know my car's a lot smaller than your truck, but I thought Emma might have trouble getting up on that high step."

"Studies show large trucks are the safest vehicles in an accident—"

"No talk about accidents today, okay, Noah? Let's talk about something pleasant. We don't want to spoil Emma's homecoming." Jesse grinned, but in his heart he was praying the kid would let go of his negativity and not spoil his time with Maddie. He looped her arm through his, laid his palm on Noah's back and ushered them both toward the restaurant. "I'm starving."

Once Noah returned from his hand-washing, the meal was a success. But that was only because Jesse refused to allow Noah's negativity to spoil it. When Maddie left for the ladies' room before their food was served, he asked Noah to stop nattering at her about his rules.

"Your mother loves you very much, Noah, but if I were her, I'd be getting pretty fed up with the way you're acting," Jesse told him in a no-nonsense voice.

"Me? Why?" Noah tried for an innocent look, but

ducked his head when Jesse pinned him with a severe glance.

"You're deliberately being mean to her and I don't like it. I don't think your father would like it, either, if he were here," he said in a firm tone.

"He was mean to her all the time." Noah shredded part of his napkin.

"Does that make it right?" Jesse watched the kid struggle with the question. "I don't think so. It isn't the way God tells us to treat people we should love."

"He had to be mean 'cause she wouldn't follow his rules." Noah's tone was defiant. "It's important to follow Dad's rules."

"It's more important to follow God's rules and you're not doing that when you talk back to your mom and say mean things." Jesse didn't like to see Noah hurt, but how else to point out his mistake? And he was determined to do that. He would not sit back and watch Noah cause Maddie more distress. He couldn't stand to see her green eyes shadowed with heartache.

"I always follow Dad's rules." Noah's glare dared him to challenge that.

"Do you? Even if they're wrong?" There, he'd said it. "Anyway, I don't think you can follow any rules all the time. Sometimes I think you use your rules against other people to get your own way." Jesse felt like he was skating on thin ice, but he continued on. "I think you use your rules to force other people to do what you want. Your mom, me, even Kendal."

"How could I do that?" Noah scoffed.

"You didn't like it when I gave Kendal a solo for our Easter concert, did you? That's why you coax him to act out at band practice. You think that will make me angry and I'll take his solo part away." Jesse leaned forward. "Friends don't do that to friends, Noah. Because it's not keeping the rules that's most important. It's what's in your heart."

"My dad said keeping the rules is necessary." Noah's stubborn jaw lifted.

"How is that working for you, Noah? Are you able to keep all of them? Are you happy?" Jesse broke his stare only to smile at Maddie when she returned and sat down beside him. "Okay?"

"Perfect." Her eyes narrowed as she glanced from him to Noah. "What were you guys talking about?"

"Friends and how we treat them. Ah, here's our food." Jesse focused on helping Maddie enjoy their time together, surprised by how much her pleasure mattered to him.

He loved hearing her unbridled laughter, loved seeing the way she dabbed at her lips, trying to get all the maple syrup off. Loved the rub of her shoulder against his and the way she worked so hard to engage a recalcitrant Noah.

Jesse wanted to protect her, cherish her, erase the memories of the past and the harsh things Noah had hinted at. He wanted to spend hours with her discussing all the dreams she kept hidden inside. He wanted to know her secret hopes and fears. He wanted to help her teach Noah to embrace life and let go of his fear.

Jesse wanted a future with Maddie McGregor. But that was exactly what he didn't have to offer.

"Have all those carbs put you to sleep, Jesse?" she teased, nudging his side with her elbow.

"Nearly. I might have a sleep on the way home," he joked.

"While you're driving?" Noah looked and sounded aghast. "The rules—"

"Don't allow it. I know." Jesse winked at Maddie. "I was thinking your mom could drive."

She nodded. "I could. Let's go get Emma."

It was exactly what Jesse wanted to hear and he drove to the care center with a song in his heart, delighted to embrace his precious grandmother once more.

"I've missed you," Emma whispered in his ear as her arms tightened around him. It was the homecoming he'd longed for and Jesse reveled in it. She said the same to Maddie, hugging her tightly before commending her for the wonderful job she'd done at Quilt Essentials. "You're a great businesswoman, Madelyn McGregor. My bookkeeper says we've done better with you in charge than I ever managed."

"I'm sure that's not true," Maddie demurred. Though the sound of her formal name surprised him, it was easy for Jesse to see she was well pleased with the praise. "I hope everything is in order."

"I'm not worried in the least." Emma studied Noah for a moment before squeezing him close. "Noah, you've grown about two inches. How are you?"

"Good." He didn't exactly return her embrace, but he didn't wiggle away as Jesse had feared he would. "I'm sorry you got hurt," he said in his solemn voice.

"I'm much better now, thank you." Emma stood with the help of her walker and let her gaze roam over all three of them. "What are we waiting for? God's answered my prayers. Let's go home."

* * *

Maddie insisted on sitting in the backseat to give Emma room in the front, but trying to ensure she was comfortable wasn't easy, especially during Noah's steady stream of musical numbers. Her son didn't even pause in his guitar playing and ignored her soft-voiced requests for a break, but eventually fell into sullen silence when Jesse broke in to say he wanted to talk to Emma.

Mortified, Maddie shrank into her corner. What kind of a mother was she that she couldn't control her eight-year-old son? And why was Noah deliberately disobeying?

Eventually Emma fell asleep. Maddie was glad, even though it meant they didn't speak for the rest of the journey. Sometimes silence was better than trying to combat Noah's dark moods. Besides, she could spend the time admiring Jesse's good looks and the tender way he periodically glanced at his grandmother. She admired him so much.

Admired?

Who was she kidding? She loved him. Maddie squeezed her eyes closed and prayed desperately that God would make him love her, then returned to her senses and realized that was a foolish prayer. It would be absolutely right if He didn't answer that prayer, because Jesse was a pastor.

Oh, maybe not at this moment, but the way he worked with the kids at Wranglers Ranch told her he had a pastor's heart and sooner or later he would return to the work he'd been called to, work he loved. Work she couldn't share.

Hadn't Liam told her how useless she was in that regard? Hadn't she failed to be the leader the church ladies were supposed to find in their pastor's wife? Maddie had stopped going to their Bible studies because she'd never be able to offer insight on the Scriptures they studied, never felt she had anything to offer a hurting heart. She'd never given a talk on her faith or shared the sweet sorrows of other women or made a close friend of any of them. She certainly couldn't be the kind of helpmate that Jesse would need.

But she wanted to. Oh, how she wanted to be the woman who supported him through good times and bad. If only she could finally put her complete trust in God and truly believe that whatever path He led her on would be where He wanted her. If only God would let her be the one Jesse turned to.

It was a good thing Emma was back, Maddie thought as they pulled into her driveway. Once her friend was settled, maybe she'd help Maddie understand how to accomplish the hardest part of the Bible study by finally letting go of the fear of love that her marriage to Liam had caused. Maybe then she could let herself be vulnerable to live and finally trust in God's love for her future.

If only Jesse could be part of that future.

Chapter Eleven

On Tuesday afternoon Maddie was up to her ears in Quilt Essentials' annual fabric sale when her phone rang.

"Could you go to Emma's? Now?"

She froze at the starkness of Jesse's voice. "Why?"

"Emma texted the word *help*. Something's wrong. I'll meet you there." There was a moment of silence, then he added, "And Maddie?"

"Yes?"

"Pray."

During the drive to Emma's Maddie begged God to remember that she wasn't asking help for herself, but for Emma, sweet wonderful Emma, and for Noah, who'd grown increasingly troubled and was spending more and more time with her. Maddie pulled up to the house a second before Jesse jumped out of his truck. He grabbed her hand and offered her a smile that calmed her. Jesse was here. They would handle this together.

Inside, they found Emma, her face contorted in a grimace, sprawled on the floor, with Noah kneeling beside her, his skin drained and sallow. Tears rolled down his cheeks as he muttered over and over, "It's my fault. You can't break the rules. That's why bad things happen."

Fear grabbed Maddie's heart. What had he done?

"Gran?" The tenderness in Jesse's voice and the way he carefully touched his grandmother's cheek made Maddie's heart swell. What a wonderful man he was.

"I'm fine, but I've twisted my ankle. Help me up, would you, please?"

With careful manipulation Jesse eased her upright, then lifted her in his arms and set her in her favorite armchair. Once seated, Emma turned to Noah.

"Honey, it's not your fault. It's mine."

"No." Noah's appearance echoed his ragged voice. "I broke the rule."

"What happened?" Jesse glanced from her to Noah and back.

"I didn't use my cane like I'm supposed to." Emma made a face. "So there was nothing to balance on when I tripped on the edge of the carpet. It's my own fault."

"Noah, you promised that if you could stay with Emma after school you'd help her." Maddie knew something was wrong because he wouldn't look at her. "Why didn't you bring her the cane?"

"I wasn't paying attention. I was playing my new song." The words emerged muffled because his chin was pressed against his chest. "I'm sorry, Emma." Noah hesitantly touched her hand, then backed up. "I wasn't playing a hymn. Dad said when you break the rules God makes bad things happen. He was right. Emma got hurt." He picked up his guitar and held it out. "I can't play this anymore."

Maddie lifted her head and stared straight at Jesse, hoping he had an answer. It was clear from his frowning face that he was as confused as she was.

"Playing songs that aren't hymns isn't breaking God's rules, Noah." Jesse's stare moved from the outstretched guitar to the boy's face. "Did you push Gran so she fell?"

Noah's head jerked and his eyes widened. "No!"

"Then how could it be your fault that she fell? She tripped. But she's all right now, aren't you, Gran?" Jesse smiled at her forceful nod.

"Yes. I thought I'd progressed past the wobbly stage, so I didn't use the cane. *I* broke the rule, Noah. Not you," she insisted.

Noah didn't look convinced as he returned the guitar to its case. He took a seat far away from it but his longing gaze kept returning to the instrument.

Maddie squelched a rush of frustration. Why couldn't she understand what was at the bottom of Noah's issues? Then Emma's pale face drew her attention.

"Would you like some tea?" Maddie hurriedly offered.

"I would love a strong cup of coffee," her boss said emphatically. "Would you make some, dear?"

"Of course." Maddie went to the kitchen and prepared a pot of coffee, her mind still on Noah. She smiled when Jesse appeared and sat at the breakfast bar.

"Any idea why he keeps on about breaking the rules?" he asked.

"No, but I'm beginning to believe he'll never get past that," she admitted, feeling she was failing her child. "I had reservations when Emma insisted he come here again today. Noah's been—I don't know. Not exactly acting out, but pushing against every restriction I make. His behaviour is getting stranger and I still feel that his coming here so often overtaxes your grandmother. She hasn't fully recovered."

"Emma's fine." Jesse frowned and scratched his chin. "Noah's issue is these rules your husband instilled in him. I think we need to stress that God wouldn't hurt Emma just because Noah broke a rule."

"It's kind of you, Jesse. I appreciate you taking an interest." She certainly did. "I have talked to him about the rules, but he doesn't seem to hear me. He's so angry at me and he won't say what it is that I've done wrong. He just keeps talking about the rules." Tears welled and there was no way she could stop them.

Suddenly Jesse's arms were around her. He gathered her against his chest, smoothing his hand down her back as he crooned words of comfort.

"You didn't do anything wrong, Maddie. No way. This is some crazy idea his father put in his head, or something Noah's twisted to understand." She felt Jesse's lips brush against her hair as he held her in the shelter of his embrace. "You've been sweet and loving to Noah, a truly caring mother. This isn't your fault."

Maddie stood silently absorbing the comfort as he stroked her back, encouraging her confidence.

"Dry your eyes and put on a happy face now," Jesse chided a few moments later. He held her at arm's length and smiled. "Or else Gran will know something is wrong and bawl me out for upsetting you."

Maddie sniffed and tried to nod. Then Jesse's hands cupped her face. She couldn't speak when he peered into her eyes. His own swirled with things she couldn't understand, while his thumbs grazed the skin of her cheeks, so lightly, so tenderly. She had a feeling he was struggling to decide something. Finally, he leaned forward and brushed his lips against hers in a brief touch that lit a fire in her heart and made it sing.

"You're so beautiful, Maddie. Such a precious heart you carry inside despite what you've been through. I don't think I've ever known anyone with a heart like yours." Then he kissed her again, and this time it was no mere brush of the lips. This time Jesse kissed her as if she was the person he prized most in the world.

Maddie gave herself to that kiss, trying to show him without words what he meant to her. She loved this man, loved him with all her heart. He was kissing her, so did that mean—

The creak of a floorboard made her draw back, breaking contact. She couldn't allow Noah to see them like this, so she turned away and busied herself setting out three mugs, which she filled with coffee. She picked up two and turned, leaving Jesse to carry his own.

"Emma says she could manage a cookie or two." Noah frowned. "You look funny."

"Do I?" She shook her hair off her face and scrounged up a smile. "I was worried about you and Emma, so I guess what you see is relief. But Noah, you—"

Jesse's hand on her arm stopped the rest of her words. He gave the merest shake of his head, then said, "There's juice in the fridge, Noah. Why don't you get some? You and I can have our coffee break in the backyard while your mom and Gran share theirs in the living room."

"Cookies?" he reminded them.

"I've got some for Emma. You and Jesse share the rest." Maddie wasn't sure what the former youth pastor could say to uncover her son's thoughts, but she hoped he'd fare better than she had, because Noah needed to talk about whatever burden he was carrying.

But when man and boy returned, Maddie knew from Jesse's face that he was still as much in the dark about Noah's rules as before. While Noah stowed his guitar in the car, Maddie paused on the doorstep beside Jesse.

"I'm sorry," he said.

"I know you tried," she murmured. "Thank you. I appreciate everything you've done for him. For us." She stepped back a little when he leaned forward. She couldn't afford to let Jesse hold her again lest she blurt out her feelings.

"Maddie," he said, frowning when he noticed her retreat. "About earlier—"

"Thank you for being our friend. We both appreciate you and Emma so much," she said as casually as she could, while forcing herself to walk toward the car, both loving and hating that he followed her. She wanted to be in his arms again. She pulled open her car door. "Don't forget we're decorating Wranglers Ranch on Good Friday afternoon. It's going to be a wonderful Easter."

"Easter always is." He nodded, though it was clear he had not said all he'd intended to. But Maddie drove off anyway. Jesse had kissed her as a man kisses a woman, but she couldn't tell if he'd meant it to be anything special.

And like the 'fraidy cat she was, she didn't want to ask. What if he told her no?

"Emma said I have to keep trusting You," she prayed

as she drove. "And I'm trying to do that. But please put a bit of love for me in Jesse's heart, because I really, really love him."

The usual doubts assailed her later that night when she was alone, sitting on her deck and watching Mars appear in the night sky.

Why would Jesse care for her? Sure, he'd said some nice things, but that's who Jesse was—a nice guy. She was a widow with a bad marriage behind her and a troubled child she couldn't seem to help.

What in the world would a man like Jesse see in Maddie McGregor?

On the afternoon of Good Friday Jesse tried hard to rein in the band as they practiced playing the final chorus of the Easter hymn he'd sung since he was a kid. And then, with a grin, he gave up and just listened.

"Make a joyful noise unto the Lord," the Bible said. This certainly qualified as noise. Who cared? Most of these kids had only recently learned to pluck out the melody of the hymn on their chosen instrument. Little things like tempo, loudness, timing—those didn't mean a thing to them. That they played at all was what mattered.

After the girl on the far end bashed her handbell in a grand finale, the last notes died away and the familiar sounds of horses and cattle at Wranglers Ranch returned.

"Amazing!" Maddie stood on the sidelines, eyes shining, clapping as hard as she could. "You guys are going to sound awesome on Easter morning."

Pride filled the kids' faces. Some of them half bowed

while others grinned, tucking their chins into their chests to hide their proud reactions.

"You did good, guys," Jesse affirmed, smothering the rush of love that took over his brain whenever he saw Maddie. "Remember to get here early on Sunday morning and to play with all your hearts, because Easter is above all a celebration."

He chatted with the kids as they packed up and left until only Noah remained, his guitar safely secured in its case.

"Did you enjoy playing today, Noah?" Jesse knew what the answer would be.

"I guess. If you're sure that's a hymn." The boy didn't look happy.

"You'll have to trust me." Jessie sighed. "I've studied the Bible a lot, Noah, and I never saw any passage that said making music was only okay if it was a hymn."

"Did they even have hymns in Bible days?" Maddie murmured.

"Not the same hymns we have now for sure," he said with a sideways look at Noah. He strummed a few notes on his own guitar, searching for a way to help, though it seemed that nothing he'd said thus far had made much difference. "Music is a way of expressing yourself. Sometimes happy, sometimes sad. Hymns are songs made up by somebody. They're nice, but you don't have to sing them, any more than the only way you can talk to God is by saying the Lord's Prayer. It's what's in our hearts that matters when we talk to God."

"But my dad said—"

"Your father did his best to teach you the right things, son." An urgency to help this child gripped Jesse. He hunkered down next to him. "But I think your father made mistakes. We all do. And I think one of his mistakes was about music."

"That's what you and Mom say, but how can *I* know the truth?" Noah whispered, his eyes stormy with confusion. "I have to know."

The same old quicksand of failure reached to grab Jesse. He wanted to leave, wanted to foist this off on somebody else. Let them give Noah advice. Let the consequences fall on their heads.

But there was no one else. Maddie had disappeared, as had Tanner, Lefty, Sophie and all the others. Right now Noah was looking to him for answers. How could Jesse fail this child?

Help me, Father, his soul begged in a silent plea.

And another voice seemed to answer. *I am the way, the truth and the life. No man comes to the Father but through me.*

"Noah, I don't have the answers you want," Jesse said as inspiration filled him. The boy's face fell, and he hurried to explain. "But I know who does."

"Who?" Noah waited, eyes wide.

"God. In 1 John 5, verse 15, it says that if we really believe that God is listening, when we talk to Him and ask Him what we need to know, He will answer us." Jesse crouched to Noah's level again so he could meet his stare head-on. "If you want to know what God thinks about this you need to ask Him."

"You think God is gonna talk to me?" Noah looked dubious.

"He talked to David and Samuel when they were kids. God speaks to our spirit and He can talk to anybody. You just have to listen with your heart." Jesse noted Lefty's urgent wave and rose. "I've got to get to work now, but try asking God about your rules."

"How?"

"Find a quiet place to pray and then be prepared to wait, and to listen for a whisper in your head and your heart. He'll let you know which rules are right."

Jesse hated to leave the kid but this was work and there were a hundred things to do to prepare for Wranglers' Easter Sunday service. As he walked away, he sent a heartfelt plea that God would use his words to help Noah but that feeble request didn't do much to assuage the lump of worry inside. Had he said the wrong thing again?

Jesse didn't want to even consider what his failure could cost Noah, and Maddie, too.

Chapter Twelve

"Doesn't Wranglers Ranch look fantastic?" Maddie twirled around, loving the festive decorations that were tucked here and there. "Beth's bunnies are perfect."

"I'm surprised she let you move them into that crate." Jesse's smile flicked up the corners of his lips.

He was such a handsome man, especially in his jeans and boots and that white Stetson. He always made her heart race when he shoved his hat to the back of his head, revealing his blue eyes.

"Tanner said his stepdaughter is very possessive about her bunnies."

"I promised they'd get carrot treats for their Easter breakfast." Maddie giggled when Jesse rolled his eyes. "It's almost time for the campfire sing-along," she said as she glanced around. "I haven't seen Noah for a while. Have you?"

"Not since we roasted our dinner." Jesse also surveyed the area.

"He only ate one hot dog and seemed pretty quiet."

Maddie frowned as she scanned the ranch grounds. But she didn't see Noah anywhere.

"Maybe I'll go look for him," Jesse said.

"I'll go with you." She slid her hand into his, needing the comfort of his touch as worry feathered across her heart. "Noah usually sits on that log over there and plays on his tablet while he waits for me. But now that I think about it, though Tanner's kids were around while we were decorating, I didn't see Noah." Fear clamped a vise around her throat. "Where could he be?"

She felt Jesse tense and was about to ask his thoughts when Tanner appeared.

"Have you seen Noah?" she asked. "Is he with Davy and Beth?"

"No. Sophie took the two of them in to bathe. They're allowed to be at the campfire for a little while before they get tucked in." He frowned. "Where have you looked?"

Jesse told him, because Maddie couldn't say anything. Fear filled her, growing by the moment as a voice she thought she'd finally silenced began to repeat her failures.

How could you lose your son, Madelyn? Noah's a child. He can't manage on his own. You're his mother. You're supposed to be the responsible one, but as usual you've failed. Nothing's changed. You're as incompetent as ever. You should never have had a child, never have been a mother. You're unworthy of that trust.

She gulped, tears welling. She'd tried so hard to have faith, to believe God cared about her. But if He did, then why—

"Don't look like that, Maddie," Jesse begged. "Noah's fine. He's probably playing a game, hiding some-place and trying to fool us."

"Maybe." She knew it wasn't true. Noah didn't play games. Ever.

"I'll organize the hands. We'll do a search of the ranch. Does he have his backpack?" Tanner's face tight-ened when Maddie told him it was on the backseat of her car. "We'll find him. Just keep praying."

"I should have been watching him more closely," Maddie whispered, her heart squeezing at the thought of what could happen. "Instead I got so caught up in decorating Wranglers, in preparing for Easter—" She shoved her fist into her mouth to choke back her tears.

"Maddie's, it's going to be okay." Jesse hugged her close. But although Maddie desperately wanted to be-lieve him, fear had crept in and held her heart captive.

"You don't know that," she whispered. "The days have warmed with spring. There's a lot more talk of rat-tlers coming out. There have been sightings of cougars, even coyotes. If something happened…" She couldn't give voice to it. "It's my fault. I haven't been the mother Noah needed. I should have—"

"Stop it, Maddie." Jesse's hands tightened on her shoulders. She lifted her gaze to meet his and forced herself to listen. "Noah will be fine. God is with him. He will protect your boy until we can find him. But you have to trust Him. Okay?"

"I'll try," she whispered, trying but failing to return the smile he gave her.

"You have to do more than try," he pleaded, his eyes dark and serious. "Now, right now, is the time to show God you trust Him. No doubts, no fears. Push them all away. You are a beloved child of God. He is your father, a father who cares for you so much He sent His beloved son for you. He made you and He has great things in store for your future."

Maddie stared at Jesse, loving the way he spoke, so calm, so certain. Then he took her hands in his. His voice dropped as he said words meant for her ears alone.

"I've seen how wonderful a mother you are. You'd give anything for Noah. God knows how much you love your child because that's exactly how He feels about you. He sees every tear you shed, hears every prayer you pray. God loves you, Maddie, and He is going to bring Noah back safe and sound. Don't let go of that, okay?" Jesse waited a moment for her nod, pressed a kiss into her palm and closed her fingers around it.

In his arms Maddie felt safe, free from her constant self-doubt, whole. With Jesse trust was simple.

"I have to go look for Noah now, Maddie." He hugged her close, then pulled back to stare into her eyes. "Will you trust God?"

That's when she understood. Trust was a decision. Trust wasn't something that fell on you like manna had fallen for the Israelites. Trust was a verb, an action.

"I will trust," she whispered.

Jesse leaned closer to hear, so she said it again, this time a little louder. A big smile stretched across his face. He bent forward, pressed his lips to hers, then drew back.

"Keep that up, daughter of God," he said. After a long look that made Maddie feel confused and oddly shy, he hurried away.

"Daughter of God," she mused, when he'd disappeared. She needed to think about that. "That would make Noah God's grandson."

And what grandfather wouldn't want his grandson returned to the home where he was loved?

Maddie's phone rang.

"Jesse explained. I'm in a taxi on my way to Wranglers Ranch," Emma said. She cut through Maddie's protests. "I'll be there in twenty minutes. They'll find him, sweetie. Noah is going to be just fine. 'The Lord your God is God, the faithful God. He will keep His agreement of love for a thousand lifetimes.' Remember that, honey."

"I'm trusting God," Maddie told her. A burst of confidence began to seep into her heart as she walked toward the house.

God loved her. Trusting would get easier, but she'd have to practice. She would practice with Emma, because her friend always knew the right words to say to God. Right now Maddie could only repeat, "I'm trusting You."

He couldn't watch Maddie's face when Tanner told her they hadn't found Noah.

Jesse veered his horse away from the other searchers while his heart begged God to direct him to Noah. He rode away from the house on the track where he'd helped with so many lessons, away from where the other hands were unsaddling their horses. He was as weary as they after a fruitless night of searching, and yet he was still plagued by that unanswerable question. Why?

It wasn't yet dawn. He dismounted under a sprawling eucalyptus tree, chilled from the bitter wind blowing off the mountains and across the desert floor. Noah was out in this, without his jacket, alone, hungry and thirsty, and probably terrified because his rules weren't working. Bleak despair fought a battle for Jesse's mind.

Why? Why hadn't God shown them where the boy was, given them a sign to follow, something? Why couldn't they have found him and brought him back to his worried mother? Why would God want Maddie to go through the torture of not knowing where her child was?

It was always why, ever since Scott had died. And still Jesse had no answer.

Frustrated, he tied his mount to a fence rail and sat down on top of a massive rock. There had to be something, some clue that would tell him where the boy had gone. He closed his eyes and tried to think of what had happened when he'd last seen Noah.

And then Jesse caught his breath. His eyes blinked open as horror filled his heart and soul.

"Find a quiet place to pray and then be prepared to listen for a whisper in your head and in your heart. He'll let you know which rules are right."

A quiet place. Had Noah interpreted a quiet place as somewhere away from the hubbub of activity on Wranglers Ranch? Had he gone into the desert alone?

"I'm begging you God," Jesse pleaded aloud, his heart aching at the horror of reliving another mistake. "Don't let this child be lost because of me. Not again."

"Jesse?" Maddie stood staring at him, her face confused. "I was looking for you. What do you mean? How could it be your fault that Noah's missing?"

"I—I might have said something, Maddie." He

wanted to beg her to understand, but there wasn't time. It would be sunrise soon. Noah had been alone all night, perhaps suffering from hypothermia by now. So Jesse repeated what he'd said to Noah.

"Yes, but…" He could tell she didn't understand.

"Don't you see? It's my fault he's missing. It's just more proof that I shouldn't be in the ministry. I've made another mistake and this time I'm not sure…" He couldn't go on, couldn't say the unthinkable.

"Oh, Jesse." Maddie's arms went around him as she hugged him close. "You're as wrong as Noah is. God isn't punishing you. Remember what you told me? We're His beloved children."

"Yes, but—" He stopped, because she laid her fore-finger over his lips and shook her head.

"We don't know God's ways. Even if we did I doubt we'd understand. But we do know that everything God does is for a purpose." Her soft smile begged him to hear her words. "I don't know why Noah's missing, Jesse. But I do know that God is watching over him, caring for him, because you taught me that's what a loving father does."

Maddie's face shone. Her green eyes glowed with inner peace as she pushed a hank of hair out of his eyes and grazed his cheeks with her fingers.

"I'm Noah's mother and I love him dearly, but God loves Noah way more than I ever could. He cares like that for you, too. It wasn't a horrible tragedy that brought you to Wranglers Ranch, Jesse. It was God. He has a reason and I believe it was so you could help Noah. And you have."

Tears welled in her lovely eyes as she gazed at him.

Tears and something else, something Jesse was afraid to believe he was seeing, something he was afraid to trust again—love?

"Before you came Noah was so reclusive. He shut out the world, would hardly speak to anyone, let alone interact. Everything had to fit into his rigid rules." She held his face between her palms. "I'd almost given up on him changing. Until you." Her smile made his heart gallop. "You refused to let Noah keep his walls up. You kept breaking through them, forcing him to see the world and to see good. I will never forget you did that, Jesse."

"But Noah's missing," he said, when he could get his voice back.

"Yes." She nodded. "And I don't know why. I only know that if God is God in my life, I have to let Him be in charge right now." She pushed Jesse's Stetson off his head and ran her fingers through his hair. "Children can't always understand why their parents do what they do. Neither can we always understand our Father's ways. But God's in control, Jesse. He *will* do what is best for my son."

The calm way she spoke, the peace in her green eyes, the gentle way she touched him—all of these told Jesse that Maddie had undergone a spiritual transformation.

"You prayed and asked God to work in your ministry and He has. Tanner told me that you touched the lives of a lot of kids in Colorado. And then God led you here, because He works all things together for those who love Him," she reminded him. "Even bad things, things we don't like, things we don't understand. So either we trust Him or we fuss and complain and fight to understand. And stay frustrated."

"How did you get to be so smart?" Jesse wove his arms around her narrow waist, loving the way her lips curved up in that Maddie smile that no one else could copy.

"I had your grandmother as my coach," she said with a wink. "But think about it. What if God asked you to stay at Wranglers Ranch? Could you live with that, do your best and trust God to make it work?"

As Jesse stood holding Maddie in his arms, truth dawned, a truth he hadn't been willing to accept before now.

Be still and know that I am God.

God didn't owe him any answers. He was God. That had to be enough. Either Jesse trusted Him and did whatever work he was sent, or he kept trying to understand what wasn't his to comprehend. In sudden clarity he realized that if he hadn't been forced to leave Colorado he'd never have come to Tucson, would never have met Maddie, never felt this heart-pounding reaction to her.

Never known what real love was.

Whatever you do, work at it with all your heart, as working for the Lord, not for human masters.

Time to get to work for the Lord and leave the results to God.

"You are a very wise woman, Maddie McGregor. And I love you." He kissed her squarely on the lips, not caring a hoot if Tanner or Lefty or even Gran was watching them. "Your heart is pure and honest, and you see God as I haven't been seeing Him for a long time. I know it seems soon. I know I should have led up to this, done things differently. But I didn't. That doesn't change the fact that I love you."

"That's good," she said demurely, fiddling with his collar before she looked at him from between her lashes. "Because I love you, too. I didn't want to. Romance never turned out the way I expected so I thought I'd just shut love out of my world. But I don't want to shut you out. You're what makes my world fun and interesting and happy. I love you, Jesse."

They shared a sweet kiss that didn't last nearly long enough but soothed the hearts of both, for now. Then Jesse drew back and bowed his head.

"God, thank You for Maddie and her love. I don't know why she loves me, but I don't have to. I'll gladly take whatever You give me." He opened his eyes to smile at her. "But now will You please help us find Noah? Because we love him and we need him with us to make our family complete. Thank You for caring for him and for us. Amen."

"Amen," Maddie whispered in a teary voice, but her smile was happy. She held out her hand. "Let's go find him, Jesse."

They'd gone about two feet when Jesse heard a noise.

"Listen," he whispered. "Someone's in that old shed. Crying."

"It's Noah." Maddie hurried forward and yanked on the weathered door, which creaked open. "Honey, are you in here?"

"Go 'way."

"We can't do that. We've been looking all over for you," Jesse said. "Your mom and I have been really worried."

"Why?" Noah sniffed. "You tol' me to find a quiet place and ask God about the rules." Tears were rolling down his cheeks. "I listened and listened but I can't hear nothing."

"Oh, sweetheart." Maddie surged forward and wrapped her arms around him. "I love you, Noah. I don't ever want you to hide out like this again. Everybody's been looking for you," she said, after she'd kissed his forehead.

Noah pulled away from her, but only a little.

"Looking...why?" he asked, his brows drawn together.

"Because you've been gone all night and we couldn't find you."

"All night?" Noah seemed confused. "Did I sleep through Easter?"

"No, honey. Easter is tomorrow. But we were very worried." Maddie fixed her gaze on her son. "Why did you come in here, Noah? What's been troubling you?" When he didn't answer, she leaned closer to brush a kiss against his cheek. "Jesse and I love you. So does Emma. We care that you haven't been happy. Can you tell us why?"

"I can't keep Dad's rules." Noah burst into tears again, his agitation growing. "I tried really hard, Mom, but I can't do it."

"But Noah, we've tried to tell you that you don't have to keep all your father's rules." Maddie looked to Jesse for confirmation, and he was ready.

He knew now that Noah was the reason he'd been sent here. There was something God needed him to help this child understand. Jesse had been called to be a pastor and it was about time he did his job and helped this child find the answer he craved.

"Why do you have to keep all your dad's rules, Noah?" Jesse kept his voice low, but every sense was on high alert. He slid his hand into Maddie's, loving that she was whispering a prayer for them all.

"'Cause I promised." Noah sniffed.

"Promised whom?" Maddie glanced from him to Jesse, then lifted her shoulders to show her lack of understanding.

Noah's face tightened and his dark eyes started to get that blank look. In that moment Jesse knew.

"You promised your dad, right?" The boy nodded. "When did you promise him, Noah?"

"The day he died. It was my fault he died," Noah wailed.

"Honey, no. You weren't even there."

"Yes, I was, Mom. I got home from school early. I was waiting for you and I got hungry. So I hid behind that big hanging that was at the front of the church and ate an orange I had left in my lunch. But I got some of it on the hanging." His face was a picture of misery and shame. "I tried to wash it off but it got worse, and Dad saw me. I broke his rules about not eating in the church and he was so mad. He was yelling at me and then his face got a funny look. I was really scared when he sat down on the chair, like he couldn't stand up."

Jesse glanced at Maddie, who was staring at Noah as if she'd never seen him before.

"And then what happened?" he coaxed gently, while Noah sobbed as if his heart would break.

"Dad said really loud, 'Bad things happen when you break the rules. Obey.' Then he flopped over, like this." The boy slumped facedown to demonstrate. "I shook his arm 'cause I thought he was sleeping," he whispered, his voice breaking. "Th-that's what made him fall off the chair and die. I killed Dad when I broke the rules."

Noah wept uncontrollably. Maddie blinked, her mouth working as if searching for the right thing to say to console her son. Jesse took her hand and squeezed it. And when she glanced at him he shook his head, knowing Noah needed to say it all, to get his secret completely out in the open. It had been festering in him for too long.

"I tried and tried to keep his rules, but I can't. There are too many. I keep making mistakes. I'm sorry, Mom. I'm really sorry." Noah threw himself into her arms, holding tight.

"You were mad at your mom because she said it wasn't important to keep your dad's rules, is that right?" Jesse nodded at Maddie's surprised look.

"Yeah." Noah pulled away. "I *gotta* keep his rules, Mom. I promised."

Finally. Jesse couldn't smother his grin, even though Maddie frowned at him. He leaned over to brush his lips against hers, knowing beyond a shadow of a doubt what he needed to do.

He was a pastor, would always be a pastor for as long as God needed him. This was what he was created to do. Jesse inhaled, sent a silent thank-you heavenward, then got about His Father's business.

"Listen to me, Noah." He smiled at Maddie to reassure her then continued. "The Bible says man looks at the outward things, but God looks at your heart. That means all the rule-keeping in the world won't help you one bit if you don't have love in your heart. That's what

God cares about. When you have His love, you don't need to worry about all the rules, because inside, in your heart, you'll want to do the things that please God and He'll help you keep His rules."

Noah looked confused. Jesse's heart ached for him. How he cared for this child, wanted him to be free of his guilt. How he wanted to help Noah find freedom and joy and happiness in life.

He stared at Maddie. Their precious time together would come, but for tonight he needed to focus on her son.

"I know tomorrow's Easter," he whispered in her ear. "And you and I have some talking to do. But I was wondering if it would be okay if Noah and I camped out in my tent tonight. I think it's going to take some one-on-one time to help him let go of the rules."

Maddie's glorious smile flashed across her face even though her lovely green eyes brimmed with tears. She lifted her hand to cup his cheek.

"One more reason why I love you, Jesse Parker," she said softly. "And yes, I think Noah would love to go camping with you."

"Did you say camping? With me? Well, did you?" Impatient when neither his mother nor Jesse responded immediately, Noah repeated the question, then danced for joy at their response. "I'm going to tell the others. I'm going camping!"

"I love you, Jesse."

"I love you, Maddie."

Chapter Thirteen

It wasn't even 6:00 a.m. but Maddie couldn't sleep.

She pulled on her cotton housecoat and slippers, then padded to the kitchen to make coffee, unable to suppress her smile.

Thank You, God, her heart sang. *Thank You for Easter, thank You for Your love and thank You for Jesse.*

She stepped outside onto her deck and froze, surprised to see the love of her life already seated on her porch swing.

"Happy Easter." Jesse rose, wrapped her in his arms and kissed her, then pressed her into the swing and knelt in front of her.

"My darling Maddie," he said softly, as the first faint rays of sunrise peeked over the craggy mountaintops. "God put you into my life because He knew you are the perfect woman for me. I love you. I want to marry you. Not today, not even tomorrow. First I want to court you, get to know you and Noah better, maybe wait till you finish cooking class—"

"Jesse!" she giggled.

"But when the time is right for us, will you marry me, Maddie?"

"Yes," she whispered, her heart aching. "Because I love you. You build me up and encourage me and make me stronger. Together we are whole. We can trust God with our futures because He works all things together for good. When the time is right, I'll marry you, Jesse."

Jesse rose and pulled her into his embrace. They exchanged kisses in a silent promise to cherish each other.

"You guys are missing the sunrise," Noah chided. He flopped down on the deck, one arm around Cocoa's neck, his guitar case at his feet as he studied the peach-toned sky flaming across the desert.

"Not a chance." Maddie pulled Jesse to sit beside her on the porch swing and savor God's latest masterpiece.

"Happy Easter!" A grin splashed across Noah's face. "Want to hear my new song?"

"Yes," they said together, then laughed for the pure joy of it.

"What's your song about, son?" Maddie asked, keeping her hand tucked inside Jesse's.

"Love." Noah plucked a few strings on his guitar. "I'm going to sing it at your wedding."

"You mean at the band concert today?" Jesse asked, glancing at Maddie.

"Uh-uh. That's Kendal's solo. This one's for your wedding."

"And you're okay with us getting married, being a family?" Maddie glanced at Jesse and felt the comfort of his reassuring smile.

"Sure." Noah nodded.

"How come?" Clinging to Maddie's hand Jesse leaned back, waiting to see if his talk had done any good.

"Well, God brought you here 'cause He knew we needed you," Noah explained. "I needed you to help me understand that keeping God's rules is what matters."

"Right." Jesse squeezed Maddie's hand while they waited for Noah to continue.

"And Mom needed you to help her not feel so bad about her cooking," Noah explained in his most serious tone. "We need you to love us and you need us to love you. 'Cause God is all about love."

"You are so right, son." Maddie told herself not to cry.

"I'm glad God sent you for another reason, too, Jesse."

"Really?" Maddie smiled. Noah's flattery was making her beloved's chest inflate. "What reason is that?"

"'Cause He knew I needed someone to show me how to make s'mores and go camping and roast hot dogs." Noah's grin made them both laugh. "I think we're gonna make a good family. I figure that as long as I make sure I have love in my heart He'll make sure you and Mom do, too."

"You're a very smart boy, son." Maddie kissed the top of his head and proudly grinned at Jesse.

"Like mother, like son," he quipped.

"You've always loved Easter, Jesse." Emma smiled as he helped her into a chair beside Maddie at Wranglers Ranch, ready to share in the Easter service.

"Always," he agreed.

"I have a hunch you're going to enjoy this one best of all." Emma struggled to keep her expression blasé.

"This is the beginning of many happy Easters, Gran." He hugged her tight, so thankful she'd been praying for him his entire life.

"I gather this means you've figured out God's leading and don't require my help?" Emma's soft chuckle as she glanced from him to Maddie and back said that, as usual, she understood.

"Maddie and I will always want your help," he assured her.

"I should hope so since I'm the one who brought you together," she said with a wink. "Only took a little time in hospital for the two of you to figure out what I've known for ages. That's why I've been praying God would lead you here."

"You—" Jesse caught Tanner's eye and knew he had to leave. "We'll talk about this later." He wasted a few more minutes gawking at Maddie, still not quite believing this wonderful woman had promised to marry him.

"They need you now, Jesse. It's going to be wonderful." Her smile sent his heart racing. "I'll be praying."

Dazed with happiness he walked to the front while marveling at their creator. God loved mankind enough to send His only son. That was the true message of Easter. And that love was what had grounded him through the most difficult time in his life.

That love had given him Maddie.

Jesse turned, searched until he found her smiling face among the group and basked in the peace he saw there. Then he faced his band.

"Ready?" he asked sotto voce. They looked so

scared. He tapped his baton on the music stand and asked again, "Ready?"

No one spoke. Was this all for naught?

Trust.

"Ready," Noah called out.

A second later every band member responded.

"Good. Now remember, this is the day that the Lord has made. We will rejoice."

Knowing Maddie would be praying through the entire concert, Jesse lifted his hand and led his students in playing the Hallelujah chorus. Deep satisfaction filled him.

Wranglers Ranch was where he belonged.

With Maddie and Noah, and any other children God sent his way.

Epilogue

At five o'clock on the longest day in June, Maddie walked down the aisle of her church on Noah's arm. Jesse felt confident and secure in the knowledge that the woman who was walking toward him loved him as much as he loved her. Today their Easter family wish would come true.

After Noah placed Maddie's hand in Jesse's he stepped to one side, lifted his guitar and began to sing the beautiful song he'd first played for them on Easter morning, a song of God's grace and love, of understanding and forgiveness and, of course, of joy.

Amid the sweet, poignant silence of its ending Noah took his seat beside Emma, whom he now also called Gran, grinning as she hugged him close.

"Noah, the rings," Maddie reminded him in a whisper.

Noah gave the bride and groom a broad wink then put his fingers to his lips. A shrill whistle filled the sanctuary.

Gasps turned to laughter as Cocoa stepped smartly

down the aisle bearing a white satin pillow with two rings tied on top. She stopped in front of the bridal couple just long enough for them to remove their rings, then raced over to sit by Noah.

He hugged her tightly, then announced, "I taught Cocoa to do that, Jesse. She's part of our family, too, so she had to be part of the wedding."

Laughter finally died away when the minister cleared his throat. And then, with the past settled and the future waiting, he and Maddie made their promises of love to each other.

"Jesse, every day you show me what real love is. You encourage and support me to be the best I can be. I am blessed to be loved by you." Maddie slid the ring on his finger, then touched her lips to it. "I promise I will always be there supporting you in whatever God gives us to do. I love you."

"Maddie, you are the most beautiful woman I've ever known." Jesse cupped her scarred face in his hand and stared into her eyes. "Your heart shines with the love that you give so freely. I had no idea that God would bless me so much when He led me to Tucson and you. I will spend the rest of my life loving you and Noah. Together we'll trust Him to lead and guide every step along our life's journey. I love you, Maddie." He slid a slim gold band onto her finger next to a shiny solitaire he'd bought the day after Easter.

"Having exchanged their vows before God and these witnesses, and pledging their commitment each to the other, I now pronounce that they are husband and wife. You may kiss the bride!"

As the couple sealed their promise with a kiss, their

guests applauded. Jesse knew Noah waited as long as he could, but apparently he felt they'd never stop kissing because he strode forward and tugged on Jesse's pant leg to get his attention.

"Isn't it time to go to Wranglers Ranch for the party?"

Jesse smiled at Maddie and wondered when they'd get a few minutes alone. "What's the rush?"

Noah motioned for him to bend down. "Sophie said the food is gonna be in triangles. *All* of it," he emphasized, his eyes huge.

"Really?" Jesse tried to look suitably impressed. "And you love triangles, I know."

"I like triangles," Noah corrected. He smiled at his mom. "I like triangles a lot. But I love God. And you guys, and Gran, and Cocoa, and…"

"Our brilliant son sure has his priorities figured out." Jesse looped his bride's arm through his. "Lead on to the party, Noah."

Smiling, he and Maddie followed Noah down the aisle and out of the church, to where Lefty waited by a horse-drawn carriage.

"And that's not all." Noah fed Amos a sugar lump, waiting as Jesse helped his bride into the decorated carriage. When he whistled for Cocoa to jump in, too, lifted Noah inside and followed himself, Noah continued. "Me and the band are gonna play a special song."

"Really?" Jesse grinned in delight.

Noah's face drooped. "Oops. That was supposed to be a secret."

"I didn't hear anything. Jesse, did you?" It seemed Maddie couldn't stop smiling at him and Jesse didn't mind that one bit.

"They're kissing again," he heard Noah mumble before turning his face forward.

"Reckon you better get used to it, son, 'cause I'm thinking there's gonna be a whole lot of that in your future," Lefty chuckled, picking up the reins.

"I know," Noah replied, as the horse clopped down the street toward Wranglers Ranch.

Delighted by his acceptance, Jesse hugged Maddie and whispered, "This is the start of our future, Mrs. Parker."

"You'll be helping kids just like God told you so long ago."

"And Noah will want to go camping with me at least once a month," Jesse predicted in a louder voice, shooting the boy a grin. "While my wife will be running Quilt Essentials with Gran and taking care of everybody who touches that sweet heart of hers."

Her cream Stetson dipped demurely.

"In between caring for my family," she reminded him.

That sounded absolutely perfect to Jesse.

"I love knowing that God's in charge, don't you, Maddie?"

"Yes." Maddie winked at Noah, then motioned for him to turn around.

Their precious son pretended he didn't see a thing as Jesse's wife told him exactly how she felt without using a single word.

* * * * *

Get 4 FREE REWARDS!

We'll send you 2 FREE Books plus 2 FREE Mystery Gifts.

FREE
Value Over
$20

Both the **Harlequin® Special Edition** and **Harlequin® Heartwarming™** series feature compelling novels filled with stories of love and strength where the bonds of friendship, family and community unite.